# Goodness
# and
# Mercy

## Also by Vanessa Davis Griggs

*Ray of Hope*

*Redeeming Waters*

*Forever Soul Ties*

## The Blessed Trinity Series

*Blessed Trinity*

*Strongholds*

*If Memory Serves*

*Practicing What You Preach*

*Goodness and Mercy*

*The Truth Is the Light*

*The Other Side of Goodness*

*The Other Side of Dare*

*The Other Side of Divine*

# Goodness and Mercy

## VANESSA DAVIS GRIGGS

Kensington Publishing Corp.
http://www.kensingtonbooks.com

DAFINA BOOKS are published by

Kensington Publishing Corp.
119 West 40th Street
New York, NY 10018

All Kensington Titles, Imprints, and Distributed Lines are available at special quantity discounts for bulk purchases for sales promotions, premiums, fund-raising, and educational or institutional use. Special book excerpts or customized printings can also be created to fit specific needs. For details, write or phone the office of the Kensington special sales manager: Kensington Publishing Corp., 119 West 40th Street, New York, NY 10018, attn: Special Sales Department, Phone: 1-800-221-2647.

Dafina and the Dafina logo Reg. U.S. Pat. & TM Off.

ISBN-13: 978-0-7582-6330-8
ISBN-10: 0-7582-6330-9
First trade paperback printing: December 2009
First mass market printing: October 2011

10  9  8  7  6  5  4  3  2

Printed in the United States of America

*To Barack and Michelle Obama
for showing the world, in real life,
the type of love my fictional characters
George and Johnnie Mae Landris
have been showing people in my books for years.*

*To those who know or have known and experienced
what real and true love feels like.*

## Acknowledgments

I am always humbled and awed by God and all that He has done and is doing in my life. Thank You, God, for your faithfulness and for loving us so much.

To my mother, Josephine Davis: Yours was the first heart I ever heard, the heart of our God that I hear even now. Mama, you've always believed in me, and your belief has been a fuel that continues to propel me to keep moving forward in the work of the Lord. Thank you for always being there for me. I pray that you know (without a shadow of a doubt) that your labor in the Lord's work has not been in vain. To my father, James Davis Jr.: my daddy, the man I grew up believing could do anything. You've taught me a lot, and not always by what you've said, but by the life you have lived before us. You don't just talk about keeping on even through adversity or challenges. You've become a living example for all to see. I witnessed you having been knocked down. But, most important, I've seen you get right back up. Maybe not as strong as you were before, but still, you got back up. You didn't allow things to keep you from "fishing." You merely found another way to cast your line.

To my husband, Jeffery; my children, Jeffery, Jeremy, and Johnathan Griggs; my granddaughters, Asia and Ashlynn; sisters, Danette Dial and Arlinda

Davis; brother Terence and sister-in-law, Cameron Davis; and brother Emmanuel Davis: Each and every one of you adds a special richness, individual to you, to my life that makes me smile. I can see just how good God really is. God has a call on each of your lives in a very special way. I'm thankful for the times we as a family have been blessed to enjoy together.

To Vanessa L. Rice: Who would have thought your reading my novel *Promises Beyond Jordan* all those years ago would have led to such a friendship! A special thanks to Vina Lavendar for the support in spreading the word about my books when no one much even knew *who* I was. Rosetta Moore: I know things are tough at times, but God promised never to leave us or forsake us. Continue looking to the hills from whence comes all of our help. Stephanie Perry Moore: You are such a special person. I know that God has great plans for you. I laugh every time you repeat the word I once spoke to you: completion. To Mary Monroe: We had such a great time at that restaurant (Nikki's West) while you were here in Birmingham. What a blessing and a delight you are!

To Regina Biddings, Gregg Pelt, Irene Egerton Perry, Zelda Oliver-Miles, Linda H. Jones, Bonita Chaney, Ella Wells, Pam Hardy, Shirley Walker, Doretha White, Diann Cylar (and other members of the WBRT Society Book Club), Adrienna Turner, Ron Marshall of Sunday Morning Gospel Sounds 98.7 KISS FM, Sylviaette Simmons, Ms. Johnnie Hamby (you hung in there with me for as long as you could), and Stanley and Greta Hamby: I thank you for your support, encouragement, and for being there in your own ways cheering me on as I've continued to travel along my writing journey.

To my editor, Selena James: It was a joy working with you on this book. I appreciate you for caring the way that I see that you do. I especially thank you for allowing me to be me. That means more than you'll ever know! To the wonderful staff of Kensington/Dafina: Thanks for everything! And thanks for yet another beautiful cover.

ReShonda Tate Billingsley, Angela Benson, and Cheryl Robinson: Thank you for the lovely words you wrote about me and my work that now grace this book. Angela, every time our paths cross, you never fail to bring a smile to my face. Thanks for sharing your gift of laughter. Thank you to the book clubs that choose my books, online sites, print media, radio shows, churches, and the church groups that have invited me (one way or another) into your lives. God's rich with no-sorrow-added blessings to you!

It's impossible for me to name each and every person who has touched my life in a positive way. If you have bought my books, read my books, told someone about my books, e-mailed me, called me, written me through regular mail, come to a book signing or one of my speaking engagements, then you are who and what has kept me going during those times when I might have wondered why I continue to do this. (I know you know that in this type of walk, things aren't always easy.) You're the blessing God blesses me with while I'm down here on earth. You give what I do meaning. And from the bottom of my heart, I thank you. Yes, God called me to do this. Yes, He keeps me and blesses me as I press onward. But you're the icing on top. You make this journey that much sweeter. Continue to walk in God's exceedingly, abundantly, above-all-you-can-ever-ask-or-think blessings.

Now, get comfortable, and let's get started with *Goodness and Mercy*. I can't wait to hear from you!

*Vanessa Davis Griggs*

www.VanessaDavisGriggs.com

# Goodness
# and
# Mercy

# Chapter 1

*Come now, and let us reason together, saith the Lord: though your sins be as scarlet, they shall be as white as snow; though they be red like crimson, they shall be as wool.*

—Isaiah 1:18

"If you're here today," forty-eight-year-old Pastor George Landris began, "and you feel there's something missing in your life. If you admit that although there are billions of people on this earth, you still feel like you're all by yourself—that sometimes it feels like it's you, and you alone. If you feel as though no one truly loves you. If you're *fed up* with being fed up." He paused a second. "If you'd like to be born again . . . you want to know *Jesus* in the free pardon of your sins. Then I want you to know that your being here today is neither an accident nor a coincidence. I want you to know that it's time for a change! You see, I've been told that the definition of insanity is doing the same thing over and over again but somehow expecting a different result." He shook his head slowly, then took one step to the side.

"Well, to that someone who's here today, your

change has come. If you're looking for change, change you can *truly* believe in, then the Lord is extending His hand to you today through me. He's asking you, on *this* day, to accept His hand. I know I'm talking to somebody today. In your life, it's time for a change." Pastor Landris nodded as he narrowed his eyes, then ticked his head three times to one side as he smiled.

"Oh, I know we heard the word *change* a lot last year. We *talked* about change. Some of you even voted for change. Some of you voted for the first time in your life *because* of change. Well, on November 4, 2008, change took a step forward in these United States of America . . . a change that's *already* had an impact on the world. But on *this* day"—he pointed his index finger down toward the floor—"on this Sunday, January 4, *2009,* sixteen days before that embodiment of change is to be sworn in as the forty-fourth president of the United States, it's time for your own personal change. A change, a wonderful change."

Many in the audience began to clap while others stood, clapped, and shouted various things like: "Change!" "A wonderful change!" and "Thank God for change!"

Pastor Landris bobbed his head, then continued to speak. "For those of you here who are tired of fighting this battle alone, let me assure you that there *is* another way. And in case you don't know or haven't heard, *Jesus* is the way! He's the truth, and He's the light.

"And today—just as Jesus has been doing since before He left earth boarded on a cloud on His way back to Heaven, where He presently sits on the right hand of the Father—He's calling for those who have yet to answer His call, to come. Come unto Him all you that labor and are heavy laden. Jesus desires to be Lord of your life. Won't you come today? Won't you come? Come and cast your cares on the Lord, for He cares for you. Oh, yes, He cares . . . He cares. He cares. He . . . cares."

Pastor Landris extended his hand. He looked like someone waiting on a dance partner to take hold of his outstretched hand in order to continue the next step of a well-choreographed dancing routine.

Twenty-six-year-old Gabrielle Mercedes heard his words. She felt them as they pierced her heart. She doubled over as she sat in her seat. Quickly, she felt the warmth wash completely over her, starting at her head. It felt as though she was being covered with pure love and peace, as though buckets of warmth were being poured on her, the warmth quickly making its way down to her feet. Her feet heard the music inside of the words "Come and cast your cares on the Lord, for He cares," and they began to move, to tap rapidly, all on their own.

The music that played inside her was not the usual music one might expect to hear in church. It was music that no words she knew could aptly describe—angelic. Her body instinctively knew what to do; her legs summarily stood her upright. She hurriedly, but gracefully, started across—one–two, one–two, side step, side step—from where she'd been sitting, quietly excusing herself past those who shared the row with her. Then, forward she glided, with long deliberate strides down a wide center aisle—flow, extend, now glide, glide, faster, faster—toward the front of the church building's sanctuary. Everything happening before the right side of her brain was even able to effectively launch a logical and methodical discussion about any of this with the left side of her brain. She was moving forward, refusing to look back.

And when she shook the hand that continued to remain extended for any and all who dared to reach toward it, she didn't see the man of God's, Pastor Landris's, hand. All she saw was the Son of the living God called Jesus, Emmanuel, the Prince of Peace, the King of kings, the Lord of lords, the President of presidents. She began to leap—higher, higher.

And as she'd shaken Pastor Landris's hand, at least twenty other people also had come forward and stood alongside her. But she'd only felt the hand of God holding her up as she stood there and openly confessed she was indeed a sinner. She knew—without any trumpets sounding, any special effects, and any special feelings—that in that moment of her confession, she was saved. Saved by grace. Now.

*Now faith is . . . now . . . faith is now . . .*

And the feeling she did have? It was the Lord leading the dance of her life, whispering throughout her every being that she now only needed to follow His lead. She needed to allow Him to take her to the next step, and then the next one, and the next one, without knowing what the next step might be. Fully trusting His lead. *One–two–three.*

Oh, how Gabrielle loved to dance! But until this day, she'd never known the true grace in dancing.

That amazing grace. God's amazing grace. The feelings she had now were a by-product of the new knowledge she possessed: the knowledge of knowing Jesus Christ in the free pardon of her sins. All of her sins, every single one of them, Pastor Landris was saying, were officially pardoned. She was free!

"Pardoned—your slate, wiped cleaned," Pastor Landris said to those who came up. "Your sins, totally purged from your record. It's as though they never happened. God says your past transgressions have been removed as far as the east is from the west, the north from the south. All of your sins— the ones folks know about, and yes, the ones only God knows. Gone. Gone! Whatever sins were in your past, from this day forward, as far as the Lord is concerned, they're gone." Those standing were being signaled by a ministry leader to follow her to an awaiting conference room.

"Hold up a second," Pastor Landris said, halting them before they exited. "I want you to say this with me: My *past* has been *cast* into God's sea of forgetfulness."

They did as he asked—some of them leaping for joy as they shouted the words.

"You are forgiven of your sins," he said. "Look at me." He waited a second. "And God is saying to you, don't allow anyone . . . *anyone,* to ever bring up your past sins to you again. Did you hear what I said? Don't let *anyone* use your past against you. If they bring it up, you tell them that it's under the blood of Jesus now."

The entire congregation erupted with shouts of praise as they stood to their feet.

# Chapter 2

*For I know the thoughts that I think toward you, saith the Lord, thoughts of peace, and not of evil, to give you an expected end.*

—Jeremiah 29:11

"Do you have a Bible?" one of the ladies asked Gabrielle as they stood in the conference room where the new converts were taken after they left the main sanctuary.

"No, I don't. But I can buy one," Gabrielle said.

"Oh, we have one for you—a gift from the church." The petite woman smiled as she handed Gabrielle a six-by-nine-inch maroon Bible. "I'm Tiffany Connors. I'm part of the ministry that welcomes converts who come to Christ through Followers of Jesus Faith Worship Center. Our goal is to ensure that you have as many tools as possible at your disposal to get you started in learning all you can about the Lord. Pastor Landris insists there's nothing worse than having something new and either *not* receiving or *not* reading the manual that comes with it—oblivious to its features, benefits, and the instructions to operate it. And of course, any good manual contains troubleshooting information to help in understanding when something is not working properly, and what is needed to correct it. We believe there's no better manual for Christians—novices and veterans alike—than the Bible." Tiffany tapped Gabrielle's Bible twice, then held out her hand for a handshake.

Gabrielle glanced at the Bible she'd been given. She smiled at Tiffany as they shook hands. "I'm Gabrielle Mercedes, and it's a pleasure to make your acquaintance."

Tiffany tilted her head in a quizzical way. "Is Mercedes your married name?"

Gabrielle smiled. She wasn't offended or felt Tiffany was moving too quickly into her business. She knew exactly what was going through Tiffany Connors's head. It was what she encountered a lot since she'd legally dropped her last name of Booker and adopted her middle name as her last. Most people could tell by looking at her smooth brown skin; hair that was, without fail or excuses, relaxed every four to six weeks to keep it from going back to its natural state of afroishness; and a signature behind that defined many a black woman as a black woman (there always being an exception to any rule, as folks like J.Lo have proven) that she was not Hispanic, as her last name might somehow suggest.

The next logical thought was that she, being a black woman, must have married someone with the last name of Mercedes to have acquired it. She could have easily explained how she ended up with it, but didn't bother to. That would defeat the whole purpose of her having changed it in the first place.

"No, I'm not married, and I've never been married," Gabrielle said. She just happened to look down and realized she was hugging her Bible. She let her arm down by her side, along with the Bible she held in her hand.

"Gabrielle Mercedes. Well, it certainly is a beautiful name," Tiffany said. She glanced at her watch and grimaced. "Listen, I hope you don't mind my having to leave so quickly—kind of drop the Bible and run—but I have to go pick up my children from children's church so the workers there can leave."

Gabrielle smiled as she tilted her head only slightly. "Forgive me, but did you say children's church?"

"Yes. We have a church for the children. They call it children's church even though it's still part of this same congregation. There's also a teen church with activities geared specifically for the teenagers and their style of praise and worship. Today was my day to work in this ministry. And since Darius, that's my husband, didn't make it to church today, I'm the only one available to pick up my little ones by the cutoff time."

"How many children do you have?"

Tiffany appreciated that Gabrielle asked. She loved talking about her children. "I have three. My oldest daughter is Jade. She'll be eight this year. Dana, our middle daughter, turns six in a few months. And our son, Darius Junior, we call him Little D., just turned two this past November. He's in the toddler's section of children's church."

Gabrielle nodded. "That's nice of the church to have a children's church and a teen church within the main church. I only went to church a few times when I was growing up, although I went all the time when I was a baby up until I was about three. My mother used to take me every Sunday. . . ." Reflecting on her mother when she was too young (her aunt and others had constantly countered) to remember anything that had to do with her or anything else that may or may not have happened during that time caused her to discontinue, at least aloud, this train of thought.

Gabrielle smiled, pretending it was perfectly normal to switch topics and entire conversations in midsentence. "Suffice it to say, there was nothing separate for children or the teens to do in the churches I attended growing up. And the preacher where we *did* go those times mostly put folks to sleep. I mean, they would be sleeping good, too. Until he reached the end of his sermon and started whooping and hollering—startling babies, men, and old folks alike right out of their naps." She laughed. "I'm sorry. Here I am going on, holding you up when you clearly said you needed to go. Please, go on and pick up your children. And thanks for the Bible." She patted the Bible's cover. "It's beautiful."

Fatima Adams walked over to Gabrielle and Tiffany just as Tiffany was about to leave. "Well, hello. It's Tiffany Connors, right?"

Tiffany nodded. "And you're Fatima . . . ?" She frowned as though that would help her recall Fatima's last name.

"Yes, Adams. Fatima Adams," Fatima said as she politely shook Tiffany's hand.

"Well, Fatima, I must say that you have *impeccable* timing. I'm hurrying to get my children from children's church. Now I don't feel so bad leaving like this. Great meeting you"—she said to Gabrielle— "and great seeing you again," she said to Fatima.

Fatima turned to Gabrielle. "Well, hello there. My name is Fatima Adams, as I'm sure you just heard." She smiled and held out her hand to shake Gabrielle's, then suddenly leaned in and hugged her instead. "I just wanted to come over, introduce myself, and welcome you to the body of Christ, as well as to Followers of Jesus Faith Worship Center. We're so excited you've chosen to accept Jesus into your life. And believe me when I say that your decision is an eternal, life-changing, and life-saving one."

Gabrielle felt Fatima's hug had been sincere. Still, she quickly pulled away, and even took a step back. "Thank you. I'm Gabrielle Mercedes. And before you ask, I'm not married, so it's not my married name." She laughed a little. In truth, the hug had taken her a little off her stride. Gabrielle wasn't accustomed to being hugged. She hadn't been hugged much since her days with Miss Crowe, a teacher who had been a rock in her life. In fact, as she thought about it, the last time she'd actually allowed anyone to hug her, to really hug her, was the last time she'd seen Miss Crowe— some nine years ago. Right before that horrible accident that ended up dramatically changing both of their lives. Any other hugs didn't mean anything to her; they were merely perfunctory.

Miss Crowe was the only person who had really cared about her. She'd cared about Gabrielle's dreams and aspirations. Cared that Gabrielle was treated fairly and with respect. In a nutshell, Miss

Esther Crowe had cared about what Gabrielle cared about. So, whenever Miss Crowe hugged her, she knew that Miss Crowe wasn't hugging her for what she could get out of her. She was hugging her because she knew Gabrielle needed it. After Miss Crowe was no longer in her life, she didn't want or care for anyone to hug her.

But she had to admit, there was something different about Fatima's hug—a hug that quite honestly she hadn't seen coming before it happened. A hug that felt rather sisterly, just one more thing she wasn't all that familiar or comfortable with.

Technically speaking, Gabrielle was an only child, born Gabrielle Mercedes Booker. Her mother and father were married before she was conceived. That was a big deal to her since it was the only thing she actually held over the four cousins she'd grown up with who could—and rightly so—be considered more siblings than cousins.

"Thanks for the information, but I hadn't planned on asking if you were married or not," Fatima said. "Not at this point, anyway. I wouldn't want you getting the wrong impression about us here."

In fact, Fatima had noticed the slight cut above Gabrielle's right eye. She couldn't help but wonder what the real story was behind that. And that pukey green, bright sunshine yellow, hot fuchsia, orange, and red scarf carefully tied around her neck didn't seem to match the classy outfit. Fatima pondered whether Gabrielle had possibly worn that scarf to merely cover up some infraction surrounding her neck. That cut above her eye had given Fatima plenty of reason to pause. And Fatima was leaning more toward some act of violence having been done to her than any act of love.

"Well, I wanted to come and personally welcome you to the body of Christ, as well as to Followers of Jesus Faith Worship Center," Fatima said, maintaining her upbeat manner. "I'd also like to give you my phone number and possibly get yours. That's if you don't mind me having it. With thousands of members, Pastor Landris wants to ensure any new people who attend here have at least one person they can easily reach, in case they need something or have any questions. A point of contact, if you will. And I am indeed delighted to say that I am your contact."

Gabrielle flashed Fatima a quick smile. *Indeed.* She'd caught Fatima's glance at the cut above her eye that honestly she'd forgotten was even there. And had she known she would end up going forward to be saved, ultimately placing herself visibly in front of other people instead of the come-in-and-leave-without-talking-to-anyone plan she'd originally had, she might have put off coming to church altogether. At least, until her impossible-to-hide-without-big-shades cut had completely healed.

Gabrielle touched the scarf she'd tied around her neck—happy now she'd chosen to wear it. Scarves were definitely not her thing. They were too old fogey for her. And she was not a scarf person. But leave it to her aunt on her father's side, Cecelia "Cee-Cee" Murphy, to give her something she didn't want but would later possibly need. The only time Gabrielle ever considered wearing a scarf was on her job, and only then if it was requested. Truthfully, even then, she didn't keep it on long enough for it to irritate her the way this one was beginning to do. She pulled at the knot to loosen it a little more, careful that it not become *too* loose and expose the black and blue bruises on her neck.

After leaving the building, she slid into her pearl-colored, automatic five-speed, V6, 2008 Toyota Camry Solara SLE convertible. She draped her off-white wool coat on the passenger's side headrest. She then placed on the passenger's seat her new Bible and the New Convert / New Member's Handbook she'd received from another person who came over right before she left the conference room. She cranked the car, turned the heat on full blast, and pressed a separate button to heat up her tan leather seat. The seat began to warm quickly. When she'd bought this car, that was one feature the manual spoke of that she thought she'd never use, especially living in the South. But on a cold day like this, she absolutely adored this benefit of her car.

Gabrielle reached for the Bible, retrieving the handwritten card Fatima had given her with her contact information along with a message she'd written. Gabrielle couldn't help but smile as she read it.

*You are now a new creature. Those old things are officially passed away. It's time to let go of past mistakes made by you and even those made against you. It's time for you to walk in your godly call. If you need anything, have questions as you embark upon this new and wonderful faith journey, or you*

*just need a friend, please trust me when I tell
you that I'm only a phone call or an e-mail
click away.*

Fatima had included her home and cell phone numbers, as well as her e-mail address.

Following that were the words *P.S. Read Jeremiah 29:11.*

Gabrielle looked at the Bible and suddenly realized she'd never really opened a Bible before, and especially not to seek out a specific scripture. Those few times as a child she *had* gone to church, the deacons usually read from their Bibles while the congregation passively listened, and nodded with occasional amens. When the pastor stood and read his selected scriptures before giving his text, the congregation was neither required nor encouraged to open their Bibles and read along with him.

Even her beloved Miss Crowe, who had told her some things about God, had never opened the Bible or read anything out of it in her presence. Miss Crowe merely quoted a scripture when she felt the need.

Starting at the front, Gabrielle turned in search of a table of contents. Most nonfiction books contained one. Surely the Bible had to have one. Surely it had to.

She smiled when she found it. *Old Testament. Jeremiah. Page 1099.*

# Chapter 3

*The thing that hath been, it is that which shall be; and that which is done is that which shall be done: and there is no new thing under the sun.*

—Ecclesiastes 1:9

With the handbook, the Bible, and the note, Gabrielle could see she would have enough to keep her occupied. She would now have to decide what her next move would be. There would have to be some changes in her life as well as her lifestyle. She knew that without anyone having to tell her. She was already beginning to see things differently. For her, accepting Christ was not a joke. She was ready for a change.

After she arrived home and got up to her bedroom, she removed the scarf from around her neck and looked again closely in the mirror. The bluish-black bruises were still very visible, thumbprints etched into her neck. Proof positive that things had to change in her life and that time was of the essence. Because the next time . . . well, the next time could possibly leave her without a next time. She had to face that likelihood as undisputable.

Then, there was Miss Crowe. Right before the neck incident, as she slept, Miss Crowe had come to her in her dreams. Miss Crowe hadn't spoken her words harshly, but Gabrielle instantly knew she was disappointed in how Gabrielle's life had turned out. In the dream, Gabrielle hadn't seen the beautiful smile Miss Crowe was known for. It was more of a pained smile. And it hurt Gabrielle's heart to know she was the cause of that pain.

"There's so much more God requires of you," Miss Crowe had said as she stood shimmering in a stunning lavender chiffon dance outfit in her dream. "God gave your gift to you. Me? I was merely a vessel He used to pour everything left inside of me into you and your gift. Gabrielle, you have to stop selling yourself short. Listen to me. It's time for a change. Listen to what God is saying to you. Listen to your heart. God is speaking to you whether you realize it or not. He's telling you, 'No God, no peace. To know God you will know peace.' God is trying to get your attention. Don't continue to look the other way as if He isn't."

Gabrielle had awakened in a sweat. She hadn't known what was going on. She had looked around her darkened bedroom. *It had only been a dream.* But it had felt so real. She hadn't seen Miss Crowe since a few days before her accident. Gabrielle had been seventeen and a few months into her senior year of high school. Miss Crowe had encouraged her to keep working hard and to keep her grades up no matter what else she did. She'd grinned uncontrollably when she told Gabrielle she had a huge surprise for her. Gabrielle had been able to tell from the joy that resonated in her voice and her face that she was bursting to tell it. But she hadn't, no matter how hard it was for her to keep.

"It's a surprise, but a good surprise. I promise you, you're going to be thrilled, absolutely thrilled! I've been working on this for some time now. And I must confess right here and now that this surprise has not been easy, either. But we're almost there," Miss Crowe had said. "I've been praying and working hard, and we're almost there!"

A sixth-grade teacher who lived in their neighborhood, Miss Crowe taught in a different school system from the school Gabrielle attended. She was an old woman when Gabrielle met her . . . old by an eight-year-old's standard of old. In truth, Esther Crowe was only thirty-six when Gabrielle first met her. A gorgeous, perfectly flawless dark-skinned woman, Miss Crowe stood five feet eight in her stocking feet. Nine years later, when Gabrielle turned seventeen, Gabrielle stood one inch taller than Miss Crowe.

"I do believe I'm shrinking," Miss Crowe had said in a high-pitched voice as though she really believed it. "I promise you, I used to be five nine, the same as you." They had just finished measuring each other's height. "It must be my bones. Must be. Maybe I really should have taken more heed to my calcium needs."

Gabrielle loved going to Miss Crowe's house. And she'd never allowed Aunt Cee-Cee to know just how much she loved going over there. Nor did she ever tell what they did when she went.

"Your aunt believes you're coming here to do some housework for me. I don't mean to be deceptive, as truly that is not my nature. But I fear that if she knew what was really taking place, she wouldn't allow you to step foot my way again," Miss Crowe had said when Gabrielle reported to her house for her second day of work. Miss Crowe told her the real intent of having her come to her house. She had asked Gabrielle if what she *really* planned to do was something they could keep between themselves.

Gabrielle enthusiastically said, "Yes!"

It all began the middle of June. Miss Crowe was out walking in a neighborhood she'd just moved into a few months earlier. She'd decided to expand her usual walking route, and this was her first time down that particular street. As she pumped her arms with each step, power walking as she called it, she noticed children in a front yard. And there was one child running around picking up toys and other things the other four children were either throwing down or dropping on purpose without a second thought.

Originally, Miss Crowe thought nothing of it, concluding it was some game the children were playing as children do. But as her power walk brought her closer to the yellow split-level house, she saw a woman sitting in a lawn chair occasionally yelling at the one child to go get this or hurry up and pick up that. She could tell from the woman's screech to undo what the other four children were doing that the child doing all of the work was called Gabrielle.

It didn't take much to deduce that Gabrielle was being treated unfairly. And that broke Miss Crowe's heart. She understood how it felt to be mistreated. And if her treatment was coming because of something she'd done wrong and she was being punished, even bad children—if that was indeed the case with Gabrielle—needed to be loved. So, she devised a plan right then and there in her stride. She walked up to the woman, who looked to her to be in her midtwenties, and introduced herself. She told her she lived on Bell View Drive, which was two streets over. She told her she was a sixth-grade teacher in the Jefferson County school system. That she'd moved into the neighborhood in December, just in time for Christmas. How eleven years ago, at the age of twenty-five, she became a widow after being married for only two years when her then twenty-eight-year-old husband died from complications with lupus, the autoimmune disease he'd been diagnosed with at age twenty-three.

"He was the love of my life. I don't believe I'll ever marry again," Miss Crowe said. "I don't think I'll ever meet another man who can move me the way he moved me."

"How did lupus kill him?" Aunt Cee-Cee asked. "I have a relative who has that, and I know a few other folks with it. But I didn't know lupus could kill a person."

"In his particular case, it was a blood clot. It broke loose from his leg and entered into his lungs," Miss Crowe said.

"So, if you were married, then why do you still call yourself a Miss?" Aunt Cee-Cee asked, having thought about what the woman had said when she introduced herself. She'd said her name was Esther Crowe, but that her students called her Miss Crowe, loving to overexaggerate the double *s* in the word *Miss.*

"When I write it, I write Ms. My students just find it easier to say Miss Crowe."

"Then, why not make them call you Mrs.? I mean, you *were* married. If I was ever a widow, I would still call myself Mrs."

Miss Crowe held back her normal inclination to smile, mostly because she didn't want to appear overly friendly, at least not at this stage. She didn't need to trigger any suspicions toward herself. Not appearing *too* friendly was part of her strategic plan. "Well, technically, I'm really no longer married. Besides, it's easy on everyone, including my students, to just call me Miss Crowe and be done with it. Calling me Miss doesn't offend me."

"Sounds fine by me," Aunt Cee-Cee said. Speaking with folks with college degrees normally intimidated her. Aunt Cee-Cee felt that because she'd married right out of high school being three months pregnant (twins it turned out), and she'd never gone to college or worked outside the home, college graduates had a tendency to look down their noses at her. She enjoyed the rare times when she could put someone with a college degree on the spot, as she was obviously doing with Miss Crowe now.

"Your daughter over there—"

"Who you talking about? You talking about Gabrielle there? The tall lanky one?" Aunt Cee-Cee said. "I declare that child grows like a weed. Resembles one, too."

Gabrielle dropped her head and started gliding

one of her feet into the wind. She hated when people called her lanky and referred to her in the
same sentence as a weed.

Miss Crowe pressed her lips together. "Yes, that
one. Gabrielle." She pointed at Gabrielle, who
lifted her head up briefly just to be sure she was
the one being talked about. She lowered her head
again and continued her foot dance with the wind.
She then began to spin around with her arms out
as if she were a bird caught in a whirlwind. Miss
Crowe's heart went out to her. But it was important
for her to maintain her pretense of not caring if
her plan had any chance of succeeding.

"She's not really my daughter," Aunt Cee-Cee
said. "Technically, she's my niece. Her mama died
and her daddy has been injustly incarcerated."

"You mean unjustly incarcerated."

"No. What happened to him is an injustice, so I
mean *in*justly, just like I said."

"Okay," Miss Crowe said, opting not to waste
time arguing about it.

"But those four little darlings right there"—she
pointed at the children balling up paper and
throwing it as well as handfuls of popcorn at each
other as they ran around laughing—"are mine.
Gabrielle, will you *please* pick up that popcorn and
paper they keep dropping! I've told you I don't
want our yard looking like a bunch of hillbillies
live here. That's exactly why white folks don't like
us moving into their neighborhoods." She sat back
in her chair and turned back to Miss Crowe. "What
about Gabrielle?"

Miss Crowe pressed her lips tightly together.
*These poor children,* she thought. This was a lot

harder than she'd first thought it would be. She relaxed her lips. "I'm looking for someone to help me do a few chores around my house. Nothing big or heavy, mind you. Definitely nothing that would constitute breaking any child labor laws. Someone to help me out one or two days a week maybe. In return, I can put a little change in their pockets. Your niece there appears like she'd do a great job. Do you think you and she might be interested in such an arrangement?"

"You want to hire Gabrielle?"

"Yes. And I promise not to keep her but an hour, two at the most. She would be doing things like vacuuming, sweeping, dusting, on occasion possibly helping when I mop. You and I can discuss the terms and what you believe would be fair to pay for this kind of work as well as for her time."

Aunt Cee-Cee sucked her teeth, then smiled. "Sounds interesting. But the problem is that I don't really know you. How do I know you're not some criminal, a pedophile"—she loved that she not only *knew* a big word but knew how to use it appropriately in a sentence—"or something else shady like that?"

"Mrs. Murphy—"

"Call me Cee-Cee. After all, we *are* neighbors."

Miss Crowe smiled. She could see they were close to striking a deal. "All right. Cee-Cee, I'm a teacher. And you're more than welcome to call the school where I'm employed and inquire about me. I'll be happy to give you the school's phone number and a person to call."

Aunt Cee-Cee leaned over so she could see the children better. Gabrielle was still running around picking up after the others. "Gabrielle, run in the house and get me a pen and some paper."

Gabrielle started for the house, even though Aunt Cee-Cee was closer.

"Will you *please* hurry up, child! Goodness and mercy, please deliver me. You're as slow as a snail. You move like you're carrying lead in your feet or something. Pick it up, and let's go!"

*On the contrary,* thought Miss Crowe. She forced back her smile as she watched Gabrielle. Gabrielle moved more like a feather . . . like a dandelion seed attached to small, white feathers floating silently . . . caught in the updraft of a soft and quiet wind.

# Chapter 4

*A hypocrite with his mouth destroyeth his neighbor: but through knowledge shall the just be delivered.*

—Proverbs 11:9

After the automobile accident, someone from Miss Crowe's family had come down from Chicago, packed up all her things, and quickly sold her house. Gabrielle wasn't even sure Miss Crowe was still alive since she didn't have a way of getting in touch with anyone in Miss Crowe's family. But Miss Crowe did have *her* address or, at least, she had their phone number. Miss Crowe would have known how to get in contact with Gabrielle. The only way she wouldn't have was if she was either seriously injured or dead.

Gabrielle hated to think that someone like Miss Crowe was no longer in the world. Although Miss Crowe would be the first to say, "No one ever really dies as long as someone somewhere is keeping a piece of them alive inside of their heart." Even though it had been nine years since Gabrielle had heard anything other than that Miss Crowe had been in a car accident on her way to see her brother, she had still continued to keep a piece of her inside of her heart.

Early Thursday morning, January 1, 2009—New Year's Day—Gabrielle had been attacked. Visibly, it left a nasty cut above her right eye from the large diamond-ringed backhanded slap she didn't see coming, and a bruised neck from the attempt to strangle her. It had been her quick thinking that had saved her life. But what wasn't visible was the emotional impact the attack had on her. She didn't report the attack to the police. She didn't even go to the hospital to get checked out. She'd merely pulled herself together after it happened, with a little help from a few of her friends. She turned off all her phones, then took a sleeping pill that effectively knocked her out. Sleep quickly transported her from the world of reality and what had actually happened to a world of pure nothingness, not even peppered by dreams. She'd uncharacteristically slept all day and all night Thursday, and most of the day Friday—happy that Thursday was a holiday night and she didn't have to go in to work. Friday night, it was back to business as usual.

Sunday morning, a woman showed up as Gabrielle was leaving work. She'd seen the woman before but had never allowed her to get close enough to her to hear anything she'd had to say. As Gabrielle went to her car, the woman came and began to walk lockstep alongside her, telling her she wanted to talk to her about Jesus, someone who loved and cared tremendously about her. She wanted to talk to her about the importance of finding a good Bible-teaching church so she could learn even more about Christ and His love.

First of all, Gabrielle wasn't interested in going to anybody's church, and she told this woman as much. She believed that after she finished giving this woman an earful, she wouldn't have to be bothered ever again with her nonsense. Besides, all of the church folks she'd ever met in life and even there on her job happened to be the biggest hypocrites she'd ever encountered. At least sinners (if that's what the rest of the world who didn't go to church were) didn't pretend to be something that they weren't. *Why bother going to church if you aren't serious about what you're being taught? The true great pretenders.*

Second, she wasn't interested in hearing anything about Jesus or God. When the woman tried to emphasize it wasn't about people being perfect, but about God, who is, Gabrielle wasn't interested in hearing any of that, either.

Where had God been all of her life? When her mother had needed Him to protect her, to save her life, where had God been then? When, as a helpless child with no one else around, she'd needed someone to step in and protect her, had God been asleep on the job? When she'd prayed to Him, asking . . . begging, even, for His help—although at the age of seven, she wasn't quite sure how to pray—did God care? Was He not paying attention? Did you have to be a member of the club already for Him to hear you when you cried? If so, then how did you get into this exclusive membership?

At school when they were allowed a moment of

silence, code word for prayer time without breaking some law, she couldn't learn how to pray from anyone else because if anyone *was* praying, it was being done silently. And did anyone *really* pray during those times, or did they merely pretend, the same way she did? Did they think about other things to whittle those silent moments away? Had God overlooked the fact that, even though she didn't know what to say when she tried to pray, at least she'd tried? And the one time, the one time she'd gotten up the nerve to ask a fellow classmate—a friend, she thought—how to pray, her friend had laughed at her instead of helping her. She was then mercilessly teased by other children for not even knowing the Lord's Prayer. Did God give her any credit for at least wanting, at such a tender age, to know Him, even though her aunt Cee-Cee had discouraged them by rarely ever attending church?

"It's just too much trouble to try to get yourself and five kids ready for church. It's just not worth it," Aunt Cee-Cee had said. "Especially when it seems most folks are really only there to try to impress a bunch of other people who are there trying to impress yet another set of people. Well, I believe that God knows my heart. He knows I'd like to go. It will be all right if we don't make it to church every Sunday."

Yes, they'd gone to church a few times, mostly on Easter Sundays. They'd even gone once during Christmastime when Christmas fell on a Sunday.

"Wait 'til those snooty church folks get a look at y'all's Easter outfits this time around," Aunt Cee-Cee had said. "I bet you a whole lot of them are gonna be so jealous that their faces gonna turn the same disgusting green as an overcooked egg yolk."

And for that one Christmas Sunday they'd attended in 1988, Aunt Cee-Cee had merely said, "You kids are always looking for a bunch of toys. Well, it's not *your* birthday; it's Jesus'. That's why you didn't get much of anything for Christmas this year. It's high time we focus on the real meaning of Christmas, and not get all caught up in the commercial aspect like everybody else. Forget Santa Claus! Today, we're going to church. Now, go put your clothes on so we can go to church!"

Of course, Gabrielle would later learn that money had been short that year. That was the year Aunt Cee-Cee and Uncle Bubba (his real name was Dennis) had tried giving a barbeque joint a shot, only to learn that more was needed to run a business than just a knack for being able to cook great-tasting, finger-licking ribs.

Gabrielle's outfit for their Easter church visits was usually the plainest of the five children's. And she knew, without it ever being formally announced, that her clothes were always the cheapest of them all.

"Gabrielle, I'm really sorry about this dress, but it's the best we can do." Aunt Cee-Cee twirled her hand in a circle, causing Gabrielle to turn around in front of her as though Gabrielle's body were connected to her fingers. "You know it's been hard, having to take you in the way we did. And you keep having these growth spurts. You grow like a weed. You'll likely be done outgrown this dress in a month or two anyhow. But you *can* be thankful that you have a roof over your head and food on the table. There are lots of kids who don't even have that much. And you know what? They wish they were you. There are plenty of kids, just like you, who find themselves in foster homes. They don't have good relatives like me to take them in. Not like we did with you. You understand?"

"Yes, ma'am," ten-year-old Gabrielle had said.

"And folks aren't exactly lining up to adopt little black children, either. Nope. If you're not some cute little baby, preferably a newborn, you can almost forget about anyone ever wanting to make you a permanent member of their family. Oh, somebody will take you in for the check they'll get. But you're just a means to some extra income. I hope you know and appreciate what me and your uncle are sacrificing just so you don't have to become one of those children without a real family, possibly being abused."

"Yes, ma'am."

"Now, go help Luke and Laura find their shoes while I finish putting on Angie's and Jesse's clothes." Aunt Cee-Cee looked up at the clock on the wall. "Look at the time! We gonna end up being late getting to church again this year. It doesn't matter how early I start, time flies like a 747 jet. But at least we gonna make an entrance this year when we walk in. Yep. All eyes gonna be on us. Hurry up now. Get the lead out of your tail. Go help Luke and Laura get ready."

Luke and Laura were twins, one year younger than Gabrielle. Angie, born a year after Gabrielle came to live with them, was four years younger than Gabrielle, and Jesse, born a year after Angie, was five years younger. It happened that Aunt Cee-

Cee was a dedicated soap opera fan, *General Hospital* and *All My Children* being her all-time favorites. So, it made sense to her to name her twins after the hottest couple in daytime television, Luke and Laura of *General Hospital.* As a fan of *All My Children,* she proudly named her third child Angie and her fourth (a boy) Jesse, after the second hottest couple, in her opinion.


So, here was this woman approaching Gabrielle when she got off work Sunday morning, talking about God. After all Gabrielle had suffered in her short life, the last thing she wanted to hear about was the goodness of God. Admittedly, this woman did seem different from any Christian Gabrielle had met before. She'd started off by telling Gabrielle that she'd once been exactly where she was now. She understood. She knew the thoughts and feelings Gabrielle was likely wrestling with. How she likely felt too trapped to make a change, even if she really wanted to. The woman kept walking alongside her and wouldn't stop talking even after Gabrielle told her she *really* needed to go.

Gabrielle was exhausted. And all she wanted to do was to go home and get some rest. She opened up her car door and slid in, yet the woman continued to talk. Gabrielle reached over and grabbed the handle to close the car door.

The woman held out a brochure with information about Jesus' love, as well as several churches Gabrielle could look into attending to learn more about Jesus and His unconditional love, if she chose to later. Gabrielle wouldn't take the brochure at first.

"Please, at least take this and read it," the woman said. "Please. This is about your life, both now and your life to come. Please."

Gabrielle took the brochure, believing it was easier to throw it away later than to continue having this woman bug her about it. And then, the woman said something that stopped Gabrielle cold in her tracks.

"To whom much is given, much is required," the woman said. And, "There's so much more God requires of you."

Gabrielle looked up at the woman. Tears began to sting her eyes. The woman said it again. "To whom much is given, much is required. There's *so* much more God requires of you."

Gabrielle didn't know enough about the Bible to realize that the first sentence the woman had spoken was actually a scripture. But she did know enough to recognize that the last sentence was the same words Miss Crowe had spoken to her in her dream. Perhaps it really was time she stopped running from and starting running toward God. Maybe God was trying to tell her something. Maybe, just maybe, it was time she found out exactly what God had in mind for her, and for her life.

Why not give God a chance? At least see what He has to say. *Why not?* she thought. She'd tried practically everything else.

Perhaps one day, she would do just that.

# Chapter 5

*Wherefore I praised the dead which are already dead more than the living which are yet alive.*

—Ecclesiastes 4:2

Gabrielle had come home from work that Sunday morning. She'd taken a longer-than-normal shower, eagerly looking forward to crawling up in her nice warm bed. But those words kept pecking at her mind, playing over and over again in her head like a woodpecker that won't go away. *"There's so much more God requires of you."* She went to her purse, took out the brochure, and looked at it.

*"There's so much more God requires of you."* In her dream, Miss Crowe had said it. Now, a stranger had said it.

Meeting that woman in the parking lot after work on this day of all days, Gabrielle now believed, was neither an accident nor a coincidence. If it had been, then why today? Of all days, why a day when she was probably the most vulnerable in allowing the woman to get that close? Why had she successfully avoided her the past few times she'd shown up at their place of work doing the exact same thing? But on this day, Gabrielle had let her guard down and allowed her to get close enough to hear her speak. And why had this woman spoken the exact same words Miss Crowe had spoken in her dream?

Something was definitely going on. Gabrielle knew she needed to follow it all the way through if she was ever to find out what it was. Then again, maybe it really was nothing. But isn't this what people do? They take a simple nothing and, at times, make it into something greater than it really was supposed to be? Whatever was happening, she knew she needed to go wherever it was leading her. And right now, for whatever reason, it seemed to be leading her to church.

She looked up at the clock. It was fifteen minutes past nine o'clock. According to the brochure's information on churches, she had time to make it to either one of the listed four churches. But which one? Followers of Jesus Faith Worship Center jumped out at her, as did Divine Conquerors Church. And what to wear? She didn't have church clothes. She knew whatever she found in her closet would need to be dressy, but not over the top.

Quickly, she got dressed and headed to Divine Conquerors Church. Reverend Marshall Walker was listed as the pastor. There was just something about the name of the church that instantly appealed to her—Conquerors. To be a conqueror implied there was something in one's life that either needed to be, and ultimately could be, or had been conquered. This was a start.

Divine Conquerors was a large church. As soon

as she stepped into the sanctuary, she took off her off-white wool, full-length coat and draped it over her arm. She was early. There were lots of empty seats up front. She decided to pick a place about seven rows back of a fifty-row seating. Before she could sit down good, she was approached by an usher and asked to follow her. She was told she needed to sit more to the back, even though there were obviously plenty of empty seats in the front and the middle. Sitting in the back didn't bother Gabrielle. Admittedly, she wouldn't have gone *that* far back were it up to her. But what really bothered her was the reason the woman dressed in all white from head to toe had given for moving her.

"Honey, you're a very pretty girl, *very* pretty. But what you're wearing, goodness gracious, it's not exactly appropriate for our church service. Especially since we tape our services and it's broadcast around the country. Our pastor has strict instructions with regards to what ends up on tape. We wouldn't, and I'm certain you wouldn't, either, want anyone to get the wrong impression of our church just in case the cameras accidentally get you in one of the audience panned shots."

Just as the usher smiled and pointed to a satisfactory row for Gabrielle to choose any seat she desired, she handed her a program of the morning services. "Welcome to Divine Conquerors," she said gleefully. "We're so glad you're here."

Gabrielle looked at the program, smiled, then handed it right back to her and politely strutted away.

"Goodness!" she heard a man who looked to be in his sixties say as she walked past him. "Have mercy," she heard a woman say in disgust as she passed her. "Mercy, you sure are something, my sweet sister," a middle-aged man said as she walked into the vestibule prior to reaching the door to exit the building. "You're not leaving us, are you?" She stopped and momentarily glared as he grinned and slightly gawked at her.

Gabrielle decided she was just going to go home and ditch this church nonsense. But an uncomfortable feeling began to gnaw inside of her stomach. It felt like a knot forming, the way she felt when she was scared or nervous about something. That sinking feeling caused her to pause as she sat in her car trying to decide what to do now. She retrieved the brochure and opened it to the church section.

And once again her attention fell on the name Followers of Jesus Faith Worship Center. She had originally looked at it, but the name had frankly intimidated her. First of all, she was not a follower of Jesus, and second, she wasn't sure she ever wanted to be. But everything seemed to be pointing her to that church. She was familiar with the area where it was located so it wouldn't be hard to find. And according to the brochure, they had two services. The second service would be starting in about forty-five minutes, giving her more than enough time to get there.

As soon as she arrived, she was warmly greeted by one of the many parking attendants running around directing people as to where to park and where to go if you were new to the church. When she walked inside, the woman who greeted her inquired as to whether she was a first-time visitor. Acknowledging she was, Gabrielle was asked to fill out the information connected to a stick-on name badge. She gave the greeter the information and stuck the badge on the top of her dress.

Inside the sanctuary, she was seated by an usher, without any fanfare, in a prominent spot three rows from steps that led up to where she was sure the pastor stood when he preached. Definitely close enough to be in the line of a camera, were they to also tape their services.

No one there commented that the Nanette Lepore, black ruched spaghetti strap dress she was wearing was inappropriate for church. Or on the scarf around her neck, which her aunt Cee-Cee had given to her as a Christmas present a week earlier.

"I asked myself, Cee-Cee, now what do you give someone who pretty much has everything, or at least is able to buy herself whatever she wants?" Aunt Cee-Cee had said after Gabrielle unenthusiastically opened the box and held up the scarf. "Well, *I* thought it was cute when I saw it," Aunt Cee-Cee said when she noted Gabrielle wasn't all that thrilled about it.

What Aunt Cee-Cee failed to say was *when* she'd actually seen it, which happened to be when Angie, one of her children, had given it to *her* as a gift. She was regifting it to Gabrielle because she didn't really like it that much, either, and she hadn't bought Gabrielle anything for Christmas, but she had a need to see her. It would be tacky to show up at Gabrielle's house at Christmastime *totally* empty-handed.

After Gabrielle left her aunt and uncle's home

upon graduation, or more correctly, after she was *told* to leave their home and find a place of her own following her graduating high school and upon her turning eighteen on May thirtieth, she didn't visit their home much at all. Especially after the first two years of being on her own. It didn't take Gabrielle long to see they hadn't changed toward her at all, even with her being out of their house. The past five years, she hadn't stepped foot near their home.

"Now, just because you left our house"—Aunt Cee-Cee rambled on that Sunday night after Christmas—"doesn't mean you can't come visit us. The only time I see you these days is if I happen to come over here." Aunt Cee-Cee scanned the den, where they sat watching a fifty-two-inch HDTV. "We're over there struggling while you seem to be doing quite well for yourself, *quite* well—living in the lap of luxury. In spite of everything, you certainly did make something of yourself. But money has been hard to come by at our little place. And everything seems to be breaking down or falling apart."

Gabrielle looked without cracking a smile as her aunt continued to talk.

"And President Bush seemed to have been asleep at the wheel. I tell you, I just don't know about people. And then McCain had the nerve to say, back in September, that the fundamentals of our economy were strong. Humph." She turned up her nose. "Maybe the fundamentals were strong at *his* house, but we've been struggling for some time at ours. And of course, all of our children are living at home. None of them seem able to keep either a job or a spouse, or a spouse with a job, for that fact. I don't know if you've heard, but Angie is expecting another baby. This will be number three for her. You would think she would have figured this out by now and stop having babies she can't take care of. That's just gonna add one more mouth to feed, placed on me and your uncle's backs, of course. Another person we'll have to take care of. I don't know what I did wrong with those children." She shook her head. "I just don't understand."

Gabrielle sat back against her burgundy leather couch and continued to swing her crossed leg out as her aunt went on and on without any regard or input to or from her. She watched her turn up the can of cola to drain it of every drop, shaking it when it was obviously empty.

"Would you care for another soda?" Gabrielle asked after at least five seconds of her continuing to shake and tap the turned-up empty can.

Aunt Cee-Cee smiled and held the can out to her. "Yes, thank you. And you can carry this with you and throw it away."

Gabrielle couldn't believe that even in her own home, her aunt, who, to her credit, *did* take her into her home after her mother's death, was still treating her as though she were her personal maid. The few times Gabrielle *had* visited the family after she moved out, no one waited on *her* like she was company. Instead, they continued to command and demand that she get this and do that for them.

When Gabrielle handed her the new can of cola, Aunt Cee-Cee took the napkin wrapped around the cold can and wiped the top off, even though she knew Gabrielle had already done the same.

"But look at you," Aunt Cee-Cee said, picking up the conversation right back where she'd left off, without missing a beat. "We must have done *something* right. Just look at how you turned out. You own your own home, drive a nice car, and wear the most beautiful clothing, when you're not lounging around, that is. You certainly have made up for what you didn't get growing up as a child. The clothes, I mean. And you appear to have money to spare. At least, you're not asking me or your uncle for money like my children constantly do. Yep, you're doing okay for yourself, kiddo. And I, for one, am proud of you."

"Thank you," Gabrielle said, knowing full well where this conversation was heading.

Aunt Cee-Cee tapped her index finger against the side of the can a few times. "Listen, Gabrielle. I know I already owe you money from the last time we found ourselves in trouble. But things haven't gotten any better. Your uncle Bubba lost his job. And I really don't want to ask this of you again, but I don't have anywhere else to turn. Could we possibly borrow another thousand dollars from you? I know I still owe you two thousand, but I promise I'll pay you this back, plus what I already owe. We're going to file our income tax returns as soon as we can. I figure we should get back a hefty refund this year, what with all the dependents living in our house. And if that second government stimulus plan goes through that people have been saying is likely to be coming, we're really going to be doing okay. They won't have to worry about *us* when it comes to doing our part to stimulate the economy. We black folks know how to spend some money. Am I right? Most of us do, anyway. If they really want to get the economy going, all they need to do is put more money into the hands of black folks. They won't have to worry about us saving it like they worry about other folks doing."

"What makes you think I have any money to loan you?" Gabrielle asked.

Aunt Cee-Cee turned her now size 16 body squarely toward her. "You were always the smart one. When you were a child growing up, I saw something special in you. I know I never told you that, nor did I reinforce it very much. But I did see it. Look, Gabrielle, I admit I didn't always do right by you. But when you had nowhere else to go—"

"You took me in," Gabrielle said, finishing the worn-out sentence for her. "Yeah, I know. I've heard that scratched CD all of my life. But the part you fail to mention, Aunt Cee-Cee, is that you received a monthly check from my mother's social security benefits for me. Or what about that twenty-thousand-dollar life insurance policy her company paid out to you on my behalf as my legal guardian?"

Aunt Cee-Cee smiled a phony smile. "You know, I hate you ever learned about either of those things, because now it makes it look like we mistreated you, when that was not the case."

"According to whom?"

"According to anybody who saw how well you were taken care of. You had a roof over your head, you had a place to *lay* your head, clothes on your back, shoes on your feet, and—"

"Food on the table," Gabrielle said. "Yes, yes, yes, I know. I know how *lucky* I was to have had a family to take me in. I know that other children were being abused in foster homes, and at least I was somewhere where people really did care about me. 'Do this, Gabrielle. Go get me that, Gabrielle. You move like you have lead in your behind.' I know, Aunt Cee-Cee, that I should be glad you let me stay with you because people weren't crazy about adopting or taking in little black children."

"I never said that."

"Yes, you did."

"No, I didn't. I never said people didn't want to take in little black children."

"You told me that people weren't lining up to adopt little black children," Gabrielle said. "That's what you would tell me over and over again. You let me know every chance you got that no one out there wanted me or would ever want me."

"No. No, what I said was that people weren't lining up to adopt *older* little black children. I said that if they didn't adopt a black child as an infant, you pretty much got stuck in the system. Now, *that's* what I said. If you're gonna throw your ingratitude back in my face, at least be accurate about what I said." Aunt Cee-Cee sighed hard.

"Listen," she continued as she held her hands up in surrender, "I don't want us to fuss or fight. It's the holiday season—a time for people to put aside their differences. We have a new president coming into office next month. Why, he's already working. Just like the black man—has to start working before he even starts getting paid. Then, they have the nerve to complain that he's not doing enough. Give the man a break!" Aunt Cee-Cee shook her head quickly as though she realized she was getting sidetracked. "Look, I admit I made a few mistakes in raising you. I admit it, okay? But I *did* try. I did the best I knew how at the time. Your mama had just died—"

"My mama was killed," Gabrielle said with deliberate measure. "She didn't just *die*. She was helped to die. My mother died against her will."

"Okay. Your mama was killed. And my brother was unjustly charged with her murder."

"No, your brother"—Gabrielle spoke slowly—"my father *killed* my mother."

"Honey, now I know that's what you believe happened. But I have told you time and time again that that is not what occurred. You were three years old. Three—too young to remember or know what happened. Look, as hard as I try, I can't remember anything much that happened in my life before I was five. Now, how could you, at the age of three, remember anything?"

"My father beat my mother, and then he strangled her until she lay lifeless on the floor. She was not just asleep like he tried to tell me when he carried me out of my room to the back porch. She was dead! I saw it. I saw *everything* with my own two eyes. And I remember it."

"Gabby, if—"

"I've asked you not to call me that! My name is Gabrielle. That's what my mother named me, and that's what I prefer being called."

"Okay. Okay. I'm sorry. I forgot. Okay, you don't like being called Gabby. Fine. And Booker is no longer your last name, so you are therefore no longer a Booker, either." Aunt Cee-Cee took a deep breath and released it slowly and with determined control. "Gabrielle, come on now. If it was your father that killed your mother, why were his thumbprints not found on her neck? Huh? The killer was wearing gloves. He had planned it all out beforehand. See, that's what I'm trying to tell you. It was a setup. They set my brother up. They set your father up to take the fall for the death of your mother because they wanted to close the case and be through with it. That's all that was. Those police didn't care all that much about some black woman being murdered. And they cared even less than that about putting another innocent black man in prison as long as they got one."

Gabrielle stood up. "I saw him strangle her. Do you hear me? I saw him beat her as she pleaded for him to stop. She even pleaded for him not to do what he was doing in front of me. But he kept slapping her around, pulling on her, like she was nothing." Gabrielle was crying now.

"Okay, if he did it, then why weren't his fingerprints found on her neck?"

"I don't know! Maybe because he was wearing work gloves!" Gabrielle knew she needed to calm down. "He had come home from work and hadn't taken off his gloves. But I saw him strangle her. Then, when the police arrived, he was crying and acting like he was all torn up about having come home and found her like that. He told them someone had evidently come into our house and killed her. It wasn't a forced entry, so she had to have known the person. Then he had the nerve to act like he hadn't been able to find me when it was he who took me and put me outside on the porch next to that old washing machine. He told me not to say a word to anyone no matter what they said to me or they would haul me away. That I would never see either him or my mother again. Well, even with me not saying anything—not that I was able to anyway—that pretty much came true."

"You see, that's what they put in your head. You were in shock. You barely spoke for over a year. I know you think all of this happened because they told you it did. You didn't remember because it never happened. Your father told them her boyfriend must have done it," Aunt Cee-Cee said. "You were mistaken. It was her boyfriend that did it."

"Then why didn't they ever find any evidence of a boyfriend?"

"Because your mother was great at keeping secrets. They couldn't figure out who she had been cheating with," Aunt Cee-Cee said. "I know you don't want to hear this, and I don't like speaking ill of the dead, but Gabrielle, your mother's boyfriend was the one who did it. He'd worn gloves to keep from leaving his fingerprints in the house. You saw her boyfriend. Then, your daddy came home. Your mind mixed up the two events; it merged them together. I know you *think* you know what you saw, but you were three years old. Three! Your little mind played a terrible, terrible trick on you. I don't blame you for what your mixed-up mind has you believing."

"No, it was my father. He told me that if anyone asked me anything, I was to tell them I had seen a stranger in the house. He said I had to do that to protect my mother or else she would be in a lot of trouble. But there was not a stranger in our house. There was only my father! My father killed my mother, and now he's paying for it in prison. And no, I will not accept any collect calls from him. No, I don't want to go see him in prison ever again. Not ever again. And I would appreciate it if both you and he would just leave me alone!"

Aunt Cee-Cee stood up. She reached out to try to hug Gabrielle. "I know that's what you think happened. The police and those social workers were the ones that put all these thoughts into your head. That's why you believe that's what happened. Come here. I'm here for you, Gabrielle. We'll sort this out, once and for all. You and me." She held out her arms for Gabrielle to come into, even though she had rarely hugged Gabrielle when she was growing up. "Come here." She reached over and tried to pull Gabrielle into her embrace.

Gabrielle snatched back. "Don't touch me."

"Gabrielle, don't be like this. I know it hurts. Look, I'm sorry, okay? I'm sorry I ever said anything that would even bring this conversation up."

Gabrielle backed away from her. "You're not sorry about anything." She shook her head incessantly. "All you're sorry about right now is that you need some more money from me and you realize causing me to be upset at this point doesn't work in your best interest. All you care about is you and your bratty children. All you care about is yourself and that sorry excuse for a husband. That's all you've ever cared about. Well, Auntie Cee-Cee, I don't have any more money to loan you. All right? So you can get your purse and leave now."

"Is it you don't have any *more* money? Or is it you don't have any more money to lend to *me*?"

Gabrielle laughed. "Good-bye, Aunt Cee-Cee. It was lovely seeing you again."

Aunt Cee-Cee slowly picked her purse up off the couch. "Gabrielle, I never meant to hurt you. I admit I've made my share of mistakes. I admit that. And if I could go back and do some things over again, I promise you I would. But please, please, I beg you; think about the good that I *did* do for you. Think about all those times I let you go over to Miss Crowe's house even though it didn't take me long to figure out she wasn't working you all that hard when you went."

"Is that right? And pray tell how did you figure *that* out?"

"You were always just a little too eager to go over there. I don't know too many children who get that excited about work," Aunt Cee-Cee said. "Not any that I know of. And then there were the dance videos she obviously gave you that you called yourself sneaking back to the house and watching. You enjoyed working a little too much for me to believe that was all you were doing when you went over there."

"Yeah, but you must have forgotten. I got paid to work for Miss Crowe, remember? Money is always an incentive to do something with a smile you might not otherwise like or want to do. Money has a way of easing the pain and embarrassment."

Aunt Cee-Cee nodded. "Yes, you did get paid. And before you bring it up, yes, I did take every bit of that money from you except the dollar I allowed you to keep each time she paid you ten. And I really didn't care that you enjoyed it, because it was at least financially helping with expenses that popped up around the house. And no, I didn't save it for you and your college like I told you I was doing. But at least the money was spent on things we needed around the house."

"But hey, at least I got a tenth of what I made, right? I've had to pay my way all the way through life. Remember, Aunt Cee-Cee? You and Uncle Bubba were the ones who told me that I needed to get a reality check about life. That I needed to get my head out of the clouds, to stop dreaming about what kind of life I'd like to have and deal with life the way it was. How dare I think I could possibly attend The Juilliard School of Dance in New York or any other dance school. Or that I might someday dance with the Alvin Ailey American Dance Theater. All merely dreams. I needed to grow up and live in reality."

Gabrielle opened her front door. "Well, Aunt Cee-Cee, I think that was great advice then, and I'm sure you'll agree that it's great advice now. I'm certain that you and Uncle Bubba, Luke, Laura, Angie, Jesse, and those darling little grandkids of yours together will find a way to work out your financial woes. Give everyone my love, won't you?"

After Gabrielle closed the door, she rested her back against it. Thoughts of Miss Crowe and the days she'd spent at her house were the only things that eased the pain of the memories her aunt had just evoked.

That was the last Sunday of December. Now that Gabrielle thought about it, that may have been what caused her to dream about Miss Crowe that

Tuesday. Maybe her aunt had triggered something, causing her to bring Miss Crowe back into
her life, albeit in a dream, at a time when she
needed to see and hear her the most. A time when
she needed to be warned to change her life and
soon, before what happened to her mother ended
up becoming her own fate.

Gabrielle touched her neck as she remembered
these things. Tears began to flow.

# Chapter 6

*That which is crooked cannot be made straight: and that which is wanting cannot be numbered.*

—Ecclesiastes 1:15

Fatima had called Gabrielle on Sunday night to tell her that for the scheduled baptism next Sunday night, the church would provide a white gown for her. All she would need to bring was something to keep her hair from getting wet. They both laughed. They knew black women didn't play when it came to their hair getting wet, and especially if they'd just gone to the beauty shop that week. Gabrielle realized what she had done in giving her life to Christ. This was a sacred matter and nothing to play with.

"I hope you get a chance to look over the New Convert/New Member's Handbook if you haven't already," Fatima said. "It tells how the baptism on next Sunday will merely be an outward show of what has taken place on the inside. You'll be no more saved next Sunday night when they submerge you in the pool than you are right now."

"Really?" Gabrielle said.

"Really. Salvation comes from faith and confession. Water baptism merely symbolizes the death, burial, and resurrection of Christ in your life. When you step down into the water, it shows Jesus being taken down from the cross after the crucifixion. When they submerge you briefly under the water, it shows the burial. And when you're brought back up out of the water, it shows Christ being raised up from the dead and your being raised with Him. That He didn't stay dead or buried for long before God raised Him up. It's symbolic of how you're now raised up with Christ, just as the scriptures say. You'll be fine. I just didn't want you thinking you're not saved until next Sunday night when you're officially baptized. I wanted you to understand that you're saved right now."

Gabrielle appreciated her talk with Fatima. She could tell they were going to get along wonderfully. Fatima also invited her to come and help out with the day of service people were participating in on Monday, January nineteenth, in honor of Dr. Martin Luther King Jr. Day. She also told her a little more about the Inaugural Ball the church was planning to have in the church's banquet hall on Tuesday night, January twentieth, in honor of Barack Obama's inauguration.

People all around the country were preparing various celebrations for the inauguration day to feel part of the event. Since everybody couldn't fit into Washington, D.C., even if they'd wanted to, various events were being planned around the country in neighborhoods and cities to coincide with the celebrations in D.C. Even churches were getting in on the nightly celebrations.

Gabrielle realized Sunday when she confessed

Christ, it was time for things to change in her life. And Fatima had explained the baptism process beautifully.

Now her first order of business would be to quit her job. She called her boss and told him that effective immediately, she would no longer be working at his establishment.

"Why?" asked thirty-four-year-old Clarence.

"It's time for a change."

"I knew it. I knew this was going to happen. It's this Obama thing, ain't it? That's why I didn't want him to win. I knew it! I knew black folks would start looking at their lives introspectively and wanting their own change. What does change have to do with you working here?"

"It's not Obama, although I am *so* proud that he won. It's me. It's who I want to be. What I was doing was fine for a past, but it's not what I desire now or for my future."

"Oh, Lord, don't tell me. That woman got to you, didn't she?"

"What woman?"

"That meddling woman I've caught hanging around trying to tell folks about Jesus and how much He loves them. I've chased her away more than a few times. I told Blue to keep an eye out for her. I bet he was somewhere asleep. You know she's crazy, right? You know she needs to be on medication," Clarence said. "Any time a person tells you they heard a voice speaking when there's no one visible to be doing the speaking, that's a person who needs to run, not walk, but run to the nearest doctor and get some help. There's medication that will shut those voices right up."

Clarence released a sigh, then continued. "Will you think about what you're doing? Goodness, you can't just leave me like this. You're the best I got, and I mean that. Do you know how many people come here because of you? A lot. And I'm not fooling myself. Do you want a raise? Is that what this is all about? The economy's been tough on everyone. If you want more money, I can do that. I did sort of cheat you when you first came to work here. I actually do owe you."

Gabrielle smiled. She knew he'd cheated her in the beginning. But he'd also been the only one to give her a real chance. She could never be mad at Clarence. "I'm saved, Clarence. And that means I can't continue doing some of the things I used to do. You know what's funny? I don't even *want* to do it anymore. Something has changed inside of me. I'm a different person now. I need to do different things in, of, and with my life. I can't explain it. But I wish you would come and go to church with me. Maybe you'll see the light, too."

"Oh, Lord, have mercy! Not you. Goodness, I can't believe this is coming out of your mouth. You're the woman with big dreams, remember? Do you know how close you are to reaching those dreams? Do you have any idea what you've accomplished just in the eight years you've worked for me? You worked your way up the ladder. That's the American way. And *you* did it. Nobody gave you anything! *You* did it."

"Clarence, I'll tell you right now what I *do* know. I know one scripture at this point. A woman at church gave it to me. She told me to read it in the Bible. I memorized it because there's a lot in that one scripture. It says, 'For I know the thoughts that I think toward you, saith the Lord, thoughts of peace, and not of evil, to give you an expected end.' That's Jeremiah 29:11."

"Goodness, will you listen to yourself? Mercy, you sound like those people who've been brainwashed by church fanatics. It was that attack, wasn't it? Thursday morning when you were attacked? That's what's got you all messed up now. Look, I'll protect you."

"It wasn't just the attack. The attack didn't even happen on your property. So, are you planning on protecting me everywhere?"

"I can hire a bodyguard for you if that's what it takes to keep you," Clarence said.

"I bet you would do that, too," Gabrielle said.

"If that will make you stay. At least until my people can find that sicko still running loose out there and take care of him."

"I believe that attack was something God used to help me to see clearer."

"Oh, so you believe God had that clown attack you so you would come to Him? Is that how you think God operates?"

"No, Clarence. I'm no expert, although I can't wait to get to know more about how God operates. But I do believe things happen in our lives, and sometimes God will use what was a bad thing and make something good come out of it. The fact is: I was attacked. Part of it, one might argue, was my fault, part definitely due to my stupidity."

"Goodness, girl! I'm sorry, but I'm not going to sit here and allow you to take the blame for something that was undeniably not your fault or your doing. No one, no one has the right to physically attack anyone, I don't care what or why they claim they did it."

"But I'm the one who put myself in that position. What else was I to expect? Well, today I went forward, gave my life to Christ, and now, I'm saved. And do you know what? It feels wonderful! I feel free. That old creature you used to know is gone. Dead! I'm a new creature in Christ. Do you have any idea what I'm talking about?"

"Sort of." He paused, then continued. "You know, I *could* tell you that you have to give me at least two weeks' notice before you can just up and leave. That *is* standard protocol when you leave a job. That's if you want to leave on good terms, at least."

Gabrielle laughed. "But you won't do that. And you know why, Clarence? Because deep down in your heart, deep down in your soul, you know what I'm doing is right."

"You're just going to end up getting hurt," Clarence said. "I'm telling you. I know a thing or two about church folks. And I'm telling you up front, they're going to hurt you. You're going to be greatly disappointed. But you and I have always been straight with one another. So, let me say this. You never tried to do me in or double-cross me while you worked here. So, if you ever want to come back and work here, I don't care how far down the road that might be, know that there will always be a place for you. As long as I'm the owner here, and I'm paying the bills, there will always be a place for you."

"Thanks, Clarence. I hope you know how much I've appreciated working for you. And, Clarence?"

"Yeah?"

"If you ever want a real change in your life, change you can believe in, I would love for you to come and go to church with me. It's called Followers of Jesus Faith Worship Center. George Landris is the pastor. It seems to be a good place."

"Followers of Jesus? Are you sure this isn't some cult? 'Cause I have peoples," he said, purposely misstating the word *people*, "and if we need to, we can come get you out of there. I have peoples; we can break you out."

Gabrielle laughed again. Clarence could always make her laugh. "You have peoples?" she said. "Thanks, Clarence, for understanding. And my invitation to go to church with me is always open."

"Yeah, well, don't take this the wrong way, but me and church don't mix. Just be thankful you didn't join up with Divine Conquerors Church."

"Actually, that's where I went first this morning."

"You did? What happened? Why did you end up at the other place?"

"I guess I was too much of a sinner for them to want me contaminating their precious sanctuary."

"Yep. I believe you hit that one dead on the head."

"How do you know about Divine Conquerors, or any church, for that matter?"

"What? You mean I never told you?"

"Told me what?"

"That I was a PK. Yep, that's right. Clarence

grew up a preacher's kid. On the serious side, you mind what I'm telling you. You be careful over there with those church folks. Watch your back. Thorns on a rose by any other name will still prick you if you're not careful. You might have signed up to follow Jesus, but everybody at church ain't walking the straight and narrow the way you might think they are. Hear me when I tell you that the church has its share of hypocrites as well as vipers."

"I'll keep that in mind. Well, I guess I should get off the phone now. Good-bye, Clarence. You take care."

"You too." He was about to hang up. "Goodness, I just about forgot. What do you want me to do with your final check?"

"You can put it in the mail."

"I can do that. But if you want, I don't mind running it by your house. Trust me, you're going to need it sooner rather than later. Trying to find a decent-paying job, especially in this jacked-up economy, ain't gonna be a picnic."

"It's okay. You can mail it. That will be fine. You take care, Clarence."

When she hung up, she couldn't help but feel the love she knew Clarence had for her. She started to smile. "Bad boy Clarence was a preacher's kid? Mister 'I have peoples' was the son of a preacher?" She couldn't help but burst into a laugh at the sheer thought of that.

# Chapter 7

*And say, Thus saith the Lord God; A great eagle with great wings, longwinged, full of feathers, which had divers colors, came unto Lebanon, and took the highest branch of the cedar.*

—Ezekiel 17:3

"Historic." That's what Johnnie Mae Taylor Landris called this day as she spoke to her two children sitting on the sectional sofa close by. Although it was Tuesday, many schools in Birmingham, Alabama, had given the children the day off, in addition to their already being scheduled off that Monday for Dr. Martin Luther King Jr. Day. That's why so many people, including school-age children, happened to be home witnessing history as it was being made.

Princess Rose took notes as she sat on the sofa in front of the television on January 20, 2009, watching Barack Hussein Obama being sworn in as the forty-fourth president of the United States of America.

Johnnie Mae smiled at the diligence of her oldest child. Earlier, she had said, "Princess Rose, pay close attention. This is historic. You and your brother are officially eyewitnesses to history being made right before your eyes. You'll be able to tell your children one day when they read in *their* history books that you saw this as it happened. You'll be able to tell your children and your grandchildren that you witnessed this day when it happened. Barack Obama"—she momentarily placed her hand over her heart, struggled to swallow, then took her hand down—"our nation's first black president."

Johnnie Mae cried through the entire morning ceremony, much as she'd done on that Tuesday night, November 4, 2008, when the news station she was watching quickly, and at exactly eleven o'clock on the dot central standard time, declared, "Barack Obama will become the forty-fourth president of the United States of America."

She got chills every time that announcement replayed, just as she had the first time she'd heard it.

Princess Rose Taylor turned ten on December eighteenth, finally reaching that coveted double-digit number. Her little three-and-a-half-year-old brother, Isaiah Barron Edward Landris, would turn four on June fourteenth. Princess Rose and Isaiah's last names were different because they had different fathers. Princess Rose's father was Solomon Taylor, killed in an automobile accident in 2000, right after her second birthday. Her mother, Johnnie Mae Taylor Landris, a famous author, married Pastor George Landris, considered to be famous in his own right, on September 8, 2001.

Many still called her mother Johnnie Mae Taylor because that's the name she continued to use on her books even after her marriage to George

Landris. Princess Rose didn't mind that at all. The name Taylor allowed her to feel connected to the family and not the odd person out. The way things stood, she was the only one in her immediate family who didn't possess the last name of Landris. George and Johnnie Mae had discussed possibly legally changing Princess Rose's last name to Landris. But Johnnie Mae felt Princess Rose should have a say-so about it. She decided it best to wait until her daughter was old enough to understand what that meant and have some input.

A few people called her Johnnie Mae Taylor Landris.

"No hyphen, please," Johnnie Mae would quickly inform anyone who was intent to write it the wrong way. But the majority of people, mostly church members, called her Sister Landris, while everyone else referred to her as Mrs. Landris or simply Johnnie Mae.

One of Isaiah's two middle names, Edward, was after his father's, George Edward Landris's, middle name.

"Daddy Landris," Princess Rose said, looking over at her stepfather as they watched the inaugural events. "Mr. Barack and Mrs. Michelle hug and act just like you and Mommy do. They look like they're really in love. I hope when I grow up, I marry somebody who loves me the way you seem to love Mommy and the way Mr. Barack seems to love Mrs. Michelle."

"Oh, it's going to be a good long while before you'll be getting married to anyone," Pastor Landris said.

Princess Rose swung her head around with a

smile and looked straight into her stepfather's eyes. "I know that, Daddy Landris. But I've heard you say how important it is for girls, and especially young ladies, to see men treating their wives right. That way when they grow up and get out in the world, they'll know what to look for in a man when they *do* decide to get married. I'm taking notes." She held up her steno pad.

"Is that what you're doing there with your notebook?" Pastor Landris asked. "Taking notes on what a good man and wife should be?"

"No." Princess Rose giggled. "I'm taking notes on the inauguration and everything else that's happening on this day. It's for school. We're supposed to write an essay as though we're writing it for the history books. So when Mommy keeps telling me to pay attention because this is history being made, I'm trying to pay attention so I can write things down. I'm going to write my essay when I finish as though I'm writing history. Only, I get to write mine as it's happening and fresh on my mind. I want to include the human angle as well."

Johnnie Mae laughed. "The human angle? Well, all righty, then. Go on with your bad self, Miss Lady." She high-fived her daughter, who giggled, then fell back on the sofa.

"Let's see. Now, where have I heard that before?" Pastor Landris rubbed his perfectly trimmed goateed chin. "Yes, that's right. This gorgeous, famous author named Johnnie Mae Taylor, who's actually married to some little jackleg preacher named George Landris, legally making her Johnnie Mae Landris, that's where." Smiling, Pastor Landris directed his full attention at his wife as he spoke. He then turned back to Princess Rose. "Maybe you're going to grow up and be an author, just like your mother," he said.

"Hold up! Wait a minute! Don't be calling *my* husband jackleg. He's anything *but* a jackleg preacher," Johnnie Mae said. "Them's fighting words, Mister."

Princess Rose laughed at both her parents. Isaiah glanced up on occasion as he worked with his puzzles. Isaiah loved putting puzzles together. He would take four or five different puzzles, dump all the pieces into a big pile, and mix them all together. He would then put all the puzzles together almost without batting an eye. And these were one-hundred-piece puzzles. He went through lots of boxes because he was so good at it.

A straight-A student who loved English, Princess Rose was in the fourth grade. Her fourth-grade teacher really wanted to skip her to the fifth grade, but upper management in the school system was bucking that idea. Princess Rose would have already been in the fifth grade had her birthday not come after the school's cutoff date. If you weren't five by that date, you couldn't start kindergarten. Born December eighteenth meant she was closer to six when she began kindergarten and seven for the first grade.

Princess Rose didn't mind too much. There were lots of children in her class whose birthdays didn't make the date. Her BFF (Best Friend Forever) was Shannon Henderson, an October-seventh-born baby. She and Shannon had been friends for as long as she could remember. They did almost everything together. At least, as much as the two of them could finagle. Like double clicks needed to launch a software program, the two of them had a lot in common. One was that they both had baby brothers who, at times, could be little monster brats.

Johnnie Mae would tell Princess Rose not to call Isaiah a brat or to say that he was bad. But Princess Rose knew a different little boy than they saw. And her brother could indeed be, on occasion, both a brat and bad. He just did his little deeds on the sly, and their parents only saw things when Princess Rose was trying to make him do right.

Johnnie Mae often reprimanded Princess Rose, telling her she was just a tad too bossy for her own good. Daddy Landris would merely laugh and say she just had a lot of spunk. He would then smile, lean down and, in a manner resembling a whisper (even though Princess Rose knew her mother could hear him quite clearly), say, "Truth be told, you're *exactly* like your mother."

Princess Rose would grin, then give her step-father a big hug.

Without a doubt, Princess Rose *loved* Daddy Landris!

# Chapter 8

*The elder women as mothers; the younger as sisters, with all purity.*

*—1 Timothy 5:2*

Followers of Jesus Faith Worship Center would be playing host to its own Inaugural Ball on the evening of January twentieth. Johnnie Mae had bought her dress as soon as she knew the church was planning to do this. She would be wearing an Amsale gown—a strapless, lustrous, gorgeous, rosewood brocade evening dress of rose, black, and pink, with an asymmetrical dropped waist that was shirred along one side. The fully lined dress contained netting underneath that caused the skirt to appear as though it was standing all on its own.

Gabrielle was excited about attending the church's Inaugural Ball on Tuesday. She'd heard others say (and she'd believed) that once a person gave his or her life to Christ, there was nothing fun left to do. She determined that was why so many waited until they got old to get serious about Christianity. But Monday, she'd worked alongside Fatima Adams and twenty other volunteers much of the day feeding the homeless and the less fortunate at the church. Additionally, they gave away clothing the church had collected, as a way of service. This was her induction into giving back, and she loved it! They even had evening wear for the women, suits for the men, and dress shoes for both to choose from. This would allow them to attend the church's Inaugural Ball the following night if they wanted to and not feel out of place because they didn't have proper evening attire.

Barbers and hairdressers, who as a general rule normally took off on Mondays, donated their time and talents to help the underserved look their best. It spoke volumes to what a press or perm and a curl for the women and girls, a clip and an edge for the men and boys, and a clean shave for the men could do to lift up a person's self-esteem.

Gabrielle had never known how wonderful something as small as serving someone a meal, watching the joy on a mother's or father's face as a warm coat fit perfectly on his or her little one, could make one feel. For the first time in a long while, she felt wonderfully alive. And it wasn't because she'd felt blessed to have food or clothing when others didn't. It was because she was blessed to be a blessing—blessed to be able to serve. It was an honor to take low, to help lift someone else up. No amount of money could buy that feeling. *Perhaps this was how Miss Crowe felt when she had helped me all those years ago*, she thought. Giving of one's self and time—priceless.

Having watched all the daytime events unfold, Gabrielle was looking forward to Tuesday night's Inaugural Ball. People wouldn't have to fly to D.C. to feel a part of the celebration. Oddly enough, after watching others get excited about *their* gowns on Monday, her biggest concern was still if what she was planning to wear was appropriate for a church function. When Fatima had told her about the ball that first Sunday night, she'd asked what church folks normally wore to these types of affairs.

"We wear what most people wear to a ball," Fatima said. "As long as it's not over the top, Christians are pretty much like regular folks who attend balls. Do you have a gown already?"

"I do, but it's strapless. I certainly can't wear a strapless gown to a church ball, especially now that I'm saved."

"My gown is strapless."

"Really?"

"Yeah."

"So, it would be okay for me to wear something that doesn't completely cover me from my neck down?" Gabrielle asked, no longer concerned about her neck being exposed, knowing that those nasty bruises would be gone.

Fatima let out a small chuckle. "Yeah. It's fine. I'm serious."

"I don't know. I would hate to have people staring at me because I wore the wrong thing."

"If it worries you or makes you feel uncomfortable, then get a shawl and wrap it around yourself. But you're going to find lots of women there wearing strapless gowns."

Gabrielle hesitated a second. She shook her head. "I just don't know. I don't want to come off too sexy or anything like that, and principally not at a church-sponsored function."

"I'll tell you what. If you don't believe me, I'll be happy to do a three-way call. I can add someone else from the church on the line who can affirm what I'm saying. You can ask them—"

"Oh, no, Fatima. No. That's not necessary," Gabrielle said. "And please don't think I don't trust or believe what you've said. You seem quite knowledgeable about church stuff. It's just being a Christian is totally new to me. But I trust what you're telling me. I just don't want people getting the wrong impression of me merely because I don't know all the dos and don'ts yet. I don't want to show up wearing the wrong thing."

"So, does this mean you're coming to the ball?"

"Yes." Gabrielle held her *s*, making a hissing sound.

"Great. Then, it looks like we'll be seeing a lot of each other over the coming weeks. Wednesday is Bible study, which is the time for you to attend your New Member's class. You get to ask all kinds of questions there. Next Sunday night, you'll be baptized. I plan to be there for that. I'm so excited for you! Possibly we'll run into each other at Bible study the following Wednesday. But so many people attend church service and our corporate Bible study, it's hard to say who you will or won't see at any given service."

"Corporate Bible study?"

"That's when, instead of breakout Bible study sessions in different areas of the church, we all meet in the main sanctuary as a group—the entire congregation. And Pastor Landris is teaching a great series: 'How to Stand During Difficult Times.' Thousands of congregants come to our regular

Bible studies. Attendance is almost as much as one full Sunday morning service. But I'll see you Wednesday at New Member's Bible study because this is my week to work."

Gabrielle inquired about clothing when she attended the New Member's Bible study. She later asked the teacher about what would be appropriate to wear to a church ball. The teacher confirmed what Fatima had told her.

Still, on the night of the ball, Gabrielle was unsure about her dress. She'd never known how self-conscious she really could be about something like this. All of this was so new to her.

A person who prided herself on always being on time, Gabrielle walked into the ball at six o'clock sharp. People instantly embraced her. She had never felt as though she belonged anywhere as much as she was being made to feel she was welcome at Followers of Jesus Faith Worship Center. She received compliments constantly on how beautiful she looked in her dress. She felt people were genuine with their words, and not just being polite. But things really hit home when one of the Mothers of the church (as she later learned they were collectively called) beckoned her to come over to their table and told her she looked nice. "But you really need to lose that shawl. You look like an old woman," Mother Gladys Franklin said.

Gabrielle smiled and took off the shawl. They introduced themselves, and seeing there were two empty seats, she decided to sit at the table with them.

Gabrielle was dressed in an ABS (Allen Schwartz) gown—a sage, brown, tan, and ivory ombré printed sheer silk chiffon, pleated at the top, draped insets extending from the front to the back, an empire waist, full sateen underlay, and strapless. Fatima arrived at the Inaugural Ball thirty minutes after it began. She couldn't help but laugh when she finally came upon Gabrielle sitting at the table with the Mothers of the church.

She hugged Gabrielle as they greeted. "*This* is what you thought could be construed as a floozy-like outfit?" Fatima asked Gabrielle as she grinned.

Gabrielle laughed as she looked her newfound friend from head to toe. "Now, I never used the word *floozy*. And any doubts I had about my dress, well . . . let's just say I wholeheartedly stand corrected. Please forgive me if I, in any way, offended you."

One of the Mothers began a deep, low chuckle. The others merged in. "You two look like twins. Y'all have on the same outfits," Mother Franklin said, pointing at both of them. "Except Fatima's dress is black and silver and yours is . . . exactly what color would you call that?" She directed the question about her dress color to Gabrielle.

"Sage, brown, tan, and ivory," Gabrielle said, recalling the colors touted on the Web site when, on a whim, she'd ordered the dress a few months back.

"Did y'all plan this that way or what?" Mother Franklin asked, directing her question to either one of the two.

"No, ma'am. We did not plan this. It's just how God happened to work it out," Fatima said.

"Well, I don't know just how much God really

had to do with it, but y'all look real pretty," Mother Franklin said. "Real cute."

Gabrielle smiled and gave a quick nod. "Thank you."

"Ooh, child. Take a gander at who just came strolling in," Mother Franklin said, pointing for Fatima to turn around and look.

Fatima turned and saw Trent walking in with someone she'd never seen before. She and Trent had been seriously dating now for a year. They first met about three and a half years ago. She'd just ended her three-year affair with Darius Connors and was leaving a counseling session with Johnnie Mae Landris after Pastor Landris's series on "Strongholds" caused her to make major changes in her life. She had thought it was too early and would be unfair to start a relationship with anyone so soon after Darius. So she'd kept Trent at bay. Of course, when Trent pressed her about going to a movie or out on a date, she had only told him that she needed time to heal completely after having just ended a long and complicated relationship. A year and a half later, they started doing more things together as friends.

She didn't dare tell Trent who she'd been in this relationship with or the unflattering and embarrassing sordid details surrounding it. Namely, that she had been dating a married man. Nor did she tell him that the married man was a member of their congregation. She made sure she avoided Darius as much as possible, which was made that much easier with his slack in church attendance after their breakup.

His wife, Tiffany, had recently joined the New Convert/New Member's Ministry. Fatima had to admit: she wasn't quite sure how she felt about that.

Fatima hated that she'd been the other woman. It had been easier when the wife had been an abstract composite created entirely by a deeply wronged party. A person she'd heard only bad things about, where she'd even felt somewhat justified in her actions. There were times when she had even been made to feel she was doing a good thing . . . a noble service actually, because the wife was not doing right by her man. But after she ended things with Darius, and after she'd seen this same woman working hard to take care of their three children (and Tiffany turned out to be as nice as she wanted to be), it made Fatima feel she'd been more like the scum of the earth than anything else.

Trent stopped at an empty table in the middle of the room and sat down. Fatima didn't want to leave Gabrielle there alone with the Mothers of the church. But she also didn't want to hurt the Mothers' feelings by implying she didn't want to sit with them if she and Gabrielle left them.

"Goodness gracious, child. Will you please go with your friend so she won't be standing there trying to figure out how not to hurt our feelings," Mother Franklin said to Gabrielle. The other Mothers began to nod in agreement, two of them shooing her to leave. "Go on. Go."

Fatima smiled. "Thank you, thank you, thank you," Fatima said to the Mothers. "Thank you for understanding."

"Oh, don't thank us. It's like it says in Psalm thirty-seven, verse twenty-five. Or is it verse twenty-nine?" Mother Franklin said. "No, I believe it's verse twenty-five—"

"Gladys, will you just tell us what the scripture says and quit fretting over getting the verse number right?" Mother Robinson said.

"No, now I believe the scripture with the word *fret* in it is Psalm thirty-seven and one, 'Fret not thyself because of evildoers.' Yep, I know that one fine. Done used it quite a few times myself over my lifetime. Fret is definitely in Psalm thirty-seven and one," Mother Franklin said.

"Mother Franklin, will you just quote whatever scripture you were about to quote before these young folk here turn as old as the six of us?" Mother Robinson said.

Gabrielle couldn't help but giggle a little as she stood there with a gigantic smile on her face. These women were a laugh a minute and so down-to-earth.

"I just didn't want to be leading this child here wrong," Mother Franklin said, pointing her head Gabrielle's way, a strand of her white hair looking like a lone finger wagging at Gabrielle from underneath her hat. "She just got saved a few Sundays back, was baptized two Sunday nights ago. Ain't you the one that practically Fred Astaired your way up to the altar on first Sunday and started shouting when you came up and out of the water on that second Sunday night? I declare the way you *glide* across a room . . . you seriously need to consider joining the dance ministry here at the church."

"She cain't join the dance ministry. Pastor Landris just sat that gal down that was over it," Mother Smith said. "Remember? I tell you, sin will mess you up every time. Y'all better hear what I'm telling ya. You cain't be up there in leadership and living any kinda way. Not at this church you cain't."

"Unh-uh, sho' you right," Mother Franklin chimed in. "Pastor Landris don't play that. Not here," Mother Franklin said. "All these folks thinking they can keep living like the world, sleeping with folks they ain't married to while they up in front of folks that know what they're doing. Unh-uh, that don't fly at this church. It might fly in other churches, but you can't be no leader here and think Pastor Landris is gonna overlook something like that. He'll shut down the whole ministry if he has to. Won't he do it?" She looked over at Mother Robinson and the others, who nodded in agreement. "I done seen him do it before. But he's fair now about *how* he do it. He ain't got favorites. Don't care how much he personally likes you. Right is right and wrong is gone. He does *not* play. Not when it comes to the Lord's business and the Lord's house."

"Mother Franklin, will you *please* tell this child what scripture you were about to tell her before y'all got off on this other subject that don't have nothing to do with what you were talking about originally," Mother Robinson said. "Unless one of y'all got a man sleeping with you we don't know about and you feel a need to confess," Mother Robinson said, alternating questioning gazes between the Mothers, Fatima, and Gabrielle.

"No, ma'am," Gabrielle said. "Not me. I'm as single as they come. I was too busy working and trying to get ahead to even have someone in the past to really speak of."

"Well, we know *you* not exactly single no more, Miss Fatima," Mother Smith said. "She done changed that Trent Howard so much he cain't actually be called a geek anymore. His own mother barely recognizes him. The two of you need to be making your way to the altar soon. It's about time we have another wedding around here. What are y'all now, thirty-six, thirty-seven? Too old to still be courting. It don't take that long to decide if you want to be with somebody or not. Look at that tux he's wearing. Y'all, just look at him. Most men come strutting up in here in a nice suit. Fatima got him so cleaned up, he steps in here in a full-blown tux. Looks real nice on him, too. Praise the Lord."

"Mother Smith, will you stay out these children's business. I declare, all of y'all need to get a life!" Mother Robinson looked over at Mother Franklin. "And for the last time, Mother Franklin, either quote the scripture so these two can leave or tell them you can't remember what you were gonna say so they can still go," Mother Robinson said.

"Oh, now I remember the scripture," Mother Franklin said, adjusting her silver rhinestone hat on her head better, clamping down that lone pointing strand. "I was just having a time trying to recall the actual reference." She folded her arms across her ample chest and pushed her back deeper into her chair. "Anyway, the scripture in

Psalm thirty-seven says, 'I have been young, and now am old; yet have I not seen the righteous forsaken, nor his seed begging bread.'"

"Oh, that was perfect, Mother Franklin," Fatima said. She sneaked a look back over at Trent again, who was now grinning and on the sly pointing a finger her way. "Well, we're going to run now. It was good fellowshipping with you all."

"Bye-bye, baby," Mother Franklin said. She tilted her cheek for her customary kiss from Fatima. Fatima hurried and hugged them, kissing them all on their cheeks.

As Fatima and Gabrielle were walking away, Mother Franklin said, "How come she feel she have to say 'you all'? How come she can't say *y'all* like everybody else?"

"It's a city-folk, northern, proper thing," Mother Robinson said. "I suppose folk who do that think the word *y'all* is too southern, too country for them. They don't realize we just know how to conserve. We're the ultimate conservatives. Y'all know our new president, President Obama—ooh, I just love saying that—President Obama is all for conserving energy, don't you? Well, I'm going to keep doing my part: You all, y'all. Two words versus one. Y'all." She smiled.

"No," said Mother Doris McFarland, "I don't think it's a city, a northern, or a proper thing as in a saddity way the way you're implying. It's just proper use of the English language, which frankly, I find quite refreshing in our young folk today."

"Course, *you* would say something like that," Mother Franklin said, laughing. "Will someone please pass the tea?" Mother Franklin said with an English accent.

"You need to stop. You know God doesn't like ugly," Mother McFarland said.

"No, it's God *don't* like ugly," Mother Franklin said, still chuckling. "Well, he don't."

They laughed even harder, including Mother McFarland and Mother Henderson, who hadn't said a word the whole time.

# Chapter 9

*The young lions do lack, and suffer hunger: but they that seek the Lord shall not want any good thing.*

—Psalm 34:10

Trent Howard stood and hugged Fatima when she walked over to the table. "I thought I was going to have to come and rescue you," Trent said.

Fatima laughed. "You know them. They're a fiery bunch, all right. But they did agree that you look quite debonair in your black and white tux, although they gave me *way* too much credit for the way you're dressed. I thought you said you weren't going to make it tonight?"

"Change of plans. I didn't want you to be alone on this night for this event. So, I changed my flight plans. Now I'll be leaving first thing in the morning to go to Seattle." Trent smiled. "I'm glad I did. You are beautiful."

The guy who had also stood up when Fatima and Gabrielle walked over cleared his throat.

"Oh, forgive me," Trent said, breaking his locked gaze with Fatima. "This is Zachary Wayne Morgan, known to many as Z. W. I met him when I was getting ready to come in. He doesn't know anyone here, but he heard we were having this Inaugural Ball and wanted to come and take part. Zachary, this is Fatima Adams. And I'd just like to let you know up front that she's already spoken for, even if you don't see a ring on her finger. And I must apologize, but I don't know this young lady, so I can't properly introduce the two of you."

Fatima smiled and turned to Gabrielle. "Well, this is Gabrielle Mercedes. She's new here at the church, just joined two weeks ago." Fatima mentioned the part about her recently joining the church more for Trent's benefit so he would know she was new to the church family. She didn't want to tell too much of Gabrielle's business here, mainly that she was also a new convert to Christ.

"It's nice to meet you, Fatima." Zachary shook her hand. "Nice to meet you, Gabrielle." He extended his hand out to her.

When Zachary spoke, it was as though the bass in the room was lowered all the way to the floor. His voice was, without a doubt, genuine baritone—not a hint of tenor trying to mask as deep anywhere to be found. His voice was as smooth as caramel, which also happened to be the color of his skin. His slightly wavy hair was jet black. And when Gabrielle's and Zachary's hands met for that first ceremonial handshake, there was definitely a connection felt by both. It was like a positive and a negative charge coming together and—without any real effort—ending up generating a spark of electricity. Like walking across a carpeted room and touching a stainless steel refrigerator afterward. A surprise shock—not enough to hurt, but enough to let you know that something scientific has just taken place.

For Gabrielle, the rest of the night was heavenly, absolutely heavenly. On the large-screen television, they replayed a tape of Barack and Michelle's first dance at the Inaugural Neighborhood Ball broadcast on ABC to "At Last," a song made famous by Etta James and sung by Beyoncé. Beyoncé almost lost it at the end as she watched the couple's touching and romantic old-school slow dance. Everyone at the church ball who had someone to dance with joined in as though they were actually in the room dancing along with President and Mrs. Obama. Trent danced with Fatima. The second time the church's deejay replayed the tape, Zachary asked Gabrielle to dance with him.

But if you had questioned Gabrielle on what went on that night, she couldn't have told you anything except that Zachary had the most gorgeous eyes surrounded by the thickest, longest eyelashes she'd ever seen on a man, that he made her laugh, that she loved talking to him, that he was a deep and thoughtful thinker, and that he was truly a magnificent slow dancer. Gabrielle loved to laugh, even if most of her life she'd found little to laugh about. But this night had been different. This night had belonged to the people.

Gabrielle didn't know whether any of this would lead to anything more. But so far, having accepted the Lord when she had, had brought her into the lives of people and places she'd never even known were available to her. On Monday, she'd served the less fortunate and in the process began cementing a real friendship with Fatima Adams, someone who could mentor her in her walk with the Lord. She was at a wonderful Inaugural Ball without ever having to leave the comforts of Birmingham, Alabama—home of the Civil Rights movement. *What a glorious day this has been! The ancestors must be smiling and shouting with joy,* she thought.

And she'd met an unbelievable man who, although not a member of the church, had left stating he would definitely be back to visit during a Sunday worship service.

Days later, Fatima talked to Gabrielle. "So, you and Zachary really seemed to hit it off. Did you happen to get his number?"

"No," Gabrielle said with an uptick in her voice.

"No?"

"No."

"Well, did he happen to get yours?"

"Nope," Gabrielle said, popping the *p* in the word *nope.*

"So, he didn't ask for your phone number, and you didn't ask for his? Then may I ask you why not?" Fatima said.

"Because I don't think it's appropriate for a woman to run after a man. If he wanted my number or if he wanted to keep in touch with me, he would have asked for my number or said something to that effect. But he didn't do either. I met him, we had a wonderful time, and now it's time to move on."

"Girl, please. That man was interested. Believe me, from where I was sitting, he was *definitely* interested. So, it sounds like we don't know how to get in touch with him since Trent only met him when he came to the church that night. I'm pretty sure Trent didn't get his number. You met him, and you didn't ask for his number."

"What's this 'we' business?" Gabrielle asked jokingly.

"I know. I need to back off and mind my own business, don't I? It's just the two of you really looked like there was something going on over there. And truthfully, he wasn't hard to look at, either. I'm just saying . . ."

"Yeah, well, I have enough on my plate right now. I need to hurry up and find a job. This is not as easy as I thought it was going to be."

"What happened with your job?" Fatima asked.

Gabrielle paused before answering. She was feeling close to Fatima, but she didn't know her well enough to tell her everything about her life just yet. That was why she hadn't asked Zachary what he did for a living. Why she hadn't pried much into his personal business. She didn't want him asking her similar questions in return.

"I'm sorry," Fatima said. "That was insensitive of me. I know people are getting laid off and losing jobs left and right during this recession they're trying not to call a depression."

"It's okay. You're right. People are losing their jobs. But oddly enough, I didn't get fired or laid off. I quit mine. But, it was time for a change."

"Well, hopefully President Obama and his administration will get things back on track soon. He hasn't been in office but a week, and they're trying to give him grief already. I understand change. So, until things turn around, what are you planning to do?"

"Just keep pounding the pavement," Gabrielle said. "I do have something that looks promising. I'm scheduled for a second interview, which is always a good sign. It's not exactly what I was looking for when I went to this employment agency, but if I get it, if nothing else, it will hold me over until I can get something better later."

Gabrielle didn't bother mentioning to Fatima that the only place she'd received a call back from was a maid service company. But it was good, honest, and decent work. And it would allow her to work a regular day shift—Monday through Friday—so she wouldn't miss any church services.

Gabrielle loved Sunday morning services as well as Wednesday night Bible study. As she'd looked for a job, she'd taken the downtime from having to work a full-time job to read through the Bible. She'd never known the Bible could be so fascinating. Admittedly, a lot of it didn't make sense to her . . . why some things were important enough to be in the Bible (all of those who begat whom, for instance). But much of it was about real life: love, hardship, betrayal, disappointment, triumph, joy, hope, belief, being alone, and even times of feeling that God wasn't there or He just didn't care. She was hungry for the Word, hungry to know more and more about the Lord. She wanted to know what God required *from* and *of* those who've asked Him to be Lord of their lives.

And she had learned how to pray. She'd learned that, early in her life, the way she'd originally come to God in prayer was actually the way He would have His children come to Him. *So why didn't He hear her cry?* He had. She now understood that

God had been there all along, even when she hadn't known it.

Fatima helped her so much, more than she would ever know. She and Fatima began having their own mini private Bible studies at each other's house, over the phone, immediately after Bible study if they saw each other at Bible study. Gabrielle couldn't get enough of the Word. She listened to a mountain of CDs of Pastor Landris's sermons. And she quickly learned and understood who she was in Christ. She had taken one of the pages out of the New Convert / New Member's Handbook and taped it to her bathroom mirror so she could see and speak who she was in Christ each time she looked at her reflection.

"I am accepted (Ephesians 1:6), a child of God (John 1:12), a friend of Jesus (John 15:15), justified (Romans 5:1), have been bought with a price (1 Corinthians 6:20), blessed with all spiritual blessings (Ephesians 1:3), saved by grace (Ephesians 2:5) . . ."

# Chapter 10

*A good man leaveth an inheritance to his children's children: and the wealth of the sinner is laid up for the just.*

—Proverbs 13:22

Gabrielle started work at the maid service company in February, a little over a month after she'd given her life to Christ. Without a doubt, the work she was doing at this juncture (cleaning other people's houses) as well as the money she was bringing home (minimum wage, a mere fraction of her previous take-home pay, and more like her previous tips), was a huge departure from her life before Christ. Still, she was comforted in knowing that what she was doing was right.

Clarence had mailed her check just as he'd promised. He also included a little extra—a bonus, he called it on the note he'd attached, promising her again "in writing" that she would be welcomed back with open arms should she ever have a change of heart. However, Gabrielle was determined to press forward, to press toward the mark of a high calling, as she'd heard Pastor Landris say in more than a few of his taped sermons. She hadn't joined a ministry yet. For now, it was enough for her to merely sit at the feet of the Lord, like Mary did in the Mary and Martha story, learning more and more about the Lord.

And learn she did.

But learning wasn't helping her pay bills, which by March were already starting to stack up. She'd heard her share from others regarding the concept of confessing into existence those things one desired, but she still found herself unable to land even a callback for a better-paying job. Besides, nothing out there lately promised to pay anywhere close to what she had made before. She'd had three months of expense money in her savings account. But close to the end of April—even with her working—she found herself with more month left over than money.

Her aunt Cee-Cee hadn't paid back any of the two thousand dollars she owed, even though Gabrielle had called her at the end of March and told her she desperately needed at least some of her money now. After that, Aunt Cee-Cee avoided her calls entirely.

By May thirtieth, her birthday, spiritually she'd grown immensely. But financially, she was in dire straits. Her house note payment was behind. And for the first time in her life, creditors were actually calling her house asking about their payments. Back in February, one of her two credit card companies had increased her minimum payment due. When she'd called to inquire as to why they'd changed it like that, the rep claimed the company was trying to help their customers during this awful economic downturn.

"How does it help me when you more than double my minimum payment?" she'd asked.

"It will help you pay it off quicker," a woman with an Indian accent said.

Gabrielle laughed. "The company believes it will help me by raising my minimum payment from two hundred eighty-five dollars a month to seven hundred? They really think that will help me?"

The woman had to laugh, too. "I know. But the company really is trying to help the customers."

"Well, if you ask me, it looks like they're going about it the wrong way. You can tell them they need to stop helping me, then. With help like this, I'll end up either bankrupt or in the poorhouse."

In truth, Gabrielle really didn't understand why God would allow her to struggle so much when she was trying so hard to live right and do the right thing. When she'd finally spoken with a financial adviser, he told her she had no other option but to sell her house. And that she really needed to get rid of her car she truthfully could no longer afford to even keep up. "You need to either make more money or downsize what's no longer an asset but a liability to your financial health and well-being," he said.

Saturday morning was her birthday. She got up early and went to the park for her morning jog. She began to fervently pray to God for direction and some kind of financial relief. That was the morning Clarence stopped by her house to see her. She let him in.

"How are you doing?" Clarence asked, as he held a medium brown bag in his hand.

"Blessed in the Lord and highly favored," Gabrielle said.

"I knew it," Clarence said. "I knew you were going to start talking like them before too long."

Gabrielle grinned. "But I am blessed, and I am highly favored," Gabrielle said. "So, what are you doing out and about so early in the morning?"

He raised up the bag. "I brought us breakfast. Which way to your kitchen?" he asked, following her as she led him there. "You of all people know my work doesn't end until the early morning light. You've been on my mind a lot lately. I decided to come over after work. I started to call you, but I wanted to look into your eyes for myself. That way I can determine if you're really doing okay, or if you're just trying to prop up things." He sat the bag down on the glass-top table. "I know how it can be. You make a decision, think it's the right one at the time, only to discover that things might require a minor adjustment, a little tweaking here and there." He nodded as he scanned her from her head to toe. "You're *looking* good still," he said with a smile.

She looked down at herself. "I've gained a few pounds."

"But it looks good on you, real good."

"Thank you. I feel good. Really, I do. I never knew what was missing in my life until I gave my life to Christ."

"Good to hear. Glad things are working out for you." He sat down and opened the bag, pulling out two of everything: cinnamon buns, scrambled eggs, sausage patties, biscuits, and two large cups of coffee—one black, one hazelnut and caramel flavored.

Gabrielle went to the sink and washed, then dried her hands. She took down two plates and grabbed up two forks and two case knives from a drawer, placing them on the table as she sat down.

They each fixed their respective plates. Clarence took a forkful of his eggs and hurriedly shoved it in his mouth.

"I'd like to say grace," Gabrielle said, effectively halting his next forkful in midair. She bowed her head. Clarence lowered his fork and followed suit by bowing his head as well. "Amen," she said after her short prayer that encompassed a tad more than just praying over their food.

"Amen," Clarence said. He then went back to shoveling food into his mouth.

Gabrielle laughed. "I suppose you really are hungry," she said.

"What?" he said through a mouthful of food. "You thought I was making up something just so I could stop by?"

"I know how your mind works. You try to act as if you're this tough guy, when in fact you're just a big old teddy bear."

"Well, you know that's what people used to call me," Clarence said.

"What? Teddy bear? No, I didn't know that."

He cocked his head to the side and smiled. "Yes, you did. You can look at me and see a little of it still hanging on. Sure, I've gotten in a lot better shape since those days, but don't I still remind you

of a teddy bear?" He made a cuddly face. "And I
know you've heard a few people call me Teddy."

She laughed. "Well, since I didn't know you
when you were young, I wouldn't know anything
about that part of your history. How was I supposed to know you looked like a teddy bear growing up?" She pulled loose a thick, doughy strand
from her cinnamon bun and placed it in her
mouth. "I thought those people were calling you
Teddy because of your voice and the way you think
you can sing and kind of sound like Teddy Pender-
grass."

"You make me sound so old," he said, frowning.
"I'm only what . . . ? Eight . . . eight and a half years
older than you."

"Of course I'm not saying you're old. All I said was
that I didn't know you when you were younger."

"So, are you implying that I *can't* sing?"

"Just like your apparent nickname Teddy Bear
that I didn't know about, I don't know whether
you can sing or not," Gabrielle said. "I'm just repeating what someone said to you: that you have a
nice voice that reminded them of Teddy Pender-
grass."

"Well, I used to sing a lot—in the choir at
church, in fact. When I took hold of the micro-
phone, I would have people running all over that
church. They would buck and shout, praising God
like there was no tomorrow. It was actually something to behold."

She sipped a little of her coffee. "So, why did
you leave?"

"Why did I leave what?"

"The church? Why did you leave the church? Why did you stop singing for the Lord?"

"I didn't leave the church. You could say the church left me." He grabbed a napkin and wiped his mouth hard, then his hands before throwing the napkin on the table.

"I don't get it. My understanding is that the church is the people of God. The church is the body of Christ. From the little snippets you've dropped lately, I'm starting to learn that you were part of the body, at least you were at one time."

"And the rest of the body cut me off." He sliced hard into his cinnamon bun in sync with the word *cut,* practically ramming the piece he'd cut into his mouth. He began to chew hard and deliberately. "Just like tonsils or an appendix: something that's part of the body that apparently no one has any real use for anymore or knows what its purpose is. Just get rid of it. It's not really needed anyway. But that's life. The more you live, the more you learn to let things go and move on. Because if you don't, if you stand there trying to figure it all out, you're liable to get run over." He clapped his hands together fast and hard.

Gabrielle finished her coffee and pushed her plate forward. She shrugged. "That was good. Thanks for breakfast. Now I'll have to work to get rid of that cinnamon bun."

"No problem." He finished off his coffee, then stood up and cleared the table.

"You don't have to do that," Gabrielle said, jumping up and almost grabbing the two empty plates from his hand.

"Will you let go?" Clarence said, holding on tight. "I got this. Contrary to what people say behind my back, I *do* know how to clean up behind myself."

"But you've done enough. You brought me breakfast."

"Yeah, well, I really would like to talk to you about you letting me do even more for you." Clarence opened up the dishwasher to put the dishes in. He saw it was completely empty. Any dishes to be washed were in a neat pile in the sink.

Gabrielle bounced a few times. "I told you, I'm good."

"So, where are you working?" He put the dishes in the sink.

She placed her hand on her hip. "I'm fine, Clarence." She forced a smile. "I'm telling you, for real. God is good."

"*God* may be good, but it can be hard out there. I know. I know plenty of people who have lost a lot while they believed God was going to come and magically rescue them. Believing they could pray their troubles away. Believing God was going to swoop in and save their house or their cars or their livelihood, right before they lost everything. I know how hard things can be out there. And I want to help you." He shrugged as though he'd been asked a question he didn't know the answer to.

Gabrielle began to bounce, even more this time, as she buttoned her lips, then made a popping sound. "How? How do *you* think you can help me?"

"Come back and work for me."

"No, Clarence."

"Why not?"

"Because that's not who I am anymore."

"Who are you now?" Clarence asked.

"I am a new creature in Christ," Gabrielle said.

"Yeah, okay. I've heard that one. So tell me: how's that working for you? How is it when it comes to paying your bills? And I know you have bills."

"I'm trusting God."

"Trusting God, that's good," Clarence said. "But you still have to do your part. Sure, God knows what you're in need of, but God is not moved by people's needs. If that were the case, there would be no homeless people, no starving children in Africa, no mistreatment of children in America or the elderly in nursing homes. And before you quote the next standard Christian line, 'God knows my heart,' let me remind you: That's all well and good, but a good heart won't put food on the table or pay your power bill. If you don't believe me, call the power company. Tell them you can't pay your bill this month but you have a good heart. Call and tell them that. See where that leaves you. My guess is you'll be in the dark soon. So, why won't you tell me what kind of work you're doing? If you're so confident in God, it shouldn't be a problem for you to tell me what you're doing to make a living these days."

Gabrielle looked at him. She changed the position of her head several times. "That seems to imply that I even owe you an answer."

"See, proof positive that things aren't going the way you thought they would when you decided to accept Christ and His way of life, then quit your job afterward."

"I work for a maid service, okay?" She opened up both her hands and held them, palm up, next to her sides. "I'm not ashamed of what I do. And I'm *definitely* not ashamed of my God."

He smiled. "A maid? You're cleaning up behind other folks? *You?* Goodness, I don't believe what I'm hearing here. As talented as you are, the best you could find to do when you left my establishment was to get a job as a maid? A maid? And you call *that* God supplying your need according to His riches in glory? A maid? Goodness!"

"Clarence, let me tell you something." She flicked a finger at him. "What I have with the Lord right now is better than anything . . . *anything* I've ever possessed in my entire life."

"And what exactly is that? The pleasure of saying you get to clean other folks' houses so that you can *try* . . . try, I repeat, to pay for and stay in your own?"

"I am not ashamed of what I do. And I have a peace that surpasses your understanding and a joy that nobody gave to me and nobody, not even you right now in all that you're trying to do, can take away from me. I don't care what comes up in my life, I'm going to stand, do you hear me, Clarence?"

"Come back and work for me," he said, walking closer to her. "You could do it for a few months, possibly until the end of the year. You could make enough money to pay off all your bills. You could be debt free. Think about that. Look, I've been where you are before. I know how hard things can

get. And for those who try to tell you that they
have Jesus and that's enough, they're just fronting.
Sure, they love *having* Jesus in their lives, but they
keep praying for more money, praying to be out of
debt. Let me help you. Allow God to bless you
through me. I don't know if you've seen this scripture in the Bible yet, but it says something to the
effect that the wealth of the wicked or the sinner is
laid up for the just. I don't consider myself wicked
by any means, although I'm sure you could successfully argue that I am a sinner. But if you believe
that because I don't go to church that makes me a
sinner, then think of what you're attempting to do
to help alleviate your financial stress right now as a
fulfillment of God's Word. Look at it as though
you're taking the money I'm offering to pay you as
transferring the wealth of the wicked to the just.
Goodness, that's a transfer, don't you think?"

Gabrielle started laughing. "As we heard way
too much last year about the bridge to nowhere to
the point where it got on my nerves," she said.
"Thanks, but no thanks. And I suppose it's about
time for me to put you out."

"What?"

She grabbed Clarence by his shirt and—in a
playful way that only the two of them could appreciate—Gabrielle walked him to her front door.
"Since you know something about the Bible,
maybe you're familiar with the part in it where it
says, 'If the devil makes his way into your house,
it's up to you to put him out.' Well, I might have let
you in Clarence, but it's time for me to put you
out."

Clarence laughed as she opened the door. "Girl, I know you're not calling me the devil. I know you know better than *that*. And exactly where in the Bible is that scripture?"

"I know the devil will use those we care about and those who care about us to gain entrance into our lives. I *also* know he will use people we hardly know, as well as perfect strangers. So, that about covers you. And although I'm not exactly calling you the devil, right now you *are* trying to put forth his agenda. And I'm not having it. Not in my house, anyway. Now, you don't have to go home, but you do have to get up out of here."

He laughed as he shook his head. "You know you're crazy, right?"

"No, I have the mind of Christ. And you can officially call this act: Goodness and Mercy putting you out of this house. *Okay?*" She cocked her head to the side and threw him a grin as she playfully moved her eyebrows up and down.

Clarence laughed even harder. "You know, you really are taking this Jesus stuff *way* too serious, way too seriously. But I ain't mad at cha." He stopped laughing. "But seriously, though, if you ever need anything . . . *anything*. Money, something to eat, an ear, a shoulder to cry on . . . and even if you don't want to come back and work for me, I hope you know that I'm here. I'll happily spot you whatever you're in need of until you land back on your feet. I mean that. And as far as your job goes—"

"Good-bye, Clarence."

He smiled as he took out a stick of Wrigley's Spearmint gum, unwrapped it, then placed it on his tongue—drawing it inside of his mouth as though his tongue were the landing that the bird inside of a cuckoo clock rides on. And the same way the cuckoo bird disappears before turning in until the next hour, his gum disappeared inside his mouth. "Oh, and happy birthday," he said as he left.

# Chapter 11

*Praise him with the timbrel and dance: praise him with the stringed instruments and organs.*

—Psalm 150:4

Gabrielle had made a decision. It was true, she couldn't sustain her bills on the salary she was now making. Clarence had made a compelling and generous offer for her to return to her old job. But if she did, that would be like what Proverbs 26:11 says: "As a dog returneth to his vomit, so a fool returneth to his folly."

The first of June, her house would be put up for sale. As much as she loved her house, she merely couldn't afford to keep it on her salary.

The fifth Sunday in May, Johnnie Mae Landris stood before the congregation to make a special announcement. The dance ministry would not only be starting back up again, but until they found the right person to be the director, she would be heading it up.

"So, we're looking for all interested members. Anyone from age fourteen to ninety-nine who has a desire to possibly be a part of the dance ministry, please meet with me in conference room ten immediately after services today. If you've had dancing lessons, or if you're like many who've never been professionally trained but you have a heart and a desire to become part of the dance ministry, please meet with me as soon as service is over today in conference room ten."

Gabrielle couldn't believe her ears. She loved to dance. She had a heart for dancing. This was like a dream come true. As soon as Pastor Landris ended service, telling everyone not only to be blessed but to be a blessing, she made a beeline for the conference room. She was almost the first person there. About five minutes later, she looked up and was delighted to see Fatima walk in.

"I knew you'd be here," Fatima said to Gabrielle as she sat in the seat next to her.

"How did you know?"

"Girl, please. I saw the look on your face back in January at the Inaugural Ball when the Mothers of the church were talking about the dance ministry. Your face lit up like a Christmas tree when you heard there was such a thing."

"Yeah, but I also learned it had been placed on ice for the time being. It was amazing just to hear there was a form of dancing available in the church," Gabrielle said.

"Well, not all churches have or allow dance teams. Some churches don't believe people should dance in church, even if it is spiritual. They think when you do that, you're bringing too much of the world inside of the church walls," Fatima said as they continued to wait for Johnnie Mae to arrive.

"Well, I know that Moses' sister, Miriam I believe, danced for the Lord."

Fatima was impressed with Gabrielle. She had truly been studious when it came to the Bible. Fatima was convinced that even though she'd been in church a lot longer than Gabrielle, Gabrielle had surpassed her in her knowledge of what the Bible had to say on a variety of topics.

"Ironically," Fatima said, "I believe when King David danced in the street and ended up dancing out of his clothes, that caused many to feel that dancing, even in church, is inappropriate. It's all because David couldn't keep his clothes on." Fatima smiled as she shook her head.

"Wow," Gabrielle said. "I'm sure I read that since I've now read the whole Bible, but somehow I must not have grasped that."

"Well, I've only *heard* people talk about David dancing out of his clothes—that's how I know it's in there. But I'm sure that's not the only reason some people are against dancing in church. Many of them, as a general rule, believe that dancing is just worldly."

Johnnie Mae walked in. Everyone quieted down. There was a packet handed out. Those who remained interested after the meeting concluded were asked to take it home and read it. Various new rules were being put into place to ensure the integrity of the dance ministry. There was a form that needed to be completed and turned in by anyone who was serious about joining the ministry and not just there to see what was going on.

"There will be an audition two Saturdays from

now," Johnnie Mae said. "Any questions?" she asked when she'd finished highlighting things in the packet now in all of their possession.

"Yes," a woman in her midtwenties said. "Why do we have to audition? I mean, if we're doing this for the Lord, does it matter whether we're good or not? I thought God looked at our hearts and not at the outside. I might audition and be told that I'm not good enough to be chosen for the ministry. Yet I might have a heart for ministering through dance and a willingness to give my all, whereas someone who *can* dance wonderfully may not."

"That's true," Johnnie Mae said. "But we still want whatever we do to be done with a Spirit of Excellence. God has not purposed or gifted all of us to do the same thing. We have different talents, different callings, and yes, different gifts. Sometimes a person may have a desire to do something they have not been gifted or called to do."

"But I have a problem with that," the woman continued. "With all due respect, I don't think that's the way things ought to be done in church."

"Okay, let me ask this. What if you have a person who, let's say, wants to sing. That person has a heart for ministry through song, *but* they cannot sing. I mean, that person couldn't carry a tune if you were to put an iPod in a backpack and personally strap it to their back." Everyone laughed. Johnnie Mae continued. "Would you put that person out in front to minister to people just because it's what they want to do?"

"Well, I would, because it shouldn't be about impressing other people. It really should be about a desire and a heart to minister, which I've been taught by Pastor Landris means to serve," the woman argued.

"Okay, let me try it this way. Say you have a person who wants to be an accountant. This person may love working with other people's financial books. They may feel it's a calling. But they aren't so great with math or numbers, debits, and credits. If you had a business, would you want this person to handle your books just because he or she has a heart to do it?"

"But the person may really be trying. I don't think anyone should discourage someone from trying. They *could* get good at it if they were encouraged to keep at it and given a chance. If that person wants to do it, who does it hurt?" the woman persisted.

Fatima was becoming slightly annoyed by this woman asking so many questions about this same thing. She raised her hand. "Excuse me," Fatima said to Johnnie Mae. "May I give it a try?"

Johnnie Mae pointed her hand at Fatima. "By all means. Go ahead, Fatima."

"If you have a person who says he's been called to preach, but he simply is not good at preaching, can't preach a lick. I mean, he's so awful that people tiptoe out before he gets finished. Maybe he's not awful; he's just not good. But let's say he's an awesome teacher of the Word. Would you encourage him to keep trying to preach just because he desires to do that or would you steer him toward where his gift actually lies?"

"Okay," the woman said. "I guess I understand.

What both of you are trying to say is: It's not about us. It's about the ministry and what the ministry can accomplish in the body of Christ, in *tandem* with our gifts."

"Yes," Johnnie Mae said. "We're not trying to deliberately exclude anyone. We just want to help direct people to where they can be the most effective. Actually, all of this will be about both: the gift *and* the desire to minister without it being about *us*. The body of Christ wins when people are effectively operating in their gifts and their calling. Some people have the gift of dance. Some, the gift of song. Others, the gift of praise. Some of you may be outstanding teachers. Some administrators. Some of you may have been called to be directors, choreographers, organizers." Johnnie Mae stopped and smiled.

"All these parts are needed," Johnnie Mae continued. "Just like the parts of our physical body. Everybody can't be the eye. Everybody can't be the hand. Everybody can't be the mouth. Even with the hand, there needs to be a thumb, an index finger, a middle finger, a ring finger, and a pinkie. But with all parts working together, the hand is able to function properly. It's able to pick up"— she picked up a packet and held it up—"things like this packet." She put the packet back down. "A pen." She picked up a pen. "Point." She pointed. "And snap your fingers." She snapped her fingers. "The thumb might argue that it's more important, the index finger may argue that it is. But the truth is they all must understand that they're all needed in order to get the job done. At least done without having to deal with a handicap."

"I get it," another woman said. "It would be like if I wanted to play the organ. Sure, I've tinkered around a little to know how to play 'Twinkle, Twinkle Little Star,' but I can't play anything else too hot. And in truth, I don't really play that song all that well. Yet I insist I want to play the organ because I have a heart to play. I would get my way, but it would likely not bless the people hearing it. So I really need to lay aside my own ego for the good of others."

"Precisely," Johnnie Mae said, picking the packet back up. "And speaking of this packet, we need the application you'll find inside of here turned in no later than next Sunday." She set the packet back down again. "As long as you all know, the auditions are not done to hurt anyone. Everything we do, we try to do it with love. We just want to make this ministry as strong as possible. This ministry is part of the body of Christ, and we need to ensure we're putting our best foot forward." Everybody laughed. Johnnie Mae laughed as soon as she realized the pun she'd just made. They finished up and dismissed.

"You're still planning to try out for this ministry?" Tiffany Connors asked Gabrielle after the meeting was over.

"Yeah. You?"

"I'm going to give it a shot. I took dancing lessons for years when I was young. I admit that was some time ago. I'm more than a little rusty now. But hopefully, I'll get chosen," Tiffany said. "I need something else in my life to switch things up a little. Something for me. You know? Right now I go to work, take care of my children, take care of my husband, and take care of the house. I come to church, and that's about it for fun. I'm not even working in a ministry."

"Weren't you working in the New Convert/New Member's Ministry? That's where I met you," Gabrielle said, recalling Tiffany was the one who gave her the Bible.

"I was, but I had to quit. I felt bad having to run out early when it was my time to work because I was the only one here and I needed to go get my children from children's church so the workers there could leave." Tiffany looked down at her feet, then back up. "I ended up quitting that ministry after the second month. But I think this ministry may work out better for me. After we finish ministering with dance, which will likely only be on occasion, I won't affect too many people. Plus, I would be able to serve while doing something I love to do. Did you take dancing lessons when you were young?"

Gabrielle smiled. "Yes. In fact, I did. I had a great teacher, too."

"Well, I need to get my children so I can get home and practice." Tiffany smiled. "I hope we both get chosen. That would be great."

"Yeah." Gabrielle grinned. "I suppose I need to practice myself. I really pray we're both chosen, too."

Afterward, Gabrielle got in her car. She couldn't believe how things had transpired. "God, You are truly awesome. Only You could bless me with an opportunity to do what I love. You've given me something to hold on to as I prepare to let go of what I thought meant so much to me: my house and likely even my car. Yet, over these past months of learning more about You, I've found that knowing You, and having You in my life, is the greatest love of all."

# Chapter 12

*A man that hath friends must show himself friendly: and there is a friend that sticketh closer than a brother.*

—Proverbs 18:24

Gabrielle got home and immediately looked through the packet they'd been given at the meeting earlier. She first flipped through each page to see what all it contained. There were scriptures and teachings on why to dance in church, as well as the attitude of worship and praise that should be evoked when it came to dance and what the word *minister* means (to serve). It emphasized that when they danced, they were actually ministering to the people. And that meant they would be serving others through the ministry of dance. It was not to be entertainment in any way, shape, or form. It was not to be *a* show or *for* show. The scripture they were to apply to their lives and especially in this ministry was Colossians 3:17: "And whatsoever ye do in word or deed, do all in the name of the Lord Jesus, giving thanks to God and the Father by him."

On Tuesday, Fatima and Gabrielle got together at Gabrielle's house to practice before their auditions were to take place. They'd cleared the area in the den to give themselves plenty of room. But before they began, Fatima could see something seemed to be weighing heavily on Gabrielle's mind.

Fatima took Gabrielle by the hand and pulled her over to the couch. "Instead of practicing right this second," Fatima said as they sat down together, "which, incidentally, I'm not so sure I want to do—in front of you, anyway," she joked, "let's talk. Besides, I have a sneaking suspicion you're really good at this dancing stuff and the practice is more for my benefit. After seeing you, I just might totally reconsider even trying out."

Gabrielle playfully rolled her eyes at Fatima. "Girl, please. What's likely to happen is when I get a glimpse of you, I'll see just how much I really don't know, and I'll be the one who'll sit down. Although honestly, I really *really* want this. Really I do." Gabrielle smiled nervously.

"Is that what's bothering you? You're afraid you're not going to make the final cut? Because I can tell something is bothering you."

Gabrielle sighed hard. "No, it's not that." She sighed again. "I don't like putting my business out there."

"I won't say anything to anybody."

Gabrielle ticked her head, then scrunched her mouth. "I don't make enough money to keep this house, so I've decided to sell it. A Realtor is coming by tomorrow to put the sign in the yard. I don't make enough money to keep my car either, so I'm looking at trading it in for something smaller and less expensive. I've been late with a few of my bills recently. So that's messing with my credit record and has lowered my FICO score tremendously, which doesn't help when you're trying to get another car."

"Whoa," Fatima said, pulling her body back. "What do you know about FICO scores? Most black folks don't have a clue what that is, let alone that it's something they should care about."

"Besides loving to dance, I'm really good when it comes to business matters. Although you wouldn't know it based on some of the decisions I've made lately."

"You mean like quitting a job that, from all you've told me, was great pay, then accepting a lower-paying job that's not paying enough to cover your bills?" Fatima said.

"So, you think I should have kept the job I had until I found one that at least paid me closer to what I was making?"

"Look, I don't know the circumstances surrounding your leaving. So no, I'm not saying that at all. I would be the last person to second-guess you on that. I'm dealing with enough stuff on my own job right now. So believe me, I can empathize with anyone quitting a job. I can't tell you how many times I've thought about turning in my resignation and walking right out the door. But I suspect most of us are merely slaves to our jobs, or at least slaves to our employers. Oh, we think we're free. But in truth, we're not. We get a few dollars after taxes, and we sell our lives to them in exchange for it. We're told what time to be there, what days, the amount and the days we get to be off. We're told what they want, how they want it, and when they want it done. Truthfully, many people do things they might not ever normally do, all at the altar of the almighty dollar."

Gabrielle started laughing.

"What's so funny?" asked Fatima.

"I was just sitting here thinking about the number of people who have sold themselves into indentured servitude without even realizing that's what they've done."

"Okay, I'm missing something here."

"What you were just saying." Gabrielle lifted her body up and purposely sat on her foot. "Some of us do things we really don't want to do, and we can't walk away because we really aren't free to walk away, in spite of our protest to the contrary. When most folks think about leaving a job, they have to consider the money they're receiving and whether or not they can actually afford to do it. Most people who *do* leave, leave because they're forced out through layoffs or downsizing, they get fired, or the company folds and then the workers have nowhere to report. Few people, especially these days, are free enough—after having acquired a mountain of debt—to simply walk away from their jobs just because they want to. And if they do leave on their own, you'd better believe either they have another job lined up or they're searching desperately to find another one to replace it."

"So, that's what's bothering you?" Fatima said. "Your decision to leave your other job?"

"Not *whether* I made the right decision in doing it; I had to do that. It's really complicated. I wish I could tell you—"

"I told you, you can tell me anything. I'm not

one of those people who likes to hear something and go blab it to somebody else. I'm not. We're friends—at least I consider myself your friend. Everybody needs someone they can share and talk things over with. Those things that mess with us, on the inside of our minds. It's not healthy to keep things locked up inside," Fatima said. "If we're not careful, the mind can quickly become the devil's playground. Satan loves toying with us. Using our thoughts against us, telling us things to cast shadows of doubts. Just messing with our minds."

Gabrielle nodded. She'd definitely been presented with her share of negative thoughts. "I don't think you would tell anybody, Fatima. You truly have been a great friend. I've just kept things inside of me for so long, most of my life actually. I've only had myself to confide in. And I'll admit: I don't trust easily. The only person I learned early on in life I could rely on and trust was me. Whenever something is going on, I tend to keep it to myself. It generally works out over time one way or another anyway. Of course, now that I've come into the knowledge of Christ, I can talk to the Lord about everything. He is truly a friend that sticks closer than a brother."

"That's good, Gabrielle. But God still created us to help one another, to be there for each other, to lean on each other for strength. I just want you to know that I'm here for you. If you need to talk about something, I can listen with my mouth closed. If you need my opinion or advice, I'll be glad to give that. If you're simply looking for a sounding board, I can be that for you. You don't have to do this all by yourself any longer. I would even encourage you to talk to Johnnie Mae Landris if you'd like. She's fantastically great to talk to. But you need to find someone you feel you can trust and are comfortable with. That's what it means to be sisters and brothers in Christ. And a true sister has your back."

Gabrielle settled more comfortably on the couch, readjusting her body. She closed her eyes as she spoke. "I'm selling my house. And I'm not even sure where I'm going to live after I do that. In truth, my house note is not all that more than it will cost to rent an apartment. So if I can't afford this house, I certainly won't be able to afford an apartment. I thought about getting a roommate, but that usually turns into a disaster. I've considered trying to find a part-time job to supplement my income. But if I do that, I'll miss Bible study on Wednesday nights and possibly not be able to attend church on Sundays. Who knows? So, a part-time job is not an option for me. My relationship with God is too important to me to sell myself out for a house or a car or just mere things."

"I understand what you're saying. But I know people who work two jobs. They're still able to study the Word. They just learn to do what they have to do to make it work."

"I'm sure they don't study the Word like they would at Bible study. They're likely too tired or have too many others things to catch up on. We can't do it all. Something will inevitably go lacking or be half done. It's a trick of the devil. I'm telling you, the devil is causing us to sell our souls for money. Making it appear that we're doing the noble and honorable thing like making sure we have a nice place to live, something nice to drive around in. Arguing how else will we be able to bless the people if we can't reach them? And we do have to put food on the table and take care of our family," Gabrielle said. "We just have to do what we have to do. It's okay. God understands."

Fatima frowned. "I'm not following you."

"We're selling out the way Judas sold Jesus out for thirty pieces of silver. We're selling out Jesus when we choose certain things over Him. How are we to follow somebody if we don't know where they're going? How are we going to know where Jesus wants us to go if we don't study His Word, have time to talk to Him, time to listen to what He has to say? Sure, I could go back to my old job, right now if I chose to. But that job would become a hindrance, a stumbling block with my walk with the Lord. I would have to work on Wednesday nights, among other things, when I need to be at Bible study. It would likely keep me from attending church on Sundays. I always had to work Saturday nights into the early morning hours. And did you know that Sunday mornings happen to be the best mornings to sleep in? That's why so many people come to church late on Sundays. The devil rocks their bed, making it oh so difficult to get up. Satan, telling them it's okay because God intended for man to have a day of rest."

Fatima shrugged. "I hear you. But then why not see if you can get Wednesdays off in exchange for another day? Same thing for Saturday nights if getting off early enough for Sunday morning is a problem? The way you talk, it sounds like your former boss must still be in contact with you. So that means you *had* to have been a great employee, and the company as well as your ex-boss really didn't want to lose you."

"He didn't," Gabrielle said.

"Well, that sounds to me like a person who would work with you. You both could end up getting what you want."

Gabrielle unfolded her foot from underneath her and placed both her feet on the floor. She leaned forward. "He would definitely work with me. Although, I'm pretty sure he won't be willing to give up Saturday nights since that's his busiest night. But Fatima, I just can't work there anymore. It's not even an option, not even a consideration for me, especially now that I'm saved."

Fatima considered what Gabrielle may have been doing that would cause her to feel it was not an appropriate place to work after becoming saved. Then again, this was the same woman who fretted about wearing a strapless evening gown to the church's Inaugural Ball. Working at a restaurant called Hooters was what came to her mind.

"I agree that you shouldn't compromise your walk with the Lord," Fatima said. "There are certain jobs Christians shouldn't be caught doing, specifically if it will cause them to stumble or to backslide. Personally, I don't think working at a bar is appropriate for a Christian. Yet some Christians would disagree with me on that. They'll tell you it's just a job. And if they're not drinking, then what difference does it make. Take my job: there's a potential temptation to embezzle or to at least set up deals that would benefit others who might be willing to give me a kickback—pay to play kinds of deals. Even though there's nothing wrong with me working there, if I were inclined to steal or to do anything unethical or that would affect my walk with the Lord, I would have to consider not working there."

"Precisely," Gabrielle said. "I'll just have to figure out what to do. And now that I have a chance to possibly be part of the dance ministry at church, I'm sure rehearsals will be at night. That's just one more night I need available, which is yet another argument for not getting a part-time job. I've been praying to God to help me, but so far, nothing's changed. The bills keep rolling in, and all my money keeps rolling out. There's just not enough to go around. I don't know what else to do except to keep doing what I'm doing, and to keep praying, believing, and waiting on the Lord."

"Now, *that's* faith," Fatima said. "In fact, that's *great* faith. You're working those faith muscles, aren't you, woman of God? Getting stronger and stronger every day."

"Well, God gives each of us a measure of faith. It's up to us how much our faith grows. Since Jesus came into my life, I've been hungry for the Word. I have thirsted after His righteousness. This is not a game for me, Fatima. I'm for real about my walk with the Lord. I don't want to just talk the talk like so many others. I want to walk the walk. If it says it in God's Word, I'm going to stand on it. I'm for real about this."

"I know that. I've seen you grow by leaps and bounds."

Gabrielle stood up and began bouncing up and down as though she'd built up too much energy inside and she needed to shake some of it loose. She then just as quickly stopped. "I just want everything God has for me. I want to know Him and all that He desires of me. I want my purpose on this earth to be manifested. I've lost so much time I could have spent with Him already. I just want my gift, the gift God gave to me, to be used for His service. And I know it's more than just the gift. That's why I've been deep in His Word the way I have. And if I have to lose houses and land and cars for His sake, I'm willing to do that, Fatima. I'll absolutely do it." Gabrielle started to cry.

Fatima stood up and hugged her. Gabrielle started to pull away, but Fatima wouldn't let her. She was hearing God speaking to her heart. "Hold her," she heard a small, still voice say. "Hold her."

Gabrielle stopped struggling and just let it all out. "I don't want to do anything that would displease Him. Not now. Not after knowing Him the way I have grown to know Him. I love Jesus so much!"

"I know. I love Him, too. And you know what? He loves us. And I can hear Him saying right now that everything is going to work out. For you and me both. We just need to keep trusting Him. No matter how things look. No matter how hard it might get. I hear Him saying right now for you to hold to His unchanging hand."

# Chapter 13

*Every good gift and every perfect gift is from above, and cometh down from the Father of lights, with whom is no variableness, neither shadow of turning.*

—James 1:17

Gabrielle waited for her time to audition. She paced outside the conference room, praying as she walked. "God, please. I know none of this is a coincidence. I know this is all from You. You have been ordering my steps along this life journey, even when I didn't recognize it. Please, Lord—"

"Gabrielle Mercedes?" a woman called her name.

Gabrielle stopped and smiled at the woman calling for her to come into the large conference room for her audition. "In the name of Jesus, Amen," Gabrielle said quickly under her breath as she went toward the conference room door.

Gabrielle walked into the room filled with sunlight that flooded through a large window. Sitting at a table was Johnnie Mae, Minister Denise Johnson, and a beautiful young woman Gabrielle wasn't familiar with, dressed in a dance outfit, who appeared to be in her late twenties, maybe early thirties. Johnnie Mae introduced her as Ebony, the owner of her own dance studio.

"You look excited, Gabrielle," Johnnie Mae said.

"Oh, I am!" said Gabrielle, trying hard to keep from grinning *too* much.

"Well, we're ready whenever you are," Johnnie Mae said with a nod.

Gabrielle composed herself, then nodded to the sixteen-year-old working the CD player. Gabrielle stood frozen, like a statue, as she waited for the music to begin. The song she'd chosen to dance to was "God Is Here," the Karen Clark Sheard version.

When Gabrielle finished her move to the final beat of the song, everyone in that room—including the person handling the CDs—was crying, shouting, and praising God. Johnnie Mae was on her feet, bouncing up and down, before she fell to her knees and began lifting her hands toward heaven. Ebony walked around the room waving her hands as she looked skyward. Minister Denise remained seated at the table, shaking her head and praising God as she wiped away tears that steadily flowed.

After five minutes of attempting to pull herself together, Johnnie Mae finally stood to her feet and walked over to Gabrielle, who was crying and also on her knees, thanking God for His goodness and His mercy. Johnnie Mae hugged Gabrielle and helped her to her feet. Standing now, Johnnie Mae hugged her even more. And Gabrielle hugged her back.

"Well," Ebony said with a quick and audible exhale, "*that* was some audition!"

"No. No disrespect to what you just said, but that was ministering right there." Johnnie Mae shook her head as she seemed to smile and frown at the same time. "That was pure, unadulterated ministry right there. That was a Spirit of Excellence coming through ministry. I'm almost speechless."

"Thank you," Gabrielle said, dabbing her eyes with tissue from the box the young woman working the CDs had gone out and brought in for them.

"Whew!" Minister Denise said, shaking both her hands as though she was trying to air-dry them. "Wow. Glory! Hallelujah! I wish now we had taped that so I could have taken a copy home and experienced *that* all over again. Gabrielle . . . woman of God, that was powerful!"

"It was the Spirit of the Lord," Gabrielle said. "I told God I didn't want this being about me. It's all about Him." She pointed upward. "Not I, but He who lives in me."

"Oh, that's scripture right there," Minister Denise said as she jotted down something on the paper in front of her. "That's the Word right there."

"I know," Johnnie Mae said. "So, it appears you're also into the Word?"

"Yes, I am. I love God's Word."

"Oh, yeah," Minister Denise said.

"Well, you're a wonderful dancer. Where did you learn to dance like that? What school did you attend?" Ebony asked.

"I didn't attend a dance school. But I *did* have a personal teacher," Gabrielle said.

"Nice," Ebony said, making a note on her paper.

"It costs a pretty penny to have a private teacher for dance. Believe me, I know. That's all right."

Gabrielle shook her head. "No, it's not what you think. My family didn't have the money to pay for me to take lessons, private or otherwise." Gabrielle stopped, then held up one hand. "Allow me to re-state that. There *was* money, just not money for me and anything I wanted to do, such as dance lessons like other girls my age were able to take. The woman who taught me was an angel sent by God. I know that now. She taught me everything that I know about dance. I owe a lot to her. She helped to free me. She opened my cage door and helped set me free. This is what I was created to do. There may be other things, but just as a bird is created to fly, dance is what God put on the inside of me."

"Well, I certainly would hire that woman to work in my studio. You're a great ambassador for her handiwork," Ebony said.

"I appreciate you saying that about her. She cer-tainly deserves all the great things I can say on her behalf. But I'm really looking forward to being more of an ambassador for Christ. That's what my gift, my talents, and what Miss Crowe poured into me."

"Did you say Crowe?" Ebony asked.

"Yes," said Gabrielle.

"Esther Crowe?" asked Ebony.

"Yes." Gabrielle narrowed her eyes and tilted her head a little. "You know her?"

"Who in the dance world doesn't? She's cele-brated in the top circles." Ebony could hardly con-tain her own excitement. "Esther Crowe was one of the best. She was at the top of her game. That's before she was unable to continue dancing professionally. But Esther Crowe would have been a legend outside of the dance world had it not been for that unfortunate knee injury that ended her dancing career. And you say she taught you? Personally?"

"Yes. Only I didn't know she was famous. Honestly, she never told me any of this. When I met her, she was a sixth-grade teacher, and not even a teacher at my school. She lived in our neighborhood. That is, until her car accident. I never learned what happened to her following that."

"That is *something*." Ebony shook her head and continued grinning. "No wonder you're so excellent and precise in the execution of your movements. Well, thank you. That's all for me." Ebony looked over at Johnnie Mae and nodded that she was finished.

"I think you've about answered all of our interview questions," Johnnie Mae said.

"Interview questions?" Gabrielle said.

"Yes. We have questions we're asking those who are interested in being in this ministry. It's not just about how well you can dance, it's the entire package," Johnnie Mae said. "As I said when we met about this ministry, it's not merely about performing. It's about ministering to the people. There are many who can dance, but they don't get that it's equally as important to know *Whom* we are dancing for. I must say, we're all quite impressed with you so far. There is one other thing I'd like to ask, and this will conclude your audition/interview." Johnnie Mae leaned forward. "Is there anything you feel we should know concerning you? Is there anything that could become a hindrance or might possibly derail your being able to carry out your position and duties in this dance ministry, should you be chosen?"

Gabrielle pressed her lips tightly together as she mulled over the question. "There is one thing," Gabrielle said.

"Okay," Johnnie Mae said as she thumped her pen on the table a few times waiting for Gabrielle to continue.

"No disrespect to the others here," Gabrielle said, directing her comment to Johnnie Mae, "but is it possible for you and me to discuss this privately?"

Johnnie Mae glanced to her right at Minister Denise, and then to her left at Ebony, who both nodded their approval.

"We have about eight more auditions scheduled," Johnnie Mae said to Gabrielle. "If you don't mind waiting, we could talk after I'm finished here. Or we can schedule a meeting later when it's convenient for the both of us."

"I don't mind waiting," Gabrielle said. She stood up and smiled as she shook each of their hands. "Thank you for this opportunity," she said, then she left.

Gabrielle exhaled after she closed the door behind her.

*That was easy. Now for the hard part.*

# Chapter 14

*Therefore to him that knoweth to do good,*
*and doeth it not, to him it is sin.*

—James 4:17

Johnnie Mae had met privately with Gabrielle Mercedes. She'd been impressed with her audition and blessed by the words of her interview. Gabrielle had been genuine when it came to her heart toward the ministry. Johnnie Mae felt she wasn't trying to manipulate her answers to what she felt they were looking for, especially since she'd answered any questions they'd planned to ask her prior to her ever being asked.

Gabrielle told Johnnie Mae everything, deciding not to hold anything back. Her telling was not fast in coming in the beginning. But Johnnie Mae was patient—pleased she hadn't forced this discussion immediately after Gabrielle's audition or in front of the others. This way, both were granted the time they needed.

Gabrielle talked about her life, starting from her birth, putting things in its proper context. How her mother, Constance Booker (Connie for short), and her father, Benjamin Booker (Ben-

nie), named her Gabrielle Mercedes Booker.
Gabrielle, the name her mother had fought hard
to give her because she believed it was an elegant
and beautiful name. It was as though her mother
knew her daughter—even as a newborn—was destined to become a dancer. As though she'd known
her child would require a moniker that would
evoke an image of a gazelle—fast . . . agile . . . pos-
itively beauty in motion, whenever her name was
used.

As for her middle name of Mercedes, that was
all her father's doing. Equally an elegant name,
she would have loved it if there had been some
semblance of elegance in his having chosen that
name for her. It had been a compromise, she'd
read—words written in her mother's own hand-
writing in a journal. Her father had been adamant
that his daughter would be named after his favorite car brand: Mercedes. A vehicle he was determined he would someday own. He merely wanted
to name his daughter after the car he intended to
possess. Her mother hadn't totally objected—Mercedes was indeed an attractive name. When
Gabrielle had read this, she had been thankful
that his desired vehicle of choice hadn't been a
Lincoln, a Ford, or a Cadillac. The thought of
Gabrielle Lincoln, Gabrielle Ford, or Gabrielle
Cadillac Booker was too much. Gabrielle Mercedes was a good name. And had she subscribed to
her father's way of thinking, she would have been
named Gabrielle Toyota Booker.

She told Johnnie Mae about her memories, as
small as they were, and how grateful she'd been to
have been given her mother's journal when she

was ten. Johnnie Mae could appreciate the journal since she was an avid journal keeper herself. Gabrielle loved how easy Johnnie Mae was to talk to.

Gabrielle told how her father killed her mother. How he had abused her and eventually strangled her to death. She'd seen the whole thing, although her aunt Cee-Cee insisted that Gabrielle, at the age of three when it happened, was too young to remember anything. That what she *thought* she remembered had been planted in her mind by others and had never actually happened that way.

But she knew what she remembered. And those memories were hers, and they were real.

With overwhelming evidence against him (excluding what she'd seen), her father was found guilty and was presently serving out his twenty-five-to-life sentence in prison. Gabrielle told how, in spite of her aunt's desire to take it away from her when she was a teenager, she still had her mother's journal—though worn for wear. And whenever she read it, she could still hear the calm of her mother's voice.

She told how she remembered dancing with her mother. As a baby, and then as a toddler, she and her mother would spin around the room together. She could still hear her mother laughing as she held her in her arms. Gabrielle didn't care how people said that wasn't possible. Her mother had written Gabrielle could dance before she could walk.

Gabrielle spoke of living with her aunt and uncle, growing up hearing almost every day how grateful she should be that anyone would even take her in. And then, how God sent this woman by her house one sunny June day—an angel named Esther Crowe, disguised as a sixth-grade teacher who ironically was also a Juilliard professionally trained dancer. Miss Crowe had been her saving grace. She'd taught her how to dance with technique and style. She'd taught her all of the basics, the mechanics, the art, and the moves. But most of all, she'd taught her how to love herself, who she was in this world, and to appreciate the gift God had blessed her with.

Only, Gabrielle hadn't wanted to hear anything about God. She would hold her tongue when she was with Miss Crowe and Miss Crowe spoke of God and His goodness. Because in her young mind, she couldn't conceive God really caring about her. Maybe He cared for others, but He couldn't possibly care about her. She'd never let Miss Crowe know how she felt. Gabrielle told Johnnie Mae how Miss Crowe had somehow realized she was being mistreated, even if she wasn't technically being abused. How Miss Crowe ended up tricking her aunt. Hiring Gabrielle and telling her aunt that Gabrielle would be helping her with various chores around her house. When in truth, Miss Crowe was paying her ten dollars for two hours to teach her the thing she'd loved and wanted to learn the most: how to dance and dance with grace.

Gabrielle told how when she was seventeen her uncle had come into her bedroom and tried to make a move on her. How she'd rebuffed him only to have him try twice again. And when she'd said something to her aunt after his second visit, how her aunt had said and done nothing. The third time when she said something to her aunt about it, that same uncle came into her room and found time to inform her she would need to find somewhere else to live once she graduated from high school and turned eighteen. As it happened, her eighteenth birthday on May thirtieth was only a few days out from her having received her diploma.

Just like that, she was out on her own. No job and no place to stay.

And as though all of that hadn't been enough for a teenager to have to deal with, Miss Crowe had been in an automobile accident the year she was seventeen. If that hadn't happened, after that third time with her uncle, she would have asked Miss Crowe if she could live with her.

The accident had been right before Thanksgiving. Miss Crowe had come to her house and told her she had to go out of town on an emergency. There was some problem with one of her brothers and his son. She, the baby of twelve children, was going to see what she could do to straighten things out. Gabrielle never learned what happened. A neighbor, who was around when one of her brothers came to Birmingham to lock up her house prior to finally selling it, told her aunt that Miss Crowe was alive, although barely. She had hit a sheet of black ice, skidded off the road, and crashed into a tree.

Her aunt Cee-Cee had been upset, only because Gabrielle now would no longer be bringing in the weekly money she'd previously made. That's how Gabrielle learned about Miss Crowe's car accident:

her aunt was fussing about the unexpected loss of income. Miss Crowe had been so excited, giddy even, before all of this happened. She'd talked about a surprise she had for her, hardly able to contain her enthusiasm. She said she couldn't tell her yet, but she would disclose everything after the first of the year.

Gabrielle would never know what the surprise was. And she hadn't heard *from* or heard anything more *about* Miss Crowe since she was seventeen.

She told Johnnie Mae about her search for a job at eighteen, fresh out of high school with no place to live. Originally, she'd stayed with a girlfriend whose parents were paying the rent on an apartment while she attended the University of Alabama in Birmingham. What Gabrielle had really wanted to do was attend college. But for her, that wasn't even an option. She didn't have a backup system the way her friend did. She didn't have anyone to help her, to encourage her. Then, she and her friend fell out over what her friend believed was her trying to get with her boyfriend.

Nothing could have been further from the truth. In fact, the truth was it had been her friend's very married (at the time thirty-three-year-old) father who had been making a play for her. Yet, through no fault of her own, she was forced again to find another place to live. Following that was what could only be summed up as the darkest period of her life. A time she didn't care to think about, let alone ever want to talk about. That part of her life was her secret—something she intended to carry with her to her grave. But eventually, she did manage to pick herself up, pull herself together, and she got a job waiting tables. It wasn't anything glamorous. She didn't make a lot of money. But at least it was something—it was a job.

After the guy who owned the place learned she didn't have anywhere to stay, he offered her a spot in his home. She declined his offer, even after he told her she was welcome to sleep on his couch if that would make her feel better. A compassionate man, he compromised and allowed her to stay at the place where she worked in an area in the dressing room that was just a little larger than a walk-in closet. She later learned, this was totally against his normal policy. Still, he had agreed to do it until she was able to save enough money and secure a place of her own. It wouldn't take her long to discover exactly who Clarence was—a man who competently and astutely handled his business, but also a man with a good heart.

Six months later, she started working in a different capacity, opting to continue her employment with Clarence. And that's when the money began rolling in hand over fist. And it had paid off. Three years ago, she was able to purchase a house thanks in part to the relaxed rules of securing a mortgage, rules that didn't have strict requirements like hard-and-fast proof of income or employment. The same rules the country was now blaming for the collapse in the banks and the housing market.

She told Johnnie Mae *everything*. She even told her how, on the morning of January first of this year, she'd been physically attacked.

"You were attacked?" Johnnie Mae asked, having successfully interrupted her only during the times when she absolutely couldn't hold back a question or comment.

"Yes," Gabrielle said, touching her now-healed neck as she recounted how it had felt having her air supply totally cut off. "This man had become unhealthily obsessed with me. Of course, I had no idea he was that crazy about me or that crazy, period. He'd been extremely nice to me whenever I saw him on my job. He would speak, I would speak back. I admit I was friendlier because it was part of my job description. Apparently, my pleasant demeanor caused him to think he had a chance of dating me. He had asked me out. I let him know that I wasn't interested, and that I was particularly not interested in dating anyone associated with my place of work. Three times, he asked. He must have lost it sometime after that. I didn't know it at the time, but apparently he started stalking me—seeing whom I interacted with, whom I was friendly with at work. The last time when I rebuffed his advance, he must have decided to take things a step further."

Johnnie Mae leaned back, pressing her index finger over her lips as though she was trying to keep her lips from parting to speak.

Gabrielle swallowed hard, then continued. "One of my coworkers, a friend I was very close to, had her purse stolen that morning after work. Before she'd reported her cell phone stolen to the phone company, I received a text message from her phone telling me her car had broken down. 'I need you. Please hurry. Please hurry,' it read. She had texted me where to meet her. Although I was exhausted, I went. When I arrived, out of nowhere this man grabbed me. He was wearing a ski mask so I couldn't see his face. But I knew I'd heard the voice before. He told me he wasn't going to hurt me. He just wanted me to hear him out. He wanted me to give him a chance to show me how much he could love me. He had planned this special date for me so he could prove to me what a great guy he was." Gabrielle stopped and took a deep breath.

"When he attempted to take me to another location, I recalled what I'd been told should anyone ever try to do something like that. 'Don't let them move you to a second location,' the defense instructor had said. So, I began to fight him. He held me that much tighter. I then bit his hand. He yelled, shoved me away, then grabbed me by my hair and began to slap me a few times with the full brunt of his strength. A ring he wore on his right hand cut me above my right eye when he back-handed slapped me one of those times." She touched above her eye that had also now completely healed.

"Blood ran down. He saw it, pulled me close, and hugged me, apologizing while saying my being hurt was my fault. He took off his mask. He kept saying he would never hurt me. That I had forced him to do that. All he wanted was to show me how much he loved me. He picked me up by my waist and headed for his car, popping his trunk open with his electronic key. I kicked and struggled, told him that I hated him and that he was going to jail for doing this. That's when he set me down, yanked me around to face him, and grabbed me about my neck with his hands and started to squeeze, calling me an ingrate and other names. Said I'd been a tease, just like his mother. He began to strangle me, squeezing tighter and tighter as he talked. He then said if he couldn't have me, then nobody would. Suddenly, there was this crazed look in his eyes. I tried to claw his hand from my neck. From the look in his eyes, I knew he was going to kill me. I gathered my strength, stomped as hard as I could, thankful I had on spiked heels. I then grabbed him in a place where I knew the pain would cause him to let go. He reacted as I suspected, releasing me in the process. I made it to my car and drove away as he tried to recover.

"Of course, I learned only later that he'd stolen my friend's purse to get her cell phone specifically for the purpose of luring me to him. She'd thought he was after her cash. Having *her* cell phone with my name and cell number programmed in it was his plan. A police friend told us later that people were reporting crooks stealing women's purses with the sole purpose of getting their cell phones. They would then scroll through the address book, checking for references of relationships. If it said 'husband,' the stolen phone was often used to text that spouse requesting the PIN number for their ATM. The unsuspecting spouse would text back the PIN number. By the time they figured out what had happened, the thief would have cleaned out their bank account and been long gone.

"The police friend said people should not label their phone list with words like *home, husband,* and *wife.* In my case, there wasn't much any of this information would have done to help. He knew my name; he knew what he was looking for. His plan was to lure me to him, and he used her phone to successfully do just that. What I should have done, and now know from here on out, is what the police friend said people should do in this situation. If you get a text message saying something like that, call the person back and verify it's really them and not someone who may have stolen their phone."

"So, what happened after you reported the attack?" Johnnie Mae asked.

Gabrielle dropped her head, then raised it up. "I didn't report it. But my friend reported the robbery, although she had no idea at that time what had happened with me. My ex-boss has a friend in law enforcement. After he learned what happened with me, he talked with him, which is how we learned about the scam people are now doing."

Johnnie Mae frowned at Gabrielle. "You didn't report it? I don't understand that. Why wouldn't you report it?"

"I just wanted it all to go away." Gabrielle pressed her lips together.

"So, you let him get away with doing that? He's still out there, possibly able to attack you again or someone else?"

Gabrielle let out a sigh. "Had I reported it, I would have had to press charges against him and most likely would have had to testify in court. I didn't want to end up being dragged through the mud, having folks judge me for what they felt I had possibly done to cause all of this. The defense focusing attention more on what I might have been wearing or doing that could have driven him to behave the way he had. Me being asked what I'd done to mislead him. You know they would have been more focused on what I did wrong instead of judging him solely on the fact that he had no right to attack me. After that, I just went home and slept, two days. Then Sunday morning, I met a woman who wanted to talk to me about Jesus, I came to church, I heard the Word, and I ended up giving my life to Christ. As far as I'm concerned, my life began anew on that day."

Johnnie Mae nodded. "Thank God you've made some real changes in your life. So, where are you working now?"

"For a maid service. As you can see, a great departure from my previous line of work for sure, especially financially. In fact, I have to confess that moneywise, it's been a struggle. In fact, I've put my house up for sale because the money I make now doesn't even come close to covering all of my present expenses."

"Let me ask you. Do you ever think about going back to your old line of work?"

"No. But I have been offered to since I left. You know how the devil works."

"Oh, yes," Johnnie Mae said. "He'll look for cracks to slip in and do all he can to pull you back into his web of deceit."

"Tell me about it. The guy I worked for really isn't a bad person. He even came by my house to let me know how much he wanted me to come back. Given my present financial situation, it could have been tempting. If you're not strong in the Lord, if you're trusting God in words alone, something like that could be quite appealing. And in truth, some might rationalize that there is nothing wrong with going back temporarily, you know, until God comes through with what you're praying and believing for. But I love God too much to let Him down. At least, not on purpose. Not when I know what His Word says. I wouldn't dare deliberately go against Him."

Johnnie Mae nodded. "Well, I thank you for your honesty. It speaks volumes to your character, your being as candid as you've been with me about everything."

"Fatima Adams and I have grown to be good friends over these past few months." Crying now, Gabrielle wiped her eyes with her tissue. "She suggested that I talk with you if I ever felt I needed someone I could trust. She says you're a great counselor. I'm also aware that this might weigh in your decision when it comes to me possibly being chosen as part of the dance ministry. But I want you to know that I *am* a new creature in Christ. And that I love the Lord with all my heart, mind, and soul. I may not be what I'm going to be when God gets through with me, but I'm for sure not the same person I used to be."

"I know that's right," Johnnie Mae said with a smile. "God is still working on all of us, me included. None of us have arrived. And if anyone tells you differently, then that in and of itself tells you that they haven't." Johnnie Mae stood up and held out her arms. Gabrielle stood and fell into her awaiting arms. "Keep your head up, okay? Even being a Christian, there will be times when you may feel like things aren't working for you. Trust me, I know. But keep your eyes fixed on

Jesus, and you'll get there." Johnnie Mae gently pushed her away arm's length, and smiled as she helped wipe her tears away. She hugged Gabrielle again. "I love you, do you hear me? And if you ever need to talk to me, you call the church office and leave a message for me. I promise I'll get back to you as soon as I can. And I want you to know that I'm pulling for you. I really am."

Gabrielle nodded, then smiled. "Thank you." She then left, not knowing whether what she'd told Johnnie Mae would affect her being chosen for the dance ministry or not. But at least she'd done what she knew was right. She'd told the truth, the whole truth.

Johnnie Mae couldn't deny that Gabrielle had been anointed when she ministered through dance. But she now had to consider everything she knew when deciding whether or not she should be chosen for the dance ministry. And if chosen, what part of the body should she be?

# Chapter 15

*Set your affection on things above, not on things on the earth.*

—Colossians 3:2

Fatima called Gabrielle. "I just got a call about the dance ministry. I made it!"

"You did?" Gabrielle said. "Oh, that's great! Congratulations!" She was genuinely happy for Fatima. "Johnnie Mae said if we made it, we'd know on Tuesday. I am so excited for you."

"Thank you very much. So, have you gotten your call yet?"

"Not yet. But I'm waiting by the phone, hoping and believing my call will come any minute now."

"I'm sure you're going to get one. From what I heard from LaKeisha, the girl who was working the CD player, your audition was 'crunk,' 'off the chain' as she put it. I can't see any reason why you, of all people, won't make it. They're probably going in alphabetical order. Alphabetically, Adams comes before Mercedes."

Gabrielle thought about her conversation with Johnnie Mae following her audition. What they discussed could be the one thing that might keep her from being chosen. At this point, she just didn't know. Johnnie Mae had told her the committee would pray about who should be tapped. It was all in God's hands now.

Tuesday came and went without Gabrielle receiving a call from anyone with the dance ministry. To say she wasn't disappointed would not be the truth. She had hoped and prayed so much that she would be chosen. For whatever reason, she hadn't been.

On Thursday, two days after the date they were told they would receive a call were they chosen, Johnnie Mae called Gabrielle.

"Hi, it's Johnnie Mae Landris. I'd like to meet with you if that's possible. Would you happen to be available for lunch this Saturday?" Johnnie Mae asked.

"Yes. Sure. I'm available. I would love to have lunch with you," Gabrielle said. Truthfully, this being Thursday made Saturday feel like it was much too far away to find out what Johnnie Mae wanted to talk to her about.

"Great! Then, I'll fix lunch for the two of us here at my house. Do you have pen and paper handy? I'll give you my address and the directions."

"Hold on a second." Gabrielle located a pen and paper and wrote down Johnnie Mae's address. Her car had a GPS, so she told her she would only need the address.

Gabrielle arrived thirty minutes early. She wanted to be sure she found the house okay and not arrive late, just in case she got lost. She sat outside in the car, not wanting to ring the doorbell that early. A rapping sound on her window made her jump. She let down her window.

"Pastor Landris," she said.

"Why are you sitting out here?" he asked.

She smiled. "I was a bit early for lunch so I decided I would just wait out here."

"Well, that's no reason for you to sit outside like this. You get out of that car and come on in the house."

"Are you sure? I'm not supposed to be here until one," Gabrielle said.

"Will you get out of that car and come on in our house?" He opened her car door. She raised up the window, retrieved her key, then picked up her purse off the center console.

They walked inside together. When she got in the house, the first thing she noticed on one of the walls was a large picture of a man sporting long dreadlocks standing behind Johnnie Mae, who had a then four-year-old Princess Rose sitting beside her. Upon closer inspection, Gabrielle quickly realized that the man in the photo was Pastor Landris. "That's you?"

"Yes, that's me," he said, grinning.

"You had dreadlocks?"

He ran his hand over his now low-cut hair. "Yes, I did."

"A preacher with dreadlocks? You actually had dreadlocks? A preacher . . . with dreadlocks?"

"Yes, a preacher who used to wear dreadlocks." He rubbed his head once more. "Aren't you glad God doesn't look at the outside of a man but the inside?"

"Well, hi there," Johnnie Mae said as she walked

into the foyer. She hugged Gabrielle. "Did you have any trouble finding us?"

"No, I came right here. I did leave early enough in case I got lost. I didn't want to be late, which is why I arrived so early," Gabrielle said.

"Well, everything is ready, so you're fine." Johnnie Mae hunched her shoulders. "Next time, you come on up and ring the doorbell. Even if I hadn't been ready, you could have waited in the den. But I'm like you. I was ready early . . . just in case." Johnnie Mae led Gabrielle to the dining room.

The table was beautifully set for two with fresh mixed flowers in a crystal vase. Because of the Landrises' status as a mega church pastor and famous author, Gabrielle had expected a table of foods she would likely have never heard of, let alone know how to pronounce. That wasn't at all the case. For lunch, Johnnie Mae had lasagna, salad, garlic bread, and a lattice cherry pie. Gabrielle was trying to figure out how Johnnie Mae could possibly know this was her favorite meal. She then remembered a question on their application for the dance ministry that asked that.

They were eating dessert, chitchatting on things like Johnnie Mae's children and the mammoth things President Obama had already accomplished since he'd taken office.

Johnnie Mae sat back against her chair after taking another bite of her cherry pie. "I'm sure you've likely heard that we completed our selections for the dance ministry."

Gabrielle tried to maintain the pleasant look she'd had throughout lunch, but hearing those words made it difficult. "Yes." She glanced down for a split second, then forced a smile as she recovered and held her head back up.

"I know how much being selected meant to you. And to be honest, after your audition, we were all pretty certain you had what we were looking for from a dance and ministering perspective," Johnnie Mae said. She took a swallow of her iced green tea.

Gabrielle nodded and found herself rocking a little. She quickly stilled herself. "Yeah. But you also told us that it would be about more than just our dancing abilities. We all knew going in that everyone who auditioned probably wouldn't be chosen."

Johnnie Mae smiled. "Yeah."

"And then, I had to tell you things about my past life that weren't flattering for me to tell or for you to hear." Gabrielle leaned her head back and looked up at the ceiling, then back down as she shrugged it off.

"But you were honest. And as I told you that day when we talked, I really appreciated that. You told me things you really didn't have to. Things I very likely may have never found out. Still, you told me anyway, understanding the possible consequences it might have on something that we both know meant so much to you."

"Well, the bottom line is: it's all about the ministry and what we can do to help. It really isn't about us. And if what's best for the ministry is my not being part of the dance team even though I love dancing and would have loved using my gift in the Lord's work, then I accept that." Gabrielle lifted the last forkful of her cherry pie and slowly placed it in her mouth. "This is really good pie," she said. "Did you make it yourself?"

"Heavens, no. It's store-bought. I *used* to bake things, but there are so many great bakeries available these days, it doesn't make sense if you don't have the time or just don't want to." Johnnie Mae picked up her fork and placed the empty fork in her mouth.

"Well, it was really good."

Johnnie Mae sat the fork back down. It clinked when it hit the empty dessert plate. "Gabrielle, about the dance ministry."

Gabrielle waved it off. "Oh, don't worry about it. I told you that I'm fine. I'm fine. But I do appreciate that you cared enough to have me over for lunch, although you really didn't have to do that. And if you need someone to help out with behind-the-scene things for the dance ministry, I'll be more than happy to do whatever you need of me. If you need someone to help get the outfits, help set things up—whatever the ministry needs, I'm willing and able to do whatever you ask."

Johnnie Mae smiled as she shook her head. "I'm happy to hear that you feel that way. You make this so much easier for me. Most people might have been a bit upset at this point. Especially when it's something they had their heart set on." Johnnie Mae got up and went over to the server. She picked up a yellow folder and laid it in front of Gabrielle as she sat back down. "Look that over and tell me your thoughts about it."

Gabrielle looked at Johnnie Mae, then opened the folder. After reading the top page, she looked back up at Johnnie Mae. "You have to be kidding me," she said.

"No, I'm not kidding you."

"Are you sure about this?" Gabrielle asked, glancing at the paper, then back up at Johnnie Mae. She closed the folder.

"Yes," Johnnie Mae said. "I'm more than sure. I'm aware that this is not what you were expecting or you'd originally had in mind when you desired to join the ministry."

"You got that right." Gabrielle fell back against her chair.

"So, what do you say? Or would you like to think it over, pray about it overnight, and let me know something tomorrow."

Gabrielle shook her head. She flashed Johnnie Mae a smile. "I told you whatever you needed I would be happy to do it. I meant that. If *this* is what you really want?"

Johnnie Mae touched her hand that now rested on the closed folder. "It is."

"Then, okay," Gabrielle said with a smile.

"Great," Johnnie Mae said, sitting back in her chair. "Care for more pie?"

"No, thank you. I think I'll pass," Gabrielle said.

The dance ministry met for their first official meeting on Tuesday night. Both Fatima Adams and Tiffany Connors made the team along with thirteen others. There would be two teams, divided up by age—the young adult and the adult team. The young adult team consisted of those ages fourteen through twenty-one; the adults, ages twenty-two and up.

Johnnie Mae began by congratulating them on having been chosen. She told how it had truly been a difficult decision. But the committee was dedicated to the mission and vision and felt all of them had exemplified what the ministry was looking for.

"I have just one more announcement." She paused and waited. Gabrielle came in from a side door.

Fatima began the applause—happy to see that, in spite of how it had looked, Gabrielle was somehow a part of the ministry.

"For those of you who don't know her, this is Gabrielle Mercedes," Johnnie Mae said as Gabrielle stood beside her beaming. "She will be our sixteenth member."

Fatima couldn't stop smiling. She couldn't believe Gabrielle hadn't told her that she'd made it. After Fatima called on Tuesday to let Gabrielle know she'd received her call, she was just sure when Gabrielle learned she'd been chosen, she would call and tell her. After Fatima didn't hear from her on Wednesday, she didn't want to call and ask about it, seemingly rubbing it in that she'd been chosen when Gabrielle hadn't. Now, it looked like Gabrielle had in fact made it.

Gabrielle stood next to Johnnie Mae as she continued to speak. "I have asked Gabrielle, and she has graciously agreed, to help with choreographing our first dance routine. So, she'll be doing double duty: choreography and dancing. For the rollout of this ministry, we'll be ministering as one team instead of the two teams we will minister as later. We will be ministering the third Sunday morning in August during a special Sunday celebration. So you can see, we have a lot of work ahead of us and not a lot of time to do it. Are there any questions so far?"

"You say Gabrielle will also be dancing with us?" Tiffany asked.

"Yes, she will be the choreographer as well as an active dance member," Johnnie Mae said.

Tiffany smiled Gabrielle's way and nodded.

As others asked questions about the schedule, what they would be wearing, and things along that vein, Gabrielle went and sat down next to Fatima.

Fatima leaned over and gave her a quick hug and smiled. "I can't believe you didn't tell me about this!" Fatima whispered.

"I couldn't," Gabrielle whispered back. "I was asked when I found out on Saturday not to say anything to anyone until it was announced today. You wouldn't believe how bad I wanted to call and tell you," Gabrielle said. "That's why I didn't call you back Sunday night when you called. I thought I was going to burst not being able to tell you!"

After the meeting was over, Tiffany came over to Gabrielle. "Congratulations!" She grabbed Gabrielle's hand and squeezed it. "This is so exciting! Isn't it exciting?!"

Gabrielle beamed. "I know. God is *so* good!"

"Oh, all the time!" Tiffany said.

"All the time," Fatima said.

"God is good!" Gabrielle and Tiffany said in unison. They all laughed.

# Chapter 16

*From whom the whole body fitly joined together and compacted by that which every joint supplieth, according to the effectual working in the measure of every part, maketh increase of the body unto the edifying of itself in love.*

—Ephesians 4:16

In July, Gabrielle received yet another notice: her car note payment was over two months in arrears, her car in serious danger of being repossessed. Her house she'd placed on the market at the beginning of June hadn't sold yet. She was six weeks behind in making that payment in full. Housing sales had picked up in some areas, but the valuation of houses was the problem with many houses being able to sell. Her house was definitely overvalued now. The way things looked, even if she did sell it, she was underwater and would have to sell it at a loss—the difference in what she owed on her loan and what she could get out of it. Help from the government was supposed to have been on its way, but she hadn't seen any evidence of it addressing people like her. Now for her, time had almost run out.

The bright spot through all of this was the dance ministry. She loved dancing for the Lord. It was even better than she had anticipated it would be when she learned it was a possibility. She and Tiffany Connors had grown to be friends. She'd grown closer to many other members of the dance ministry as well. And she still faithfully attended Bible study, so she was learning more and more about the Lord and growing stronger in faith.

The date for them to minister in August was rapidly drawing closer. Tiffany was struggling with being able to practice at home the way she needed to. Besides working a full-time job, she had the responsibility of taking care of her children and a home. Her husband wasn't much help since he was always working late, leaving her pretty much on her own until he came home sometimes well after midnight. By the time she got all of the children taken care of and to bed, she was exhausted. Tiffany pulled Gabrielle off to the side after Bible study when she saw her. Tiffany asked if it was possible for them to get together at her house so she could get in some extra practice to get her steps down better. After all this time, she still hadn't reached the level she needed to be, and it was showing.

"I don't want to get kicked out of this ministry," Tiffany said. "It's hard to practice at home when you have little ones to constantly see after. Especially when you don't have much help," Tiffany said.

"It's no problem. I would be glad to come over. We're part of the same body, fitly joined. So we need to work together to help each other succeed.

I can ask Fatima if she would like to come over as well, that's if you don't mind?"

"Oh, no," Tiffany said, excitement blanketing her voice. "I don't mind. That would be great! Please ask her and any other members you'd like to. I can move some of the furniture out of the way in the den, and we would have plenty of room for at least five of us."

"I was only thinking of Fatima maybe. She has the routine down almost as well as I do. Not only could she help with the dancing portion should we need it, but between the two of us, we can help with the children when necessary. She and I can take turns helping out and give you all the time you need to rehearse."

"Oh, that's too much to ask of her. I couldn't ask her to come over here to help with my children. I know her a little, mostly because of this dance ministry, but I wouldn't feel right asking her to do something like that," Tiffany said, shaking her head.

"I'm sure Fatima won't mind. She's a team player. And I believe she will love doing this. Besides, it's about the ministry, and she loves this dance ministry as much as you and I do."

"Well, my children are pretty well-behaved."

"I'll tell you what," Gabrielle said. "Let me ask her and see what she says. Then, we'll go from there."

Tiffany began to clap with excitement. "This is so great! Thank you, thank you, thank you. I really appreciate this. I don't want to not be giving my best, and I need to get these steps better. You coming to my house will be such a blessing, you just don't know."

Gabrielle called Fatima as soon as she got home from Bible study.

"How would you like some extra off-schedule practices?" Gabrielle asked Fatima.

"Am I *that* bad?"

"No, you're not bad at all. In fact, you're very good. That's why I thought of you. We have a member in the ministry asking for extra practices. She's having a hard time being able to rehearse on her own because of her home and family obligations. I was thinking you and I could help her with practice, as well as with the children while she works at getting her steps down better. It was her idea—the extra rehearsals, that is."

"Sounds good to me," Fatima said. "I would love to get more practice in myself."

"She said it was okay for us to come to her house. Would that be a problem for you?"

"Nope. Not a problem for me. And it makes sense, especially if she has children. I can help with them while you help her with her steps. That's what this ministry is all about: serving others. It's based on the principles Christ exhibited. So, when were you looking to get started?"

"How about tomorrow? That's a Thursday and nothing's going on at church that any of us have to be there for."

"Tomorrow works for me," Fatima said.

"Great. Then, I will call Tiffany and—"

"Tiffany?"

"Oh, I'm sorry. I didn't tell you who it was, did

I. Yes, Tiffany Connors. You know, she has three young children. I've met them a couple of times, and they are so adorable: Jade, Dana, and Little D. I believe I have their names right. And Tiffany is so great with them, too. So I know they're not going to be much trouble at all."

Fatima's mind was going a mile a minute now, her thoughts all over the place. *Tiffany Connors, Darius's wife. And she wants us to come to her house, her house, where she and Darius live . . . together. Darius, the guy I had a three-year affair with.*

"Did you tell her you were thinking about bringing me?" Fatima said, stalling as she continued to try to sort this out in her mind.

"Yes, and she thinks it's a great idea." Gabrielle stopped for a second. "Unless you don't want to be bothered with her children?" Gabrielle sighed audibly. "You know, I really shouldn't have done this like this. I am *so* sorry, Fatima. I didn't think that you really might not want to be bothered with someone else's children. Now I've placed you in an awkward position."

"Listen, there's nothing wrong with what you did," Fatima said as she wondered what she ought to do now that she was being given an out. "A fellow laborer in the ministry needs our help. You wanted us to help her. I don't have a problem with that. I was just trying to see whether tomorrow works for me."

Fatima was trying to buy some time to figure out what she should do. She couldn't go to Tiffany's house. That was definitely out. What if Darius was there? She had made every effort to avoid him over the past few years since she'd broken off with him. They saw each other at church on occasion, but nothing that placed her face-to-face with him for any great amount of time. The last thing she needed was to set foot into her ex-lover's house at the request of his unsuspecting wife. That was more than just tacky.

Gabrielle could tell Fatima was wrestling with this. "If you like, I can see if Friday or Saturday would be better," Gabrielle said. "Tiffany didn't give me her schedule, but she pretty much made it clear she was available whenever we were," Gabrielle said. "She's much like me: you go to work, to church, and you come home."

For Fatima, the problem wasn't the date—Thursday, Friday, and Saturday were all fine for her. The problem was the place they wanted to meet.

"Why don't we have it at your place? Or better still, we can have it at mine. You know," Fatima said, her words pumped up now with a bit of enthusiasm, "I could fix us something light to eat, and we could make a special time of it. I know Tiffany would have the extra burden of having to bring her kids over here, but it would be so much fun. I'm sure her kids will love it. And I bet you anything, Tiffany would like the change of scene. Work, church, grocery store, and home can get a little stale after a while. Why don't you see if her coming here will work for her? In fact, you know what? We could do this for any and all of the extra practices, if we decide to continue to do this. It would be a real sister-girl thing. Like *Waiting to Exhale,* only waiting to exhale with children in tow."

Gabrielle smiled as she thought about how

thoughtful Fatima was to even suggest such a thing. "I love it! I'm not sure what Tiffany will think, but I certainly will call her and find out."

"And if she'd rather do it on a Saturday during the day so the children won't have to be out late, Saturday works for me. That way we could get even longer practices in, should she find she needs it. This will work."

"Oh, you don't have to convince me. You're . . . what is it that people say when they mean you're telling me something I already know?" Gabrielle said.

"Preaching to the choir," Fatima said.

"Yeah, you're preaching to the choir now. I'm getting excited just thinking about this," Gabrielle said. "Let me call Tiffany real quick, see what her thoughts are on this, and get back to you."

Fatima hung up and waited. She prayed Tiffany would go for the idea.

Gabrielle called back ten minutes later and told her they were all set for Saturday. "Is two o'clock okay with you?"

"Two o'clock is great," Fatima said. She hung up the phone after they finished, then released a huge sigh of relief.

# Chapter 17

*Now I beseech you, brethren, for the Lord
Jesus Christ's sake, and for the love of the
Spirit, that ye strive together with me in your
prayers to God for me.*

—Romans 15:30

The three dance team members came together
for several weeks of practice outside of the entire dance team's scheduled Tuesday night rehearsals. It had truly been glorious. Even counting
their first rehearsal when Jade, Tiffany's eight-year-
old daughter, hugged Gabrielle, then gave her a
big kiss on the cheek, and out of nowhere (it
seemed) Gabrielle broke down and began to cry.
She had quickly composed herself. But she couldn't
quite explain what had been the cause of her unexpected reaction. Fatima attributed it to Gabrielle
still being deeply affected by Michael Jackson's un-
timely death. It became fairly obvious to everyone
that she and Jade developed a special bond after
that.

Fatima had purchased several DVDs for the children to watch while they practiced. She bought
pizzas and other fun foods that the children loved.
For three Saturdays in July and two Saturdays in

August, they came together even though Tiffany had long ago reached the level she needed. They'd continued meeting because the three women really loved the Christian sisterhood that had developed among them.

"It's a good thing we're dancing while we're eating all this junk food," Fatima said as she took a bite of the Pizza Hut deep-pan pizza topped with an assortment of meat she'd ordered for the adults. The children loved cheese pizzas. "Can you imagine the pounds we would have gained by now had we not been burning off these extra calories dancing?"

Tiffany chimed in. "Well, I'll be the first to admit this dance ministry has helped me to lose a little weight. And practicing at the level we've been doing, I'm in great shape since we began this ministry back in June. Even Darius commented on how good I was looking lately. All I'd been hearing from him was how much weight I'd gained since before we got married. Like we're actually supposed to maintain our prewedding weight, even *after* having children. Talking about I'm not the same woman he married. Well, he's not exactly the same size he was when I married him either." Tiffany laughed.

They had been talking for more than thirty minutes and Gabrielle hadn't said much.

"Gabrielle, is something wrong?" Fatima asked after she and Tiffany had talked without Gabrielle contributing anything to the conversation with the exception of an occasional grunt or a few properly spaced nods.

Gabrielle smiled, then shrugged. "You know, I

was just thinking. It's something how as Christians we can be so blessed on one hand while, on the other hand, things seem to be falling down all around us."

"Do you want to talk about something in particular or is this just a general observation?" Tiffany asked.

Fatima knew about Gabrielle's continuing financial situation, but she wasn't sure if Gabrielle had shared that information with Tiffany or whether Gabrielle even wanted her to know. She was just glad Tiffany had been the one to put that question out there instead of her.

"In particular, I suppose," Gabrielle said.

"Anything we can do to help?" Tiffany asked.

"That depends: Do you know anyone who's looking to buy a house?" Gabrielle said. "It's fully bricked, four bedrooms, three and a half baths, with two, mind you, two nice-size dens. Much too much house for one person when you actually think about it."

Tiffany's voice squeaked a little as she spoke. "You're selling your house?"

"I'm trying to."

"Well, it sounds like a nice house," Tiffany said. "If you don't mind me asking, why do you want to sell it?"

Gabrielle leaned her head back on the couch. She inhaled deeply, then released it. "Because"— she exploded the *b*—"I need a higher paying job. Because I can no longer keep up with the payments, along with everything else, on the salary I make now."

"Oh, I can understand that," Tiffany said.

"Things have been rather tight at our house, too. Last summer, when gas prices went up, Darius and I had to use our credit cards just to make a halfway decent dent in our gas tanks. Darius drives a Denali, and I drive my old faithful minivan. Both of them drink gas. It was costing me around sixty and him eighty dollars just to fill up our vehicles. And I have to fill up every three days. It's funny how you don't pay much attention to how often you fill up until gas goes sky-high. Now, even though gas has gone back down, we're still stuck paying off those charges. Folks are calling our house occasionally looking for their money. It's hard. Thank God for caller ID and answering machines. But those debt and bill collectors can be some tricky little devils." Tiffany sighed.

"Darius works a lot of overtime," Tiffany continued. "But it doesn't seem to be helping our household very much. By the time they take out taxes on his overtime, he says there's not much difference in what he got paid on his regular check. I told him I don't see why he works overtime if it's not making a difference in our family. Except that he's not home to help out more. And as for me working outside the home, it's the craziest thing. Do you know how much day care and after-school care cost for three children these days? And in the summertime, all three of them are in day care. It's hard, I tell you. I'm working to pay day care. Now, how crazy is that? So, I feel you, Gabrielle. I feel you."

Fatima pretended to wipe her mouth with her hand as she tried not to draw any special attention to herself. Knowing Darius as she had, she couldn't help but wonder if he was really working overtime or just had another woman on the side. If he would cheat on his wife with her, lying about what he was doing so he could spend time with her when they were together, he might be lying to her now about working overtime. Perhaps that was the real reason his take-home pay was so close to his regular pay. No extra work, no extra pay.

"Well, Gabrielle, keep your chin up. A lot of Christians are struggling these days," Tiffany said. "Being a child of God doesn't seem to exempt us from the troubles of this world. And the Bible tells us that in this life we're going to have troubles."

"But do you know what the Bible also says?" Fatima said. "It says we have not, because we ask not. We need to let God know what we need, then stand on His Word."

Tiffany raised one hand in the air as a witness. "Oh, now, I know that's right! Me personally, I believe what the Bible says. Yes! My God *shall* supply all of my needs according to His riches in glory."

"Well, I *have* been praying, and I've continued believing." Gabrielle turned up the bottle of water she was drinking and took a few swallows. "I continue to expect, standing in faith, that something good is about to happen any day now. You know, like I'll get a better-paying job that pays enough for me to keep my house. Or somebody makes an offer closer to what I owe on my house so I at least don't still end up having to pay on it after I sell it. Originally, I wanted to get the equity I'd put in. Now, I'll be happy just to break even. If I can just get what is owed, I'll be thankful."

"Now that I think about it, I believe one of our

dance team members works in the mortgage department of a bank. Maybe you can talk to her and see if she has any suggestions or ideas that can help you," Tiffany said. "You never know."

"Now, that's a thought," Fatima said, turning to gauge Gabrielle's reaction to that suggestion. "Why don't you check into that?"

"I've already spoken with a financial advisor. I'm not sure anyone can tell me anything different than what I've already been told. And what I've been told is that either I need to make more money and pay what I owe or I need to unload my house and get it out of my name," Gabrielle said. "And the sooner, the better."

"I would still check with her," Tiffany said. "You never know what God is up to. People used to say this all the time, but I know it for myself now: God works in mysterious ways."

"Okay, so who is it?" Gabrielle asked.

"Sasha Peeples," Tiffany said.

"Sasha works for a bank?" Fatima said. "Well, I didn't know that. I thought she was working somewhere else last year."

"Yeah, she works for the bank now," Tiffany said. "From what I heard, she's only been there about eight months. I'm not sure whether she can help or give you any useful information," Tiffany said, directing her statement to Gabrielle now, "but it sure can't hurt to check."

"Meantime, keep praying and believing. God is faithful," Fatima said.

"Oh, let's not just talk about it, let's do it now," Tiffany said. She rose to her feet and held out her hands for the other two to stand and take hold of. "Let's pray."

They stood, grabbed each other's hands to form a small circle, and prayed.

The doorbell rang just as they finished.

"I wonder who that could be," Fatima said to no one in particular.

"Oh, that's probably my husband," Tiffany said nonchalantly. "Let me go get the kids. Will you tell him I'll be right out?" Tiffany said to Fatima.

"You didn't drive?" Fatima asked, then realized how strange that must have sounded. "I'm sorry. I just didn't realize you didn't drive here today."

"My husband's Denali is in the shop. He needed to borrow my van. I had him drop me off and told him what time to come pick me up," Tiffany said. The doorbell rang again. Tiffany laughed. "Fatima, aren't you going to answer the door?"

"Oh, yeah. Sure," Fatima said as she started toward the door. Tiffany went to get the children. Fatima took a deep breath, then released it as she opened the door.

Darius stood there wearing his signature Kangol hat, his head cocked to the side. "Hi there," he said. "I'm not sure whether you remember me or not. But I'm Darius Connors. I'm *Tiffany's* husband." He made sure he emphasized Tiffany's name. "I'm here to pick up her and my children."

"She's gone to get the children," Fatima said. "She told me to tell you she'll be right out."

Darius was smiling at her with a sinister grin. He was like that. Fatima had hoped he would have changed by now—he hadn't. He then slowly leaned down as though he was going to kiss her on her cheek. She took a quick step back.

"So, aren't you going to ask me to come in while I wait on my wife?"

Fatima rolled her eyes at him. "Sure. Come on in," she said dryly.

Darius pulled his body back a little when he saw Gabrielle standing there in her cute little black and gold jogging outfit. "Well, hello there," he said to Gabrielle. He walked over to her and shook her hand. "I'm Darius Connors, Tiffany's husband."

"Hello," Gabrielle said as she shook his hand.

"Excuse me, but have we met before?" Darius asked as he continued to hold on to her hand. "You look *so* familiar."

Fatima couldn't help but roll her eyes in total frustration at having to stand and listen to his stale and outdated come-on line, and in her house at that.

"Maybe we've passed each other at church or Bible study," Gabrielle said, pulling hard enough to finally free her hand from his.

"No, I don't think that's it. I'm trying to picture where it might have been. I just can't put my finger on it right now. But your face looks *so* familiar. Have you ever done television, commercials, anything like that? Are you an actress, a news personality possibly?"

Gabrielle shook her head. "No. Nothing like that."

Darius scratched his head, then tapped his index finger against his buttoned bottom lip. "I'm not trying to be funny, but I'm not kidding, you do look familiar. It's bugging me trying to figure out where I know you from."

"I guess I just have one of those faces," Gabrielle said.

"Yeah, Darius. You know, maybe she just has one of those *faces.*" Fatima's words dripped with sarcasm. "You know, the kind of face that people see and think they've seen somewhere before when they really *haven't? That* kind of a face."

Tiffany came out with the children. Little D. was asleep on her shoulder, Jade and Dana beside her. She was struggling to carry him along with all of her other things.

"Hi, honey," Tiffany said to Darius. "You're right on time. I see you didn't have trouble finding the house." She lifted up a slipping Little D. "Can you help me, please?"

"Yeah. Sure." He hurried over, taking Little D. off her shoulder, laying him on his.

They walked over to the door. "Well, I'll see you ladies later," Tiffany said as she stepped last through the doorway. "Thanks for everything. I enjoyed it, as always." She hugged her two friends.

Tiffany waved one last time. Fatima closed the door after watching them get into the van. She and Gabrielle went back inside, then turned to each other.

"Jerk," they said in unison. They both laughed at the irony of their apparently thinking the same thing and saying it at the exact same time.

"You thought so, too?" Gabrielle said.

"Oh, yeah. 'Your face looks *so* familiar. Where have I seen you before?'" Fatima said, mocking Darius. "What a piece of work."

"'Have you ever done television? Are you an actress?'" Gabrielle said, also repeating the words Darius had spoken to her.

"I *know* I've seen your face before." Fatima laughed. "Where, oh where?"

Gabrielle smiled at Fatima's comment, although in truth, she had to admit: his face looked familiar to her as well.

# Chapter 18

Gabrielle decided to talk to Sasha as Tiffany had suggested. Saturday afternoon the entire dance team was having its final dress rehearsal before the celebration on Sunday morning. They wanted to make sure everything went off as planned. If anything needed adjusting, it could be done during this rehearsal. After they finished and changed out of their flowing pastel dance outfits, Gabrielle walked over to Sasha. She was in deep conversation with another dance member, Alicia, the young woman who'd asked so many questions at their first ministry meeting about people having a heart to do something who may not be good enough to be chosen. Gabrielle stood waiting for the two of them to finish so she could talk privately with Sasha.

"Now, you talking about fine, good-looking, and on top of that, the man just completed his residency and has started his own private practice in an office he shares with two other doctors, that's Doctor Z.," Sasha said, oblivious to the fact that

Gabrielle had walked up on her conversation. "He showed up at our office because he was closing on a new house he'd just bought, a thirty-five-hundred-square-foot mansion over in Mountain Brook. I'm sure it's just a starter home for somebody like him. But that's a nice-size mansion, located in a great area even in this housing market, where folks have lost some really nice homes to foreclosure. And without divulging anything proprietary, you *know* that house *had* to cost him a pretty penny."

"Wow, he does sound like something to see," Alicia said.

"Well, he's been here to this church a few times. I think I've seen him once during morning worship service and once at a Bible study," Sasha said. "But he's not a member. When he came to our office on Tuesday to close, I happened to mention that he looked familiar. We—well, it was actually more *me* than *him*—were trying to figure out where we might have known each other from."

"Don't you just hate when that happens? You see someone, and you can't for the life of you recall where it might have been?" Alicia said.

"Ooh, girl, yeah. But it helped when I told him that I'd seen him recently. That's how we got on the subject of him being a doctor in the first place. He asked if I'd had any reason to have come to the ER lately. That's where he'd done his final residency—UAB Hospital emergency room. Well, of course I told him *that* wasn't it. I haven't set foot in a hospital, not even to visit anyone, since my father was sick and died. With the exception of when I had my last baby girl fourteen months ago, which would have been before he arrived. He told me most folks call him Doctor Z. Isn't that the cutest thing?"

"Doctor Z.? That is *so* cute," Alicia said. "He must have a killer last name to have to shorten it like that."

"So then I was thinking I might have seen him at a club, since I've been there a couple of times this year." Sasha stopped when she remembered she was still in church and talking about going to a club while in church was hardly appropriate. "One of my friends from high school named Mercedes celebrated her birthday at a club," Sasha said. "That's why I was there. Then, another friend celebrated a promotion at a club. Of course, I had to go. Both of these ladies are high maintenance. And if you don't support them without a real good reason, like somebody died in your family—and it had better be an immediate family member at that—they get *major* attitudes, major."

Alicia waved her hand at Sasha for her to just finish the story and drop the extra commentary about why she happened to be at a club.

"Anyway," Sasha continued, "instead of bringing up the club, I decided to ask him where he attended church. That's when he informed me that he wasn't a member of any particular church. He'd only recently moved back to Birmingham after earning his medical degree at University of Illinois College of Medicine in Chicago. But he did admit he was looking for a church home. In the past, with his erratic schedule, it was hard for him to make it to anybody's church. Well, of course, I told him I was a member here, and that's when we made the possible connection. He said he'd visited here a couple of times. I told him that's where I'd likely seen him. He said he's been to worship service as well as one other function this year. But I knew I'd seen him before. I may not be great with names, but I never forget a face, especially not one as good-looking as his. Oh, girl! You talk about cute." Sasha shook her right hand as though she'd been burned and she was trying to cool it in a hurry.

"I hope you didn't tell him all of *that*," Alicia said.

"Of course I didn't. But I did tell him about the celebratory service we're having here tomorrow. And I think he just might come. At least, I certainly hope he does," Sasha said. "I'll be on the lookout for him. You can believe that!"

Gabrielle cleared her throat. She didn't want to hear any more of Sasha's conversation. She had hoped one of them would have noticed her standing there and acknowledged her presence so she could have at least told Sasha she wanted to talk with her when she finished. Since neither of them either realized it or acted like they saw her, she had no other option than to do something to get their attention.

Sasha turned around. "Oh, I'm sorry. I didn't know you were standing there. Do you need us for something?"

Gabrielle smiled. "Actually, I was wondering if I could speak with you when you finish here." She was directing her comment to Sasha.

"Sure," Sasha said.

"I'll catch up with you later," Alicia said to Sasha, then scurried away.

"You have been so great with this dance team," Sasha said, pouring on the praise. "Everybody is excited about the routine you choreographed and impressed by just how anointed you are when you dance. I only pray I someday reach your level."

"Thank you. I think everybody's doing a fantastic job. I believe the people are truly going to be blessed tomorrow. I know the Lord will be."

Sasha smiled. "Absolutely." She stood waiting for Gabrielle to say something else. When she saw she was slow in doing it, she said, "So, what did you want to talk with me about?"

"I hear you work for a bank, in the mortgage department."

"I do."

"They wouldn't happen to be hiring, would they?" Gabrielle said half teasing, but deciding it certainly couldn't hurt to ask even though that wasn't her original intent.

"No, they're not. In fact, they even may be laying off soon. What? You're looking for a job?"

"I have one, but I really could use one that pays a lot more. What I'm making now is not enough to keep up with all of my expenses."

"I know what you're talking about. I can empathize with you on that," Sasha said. "I got fired last year at the worst possible time, of course, and had to start all over again. That's how I ended up at the bank. I'm a divorced, single mother of a fourteen-month-old baby girl and an eight-year-old daughter, who's going on twenty-two." Sasha laughed.

"Your oldest daughter's name is Aaliyah, right?"

"Yeah. It's Aaliyah." Sasha smiled, somewhat

touched that Gabrielle had remembered her oldest daughter's name, having met her only once.

"She's something else. You had her here at one of our earlier rehearsals. She picked up on our steps perfectly, just in that brief time. In fact, when I saw her dancing that day, I was thinking how we seriously need to bring our youth into this dance ministry, not that I have any say-so about that. But your daughter is an outstanding little dancer, a real ballerina with great deliverance and technique."

Sasha began to beam with pride. "I know. She *is* something, isn't she? I was thinking maybe I was biased, being her mother and all."

"No, she's really good. She reminds me a little of me when I was young, dancing in almost every move that she makes. And she has a natural curiosity about things. That's a giant step toward becoming great," Gabrielle said.

"Well, her father certainly spoils her. He's the one who makes sure she has dance and piano lessons. He's like that. Although it did take a lot of prayer for him to forgive me about a piano fiasco a few years back. But he loves Aaliyah so much. You know Minister Marcus Peeples, don't you? He's my ex-husband, Aaliyah's father."

"I didn't know you two used to be married. I mean, I knew your last name and his were Peeples, but I didn't link the two of you together at all," Gabrielle said.

"That's because you probably see him with his new wife, Melissa, and their brand-new baby boy. Well, I suppose his wife is not so new anymore even though the baby would be considered new at six months. They dated for about four months, got engaged, and were married in July before the year was even out. She had a little girl the following July, and now they have a brand-new baby boy. Makes my head swim. She was the one who put on the church's Inaugural Ball back in January, pregnant and all. But she did a great job. At least that's what I heard, since I didn't make it to it." Sasha shifted her body.

"Personally, I don't understand all of these short courting periods between Christian folks," Sasha continued. "I think people should date for at least a year just so they can really get to know each other. Do you know why some couples get married so fast? Do you want to know why?"

Since Sasha brought it up, Gabrielle did want to know even if the conversation wasn't heading where she was trying to go. At some point soon, she would need to grab the reins and steer things back on course. She nodded her answer to Sasha's question.

"Plain and simple: they get hot for each other—hormones and pheromones. That's mostly why. And wanting somebody to want them. Then, you have Pastor Landris, who dares to teach on fornication and adultery—sermons a lot of preachers won't touch with a ten-foot pole. Not in these prosperity and breakthrough days. Who wants to hear about sins and consequences during these times? Just make the people feel good, and everybody gets what they want. Most people know how difficult it is to keep yourself while dating. Heck, it's hard to keep yourself when you're married. People who come to this church and hear the Word of

God take the scripture 'It's better to marry than to burn' literally."

"So, you're saying that you don't?"

Sasha cocked her head. It occurred to her that Gabrielle *was* in a leadership-type role with the dance ministry. Johnnie Mae had obviously been impressed with her, enough to elevate her to a status above the rest of them. Sasha realized she needed to watch what she said to Gabrielle. The last thing she wanted was to be kicked out of the dance ministry because of something that had flippantly come out of her mouth. Marcus always told her she needed to think more before she spoke.

"Of course I'm not saying that I don't. Although, I do question whether 'to burn' is referring to hell's fire or to the fact that if you're hot for somebody, it's better to marry them than to burn, you know . . . burn up with desire. But what happens when the fire starts to burn low, or worse, burns completely out? I'll tell you what. They're stuck with that person, and the question then becomes: did they really love each other, or were they merely satisfying their flesh? If it's love, then okay. If it was more lust than love and the luster has dulled, then what are they going to do?"

Gabrielle thought this was a great discussion—for another time. Sasha was indeed bringing up some thought-provoking discussion questions.

Fortunately, or unfortunately, for Gabrielle, this was not the problem confronting her right now. Not her problem at all.

# Chapter 19

*For if any be a hearer of the word, and not a doer, he is like unto a man beholding his natural face in a glass.*

—James 1:23

Presently, Gabrielle wasn't talking to or dating anyone. But that hadn't stopped plenty of men, both in and out of the church, from stepping to her and trying. For now, she was content with sitting at the Lord's feet, feeding her spirit. That way, as Pastor Landris had said often since she'd become a member, she would be prepared for whatever the devil threw at her. She was fortifying her faith shield to quench all of the fiery darts that might be hurled her way.

Darts, as she tried to be true to what God had called her to do in spite of things not going her way. She'd given her life to Christ. In the beginning, things had been grand. Folks told her that's how it appears to work when people first come to Christ. "A baby Christian," they'd called her. The best way they explained it to her was that it was like lifting weights. You don't start out bench-pressing or lifting one hundred pounds from the get-go. You start out with small, manageable pounds, then work your way up to twenty, fifty, and eventually able to lift hundreds.

"God knows how much you can bear," Pastor Landris had said at Bible study. "Trust that God is watching and that there is nothing happening in your life that He doesn't know about. Trust that if God allows it to be brought to you, God is there to bring you through it. He'll bring you through, and He'll bring you out. No matter what's going on in your life, in the end, God *will* get the glory. Even those negative things help us in the exercising of our faith."

Gabrielle was now lifting heavier weights than when she'd begun. She was deep in God's Word. That was something else Pastor Landris had said.

"Satan will bring all kinds of trouble to your household. For those of you who have children, he'll use your children to get to you. To you who are married, he'll use your spouse. Single, he'll find ways to tempt you, to try to cause you to fall, thinking he can use that against you. If you have a house, a car, or other things, he'll mess with your things to cause you distress as he whispers that God is not there or that God doesn't care. But trust God no matter what it looks like, and no matter what's going on in your life. Maintain an attitude of forever praise." Pastor Landris did a one–two step dance. Chuckles and laughter rose in the sanctuary.

"Your attitude should be that you're going to praise God no matter what—come what may. Learn to press your way through. Be focused on your desires. And no matter who or what tries to get in your way, keep pressing until you've reached *your* contact point." Pastor Landris shook his head, then walked down the steps to the main floor.

"God is looking for faith today, not fake. He's looking for faith. Real faith. And how does He know you have faith? By what you do. So, what are *you* giving God to work with?"

Pastor Landris walked over toward his right, then without saying a word, back to the left. "Let me leave you with this. In Matthew the ninth chapter"—he held his Bible up, then let it back down— "there is the story of two blind men. They were following Jesus, crying, and saying, 'Thou son of David, have mercy on us.'" Pastor Landris began to laugh. "Think about that: two blind men . . . men who *couldn't* see, but they could see *enough* to follow Jesus. Men who in the natural couldn't see but could see enough to follow Jesus. We have people right here, right now with natural eyesight, twenty-twenty vision, and they can't see to follow Jesus the way these two blind men could see enough to follow Jesus."

Some in the congregation began to erupt with shouts as they got what Pastor Landris was saying.

Pastor Landris read what Jesus said to the blind men in verse twenty-nine. "'According to your faith be it unto you.' Did anybody get that?"

The congregation was shouting and praising God.

Pastor Landris began to repeat that scripture, emphasizing different words during each time. "*According* to your faith . . . be it unto you. According to *your* faith be it unto you. According to your *faith* . . ." Pastor Landris did another two-step. "Not according to someone else's faith, but according to *your*

faith. I like to say it like this. Whatsoever you believe, be it unto you. Do you hear what I say? If you
don't want to believe, then according to *your* faith,
be it unto you. I'm not going to argue with you
about it. We're not going to fall out because of our
difference in belief. Because ultimately, and I've
seen this work too many times . . . faith works y'all,
you *will* have what you say. You will have what *you*
say. Not what *I* say. What *you* say."

Gabrielle had heard the Word as it had come
forth from Pastor Landris. Hearing the Word was
great, but doing the Word was what it was about.
Standing here, talking with Sasha now, she was trying to do what she could. She had already prayed.
She'd even held up her bills, shown the Lord what
she was faced with.

She'd shown God the notice she'd received
from the car loan company, their intent to repos-
sess if payment was not received in ten days. She
knew God was aware of all of this. The car loan
company had informed her of her "right to cure,"
which meant she could avoid the car being repossessed by making up any missed payments plus ap-
plicable penalties and fees. Unless God stepped in
and soon, there was nothing she could do to keep
her car from being taken. And her home mortgage company had written to inform her that her
contract gave them the right to initiate a nonjudi-
cial foreclosure process if she didn't catch her payments up as well.

"I need to sell my house," Gabrielle said, getting
back to Sasha and the topic at hand. "Is there anything that you know about that might help me
these days?"

"Well, I'm only a receptionist in the mortgage department, so I don't know all the ins and outs. But you could try contacting HUD. That's Housing and Urban Development. I hear they have some things that can help people who are in jeopardy of being foreclosed on. See if they can help."

Gabrielle thanked Sasha. At least it was something to go on. She would check into that tomorrow. Since she'd gotten rid of everything that wasn't a necessity back when her situation called for some real belt-tightening, she didn't have Internet access in her home any longer. She would have to go to the library to go online or call HUD tomorrow sometime.

Right now, she could no longer afford her house. Only God moving on this, and moving relatively quickly, would be able to save her.

"God, I don't have anywhere or anyone else to turn to *except* You," she said as she kneeled down and prayed before going to bed. "Please, hear my cry. Lord, I need Your help down here. I need a little relief. I don't know where else to go or who else to turn to except You. Please . . ."

# Chapter 20

*By him therefore let us offer the sacrifice of*
*praise to God continually, that is, the fruit of*
*our lips giving thanks to his name.*

—Hebrews 13:15

It was a beautiful day at Followers of Jesus Faith Worship Center, the church congregation's special day of celebration being held the third Sunday in August. They had set aside this day to invite family, friends, and the community to give thanks with them for God's goodness and mercy. A day to celebrate with a congregation that had begun the second Sunday in March 2002 in Pastor George and Johnnie Mae Landris's home before moving into a modular building in July of 2003, to their present facility moved in on December 5, 2004. This day drew an overflow crowd.

The newly named Wings as Eagles Dance Ministry was derived from Isaiah 40:31: "But they that wait upon the Lord shall renew their strength; they shall mount up with wings as eagles; they shall run, and not be weary; and they shall walk, and not faint." Johnnie Mae told the group she'd chosen that scripture and that name because she thought it was befitting of the message the ministry wanted to convey.

"An eagle is a large bird—strong . . . powerful," Johnnie Mae had said during their first official meeting as a dance team. "Eagles have exceptionally keen eyesight; able to see what other birds can't at a distance other birds can only wish for. As Christians, *we* should also be able to see what others can't. Eagles build their nests in tall trees or on high cliffs. I admonish all of you to set your sights on your home on high. We serve a big God, a powerful God, an unlimited God when it comes to what He can do. Eagles don't sweat. As Christians, we need to stop sweating both the small and the big stuff. Stop sweating stuff. Eagles are active during the daylight. That goes hand in hand with scripture that tells us to work while it's day.

"Ironically, eagles don't have vocal cords even though they're capable of making shrilling sounds when needed. Eagles' movements—grace in flight—speak volumes for them when witnessed by others. So it should be with you, your life, and your dance. Eagle wings are fashioned for soaring. They know how to use rising currents of warm air, the updrafts generated by terrains—those peaks and valleys in life as well as mountaintops—to make it to their destination. You see, eagles don't need to flap in order to fly. They have learned to rest, using what others would view as negatives, to reach even higher heights. They use the storms in life to soar, and they soar with ease. The eagle's feathers are light in weight, but they're strong and flexible. I encourage all of you—when you minis-

ter through dance and as you go through life—to
mount up with wings as eagles."

And minister to the people is just what Wings as
Eagles Dance Ministry did that Sunday morning.
After they finished, when the congregation de-
manded it by a standing ovation, Johnnie Mae had
each member step forward as she called their
names. It had been a powerful and magnificent
time of worship. They had indeed set the atmosphere for the rest of the church service.

After service, Gabrielle was approached by a lot
of people who told her how much they had been
blessed by the ministering of the dance team.
Gabrielle loved how her gift was being used in the
service of God. Her response to those who told
her how great she was and how blessed they were
having been here today was, "Thank you. I praise
God. God gets all the glory."

"Now, *that* was praise in motion," Gabrielle
heard a man's deep voice say directly behind her.

She turned around and could hardly believe
her eyes.

"Well, hello there, stranger," she said as coolly as
she could manage after seeing who stood before
her.

"So, you remember me?" he said with a smile.

"Of course I remember you. We met back in January, on the twentieth, to be exact, at the church's
Inaugural Ball. You're Zachary Morgan."

He bowed his head slightly as he continued to
smile with an added primp of his mouth. "The
dance team was awesome . . . a true blessing.
Goodness, all of you blessed me." He shook his
head. "In fact, I was so moved by the ministry

through dance, and after that, the Word coming from the pastor, I came forward to become a member."

"Really," Gabrielle said, unable to mask her delight. "That's wonderful! Allow me to welcome you to Followers of Jesus Faith Worship Center. You're going to love it here."

"Thank you. I still have that one day of orientation this week before I receive the honor of officially being 'added into this flock,' as I believe they call it here. But so far, everybody has been quite . . . quite . . . what's the word I'm looking for?"

"Loving and embracing?"

"That's more than one word, but that works." He smiled. "They certainly are loving and embracing here. You feel like you're being welcomed back home after a long period of having wandered around in life, slightly lost, not knowing who you really were before finding your way back to your family. Back to a family, I might add, that's been looking for you and praying for your safe return. I don't know if that makes sense," Zachary said.

"Oh, it makes perfect sense. Especially to me." Gabrielle smiled back.

"Well, you, Miss Mercedes, were absolutely anointed today. I can't find words to tell you how much I enjoyed the way you personally ministered to me. Not taking anything away from the others, who were also fabulous, but you . . . *you* made me and the rest of the congregation feel as though we really could mount up with wings not *like* but *as* eagles, and soar above any and every thing that might normally try to hold us down. Magnificent, that's all I can say. Bravo."

"Praise God. I give Him all the glory." Gabrielle didn't know what else to say either. He continued to gaze at her with such a sincere smile. Silence stood between them—smiles and silence, now quickly becoming an awkward sixty seconds.

He stopped grinning. "I didn't ask you this the last time we met—"

"Oh, you mean the first time we met?" Gabrielle said, unable to keep her own grin under control.

"Yeah, okay, the first and the last time we met. That's a good one," he said. "I see you're not wearing a wedding band, and I know that doesn't always mean anything, especially in today's world. So, I'll just ask. Are you married?"

"No."

"Engaged? Seeing anyone special?"

"Nope." She blushed.

"Okay, then I wonder if I *might* be able to persuade you to go to dinner with me today." There was a distinct question there.

"It depends," Gabrielle said.

"On what?"

"Are *you* married, or engaged, or seeing anyone right now?"

"No, no"—he hesitated for a second—"and no."

She pulled back. "Do you really expect me to believe someone like you has no one else? Not even someone you're merely talking to. A good friend. Maybe someone you just recently broke up with."

"To be honest with you, I haven't seriously dated in five years," Zachary said.

"Oh, come on now. I know you don't think I'm going to fall for that line, do you?" Gabrielle said.

"Well, it's true. And we *are* standing in a church.

I'm too afraid of God to lie in a church. The truth is I've been too busy to seriously date anyone. Now things are a bit better. Not tremendously, but it wouldn't be as much of a strain on a relationship now as it would have before. That is, *should* I find myself blessed to be in a relationship now."

"Okay, I'll bite," she said, referring to his comment about him being too busy to date as she compared this scenario to a fish eyeing bait on a sharp, new hook before deciding to take a swipe. "How is it you were too busy?"

"Come to dinner with me and I'll tell you anything you want to know. Anything and everything. A fire sale—everything . . . nothing held back."

"Okay."

"Okay?" He began to smile again. "Okay." He nodded. "Great! Do you want to go now, or would you prefer waiting until later in the day?"

"Let me go home, put away my things, and change. I can meet you there," Gabrielle said.

"Actually, I'm sort of old school. My mother taught me to, and I believe in, picking up my date from her home and safely returning her back there. If you'll give me your address, tell me what time you'd like for me to be there, we can go from there."

Gabrielle hesitated.

After she didn't say anything more, he asked, "Is something wrong?"

"Nothing really. I was just thinking whether it might not be better, since we are just getting to know each other, for me to meet you there." Actually, Gabrielle was thinking of several things. She'd been lured once into a trap by a man who was cunning and clever and ended up beating her up, although Zachary appeared harmless enough. Still, she wanted to get to know him a little better before giving him her home address, which led to her second concern. He would see the sale sign and might begin asking questions that could end up derailing things before they got to know each other better.

He held up his hands in surrender. "Listen, if meeting me at this stage makes you feel more comfortable, I understand. We can meet *this* time. But *next* time, we'll do it the right way," Zachary said.

"Next time?"

"Yeah, next time."

"Who said there was going to be a next time?"

"The Bible," he said.

Gabrielle cocked her head to the side and smirked just a tad. "Where in the Bible does it say you and I are going to have a next time?"

"Where it says to speak of those things that be not as though they were. So, I'm speaking those things as though they already are. Totally Bible. Next time. And if you don't like that scripture reference, how about, 'You have not because you ask not'? That can be found in the book of James. Next time. Shall I continue?"

She shook her head and laughed. "No. All that's left now is for us to decide where and what time."

He winked.

At this juncture, Gabrielle wasn't sure whether his wink was flirting, to disarm her, or some involuntary reaction he didn't even know he'd done. Either way, it was cute.

# Chapter 21

*If we confess our sins, he is faithful and just to forgive us our sins, and to cleanse us from all unrighteousness.*

—1 John 1:9

Smiling at the thought of having seen Zachary again, Gabrielle made her way out to her car. She was hanging her dance outfit on the clip over the back door's seat when she heard a voice whisper behind her, "Goodness and Mercy."

She turned around. "Darius?" she said both quizzically and startled. She wondered why he was standing so close to her, and how had he sneaked up on her without her having heard him. She looked to see if Tiffany was nearby. The parking lot was almost empty now. "Are you looking for Tiffany?" Gabrielle asked when she didn't see any sign of Tiffany.

"*Goodness* and *Mercy*," he said again, this time with a smirk as he lifted his eyebrows the way the bushy-browed comedian and actor Groucho Marx used to do in his acts. Darius moved in even closer.

Gabrielle quickly closed the rear car door, then took a few more steps away from him. She was now next to the driver's door.

"I *knew* you looked familiar. And today, while you were up there all made up, dressed in your fancy doodads, ministering in that *gorgeous* flowing dance outfit, it suddenly hit me like a ton of bricks."

"What are you talking about?"

He flashed her a teasing grin. "Oh, now . . . *you* know what I'm talking about. So, let's not play games anymore, all right? I know, and you know that I know."

"I don't have a clue *what* you're talking about," Gabrielle said, her voice escalating slightly as she tried to maintain a calm composure.

"Goodness and Mercy. How's that for a clue? Are things starting to become a little bit clearer for you now, Miss Mercedes?"

"Listen, Darius. I don't know what you're thinking, but I do know that what you're doing here is highly inappropriate. We're brothers and sisters in Christ. I think you should remember that and govern yourself accordingly."

He placed his index fingers together, formed to look like a steeple, and placed it against his nose, his thumbs under his chin. He leaned in slightly before taking his hands down from his face. "G. M., Gabrielle Mercedes. G. M., Goodness and Mercy. Did you come up with that on purpose or is that merely a coincidence?" He chuckled. "Okay, what I'm thinking is that maybe you should stop acting like you don't know what I'm talking about. How's that for starters?"

"Fine. But the Goodness and Mercy you knew no longer exists. She's dead. In fact, she was buried back in January. There were even witnesses to her death as symbolized with her water baptism. And the person who arose with Christ in her place, she's a new creature in Christ. Whatever was there before is no longer there. It's all under the blood of Jesus. I'm Gabrielle Mercedes, a child of the Most High God. And I refuse to allow you to bring up anything from my past and try to throw it in my face. I have confessed my sins. I am forgiven, and I've been cleansed from all unrighteousness." Gabrielle's words were matched with a look of sternness and seriousness.

"Goodness and mercy, lighten up will you." He laughed. "Did you catch that pun I just did? Goodness and mercy, you know, as in when you're just expressing yourself before you say something, and Goodness and Mercy as in a person whose stage name is *Goodness and Mercy*." He nodded as he grinned.

"Look, we just had a wonderful time in the Lord. You really need to stop playing, put away childish things, and grow up."

"First Corinthians chapter thirteen. Ooh, I'm impressed. So you're giving *me* spiritual advice, now? Godly advice coming from you. You, Miss-All-Respected-for-Your-Walk-with-the-Lord. So, you think you're better than me now? Is that it? Are you judging me?"

"No," Gabrielle said. "I'm not judging anyone. I'm saying that the person you obviously *think* you knew no longer exists." Gabrielle chose her words carefully. "I'm sure you're ecstatic that you figured out why you thought I looked familiar when we met last week. Now we can put all of this behind us and move on."

"Yeah, but you did leave me hanging. I bet you and Miss Fatima had a big old laugh, at my expense of course, after I left."

Gabrielle stood stone-faced, not letting on that he was absolutely correct.

"But I do understand," Darius said. "I can't say I blame you at all. It wasn't in your best interest nor was it the right place to admit another place we could have met. Honestly, you did me a favor not mentioning that place, especially not in front of Miss Righteous Fatima." He shook his head fast, then nodded. "Nope, you're one smooth operator. I like that. You've shown you can keep a secret. You, Sister Gabrielle Mercedes, know how to play the game with class and dignity. I mean, look at you today—class and dignity. A man can appreciate that. A real man can respect a woman like you."

Darius figured Fatima hadn't told Gabrielle about the two of them having had an affair that ended, reluctantly, about four years ago. He deduced Fatima cared too much about maintaining her image and pristine reputation to spill that kind of information about herself. He wasn't worried too much about her saying anything that might incriminate herself.

"Well, I need to go now," Gabrielle said as calmly as she could muster. She didn't want him knowing he was getting to her.

"Goodness and Mercy," he said with a smirk. "Hold up a minute. You know we've missed you. Okay, let me speak for myself. *I've* missed you. Things haven't been the same since you left. Of course, I didn't realize at the time you'd changed partners."

"Excuse me?" Gabrielle frowned. "Changed partners? What are you talking about?"

"You know, some would consider what you were doing before as dancing with the devil, or more accurately, dancing in service *of* the devil. Now you're dancing for or in the service of the Lord. Still dancing, mind you—you just changed partners. I think it's great myself. Although between the two of us, I have to admit, there was something extra special about watching you dance today. I guess what people say is true: it *is* better when you leave more to the imagination." Darius playfully widened his eyes.

"Seriously, though, the guys have *really* missed you. Things began going downhill after you left. People were demanding to know where you'd gone so they could come and patronize you there. But Clarence wouldn't tell anybody what happened to you. He did say you'd likely be back. But I had no idea here is where you'd end up. So close. Right here with me." He nodded. "Well, I suppose I need to start coming to church more often."

"Look, whatever was in my past is past. If you want to talk about God's goodness and mercy, we can have a word here and there. However, if all you want to talk about is my past, then you need to find somebody else to chitchat with. I have more important things to do with my life." She held up her arm and blatantly looked at her watch.

"Wow, I've heard having Jesus in your life changes a person. But I admit: this is my first time witnessing it up close and personal—seeing just how much Jesus *can* change a person. You appear totally sold out for Christ," Darius said. "But then, most Christians do."

"The correct terminology is that I am redeemed. I was bought with a price. I understand that. I welcome that. I embrace it. If you have a problem with that concept, maybe you need to talk with someone else about it. Possibly your wife, or better yet, schedule an appointment with Pastor Landris and talk it over with him."

Darius frowned as he tilted his head to one side and began to bounce his head a little. "Hmm. You know, that *is* a thought. I wonder if Pastor Landris or his lovely wife knows about your past. His wife is over the dance ministry, for now anyway, isn't she?"

"She is."

"And she allowed you to become a part of the dance ministry? Although, in truth, I have to admit, you really were the most talented of all of them. And, I'm not just saying that because I've been a longtime fan of your work."

"Listen, I really have to go." She opened her car door.

"Tell you what: I'll let you go if you agree to have lunch, dinner, or something with me, at a later date of course. I've got the family thing today—you know how it is."

"What?" Gabrielle couldn't believe what he'd just said.

He shrugged. "I'd like to see you again. In a more relaxed setting. You know, a fellow brethren and a fellow sisteren in Christ"—he chuckled at his made-up word of *sisteren*—"sitting down together, breaking bread . . . drinking a little wine, maybe. You know the Bible says a little wine is good for the stomach. Nothing too heavy—just me and you . . . making things up as we go. I'd like to hear more of your wonderful conversion to Christ."

"You're kidding, right? This is your way of being funny?"

He shook his head. "If I'm kidding, then I'm failing miserably since neither one of us is laughing. This is not a joke." He scanned her body from head to toe. "*Definitely* not a joke. And I know you're not married. Got that from the little wifey."

"Excuse me, but you don't see a problem with what you just said?"

"What?" He held out his opened hands, palms up, to her as though he were waiting for her to lay a large object in them. "You mean about you not being married?"

"No. That you got that information from your *wife*." She frowned at him. "Someone, I might add, I've grown close to and fond of over these past two months."

"And someone you probably early on learned was a little slow when it comes to catching on to things. That's the reason she needed extra dance rehearsals. It wasn't because of the children or her not having the time. She loves to use our children as an excuse for everything." Darius stood up straighter.

"Now, don't get me wrong; Tiffany's a beautiful woman," he said. "She definitely has her own gifts, believe you me. And the woman is loyal to a fault. She rarely gives me any lip about anything, which I have to admit is a rare find in today's women. Women want to brag about how independent they are. Destiny's Child, Kelly Clarkson, Ne-Yo, and any of the rest of them all singing about the independent woman or *Miss Independent*. I don't know one woman who doesn't want to be loved and appreciated. I don't care how much money she has. If you don't have anyone to share things with, how much fun is that? That's how women are. Once you figure that part out, you can keep your woman happy and pretty much out of your hair. Tiffany knows I love and appreciate her. And during those times when she might feel like I'm a little out there, I do my thing. I remind her of how *blessed* she is to have a man like me, and we're straight."

"Is that so?" Gabrielle said with sarcasm. "Well, Mister-Knows-What-Every-Woman-Wants-and-Needs, I wish you well. Not Godspeed, but well. But right now, I have Jesus in my life. And frankly—and I hope you're not offended by this, but if you are, it's all right with me—Jesus is all the man that *this* woman right here really needs."

"Mercy, if that's not what people expect you to say, I don't know what is. But on those cold nights when you're all alone . . . all by yourself, and you need someone to put his arms around you, to cuddle up with, to whisper a little sweet somethin'-somethin' in your ear, when you want someone you can talk to and hear talk back audibly to you, not just thoughts in your mind, then what? God created us for each other. He was the one who said it wasn't good for man to be alone. All I'm saying is that I can love and appreciate you the way God made you. I know about your past, yet I can talk to you and not hold that against you. In fact, I celebrate you. Now, how many men out there do you really think can feel this way? I'm talking about a good Christian man such as myself."

"Bye," Gabrielle said as she opened her door more and slid inside, then grabbed the handle to close the door.

Darius grabbed the door and held it open—forcibly restraining her from being able to close it. "You didn't answer my question."

Gabrielle glared at him. "Go home and tell your wife what a wonderful job she did today. Okay? Then, tell her how much she blessed you in dance and praise to the Lord. And you know what you and I will do? We'll both forget we ever had this little conversation." She smiled, yanked the door from his clutches, and shut it. She hurriedly locked her doors, took out her key, cranked up her car, then drove away.

Darius stood with a smile on his face as she hurried away. Biting down on his bottom lip, he made a long sucking sound as his teeth continued to press down. He then nodded. "Every dog has his day," he said. "Yep. Every dog has his day. Ruff-ruff."

When Gabrielle reached the stoplight, she laid her head on her steering wheel. "God, please, help me. Please. I'm trying so hard down here. I don't know how much more of this I can take. And I truly don't need Darius on top of everything else that's going on in my life right now. I don't. You know that I don't. And I especially don't need something like this after having had such a praise-filled day. Please, I need Your help down here."

The light turned green. A car behind her honked its horn. She lifted up her head, and drove away.

# Chapter 22

*Let not him that eateth despise him that eateth not; and let not him which eateth not judge him that eateth: for God hath received him.*

—Romans 14:3

"**I**s something wrong?" Zachary asked as he and Gabrielle sat in the restaurant. He noted how she was using her fork like a hockey stick to shuffle her food back and forth, vacillating between her salad and the food on her plate. "Is yours not good?"

Gabrielle looked up. "No. I mean, yes, my food is great." She speared a piece of lettuce and a cucumber with her fork and carefully placed it in her mouth. She smiled.

"I suppose you're still feeling the effects from earlier today at church. Ministering is something. One preacher told me that after he preaches, sometimes he has to take a nap to get his energy back. I hear that ministering can take a lot out of you. It's the adrenaline, hormones released in anticipation, that stimulates the heart rate, dilates blood vessels and air passages, things people associate more with fight or flight. . . ." Zachary stopped speaking. He leaned down to look up into her face, which remained down. "Hey? Hey? What's wrong?"

Gabrielle raised her head. "I'm sorry," she said. "I suppose if you wanted to go to dinner alone, you could have done that, huh? I just have a few things on my mind right now. I apologize. I guess I'm not being great company."

"Would you like to talk about what's bothering you? I'm a pretty good listener."

She shook her head. "Not really. I just need to shake it off, that's all. You know how things can be. You're excited about what God is doing in your life, but at the same time . . ." She leaned her head back, then back down before spearing a grape tomato with her fork and placing it in her mouth.

"At the same time, the devil seems to be intensifying his attacks on you."

She smiled and tilted her head to one side. "Sounds like you've been there."

"I know how it can be. Although I've not been attending church regularly lately, I still take time out to spend with the Lord. Occasionally, I read my Bible during breaks at work. And I pray often. In fact, I don't know where I would be had it not been for the Lord." Zachary sat back against his chair.

"I just got saved this year," Gabrielle said. "January fourth. It's been a wonderful blessing. Honestly, I don't know if I could have handled some of the things I've faced here lately were it not for the Lord on my side." She drank some of her Dr Pepper.

"May I offer a bit of advice?"

"Sure."

"Turn it *all* over to the Lord. Do what you can, but ultimately you really do need to give it to God. Cast your cares on Him because He really does care for you."

Gabrielle smiled. "You're right, and I have. I've found that there's only so much I can do anyway no matter how hard I try otherwise."

"My definition of faith is to act like you believe God's Word is true. That's something my father drilled into me early on. If you believe, if you truly trust God, then you have to believe not only that He *will* handle it, but in *how* He chooses to handle it. We often pray, but then we want to tell God how He should bring it to pass." Zachary took a sip of his lemon water. "And preferably, we would appreciate it, if we didn't have to suffer at all along the way. Make it the straightest and shortest way possible, Lord."

"The shortest distance between two points. But that's not realistic, though, is it?"

"No, it's not. There will be some things that will cause us to want to turn around and go back to what we know, even if what we know wasn't that great or in our best interest. But at least—we rationalize—it was familiar to us," Zachary said, glancing downward, then back into Gabrielle's awaiting gorgeous brown eyes.

"I get the impression that *might* have been as much of a Word for you, as it was for me," Gabrielle said as she shyly blushed.

"I love your smile," he said. "A man could get

spoiled, think he's special, blessed beyond blessed waking up to a smile like yours each and every morning."

That caused her to blush even more. "Stop that," she said.

"Stop what?"

"Stop making me forget about my troubles and having me concentrate on what I have right now, which truthfully is not so bad at this moment."

He hurried to chew the green beans he'd just placed in his mouth as she was speaking. "Do you know what I really like about you?" he said.

"You mean besides my 'wake up to' smile?" she teased, then she held tightly her bottom lip with her teeth to keep a full laugh from escaping. She then playfully rolled her eyes at him as she batted them a few times, her way of making fun of his comment.

"You see, now your eyes are messing me up. I'm trying to tell you something about your personality, but you have me falling into those beautiful brown eyes along with your beautiful smile. I'm really trying hard not to be superficial over here by only complimenting you on things like your warm smile, your striking brown eyes, the way you wriggle your cute little nose."

"I don't wiggle my nose."

"I didn't say wiggle, I said *wriggle*. Wriggle, you know, like this?" Zachary wriggled his nose to demonstrate.

She laughed. "Oh, now, that was nice. You should do that more often." She pulled her laugh under control. "Okay, now what were you about to say before you started becoming so patently superficial?"

He shook his head, then brushed his perfectly trimmed mustache with his thumb and index finger, making an expression as though he were trying to readjust his mouth.

"What?" Gabrielle said. "What? Will you *please* stop gawking and start talking?"

"Oh, so now I'm gawking?"

"Just say what you were going to say. All right?"

"Bossy, too. Real management material. I bet you're a supervisor on your job."

"No."

"Okay, I know. I know. You own a business?"

"No." As flattering as this was, she was becoming a bit uneasy with where this conversation might lead. "I work for someone else, and I'm proud to say that I'm good at what I do. Now, will you quit stalling, and tell me what you were going to say?"

"Okay, okay, Miss Boss Lady. What I really like about you is that you're real." His tone became serious. "You and I have sat down together and talked twice: once at the Inaugural Ball at church that night and here today. And what you just said earlier spoke to the type of person you are. Most folks don't want people to know they're having a hard time or a bad day. 'How are you? Fine.' Not true. But you . . . you were real and honest without managing to depress the person you were talking to—me. That's refreshing. I'm tired of phony people. I just wish people would be real with each other. Show their scars. Acknowledge what's going on." He sat back. "I like talking to you. I really do."

"Thank you. I like talking to you, too. You make it easy for me to be myself. And it doesn't hurt that you know something about the Bible."

"Oh, that's because you couldn't be a member of our family unless you knew something about the Bible, as well as the one Who inspired the words written. My father was one of twelve children. He and my mother had four children of their own—two girls and two boys. My oldest sister is deceased. I was named after my father. That's why they call me Z. W. My father was actually named Zechariah. He later started calling himself Zachary and named me that. My father's mother was quite religious, as evident in all of her children being named after people in the Bible."

"Interesting. Very few people have that many children these days."

"Yeah, I know. But it was real common in the old days. And my aunts and uncles are extremely close. I had one aunt who lived in Alabama years ago. Our family would come down once a year and visit with her when I was little. But she was in an accident some years back. She tries to talk, but sometimes it's difficult to make out what she's trying to say. My father is still holding out for a miracle, her full recovery. He truly believes that one day she's going to come back to us and be the way she was. I'm not saying it's impossible, but she has to have the will to do that. So far, nothing we've done has pushed her effectively in that direction. As I mentioned before when we talked, I moved to Birmingham a little over three years ago. I like it here. This is home now."

"You mentioned earlier today that you hadn't seriously dated in five years."

"And it's true." He put a forkful of cheesy mashed potatoes in his mouth.

"Yeah, well . . . quite frankly, I find that difficult to believe. A handsome man such as yourself, appearing—at least from all I've seen so far—to have a lot going on for yourself. So, what's the real story with you? Tell me, Zachary. What's wrong with *you*?"

He laughed. "What's wrong with *me*?" He leaned in closer, as much as the table would allow him to press in. "What do you mean what's wrong with me?"

"Has to be *something* wrong with you. You haven't had a date in five years? Are you mean? Paranoid? A jerk? Oh, wait a minute. I know what it is. You're a perfectionist, and you haven't been able to find a woman who can live up to your high expectations. So, you decided to become a priest. No, wait, a monk. And you went off to a monastery until you could find a way to drive those perfectionist demons out of your life."

Zachary tilted his head and stared intensely at her without cracking a smile. "How did you guess? Wow, I can't believe you know. Is it that obvious? What gave me away? Oh, wait a minute. I know. You know someone who knows me? Okay . . . who told you?"

"Are you serious?"

He broke his stare and started laughing. "No, I'm not serious. But I had you going there for a minute, didn't I? Truthfully, I've been *sort* of locked away a bit, buckling down with college and stuff. It hasn't been easy. I really didn't have time to date or anything else for that matter. Not if I wanted to finish up."

Gabrielle sliced into her steak. "Oh, so you were

kind of slow in college, huh?" She took a bite, her eyes rolling back as she let out a sound to indicate her delight.

"No, in fact, I graduated the top of my class. It's just, if you're going to do something, you should do it right and with all your might. I still had a *little* fun on the side. But I *had* and still *have* goals that I'm serious about reaching. Too many folks have sacrificed for me to be here. There are a lot of people who have carried me on their backs, some literally, although I'm too big for them to carry me now. But in all seriousness, I do stand on the backs and I sit on the shoulders of many who gave much for me to be where I am today. And all they've ever asked in return was for me to do my best and to not forget where I came from." He cut into his steak and placed a piece in his mouth. "This *is* good," he said as he chewed, then briefly closed his eyes to savor the taste.

"So was what you just said," said Gabrielle. "What you just said . . . that was good."

"Okay . . . your turn. What's your story?" Zachary said.

"Oh, it's the standard Cinderella tale. You know, one parent dies when the child with so much potential is merely a baby. The other parent becomes indirectly responsible for aforementioned child ending up in the hands of a wicked stepmother. Only in my case, not so wicked or my stepmother, but not all that nice of an aunt and uncle along with their four children. This said child becomes responsible for cleaning up after and taking care of the other four. A child who—incidentally—is left at home to sweep the chimney, clean the house, while the others get to play games and attend balls."

"Interesting story so far. So, who's the fairy god-mother?"

"What?"

"Cinderella had a fairy godmother," Zachary said. "Who was yours?"

"If we're to keep in line with the story, I guess I would say it's the person who taught me how to dance. She took rats and a pumpkin and turned them into a coach and coachmen. Eventually, I dressed in fine attire and came before people of great nobility and wealth, although most of them were pure sleazeballs, if you want to know the truth about it. Are Christians allowed to call peo-ple sleazeballs?" she asked.

"If the mitt fits, I don't see why not. A sleazeball by any other name is still a sleazeball." He cut more of his steak and continued to eat while she continued to talk.

"Broken from the mistreatment and the cold-ness of the world one day, she found herself sitting before the King of kings. He stood with His arms open. And without uttering a word, He let her know that He understood what she'd been through. And that it was time for her to stop trying to go this journey alone. He had plans for her life—big plans. And she was not walking in her God-given gifts the way He'd created her to do. It was time for her to step in to her rightful place; time for her to come home."

"Is this a real story, or are you just spinning a

yarn . . . a tale, as we in America call it?" Zachary placed his chin on top of his fist as his elbow steadied him. He gazed into Gabrielle's eyes.

With her fork, Gabrielle speared a slice of her steak, placed it in her mouth, and began to chew. She held up her hand to let him know she would answer him shortly. Swallowing, she smiled, then said, "Aren't all tales based on some measure of the truth?"

# Chapter 23

*My brethren, count it all joy when we fall into divers temptations.*

—James 1:2

Gabrielle's car was repossessed on Tuesday. She'd gone outside after her shift was over, only to find her car missing. Her first thought was that it had been stolen. Just as she was about to call the police, she received a call on her cell phone telling her the car had been repossessed, where it was, and that she was welcome to come pick up her personal things from inside of the car. She called Fatima and asked her if she could possibly come and pick her up from work. When Fatima arrived, Gabrielle got in the car without saying much more than "Hi" and "Thank you for being there when I needed you."

"Are you okay?" Fatima asked after she arrived at Gabrielle's house. Fatima didn't know what was going on as Gabrielle sat there without making any effort to get out and go inside of her house.

"It's *going* to be all right," Gabrielle said.

"Do you need a ride to work in the morning?"

Gabrielle smiled. "I hadn't thought that far ahead. I do need to get to work."

"Is your car in the shop? Did it break down somewhere today?"

Gabrielle began wringing her hands. She sighed hard. "Can you come inside?"

"Yeah." Fatima turned off the engine. They got out and went in Gabrielle's house.

Gabrielle picked up a stack of opened envelopes and laid them on the kitchen table, where Fatima sat. She picked up each one individually and held it in the air. "This is the notice on my car. They came and got it today." Picking up another envelope, she tried to force a smile. "Here's the letter regarding my house note and my house possibly going into foreclosure soon. And these?" She held up five other envelopes. "They're letters telling me my power bill is in arrears, my charge card rates will now be increasing to more than thirty percent because I was late with another credit card payment. I wasn't even late with this card's payments, but they're raising my rate to loan shark rates just because they can. And the relief from the government for them not being able to do stuff like this anymore doesn't come until next year after all the damage will have been done. Now, even with me continuing to try to pay on them, only a fraction will actually go toward paying off the principal amount. It's a racket, a legal racket. And it's a shame!"

Fatima looked at the envelopes Gabrielle laid back down on the table before her. "Well, you just need to pray and believe God."

"I *have* prayed. I *am* believing. I promise you, Fatima, I've *been* believing with all of my heart. I believed I would get the money to catch up on the car note right up until they came and pulled my car today. I've tried doing right. I've been deep into the Word. I've confessed only those things I desired. I've kept a watch over my mouth so I wouldn't slip and say anything negative that would hinder the Word working for me. I've given God everything I have. And still, nothing seems to be working right for me these days."

Fatima stood up and hugged her.

Gabrielle pulled away from Fatima's embrace. "And do you want to know what the funny thing is? I actually walked away from a job that would have more than taken care of all these stupid bills. And I've had the opportunity to go back. But I didn't. I've stood strong. And do you want to know why?"

"Why?"

"Because I don't want to do anything that will reflect badly on our Father in Heaven. I've watched so-called Christians profess one thing while they're out there doing all kinds of stuff that dishonor God. But when I gave my life to Christ, I meant it. I don't want to do anything that might cause God to be ashamed of me or to cause anyone else to stumble if they're looking at me and my faith walk."

"Yeah, but we all mess up. As hard as we try, all of us mess up. I've watched you. I know how much you love the Lord. Gabrielle, I don't know why God didn't come through for you. I don't. And honestly, I don't know the correct thing to say to you right now." She looked hard into Gabrielle's eyes. "Listen, I have a little money. It's not a whole lot, but I can loan you some."

Gabrielle let out a laugh. "It's not really funny, but it is. My aunt owes me money. And when I call her, she either won't answer or won't call me back. But when she needed something from me, she was all up in my face. I appreciate your offer. I do. But no, I'm not going to borrow any money from you. If I don't have it to pay now, what makes you think I'll have it later? I've done all I know how to do. I realize this is just the devil messing with me, but I can't help but wonder if God cares, then why is He allowing Satan to lean so hard on me. God *has* to see what's going on down here. Has to. Why does He allow Satan to beat us down, especially when He knows we're trying?"

"May I make a suggestion?"

"Sure," Gabrielle said.

"Call the church."

"For what?"

"Ask them for some help. Let the people over these type of matters know you're in need of some assistance," Fatima said.

Gabrielle shook her head. "No. I'm not doing that. They weren't the ones who got me into this mess. It's not their place to get me out."

"Okay, if you don't want to call the church, then call Johnnie Mae. Talk to her. Let her know what's going on. She really is a great listener. She usually has good advice."

"I'm not doing that either," Gabrielle said as she sat down. "I don't want people looking at me like I'm some charity case. Feeling all sorry for me. Everybody has something going on in their lives. Everybody's dealing with something. My situation isn't special."

Fatima flopped down in a chair. "That's just stupid. If you need some help, then you need to get rid of your silly pride and ask for it." Fatima said that before she thought about what she was saying, and how she was saying it. "I'm sorry. I'm sorry. I didn't mean to say it was stupid. I suppose I'm just frustrated right now. I know how faithful you've been, and this just doesn't seem right. It's just not right!"

"Fatima, I've prayed. I've put it in God's hands. How many times have we said we have to trust God?"

"I know but—"

"*But* nothing. I appreciate your coming and picking me up from work today. And if I may ask, I would like for you to pick me up tomorrow and drop me off at work. I'll need to be there at seven-thirty. I'm just thankful that the company transports us to our cleaning jobs. At least I don't have to have a car to get there and back. And I'll pay you."

"Of course I can. And no, you will *not* pay me either, not one red cent. I have to be at work at eight. Your job is on my way. So it's not a problem or an inconvenience."

"Fatima, if you won't let me pay you, then I'm not going to let you pick me up. That's my condition." Gabrielle folded her arms and sat back against her chair.

"Girl, you're one crazy, stubborn Christian. But I have to give it to you; I don't think I could be as cool as you if I was dealing with what you seem to be dealing with right now. And compared to me, you're still a baby Christian." Fatima shook her head.

"Baby or not is not the point. The race is not given to the swift nor to the strong—"

"But to he or she who endures until the end. I know," Fatima said. "And in truth, I do believe God is up to something, so you can't start speaking negative stuff now."

"Oh, I know. It can be hard. But God is keeping me in perfect peace."

"You just have to stand strong."

"Yes," Gabrielle said. "Do you know right off-hand where in the Bible it tells us to stand?" Gabrielle got up and retrieved her Bible off the bookshelf in the kitchen.

"Ephesians something, at least I think it's in Ephesians. Look in the concordance in the back," Fatima said.

Gabrielle flipped to the back of her Bible. "Ephesians sixth, thirteen," she said as she turned to the scripture. "'Wherefore take unto you the whole armor of God, that ye may be able to withstand in the evil day, and having done all, to stand. Stand therefore, having your loins girt about with truth, and having on the breastplate of righteousness.'"

"Oh, don't stop there," Fatima said as she sat soaking up the words.

"I already read down to the fourteenth verse."

"I don't care. Keep going," Fatima said. "I need to hear this."

"'And your feet shod with the preparation of the gospel of peace; Above all, taking the shield of faith, wherewith ye shall be able to quench all the fiery darts of the wicked. And take the helmet of salvation, and the sword of the Spirit, which is the word of God. Praying always with all prayer and supplication.'" Gabrielle stopped while reading verse eighteen and placed her hand over her mouth as she eased back down into her chair. "Fatima, this is a test," Gabrielle said.

"What?"

"All this happening right now in my life, it's what Pastor Landris preached on a few weeks ago. It's only a test. I have to be strong. This is all just a test. Pastor Landris told us these times would come in each of our lives. Some—at times—worse than others. But we are to count it all joy. Even during those times when it looks like we're losing or even have lost."

Fatima stood up. She hugged Gabrielle, then headed for the door. She turned and nodded to Gabrielle. "I'll be here to pick you up no later than seven. And before you have to ask, I'll pick you up after you get off work tomorrow afternoon. We'll work this out together, and we'll continue to trust God for the rest. You just keep standing. Stand."

# Chapter 24

*The wicked watcheth the righteous, and seeketh to slay him.*

—Psalm 37:32

*T*his is just a test. Gabrielle thought of those words. Her week of things going wrong had seemingly only just begun. When Fatima picked her up from work that afternoon, she told Fatima she'd lost her job.

"Why? What happened?" Fatima asked.

"More workers than places that need us is what I was told," Gabrielle said.

"So, did you get laid off?"

"Nope. I suppose you can say they officially downsized. I only had a little over six months of service with them. You know how it is: last one hired, first one fired."

"So, what are you planning to do now?"

Gabrielle scratched her head, then rubbed her jaw. "Let's see, it's Wednesday, so I plan to go to Bible study tonight. That's if I can thumb a ride there."

"Girl, please. You know I'll come by and pick

you up if you want to go to Bible study. But anybody else in your place right now probably would be thinking about going home and pulling the covers over their head. Definitely not trying to figure out how to make it to Bible study. I know people who don't make this much of an effort to get to Bible study when things are going perfectly wonderful for them."

"I'm going to focus on what I *can* do. I can't get a job tonight, that's for sure. I can't get a car tonight either. But I *can* go and hear God's Word." Gabrielle glanced at Fatima. "I *can* be with others who love the Lord while God is doing whatever it is He's doing behind the scenes."

Fatima shook her head. "You're undeniably teaching me something. I don't think I could take what you're taking—car problems, house problems, job problems. And you're not the least bit upset with God? Not even a little? I don't know if I could do it."

Fatima dropped Gabrielle off at home with the promise of picking her up for Bible study. As soon as Gabrielle walked inside her house, the phone started ringing. When she looked at the caller ID, she saw it was Tiffany. Cheerfully, she answered the phone. There was no reason to let others know she had reasons to be down in the mouth.

"Hello," she said in a cheery voice.

"Well, hello to you," a male voice said back just as cheerily.

"Who is this?" she asked.

"Whose name popped up on your caller ID?"

"Darius Connors," she said dryly, having seen

his name on the caller ID, but having thought it was his wife. "Why are you calling? What do you want?"

"Is that the way you talk to a fellow brother in the Lord? Members of the same church where we're admonished, encouraged even, to show each other love?"

"Look, I've had a bad day today, okay? In fact, I've had a bad week. I just got in from work, and I really don't feel like playing games with you today. Okay?"

"Hold up. So, are you planning to come to Bible study tonight?"

"Why?"

"Lighten up, will you? I was only asking. Thinking maybe I could come by after Bible study is over. You know, we could talk a little more, in private."

Gabrielle sighed, making sure he heard her. "I told you I'm not interested in having any discussions with you. We have nothing to talk about."

"Oh, now, I wouldn't be so sure about that. You see, I just so happen to know this *teeny* little secret about you. And, I'm wondering what might happen if this little secret somehow starts to make its rounds throughout the congregation."

"You wouldn't dare," Gabrielle said incredulously. "That would just be . . . wrong."

"Who said I would be the one to spread it? I mean, I might in *passing* mention something to one or *two* people. You know . . . tell them we need to pray for you so God will keep you strong. There's nothing church folks love more than to hear a good, juicy story that others aren't supposed to know about while being asked to pray for that person. Of course, they'll pass the word on to others as they solicit prayers for you. They might even preface it by saying that they don't believe in gossiping. But trust me, a lot of church folks *love* secret prayer services."

"What do you want?"

"I told you. I just want to talk, to hang out maybe. We could get together, play it by ear. I don't want to brag, but I'm quite flexible, in more ways than one. And I promise, I wouldn't ever pressure you to do anything you don't want to," Darius said.

"And what about Tiffany? You remember . . . your wife?"

"What about her?"

"She and I are friends. Even if I *was* interested, which I am *not*, I wouldn't do anything like that to her. And to think you call yourself a Christian. You really should be ashamed of yourself," Gabrielle said. "It's people like you who give Christians a bad name."

"See, now, that's the difference between you and me. You actually buy into this Christian stuff. Do you have any idea how many Christians wear two faces? The one they let other Christians see and the one they display when they're doing things with the world. Where do you think the phrase 'He's just a man' originated from? I'll tell you: some Christian trying to explain away, justify why this preacher or that deacon, this sister, that brother, the pastor's wife, that darling Mother of the church, the choir director, choir member, usher, or the musician, low and behold, fell and ended up in sin."

"Well, I'm not interested in getting with you. Not now, not ever. And frankly, I believe you have too much to lose to try to push this any further. So, let it go, okay? And you know what? I'm going to pray for you. Now, don't call my house again, okay? Bye."

"Don't you hang up this phone!" he yelled as Gabrielle clicked off the phone.

She went to take a shower. It had been a long and emotional day. When she was almost dressed, the phone rang again. Although it was obviously from a cell phone, her caller ID read "Darius Connors." Tempted not to answer it, she decided she was going to let him have it with both barrels this time. Once and for all!

"Hello," she said harshly and with a definite I'm-not-playing attitude and voice.

"Well, hello," a mild and timid voice said in return. "What's wrong with you?"

Gabrielle's voice quickly adjusted. "Tiffany, I'm *so* sorry. I thought you were . . . someone else."

"Well, I feel sorry for whomever you thought it was," she said. "I know you're getting ready to go to Bible study. I just wanted to call and let you know that we were running a bit behind, but that we're en route. We should be there in about fifteen minutes."

"Excuse me? But did I miss something somewhere?" Gabrielle asked.

"Fatima called. She said you were having car trouble and asked if I could pick you up and take you to Bible study," Tiffany said. "Dana, stop it!" she said. "I'm sorry."

"Did something happen with Fatima? I just saw her a little while ago. Why didn't she call me?"

"She called and told me she had an emergency. She asked if I was going to Bible study and asked me if I wouldn't mind picking you up and bringing you back home. That's all I know," Tiffany said. "It's not a problem. We were just running a little late, and I didn't want you thinking I'd forgotten about you. I'm on my cell phone now."

"Okay. I'll be ready when you get here," Gabrielle said. When she hung up, she saw where she had two messages on her answering machine. The first message was from a debt collector.

After pressing the delete button, she heard Fatima's voice on the second message stating that she had to rush out of town. She had called Tiffany and asked her to pick Gabrielle up for Bible study. Tiffany had said she would be delighted to. So Tiffany was coming to get her.

"I'll call you later and let you know more about what's happening on my end," Fatima said. "It's my mother. She's gravely ill. Say a prayer for us." She'd hung up.

Gabrielle hurried so Tiffany wouldn't have to wait on her. She looked out the window so she would be in position to run out when Tiffany pulled up. A white Denali drove up into her driveway. Gabrielle grabbed her purse and Bible and trotted out. Tiffany opened the passenger's side and got out just as Gabrielle approached the SUV.

"You can sit up front," Tiffany said, meeting her and greeting her with a hug.

Gabrielle stood, stopped in her tracks. *If Tiffany is on the passenger's side, that can only mean one thing: Darius is likely behind the steering wheel.* That's why Tiffany was in the Denali. Darius was protective of his precious SUV. In fact, Gabrielle couldn't remember hearing Tiffany say she'd ever driven it.

Gabrielle hesitated. She tried arguing with Tiffany about taking her seat, but Tiffany wasn't hearing it. Gabrielle stepped up on the running board and got in.

"Well, hello there," Darius said, as though he hadn't just called her not an hour ago that evening, practically threatening her.

"Hi," Gabrielle said to him, and then, "Hi, kids" to the three sitting in the back now with their mother in the mix. That was pretty much all she could manage to say their entire twenty-minute ride to the church.

She helped Tiffany get the children out. They were always happy to see her, having spent so much time together over the past few months.

Bible study was absolutely worth all the trouble she'd gone through to get there. Even Darius seemed affected by the message. On the way back to Gabrielle's house, he'd gone on and on about what Pastor Landris had said. When Darius pulled into her driveway, Gabrielle turned and thanked Tiffany for the ride to Bible study. She offered them money, which they flat out refused to accept, then told the children how much she enjoyed hanging out with them, and not as enthusiastically, she finally thanked Darius.

Darius opened his door and ran around to her

side before she could get out completely. "You don't think I'm going to let you go inside by yourself, now, do you?" he said. "What kind of a gentleman would I be if I sat here and just dropped you off without making sure I saw you to your door?" He grabbed her by the hand.

"Oh, it's fine," she said, trying to take her hand out of his without it being too obvious. "I do this all the time. It's not necessary for you to help me down or to see me to my door," Gabrielle said. "Really."

"Daddy never helps Mommy get out of the car," Dana said.

"Hush that," Tiffany said with a snap in her voice. "Daddy has opened the door and helped Mommy down plenty of times before. He's being a gentleman now, which means all of you need to pay attention and take notes."

"Including me?" Jade said.

"*Especially* you. You need to know how you should be treated so you won't end up with some deadbeat," Tiffany said.

"It's really not necessary for you to walk me to my door. I'll be fine. Thanks for the ride. I appreciate it," Gabrielle said. She took off, trying to distance herself from him.

"Oh, you must be one of those independent women who cut us men off at the knees," Darius said to her back. "I'm sorry, but I wouldn't be able to look myself in the mirror if I sat here and just let you go in your house by yourself." He turned back toward his Denali. "I'll be back shortly," he said to Tiffany. "This won't take but a few minutes."

"We're fine," Tiffany said, scooting out of the middle row of the Denali to get out, and then back to the front seat vacated by Gabrielle.

Gabrielle walked even faster. He jogged and caught up with her. "I didn't need you to walk me to the door," she said with much hostility and under her breath.

"Oh, cut me a little slack, will you? Look how awesome God is. I call you today trying to come to your house after Bible study and look what happened? I'm here at your house after Bible study. Now, tell me God isn't trying to tell you something?"

"Yeah, He's trying to tell me something, all right. He's telling me to resist the devil and he will flee." Gabrielle reached her door and pulled out her key. She started for the keyhole.

Darius took her keys out of her hand. "Allow me," he said.

"I can do it myself," she said, her teeth clenched tight as she spoke.

Darius unlocked the door, pushed it open, stepped inside, felt the wall for the light switch, then flipped it on. When he fully went inside, he grinned at Gabrielle. "You really need to learn to chill out more. All I've done is walk you to your door. That's what thoughtful and caring Christian brothers do for their Christian sisters."

"Okay, so you've done your Christian duty. You can leave now."

"What a lovely home," he said as he scanned the area.

That's when it hit Gabrielle. Now he knew where she lived. That was the last thing she had wanted. She maintained her composure. "Thank you and good-bye," she said, holding the door-knob as she stood waiting on him to get out.

"That guy you were talking to tonight at Bible study, you know, the one who was all giddy when he saw you walk in and couldn't wait to come over and speak to you."

"You mean the one that I started to ask to bring me home tonight so I could have avoided *just* this situation I'm dealing with right now with you?" Gabrielle said.

"The reason you didn't ask him is because you didn't want to hurt Tiffany's feelings. Or maybe you didn't want to have to explain why you didn't call him to come pick you up tonight instead of riding there with us," Darius said. "You now owe me."

"He wouldn't have asked. Besides, he didn't know I came with you and your family. He probably thought I drove. I could have just told him I needed a ride home."

"But you, being the strong lady that you are, would never be as forward as to ask a man to do *anything* for you," Darius said. "You're probably the type of woman who still believes a man should be the one to ask a woman out."

"And what's wrong with that?" Gabrielle asked.

"You mean besides it being old school, old-fashioned, and out of date? This is the age of cell phones, text messages, e-mails, instant messages, MySpace, Facebook, Tagged, and Twitter. Women have officially been liberated. You can put your profile in cyberspace for all the world to see. You can press a button and in nanoseconds you're letting your wishes and desires be known. If a woman sees something, she's free to go after it." He grinned. "Or him, if that's the case. No, I suspect you just might not want him knowing where you live. I take it you just met him, and you're probably still putting him through his initial interview."

"I'm sure Tiffany is wondering what's taking you so long. Can you please go?"

He nodded. "I'll handle Tiffany. But that guy who's hot to talk to you, he's not right for you. He's a bit too polished for a woman like you. He can't appreciate you. You need a real man. Someone who can take charge; someone who will tell you what's what. That guy, Mister-I'm-so-happy-to-see-you-again-I-hope-the-last-time-we-talked-helped-move-me-along-in-this-relationship, is *not* what you need at this stage. Maybe later, but not now."

Darius stepped out the door and bowed slightly. "You can take that little advice from your Christian brother who's just trying to look out for you, or not. That's all I'm interested in—you. I'd like to take care of you until you get your Christian legs under you. Otherwise, these seasoned Christians are going to have you for breakfast. And what do you think homeboy will think about you should he find out what you used to do for a living? Huh? You think about that."

Tiffany stuck her hand out the window and waved again when she saw Gabrielle still standing in her doorway. Gabrielle waved back and smiled. Darius strolled back to his SUV.

Gabrielle closed the door, then leaned back

against it. "God, please help me. Something is seriously wrong with that man. Seriously wrong. At best, he's a real pest; at worst, he could be dangerous. But honestly, right now, I don't know exactly what to do about him. I don't. Please, I need You to help me."

# Chapter 25

*Knowing this, that the trying of your faith worketh patience.*

—James 1:3

Zachary called Gabrielle shortly after she'd gotten dressed for bed. They talked for an hour. She didn't tell him about her car or her job or her house possibly headed for foreclosure. They did talk about things in the Bible and what Pastor Landris had taught at Bible study. They talked about what real faith was, and what trusting God really meant to them individually.

"How can God tell when you're really in faith or when you're merely just trying to fake it until you make it?" Gabrielle began the discussion.

"I think it's by how you stand no matter what's going on in your life, no matter if the world is crashing down around you," Zachary said. "That's how God knows you're in faith. You don't change your confession or belief in what He'll do, even when it looks like what you believe hasn't happened yet or when it looks like it's DOA."

"DOA," she said, laughing at his choice of

words. She could see he liked to watch either crime shows or those set in hospitals.

"Yeah, DOA: Dead on Arrival. God can resuscitate, resurrect if He has to, what others, including the experts, have declared dead. I know. I've personally seen what appeared to be all but gone, lost . . . come back to life—physically and spiritually."

"Physically?"

"Yeah, physically. When someone's heart stops and you get it back going, that person died for whatever brief time it might have been. When a person is given mouth-to-mouth resuscitation, that is nothing more than dealing with life and death through breath. The way the Bible said God breathed the breath of life through Adam's nostrils, think about that for a second. That was the first recorded evidence of resuscitation performed by the Master Himself. And spiritually, those hopes, dreams, and desires that you believed would come to pass, you were praying for, standing in faith for, when those things seem to have died . . . they're gone, God can bring new life to the situation. Faith is to believe in God's power to do even the impossible, then to act like you believe. Trust demonstrates your confidence that God not only knows what He's doing but can handle it without any input or direction from us on how it should be done."

Gabrielle really liked Zachary. She liked talking to him. And when it was time, she didn't really want to get off the phone with him. But he had to be at work early and she . . . Well, she didn't have a job to go to or a car to go and look for one. Yes, she *had* believed God would come through. And even though the devil was constantly whispering in her ear, talking to her mind—saying that God didn't care, that God had let her down—her mind (even through all of these trials) was being transformed. Pastor Landris's teaching had helped her so much, and talking to Zachary had given her yet another boost. She had put her life in God's hands. He knew what was going on. He could see what was happening. Now she had to trust Him, even though her whole being was screaming for her to save herself in whatever way she could or knew how.

*It's not over until God says it's over.* Those were the words she heard as she began to drift off to sleep.

She'd almost fallen asleep when the phone rang. She fumbled and picked up the phone without thinking about it, or bothering to look to see who it was.

"Hey," the voice on the other end said. Gabrielle could hear loud muffled music in the background. "You 'sleep?"

"Just about," she said, trying to get reoriented. "Who is this?"

"It's Clarence."

"Clarence? Why are you calling me?" She sat up, turned on the lamp, and pressed her back against her pillow and the headboard.

"Listen, I'm not going to front with you. I need your help. There's this big delegation in town. A few of the girls got sick, so I'm really shorthanded here. I know you're not doing this sort of stuff anymore, but I have all these hungry men here, and they are going to tear down my place if I don't deliver the service they're expecting."

She shook her head even though he couldn't see her. "I'm not interested, Clarence."

"You don't have to do anything you don't want to. I just need some help here. Please. My business has fallen away since you left. If this night goes well, it could help. You could help me tremendously. And I know you're hurting for money. You know I'll take care of you and do right by you. Think of how much money you could rake in the rest of this week." Clarence paused. Gabrielle could tell someone had walked in.

He'd either pressed his hand over the mouthpiece or pressed mute. The sound suddenly came roaring back. "Sorry about that," he said. "I tell you the truth: I work with a bunch of nitwits. I just don't know about folks these days. Now, back to what I was saying. Listen, I heard about your car."

"How did you hear about my car?"

"Now, you know I'm connected like that. One of my friends works for that repo company that came and took it. He called and told me your car had been impounded."

"Hold up," Gabrielle said, "why would someone who knows you be able to connect the name Gabrielle Mercedes, which is on my registration, with the name Goodness and Mercy?"

He started chuckling. "Okay, you kind of got me there. I sort of have a file with things in it like your loan company's name for your car and your home mortgage company. You know, you had to put your place of employment down on your application when you applied to get them. They actually verified that you worked here, so I still had all of that information. What can I say? I'm a resourceful person. After you quit, I called around and asked a few folks I knew to keep an eye out for you. I asked them to let me know if you were ever in trouble. That's all."

"So, you had people spying on me?"

"No. I just knew you would never let me know if you needed help. I told you, I know more about this Christian stuff than you think. You seem to be a lot more serious about it than I ever was, so I suspect you've totally surpassed me in the knowledge of Christ department. Still, I knew where you were coming from and where you were trying to go. I knew that it was going to be a difficult journey, especially financially. Goodness, now you know I care about you. You're like a little sister to me. I just want to help you. I know you won't take a loan from me; that's just the type of person you are. And you're too proud to ask for help or to borrow money, even from your friends. That can turn out to be a double-edged sword—whether you're a Christian or not."

"Clarence, you don't really need my help. You're just trying to figure out how to help me without me thinking what you're doing is charity," Gabrielle said.

"Oh, no, now. Don't get this twisted. I need your help for real. No joke. Believe me, I desperately need you here. What harm would it do? You could come and work tonight and the rest of this week. Next week, if you like. And I'll pay you top dollar, regardless of what job you decide to do. If you want to wait tables, hey, I'm down with that. We both know that doesn't pay as much as the other work available to you, but every little bit helps. It would be no different than you cleaning other people's toilets, which frankly causes me to cringe just thinking about someone with your awe-inspiring gifts and talents doing something like that."

Gabrielle laughed. "Well, somebody has to do it. Otherwise, even *your* business would stink to the high heavens."

"Somebody has to do it, but it doesn't have to be you," Clarence said. "You're better than that."

"Well, you don't have to worry about me doing even that for now. I lost my job today."

"Now see, now you know this *has* to be God," Clarence said. "I bet you that you've been praying for help, haven't you?"

"You know I have."

"Then maybe this is the answer to your prayers. You don't have a job; I have one begging for you to come right now. You don't have a car. I can send someone to come and pick you up *and* take you home when you finish—free of charge—while you make the money you need to get your car back. You could even make enough money to catch up your home loan."

"I don't think even *I* can make enough money in a week to do all of that."

"That's why I'm offering you two weeks, three, a month, the rest of the year if you need it. Can't you see God's hand in this? What you'd be doing here isn't illegal. It's a legitimate way to bring in some much-needed funds. People always say God works in mysterious ways, His wonders to perform."

Gabrielle started laughing. "I'll tell you what I *do* see. I *do* see you're trying to work me in all of this," she said. "Nice try, though. I give you an A for effort."

"Look, you've been praying for a while for God to move, am I right?"

"Yes."

"And so far what has happened?"

Gabrielle knew she could be real with Clarence. "I couldn't find a job that paid enough money to take care of my existing bills, my car has now been repossessed, my credit cards are maxed out while those legal loan sharks jack up my rates and there's nothing I can do about it. I lost the only job I was able to secure with my limited education and in this economy. And it's likely, by the end of the month, I'll be that much closer to losing my house that I've had on the market since June with all the equity I've put into it so far."

"And then, what happens right after all of this?"

"You call me and offer me a perfect way out."

"A boat in a storm. Now, tell me that's not God," Clarence said, smiling as he leaned back in his oversized black leather chair, causing it to make a slight squeak.

"That's not God," she said.

Clarence sat up straight. "What? See, that's just the reason why you're going to find yourself out on the street with nowhere to lay your pretty little head. You're like the story of that person who prayed to God for God to save him when a storm and a flood came through the town. He prayed for deliverance, God sent a few boats and a helicopter, and he was still on the housetop saying he was waiting on God. And do you know what happened to him? He drowned! And when he got to Heaven and questioned God on why He hadn't saved him, God told him He had sent several people to help him, but he had turned the help away. That's what you're doing now. God has sent me to help you, I'm here extending a hand to keep you from drowning, and you're just slapping my hand away without any regard to what you're doing, saying you're waiting on God."

"Oh, now, don't think I don't appreciate you, Clarence. And I know you *think* you're doing something to help me and in turn helping out God. But I've come too far to turn around now. I'm going to say to you what Esther in the Bible said: 'If I perish, I perish.' Right now, this is about me trusting God. Believe me: the easy way out *would* be to take you up on your more-than-generous offer. You're right. What you do isn't illegal. But it is, in my opinion, immoral. Yes, I could take the easy way out. But easy is not always godly. I choose to wait on the Lord. And if you think that's foolish, then I will continue to pray for you that God will open your eyes so you can see, as my eyes were opened, and I now see."

"Amazing grace," Clarence said.

"What?"

"There's a line in a hymn we used to sing a lot when I was little. The song is called 'Amazing Grace.' The line says, 'I once was blind, but now I see.'" Clarence suddenly stopped.

After too long of a silence, Gabrielle said, "Clarence, are you still there?"

"Yeah, I'm here." Clarence spoke in the most humbled voice Gabrielle had ever heard from him. She also heard what she thought sounded like a sniffle. "Darn allergies. Listen," Clarence said in his deep, strong voice again. "I commend you for taking a stand and sticking with it. I just hope you know what you're doing."

"Well, the Bible says we never really lose anything for Christ's sake and not receive it back in this life as well as the life to come. I guess I may end up finding out firsthand whether that's actually true. In any event, I refuse to go back to where God has brought me from. I think I'll run on and see what the end is going to be," she said.

Gabrielle hung up after they said their respective good-byes. She turned off the nightstand lamp, laid her head back on her pillow, and began to pray for Fatima and whatever had called her away so suddenly as well as others who had asked her—likely not really thinking that she would—to pray for them.

# Chapter 26

*And he spake a parable unto them to this
end, that men ought always to pray, and not
to faint.*

—Luke 18:1

Fatima called Gabrielle early the next day and
told her what was going on. Her mother was in
the hospital, deathly ill, having been stricken by
salmonella. The doctors weren't sure her mother
was going to pull through. Her father had gotten
her to finally go to the hospital. They just weren't
sure if he'd gotten her to go in time.

They had narrowed it down to peanut butter.
Apparently back in January when there was a huge
salmonella problem with a plant in Georgia dealing with peanut butter products, the tainted
peanut butter product had remained on a shelf in
their house. Her mother either didn't know about
the recall or never checked her cupboard—thinking the problem couldn't possibly affect them. In
any case, she hadn't thrown the product away and
now havoc was visiting their family.

"The doctors say her recovery will depend on
her immune system," Fatima said. "They're working to keep her hydrated, replacing her fluids and

electrolytes. They're giving her antibiotics. All we can do now is pray. She wouldn't go to the doctor early. She'd gotten so bad that my dad had to call an ambulance to come and get her. By the time he called me, he had lost it. I don't know what my dad will do without my mother. I don't know what I'll do. I'm not sure how long I'll be here. I'm sorry I had to leave the way I did. But my dad called, and he wasn't sure, even with me flying in to Cleveland, that I would make it in time. She's not doing well at all."

"Don't worry about leaving me. I'm just glad you're there with your family."

"Did Tiffany pick you up okay?"

Gabrielle's first thought was of Darius coming to her house and her surprise in seeing him. That wasn't cool by any means. "Yeah. Darius brought her."

"Darius? You mean he came?"

"Yes. He drove her over here to get me."

"We're talking about the Darius that Tiffany said hasn't been to Bible study in more than two years? *That* Darius? But he went to Bible study last night when Tiffany was coming over to pick you up? And I suppose it was sheer coincidence that the one night when you need a ride to Bible study, that would be the night he just *happens* to decide to go, too?"

Gabrielle knew what *she* was thinking about that situation, but she was picking up on something from Fatima now. She wondered if Darius was also trying to make a play with Fatima. Her question: *How could she bring that up without it coming off wrong?*

"You don't seem to care much for Darius," Gabrielle said, hoping Fatima might explain what was going on, so she in turn could tell what was going on from her end with him.

"It's just . . . his wife deserves better than he seems to give her, that's all."

"Yeah, but if you don't mind me saying, you seem to be taking it more personal," Gabrielle said.

"I like his wife. Personally, I think she's gotten a bum rap from him. Like when he came to my house to pick her up that time. There she was with his three children and all of her stuff. Did he run to take some of the load off of her? No. She had to ask him for help. And I still have to wonder if he didn't move as quickly as he did when she asked him because he was trying to impress us. He's just that kind of a man."

"Sounds like you know what you're talking about," Gabrielle said.

"I just know his kind. He's a snake. And I think it's awfully suspicious that he *happens* to decide to go to Bible study on the one night Tiffany would be coming to get you," Fatima said. "But hey, he's not my husband, and he's definitely not my problem. Thank God for that!"

"Yeah," Gabrielle said.

"Let's change the subject to something more pleasant. Have you talked to Zachary lately?"

"Last night. In fact, I saw him at Bible study, and then he called me before I went to sleep."

"Ooh," Fatima said in a meddling voice. "Did you get him to bring you home after Bible study?"

"No."

"See, you just don't know how to work unexpected blessings."

"What do you mean 'unexpected blessings'?" Gabrielle asked. After lowering herself to the couch, she sat comfortably on one of her feet.

"You don't have a car, unless something has changed," Fatima said.

"Nope, nothing's changed. I still don't have a car."

"Okay, you don't have a car, so last night you needed a ride to church and back. You get to church and you see your friend who has a car and would have loved taking you home. It would have been a great excuse to spend some more time with him. All you had to say to him was that you'd ridden to church with a friend, then ask if he wouldn't mind taking you home. See, an unexpected blessing. You get to ride home with him; he gets to spend time with you. He finds out where you live without you having to figure out a way to invite him over later, which is exactly what you're going to have to do if he doesn't ask if he can come over to your house again soon."

"Wow, you certainly have an active mind," Gabrielle said, chuckling.

"Well, it's true."

"How about, I'll likely be moving soon so it makes no difference whether he knows where I live or not. And if I don't have a job, I most likely won't be finding another place to live, which means I'll either be in a shelter or be living with a friend. Living with my family is out since they've made it quite clear that I'm not welcome in their home. You know, the more I dwell on my present situation, the more I think it might be best that he and I don't start up anything serious yet anyway. I have too many issues."

"Okay, I would argue with you a little longer, but I need to go back and check on my mother. I just wanted to take a break and let you know what was going on here. If you need me, my cell phone is on twenty-four seven. Just call me."

"Keep me posted on things there with you. And please know that I'm here for you, and that I'm praying for your mother as well as you and your family."

"I know, and I appreciate you. Oh," Fatima said, "would you do me a favor and call the church to let them know what's going on here?"

"Sure, I'll be happy to."

Gabrielle hung up and went to find the church's phone number. She spoke with the Care Department and reported what she knew so far about Fatima's mother.

*Now, for the hard task: trying to find a job without a car.* It was days like these when Gabrielle wished for the city life instead of the suburbs, where she now resided. At least in the city, she could walk to a bus stop and be able to get around. Not so when there's no bus running anywhere close to your community.

Gabrielle began to laugh. She couldn't look in the paper for a job because she needed a car to get to a paper box. She couldn't get to a paper box because she didn't have a job that paid her so she could get her car back, which would allow her to get to a paper box. She couldn't access the Internet because she didn't have Internet access in her house. And she couldn't get to the library to access the library's free Internet service because she needed a car to get to the library so she could get a job to pay for her car to get to the library.

And to think: the thing she'd loved most about her house was that it was off the beaten path of everything and allowed her the peace and quiet that city life couldn't.

Gabrielle kneeled down. Before she could even begin, she looked upward and smiled as she thought about something Pastor Landris had said at Bible study.

"When things seem to be going bad in your life, when it looks like everything that *can* go wrong *is* going wrong, stop and see what you *can* thank God for. If your car breaks down and it was in a good place when it broke down, then thank God for that. If it had to break down, at least it broke down where it did. Learn to praise God under any circumstance."

Gabrielle began to pray. "God, I thank You that even if I don't have Internet hookup, even if I don't have a car to get around in, even if I don't know what's coming next in my life, You know all things. I don't need the Internet to connect with You. Oh, that You would bless me indeed, and enlarge my territory. I thank You for a job. I thank You for transportation to my job. I thank You for Your blessings. . . ."

# Chapter 27

Johnnie Mae called Gabrielle on Thursday afternoon. Gabrielle thought she was calling to find out more about Fatima's mother. Early into their short conversation, she learned that was not the case.

"Is it possible you and I can meet and talk?" Johnnie Mae asked.

Gabrielle's eyes widened a little as she quickly tried to think, without a car, how to answer that question. She knew whatever she did she would not lie or attempt to fudge the truth. "I'm free to meet with you, but it's just I'm having some challenges right now."

"If it's a problem for you to come here to the church, it's not a problem for me to come to your house, right now if you're free," Johnnie Mae said.

"That would be great. I'm here and I'll be here."

"That's good. It's important." Johnnie Mae sounded deathly serious.

"Okay," Gabrielle said, fighting the urge to ask

her for a hint so she could at least mentally prepare for what was coming.

Johnnie Mae asked for her address. "I'm leaving now, so I should be there shortly."

Gabrielle paced as she waited. When the doorbell rang, she jumped. After she opened her door, Johnnie Mae greeted her with a warm and motherly hug. They went to the living room and sat down.

"I see you haven't sold your house yet," Johnnie Mae said with compassion as she pushed the sleeves of her dark truffle-colored jersey knit dress up closer to her elbows.

"No, and it's not looking promising either."

"Are you also having car trouble?"

"Why do you ask?"

"Earlier you said you couldn't come to the church because you were having a few challenges. I thought it might be car trouble."

Gabrielle tried to smile it off. "Well, I've told you a lot of things about what's going on with me already. I guess it won't hurt to tell you that my car was repossessed."

"My goodness. When did that happen?"

"Tuesday, two days after the wonderful time we had on Sunday and one whole day before I lost my job," Gabrielle said.

"You lost your job, too?" Johnnie Mae reached over and touched Gabrielle's hand. "I am *so* sorry."

"Hey, but that's life, right? We all have our cross to bear."

"Is there anything I can do to help?"

"I don't know. Do you know anyone looking to hire a hardworking Christian woman who's absolutely sold out for Jesus?" Gabrielle said half joking. "I do windows."

Johnnie Mae squinted her eyes as she thought about Gabrielle's question. Gabrielle looked at her disbelieving that she was actually taking her question seriously.

"You know, I just might," Johnnie Mae said. "Believe it or not, I received an e-mail today asking if I knew anyone who was reliable and could professionally clean a house with a Spirit of Excellence. It specifically asked for someone who was a Christian and could be trusted, since no one would likely be home during some cleaning times."

"Oh, my goodness! Are you serious? Of course I would love to be considered. I would love to do that. It's good, honest work, and it's something I know I can do well."

"Don't sell yourself short now," Johnnie Mae said. "You are also, without a doubt, an awesome dancer. I've heard nothing but praise reports for the dance ministry, and specifically how much you stood out. Maybe you should check into teaching dance."

"I don't know about teaching. I love to dance, but I don't know about showing someone else how," Gabrielle said.

"From what I hear, you taught many in the ministry. I received great reports from your associates who spoke on how you went out of your way to help them become the best they could be," Johnnie Mae said. She coughed. Then coughed again.

"Can I get you something?"

"Water," Johnnie Mae said, continuing to cough. "I seem to have a tickle in my throat."

Gabrielle went and got her a glass of water.

Johnnie Mae took several swallows, clearing her throat in between. "Ah, that's better," she said as she carefully set the glass down on a brass coaster on the coffee table. "Gabrielle, the reason I wanted to talk to you is because there is a slight rumbling beginning to make its way with some of the members in our church congregation."

"Really? About what?"

"About you," Johnnie Mae said. "From what I can tell, it's not on a broad scale yet. Just a few people calling the church saying they've heard some disturbing facts concerning one of our dance members, and they wanted to know whether it's true."

"What are they saying?"

"They're talking about what you used to do before you were saved and became a member here."

Gabrielle lowered her head. "I don't know what to say to that."

"Well, for now, it's just a *few* people talking. Hopefully, that's all it will turn out to be. Pastor Landris spoke a while back on talebearers and gossipers. He just might have to address that topic again soon. I'm sure he will if it becomes necessary. I just wanted you to know what's going on," Johnnie Mae said. "You remember when we had our talk that day? What I said to you?"

"That I am forgiven by God Himself. That if God calls me a new creature in Him, then it really doesn't matter what anyone else tries to call me. It's not what people call me, it's what I answer to," Gabrielle said. "But will you be honest with me?

How bad do you think this is? I don't want to be a problem for the dance ministry."

"As far as I'm concerned, you're not a problem. And I won't hear any more talk like that. An awesome, powerful, and incredible God created you. You've been washed in the blood of Jesus. Whatever sins you had before you came to Christ, God has thrown them into the sea of forgetfulness."

"But somebody out there apparently didn't get that memo," Gabrielle said, using comedy to deflect her uneasiness. "About me being a new creature. About my sins being forgiven and thrown into the sea of forgetfulness. They didn't get that message."

"I'd love to know who thought it so important they felt it necessary to start spreading something like that," Johnnie Mae said. "I don't suppose you would have any idea who the culprit might be, would you?" Johnnie Mae looked at her with intensity.

Gabrielle didn't say aloud who she thought. Darius Connors had told her he would do this very thing. But to accuse or implicate him without any real proof would be just as bad as what was being done to her right now. However, if Darius *wasn't* responsible, then who else could it be? Who else had an agenda against her?

Gabrielle scrunched her mouth and shook her head. "Not exactly," she said. "Not enough for me to publicly accuse anyone."

# Chapter 28

*The wicked worketh a deceitful work: but to him that soweth righteousness shall be a sure reward.*

*—Proverbs 11:18*

Sunday turned out to be worse than Gabrielle ever thought. First of all, without a car, she had to figure out how she would get to church. Zachary had called her Saturday night. They talked. During their conversation, she asked if he was going to church on Sunday. He said he was. At that point, she decided to swallow her pride and ask if he would mind her riding to church with him. He didn't even ask why she needed a ride. In fact, he was thrilled that she'd brought it up. He viewed it as another step toward the two of them getting to know each other better. He asked for, and she gave him, her home address.

But when they arrived in the church's sanctuary, she could feel a difference in how a few people, not everybody, were treating her. People who normally grabbed her to give her a hug or made sure when they saw her they shook her hand ignored her completely. Some of them looked right in her face, and when she smiled, they deliberately turned away. She even caught two people in the dance ministry whispering as they pointed in her direction. Again, it wasn't everybody, probably ten to twelve people total. It was just amazing to Gabrielle how something like that could change the atmosphere without one negative word ever being spoken to her face.

There were many who did speak to her, hugged her, and acknowledged that she had somehow crossed their paths. But the negative always has a way of getting blown out of proportion in a person's mind. Nine people can pay you a compliment, one can have something negative to say, and for some reason, it's the negative comment that sticks out the most. The one that ends up causing you to pay more attention to it than you did to the nine and, quite frankly, getting more attention than it deserves.

Gabrielle couldn't understand why Sasha and Alicia had acted that way. It both surprised and hurt her more than the rest of the people *because* she'd worked so closely with them. Just last Sunday, they were all one—ministering to the people, giving God the praise. This Sunday, she'd seen them point at her while whispering to each other. Sasha looked as though she was really upset with her. Thinking at first that whatever was going on had nothing to do with her, Gabrielle had walked toward the two of them to speak, bringing Zachary along with her. She'd waved so they would know she was headed their way. They had seen her wave, that much she was certain. But neither of them waved back. And before she could get to them, they left. *Childish,* she thought. Like middle school children. The way they acted was childish.

An RN named Jackie, also in the dance ministry, did speak to her and gave her a hug.

One person who made an effort to speak to her as well as Zachary was Darius. He had been with Tiffany, who had been another who had acknowledged her with a wave as she dashed off, no doubt to go get her children from children's church.

"Hey, man," Darius said. "How's it going?"

"Wonderful," Zachary said. "Everything is wonderful." Zachary smiled at Gabrielle as he said that.

"Well, good afternoon and praise God to you, Sister Mercedes," Darius said to Gabrielle as he also smiled at her.

She nodded toward him without a smile and without saying a word.

"Goodness," Darius said, looking at Zachary. "Mercy! Whew!"—he glanced at Gabrielle—"Pastor Landris certainly did preach today!"

"Yes, that was a powerful message," Zachary said.

"I don't believe we've met. I'm Darius Connors," Darius said when he realized Gabrielle wasn't planning on introducing them.

"My name is Zachary Morgan. But most call me Z. W."

"What's the *W* stand for?" Darius asked.

"Wayne."

"Oh, cool. So, are you a member here?"

"Yeah. I came forward last week after that awesome service." He looked at Gabrielle again.

"Oh, yeah. You mean with the dance ministry dancing and all. That was tremendous. My wife is part of that ministry, as is Sister Gabrielle here. They were all terrific, although I must admit, this one's"—he pointed at Gabrielle—"dancing makes you feel something all over. After she finished, I confess: something went all over me."

Zachary looked at Gabrielle, who wasn't smiling or even looked glad to be hearing any of this. "Yes. She's anointed when she dances, that's for sure. As long as God gets the glory, that's all that really matters. And I know God got the glory through their dance last week. Many people were affected, as I said, including myself. Couple that with that Word from Pastor Landris. It's the Word that draws us. That's the meat . . . the meal . . . the entrée. All of the rest is either appetizers or dessert."

"Yeah, like what Pastor Landris said today about presenting our bodies a living sacrifice," Darius said.

"Actually, if you're going to quote Romans twelve and one, you should finish that sentence out the way Pastor Landris did: 'Present your bodies a living sacrifice, holy, acceptable unto God, which is your reasonable service,'" Zachary said.

Darius nodded as he grinned. "Yeah. So, I see you know scriptures by heart. That's good, that's good. You sound like a serious cat for the Lord. Are you a preacher?"

"No. But all of us should study and care about God's Word, not just the preachers and the teachers of the Bible," Zachary said.

"So, you two an item?" Darius asked Zachary, using his head to point at Gabrielle.

Zachary flashed his smile at Gabrielle, who had yet to crack one. "We haven't known each other long, but you can say I'm working on it," Zachary said.

Darius nodded. "She's a good-looking woman, no doubt about that. One word of advice from one who knows: make sure you find out *everything* about each other up front. Not that I'm trying to insinuate anything or act like I'm some kind of an expert on relationships, although me and my wife have been married eight years now. Believe it or not, we're still learning stuff about each other. What I generally tell any couple at the dating stage is to ask each other about things that you should know about their past. That's usually the *very* thing that will come back and destroy a good relationship later. It can literally tear a promising relationship to shreds. And all of that could be avoided if people would just find out stuff at the beginning."

"Okay," Zachary said, glancing between Darius and Gabrielle as he tried to figure out what exactly was going on. "I'll be sure to keep that in mind."

"Well, look, it was good seeing you"—he nodded to Gabrielle—"and nice meeting you," he said to Zachary. "Welcome to our loving church family. People here really are close, and they really do care. If you need help, all you need do is to tell a few people in the congregation, and I guarantee you, they will spread the word like wildfire." He smiled at Gabrielle. "Am I right or am I right?" He then tilted his head toward Gabrielle before throwing a grin Zachary's way, giving him a solid handshake in the process.

When Gabrielle and Zachary reached his car, he

opened the door for her, then closed it. After he got in and she'd put on her seat belt, Zachary turned toward her before buckling his own belt. "Okay, so would you like to tell me what *that* was all about?"

"What?"

"Darius. What's up with that guy?"

She shrugged. "I don't know. He's married to one of the members in the dance ministry. I've met him a few times. In truth, I don't know what his problem is."

"I know that he's married, but that boy has some *serious* interest in you," Zachary said. "Serious interest."

Slightly embarrassed by what he'd just said, she dropped her head quickly, then looked back up at Zachary. "What makes you say something like that?"

"Trust me, men know these things. Homeboy has all the signs."

"Well, I hope you know that I'm not the least bit interested in him. I don't mess with married men. And even if he wasn't married, he wouldn't be my type," Gabrielle said.

Zachary fastened his seat belt, then cranked the car. He looked over at her and grinned. "And what exactly *is* your type?"

She could feel her face heat up from her blushing. She only hoped he wasn't able to tell.

Zachary smiled, then raised and lowered his eyebrows successively several times. "All right now," he said. "Looks like I just might have a chance with you after all."

She tilted her head slightly as she continued to grin. "I didn't say anything," she said.

"Yeah." He put the car in reverse and started backing out of the parking space as he looked backward, his hand touching her headrest. "But that smile on your face," he said looking at her as he put the car in drive, "is absolutely priceless. Let's go get something to eat."

# Chapter 29

*To every thing there is a season, and a time
to every purpose under the heaven.*

—Ecclesiastes 3:1

Gabrielle and Zachary went to eat, then to see a
movie. They had a wonderful time Sunday, in
spite of any damper others may have tried to place
early on in the day.

"So, I see you're about to lose your house
shortly," Zachary said as they sat in her den talking.

"Who told you that?" she asked a tad *too* defen-
sively.

He frowned. "The sign . . . in your front yard? I
saw it when I picked you up this morning, and
again when I brought you home this afternoon."
He bent his head down to get a better read of her
face. "The 'for sale' sign in your yard."

"Oh, yeah. The sign." She laughed nervously,
then tried to quickly rein herself back in. "That's
why the sign is out there. To let people know the
house is for sale."

"It's a beautiful house. I like it."

"Would you like to buy it?" She chuckled. "It's available, for the right price."

"No, I just bought a house. Although I haven't had time to move in properly and get situated. But I did buy one. And there are boxes everywhere waiting to be unpacked and things put in their proper places. I'll get to it eventually. There's only so much time in a day, and only so much a person can get done *in* that allotted time. I am a true subscriber of not sweating the small stuff unless it's absolutely essential that you sweat. Like when I work out. I love a good sweat then," he said.

"Do you work out a lot?"

"Yes."

"And to think, I just thought you naturally came that way," Gabrielle said, having noticed the size of his biceps through his white shirt when he'd taken off his suit jacket.

"Our bodies are the temple of God. It's wonderful getting a new building, but I'm a firm believer in keeping up the one you have. That means exercising and eating right."

"Okay, now you're starting to sound like a doctor," Gabrielle said.

Zachary smiled. "What's wrong with doctors? Do you have something against doctors?"

"No, of course not. I love doctors. I'm just saying, they're the ones who usually advocate eating right and taking care of your body. But from the looks of many of them, they definitely aren't practicing what they preach."

He laughed. "Yeah, I know quite a few doctors who will tell you to do one thing while they're over there abusing their bodies just like their patients.

That's a classic case of do as I say and not as I do. But I actually believe *and* do what I say should be done. Life is too short to play."

"So, you don't like to play?"

"Of course I like to play." Zachary leaned away from her. "Why would you ask me something like that?"

"You appear to be somewhat intense. Don't get me wrong. I don't mean in a bad way. Like when you said you didn't date anyone for five years because of college. That's rather intense. And you seem to know a lot about the Bible even though you said you haven't been able to attend church often over the years. You'll talk on the phone with me, but you're conscientious enough to not talk too late, so that you're ready for work the next day. You're interested and seem serious about taking care of and maintaining your body, and not just talking about doing it. Intense, serious, and dedicated. Not a *lot* of play. And not a bad thing by *any* means."

"But I also understand and appreciate balance," Zachary said, straightening his body up so he was back to being closer to her. "The third chapter of the book of Ecclesiastes speaks about time. How there's a time to everything under the sun. The problem with most people is that we want to do everything all at once. And that's not always practical, let alone scientifically possible. In the first verse, it says, 'To every thing there is a season, and a time to every purpose under the heaven.' But people are so impatient. We need to understand there are seasons to our lives. And even things that happen that we feel have no purpose actually do.

That's why I don't discount or dismiss anything in my life. Things happen, but there is a purpose that can be gleaned from it, if we would learn to trust in that, and see it.

"Things don't always happen when we'd like," he continued. "But there's even something we can get out of that. It's about appreciating the journey even more, sometimes, than reaching the destination. Everything that has happened in our lives has a useful purpose. Useful to God in Heaven, who I truly believe has placed a watch over us. And that's why, when bad things happen in my life, I take comfort in knowing that God is not asleep on the job. I know God has a plan for my life, and He can and will use whatever happens and use it for good."

"That was beautiful. Now, where can I buy your book?" Gabrielle said.

Zachary began to smile as he gazed into her eyes. "What?"

"What you just said, I know you have to have a book with that in it," she teased. "I should write down what you just said. Like what you said about the journey versus the destination. I'm in the journey stage of something right now. I know what I believe the destination will look like when I get there. But the journey has been interesting, to say the least. It hasn't always felt good, God knows it hasn't. And had I been asked my opinion on how things should be done, believe me, this definitely wouldn't be the way I would have chosen to do it."

Zachary started laughing. "Okay, you're preaching to the choir," he said. "Let the church say,

'Amen,' " he said, mocking what many preachers say when they preach.

"Amen," Gabrielle repeated the callback.

Zachary continued to chuckle. "Let the church say, 'Amen again.' "

"Amen again," Gabrielle said, laughing along with him.

He pulled his laughter under control. "But honestly, isn't it wonderful to know that whatever is happening in our lives right now, God knows and He cares? And that this is not the end of the book. That it's one chapter, possibly even only a small scene?" Zachary said in a serious tone.

"Yes. And even more wonderful to know that God already knows the ending, so He doesn't get all bent out of shape about the trials and tribulations we face," Gabrielle said. "It becomes part of our story when we tell others how we got over. It's worth the cost of admission."

Zachary shook his head. "What are you over there saying, Miss Gabrielle?" He bit down on his bottom lip to try to keep from smiling so much. *Gabrielle.* He loved saying her name.

"You know when you go to a show or certain places, and they charge a cover price for you to get in? Then, when you get in, you might discover what you're getting was not worth what you paid. Well, what you just said, and the way God works— what it ends up costing us, what we might have to give up, to pay in the process—in the end, just to watch God work it out is worth the cost of admission."

"Okay, maybe I need to find out when *your* book

is coming out so I can be the first one in line to get *my* copy," Zachary said.

Standing at the door when he was ready to leave, Zachary touched Gabrielle under her chin and lifted her head higher. "Don't you let any of this stuff get you down, okay? I don't know everything that's going on with you. I just hope you feel comfortable enough to talk to me if you ever need to. I'm a great listener. And even though you may not realize it, I'm starting to feel something for you. I only hope you'll allow the two of us to get to know each better because you seem to have a tendency to pull back from people."

"And how would you know that?"

"I know. You allow people to get but so close to you even though they think they're a lot closer. You erect walls, firewalls, like on computers, to keep people out. I just hope you'll allow me past your firewall. Gabrielle, I believe in you. And I believe in you I've found a *good thing*."

"A good thing?"

"Yes. There's a scripture that states that a man who finds a wife finds a good thing."

"But you don't know me that well. In fact, you really don't know much of anything about me. You don't know about my past. You don't know my hopes for the future. You don't even know the troubles I'm going through right this minute as you stand here acting like you know so much about me," Gabrielle said.

He nodded with a smile. "You're right. That's why I hope to get to know you. But I *will* tell you what I *do* know. I *do* know you have a good heart. I know you're a woman after God's own heart.

That's what matters to me right now. Whatever else I need to know about you will come in its own time. And you know what? We'll deal with it the way the Bible advocates. But let me tell you this: none of us is perfect. Yes, we strive for perfection, but none of us has arrived. None of us has wholly clean hands, and that includes me. So while you're beating yourself up about whatever, keep that in mind, okay? If you have things right with God, what difference does it make what others think? And only you know if what concerns you is right with God."

He leaned down and gave her a quick hug. "I'll call you later. Okay?"

She nodded.

After he left, she slowly closed the door and wiped away an unexpected tear that had made its way down her cheek.

# Chapter 30

*A time to weep, and a time to laugh; a time to mourn, and a time to dance.*

—Ecclesiastes 3:4

Johnnie Mae called Gabrielle Sunday night. It was a little after nine.

"I hope you'll forgive me for calling you this late," Johnnie Mae said.

"Oh, you're fine. I'm not one of those who goes to bed with the chickens," Gabrielle said. "Service was *so* great today. Pastor Landris's sermon hit home for me: 'Being not conformed to this world but being transformed by the renewing of our minds.' I'm still in the renewing process, but I'm further along than when I started," Gabrielle said. She didn't bother to mention the cool reception she'd experienced from some, no doubt because of the gossip Johnnie Mae had told her was circulating throughout the congregation. "And how are you and your family?"

"Doing great. In fact, we're all doing great here. My mother's staying with us this week. With her Alzheimer's, she has her good days and her bad. But we're hanging in there, making the best of it."

She paused. "Okay, so let me get to why I called. Remember I told you about an e-mail I'd received looking for someone to do housecleaning work?"

"Yes."

"Well, I sent the person an e-mail, telling her I had the perfect person for her. She called me, and I just got off the phone with her. I told her all about you, and she wants to meet with you tomorrow morning, possibly starting work tomorrow. She was impressed with my high recommendation of you."

"Thank you," Gabrielle said with excitement, although her mind was already working on how she would get to the interview, and then to this place of work, should she get the job and be asked to start tomorrow.

"Now, I know you're having car problems. We have a car here you're welcome to use until things straighten out for you. No one's using it right now. In fact, we have to crank it periodically just to ensure the battery doesn't run down. It's nothing fancy, mind you. My sister used to drive it. But it runs, and it will get you where you need to go."

"Are you serious? Of course I'd love to use it! Thank you so much! Oh, thank you! Man, God is *so* awesome! He's *so* awesome!"

"Oh, God is certainly that and so much more," Johnnie Mae said. "Now, I can bring the car to you tonight so you'll have it in the morning to get to your interview on time. She wants to meet you at eight AM."

"I hate having you coming out so late. But yes, yes, I'm here. Oh, thank you!"

"I'll bring the name of the person and the address. I'll see you in a little bit," Johnnie Mae said with a smile in her voice.

Johnnie Mae and Pastor Landris came to Gabrielle's house. Pastor Landris drove the gray Corsica to Gabrielle's. Johnnie Mae drove her black Chrysler 300 C. Giving Gabrielle the key, Johnnie Mae told her that the insurance card was in the glove compartment along with the vehicle registration, in case she needed it.

After Johnnie Mae and Pastor Landris left, Gabrielle put on a CD and began to dance around the room, giving God praises for His goodness and His faithfulness. She laughed as she thought, *Who would have ever believed I would be praising God about acquiring a Corsica, on loan no less, so I could apply for a job to clean somebody else's house?*

"Lord, you are good, and your mercy endureth forever!" Gabrielle sang one of Israel & New Breed's songs taken directly from Psalm 106:1.

But there she was, thanking God and dancing as though she were auditioning for the lead role in a major production paying thousands of dollars a night.

Fatima called after Gabrielle finished her praise time. Gabrielle answered the phone with such joy in her voice. She couldn't wait to tell Fatima what had happened so far. And even though she hadn't interviewed for the job yet, she felt she was going to get it.

"How's your mother?" Gabrielle asked before forging into how God was moving in her life.

"She died," Fatima said solemnly. "They just called us in and allowed us to be there with her.

She died peacefully. All of us were in the room."
Fatima broke down and began to cry. Gabrielle
tried to think of words to comfort her, but all she
knew to do in that moment—then and there—was
to pray aloud for her friend and her friend's family.

# Chapter 31

*Withhold not good from them to whom it is due, when it is in the power of thine hand to do it.*

—Proverbs 3:27

Gabrielle arrived an hour early for her interview. Ms. Daniels, the person she was scheduled to see, was impressed to see Gabrielle sitting there when she walked in at seven-thirty. The company was an employment agency used by those who desired a reliable way to hire screened people to clean and take care of their homes. Prospective employees were subject to various things such as a drug test and a criminal background check, which were done at the office and with instant results. References also carried a lot of weight in their hiring decision.

Gabrielle was so excited when she was told she got the job. She was even more excited to learn that her pay would be much higher than it had been with her previous employer, though nowhere close to what she'd garnered at her job before that. With this job, her salary would be paid by the owner of the home. The employment agency received a finder's fee for their services from the employer. Gabrielle liked that because it meant she wouldn't lose any of her money to them. The employment agency's clients were thrilled to pay it because of the caliber of employees they consistently delivered, matching skills and personalities of the employees with the personalities that the prospective employer desired and requested—a fact the company not only publicized but prided itself on.

Gabrielle was given special training the agency's new hires were required to go through to ensure the standards promised to the prospective employers. Gabrielle was also required to sign a confidentiality agreement that required she not disclose any information attained or that she may become privy to while employed in the home. She was told the house belonged to a doctor (she would learn the doctor's name when she arrived at the house), and only given the address and time when she was to report. They were expecting her, so someone would be there to greet her tomorrow and let her know what was needed and expected of her. After that, Gabrielle was informed, there would likely be days when she would be at the house alone, which is why they were extremely cautious about hiring someone who could be trusted and could work without direct oversight and supervision.

After Gabrielle arrived home, credited with a full day's pay that included her interview time, testing, and training, she called Johnnie Mae to let her know she'd gotten the job and to thank her for all she'd done to help her secure it.

"All I did was give them your name," Johnnie Mae said, "and tell them what an incredibly dedicated, hard worker I believe you to be. That's all I did. You did the rest."

She and Johnnie Mae also talked about Fatima and her mother's passing.

The dance ministry would be meeting as usual on Tuesday night, so Gabrielle had a full and exciting day ahead of her tomorrow in tandem with starting her new job.

She called Zachary to tell him about her job, but his phone went straight to voice mail. Two hours later, she tried calling him again, and the same thing happened. The third time, she decided to leave him a message to call her back. She wanted to surprise him with her great news. For whatever reason, she didn't hear back from him at all that night.

Tuesday, she arrived at her employer's house in Mountain Brook. From the outside, she could see it was large. She understood why the agency wouldn't give out the client's name until the job started. That kept workers from checking out their new employers over the Internet (not that she had Internet at home to do it) before meeting them.

A twenty-five-year-old woman answered the door. Pregnant, she was wearing a beautiful royal blue satin pantsuit. Her hair was perfect—jet black, free-flowing, and cut into layers—which impressed Gabrielle because it was eight AM. *A beautifully flawless, dark-skinned, African-American woman,* Gabrielle thought. *Maybe she works here, too.*

"Hello," the woman said. "You must be Gabrielle Mercedes."

Gabrielle reached out and shook the extended hand. "Yes, I am."

"I'm Queen. I received a call from the agency yesterday saying that you'd be coming this morning. You're right on time. Please, come in." She held the door open for Gabrielle. "I'm so excited to have you working here. There's a lot to do for sure."

Gabrielle realized she didn't work here; this was her house. She looked around the foyer, with its marble floor, crystal chandelier, and winding staircase. Sneaking a peek into two adjacent rooms, she saw nothing but boxes. Obviously, they'd just moved in.

Gabrielle didn't want to ask *too* many questions, but she was at a disadvantage. "Are you the doctor?" she finally asked Queen.

Queen laughed. "Oh, heavens no. Doctor Morgan's not here. He was at the hospital all day yesterday. There was this horrible accident. You may have seen it on the news—an explosion at a plant. They called him to come help at the hospital because of his expertise. When I spoke with him briefly, he was stretched to the max. I wanted to let him know the agency had called to let us know they'd found someone for this job. He was so busy, he didn't even have time to hear about it. So, of course, everything is left to me to handle. He called this morning around one, knowing that I'm a night owl and was still awake, to let me know he would be sleeping at the hospital because there was so much left to be done . . . lots of patients that still needed his attention. He's *such* a dedicated doctor. I am *so* proud of him, I can't begin to tell you how much."

So far, Gabrielle was able to deduct that Dr.

Morgan was the name of the doctor she was working for. She hadn't heard of him, so he wasn't *that* famous.

"Is Queen your real name?" Gabrielle asked, then thought that might not have been a good idea considering she'd just walked in and could easily be sent right back.

"Actually, it is. Those close to me call me Queen Esther, which is really my first and middle name, taken from the book of Esther in the Bible. Some people call me Q, although I don't care much for being called that. The only one who consistently calls me Q is one of my two brothers, so I suppose I really don't mind all *that* much."

"It's a fitting name. Queen, I mean. You're definitely as beautiful as a queen."

"Well, thank you." Queen looked around. "I suppose I should show you what needs to be done today." They walked into the dining room first, since it was equally as close as the living room. "As you can see, most things are still in boxes. The heavy furniture's in place. But all the whatnots and knickknacks are in boxes. Most of the rooms look just like this one. Heavy furniture set up, but things needing to be put away."

Queen showed her the rest of the house, each room awaiting her attention.

When they finished the tour, Gabrielle asked, "Are you planning on being in the rooms to show me where you want things to go? I mean, I would hate to put up something somewhere and no one is able to find it later."

"Oh, it's fine. We trust you to put things in their proper places. However you decide and wherever you put things will work, as far as we're concerned. If it's not where it's wanted or desired, it can always be moved or changed later. The immediate goal is to get things out of these boxes and into, say, the china cabinet if it's china, the closet if it's clothes. Seriously, however you want to arrange things at this stage of the game is fine."

Glancing at Queen's pregnant stomach, Gabrielle understood why she didn't need to be lifting anything. "All right, then," Gabrielle said. "Which room would you like me to start with?"

"The kitchen, please," Queen said. "I've taken a few things out of the boxes because there was nothing to eat on or with. And I hate eating with plastic and out of containers if I don't have to. You can start by putting the things in the kitchen up, then the dining room, and the master bedroom after that. I'll be in the master bedroom putting away papers and things like that since I know where they all need to go, and it's not that heavy of a job."

"Okay," Gabrielle said. She went to the kitchen and began.

Gabrielle loved the large kitchen. There was plenty of room to put away the pots and pans and other dishes without crowding. Most of the things were brand new, still in their boxes. Gabrielle washed them before putting them up. She speculated either they'd just gotten married and had received these new dishes as gifts (opting not to take them out of their boxes until they moved into their new house) or when they bought the house, they decided to buy all new things. *People with money can do stuff like that.*

Gabrielle left at four o'clock. She was tired, but it was a good tired. Queen had been wonderful. She'd ordered lunch for them, so they'd sat in the kitchen nook and ate Chinese food. Queen loved Chinese food and confessed to having eaten it three times in the past seven days. They talked while they ate, but it was mostly Queen asking things about her. Gabrielle figured this was her way to conduct a different kind of background check. She didn't mind. In spite of her name, Queen was down to earth. And it didn't hurt that they were close in age—Gabrielle twenty-seven, Queen turning twenty-six on December twenty-seventh. The big difference was that Queen had a college degree, and she didn't.

Zachary called Gabrielle just as she was about to walk out of the door to go to church for a dance ministry meeting.

"Hey, I got your message, but it's been mad crazy at work these past two days," he said. "This is the first time I've gotten a chance to call you back. I'm exhausted."

"It's okay. I understand. I was just calling to let you know that I got a job."

"You did?" Zachary said through a loud yawn. "Oh, that is great." He yawned with even more sound effects this time. "Congratulations."

"Look, you go on and get some rest. I'm on my way to a dance ministry meeting. And I *would* call you back when I finish, but I can tell you're going to be knocked out. Maybe we can talk tomorrow evening after I get off work?"

"That sounds good. Then you can tell me all

about your new job." He yawned again. "I am *so* sorry. I just can't help it. I am beat!"

"Well, you get some rest," she said as she smiled at the phone. "We'll talk later."

"Okay. And you have a good ministry meeting." He hung up.

Gabrielle shook her head. She really liked him. And the more she thought about it, the more she believed Zachary just *might* be the one. He could be the one to bring down the thick walls she'd erected to protect her heart.

# Chapter 32

*Forbearing one another, and forgiving one another, if any man have a quarrel against any; even as Christ forgave you, so also do ye.*

—Colossians 3:13

At the dance ministry meeting, Gabrielle could feel the difference in how some of the members of the team were toward her than in the past. Sasha and Alicia were especially different. She had spoken to both of them, and they'd thrown up a slight wave without even looking at her. Her first reaction was to say "forget them." If they wanted to act that way when she'd done nothing to them, then so be it. But Pastor Landris had taught all of them about confronting with love, and that confrontation was not a bad thing, if done right.

The way things were, the two of them were upset with her either for something she'd done and not known, or for some other reason she was not privy to. If she'd done something to them unknowingly, she wanted to make it right. If they'd merely heard the whispers about her past that Johnnie Mae had told her were circulating throughout the congregation, then they were wrong, but they still needed to talk it out. If the two of them were having a bad day or just had an attitude toward her for no reason, then there wasn't much she could do about that except to still show them love and keep going.

After their ministry meeting dismissed, she walked over to them.

"Excuse me, may I speak with you two?" Gabrielle said to both Sasha and Alicia.

"I really don't have a lot of time," Sasha said. "I need to get out of here and go pick up Aaliyah and Ashanti from Aaliyah's father's house. I told him and Melissa I wouldn't be long tonight."

"It shouldn't take but a few minutes," Gabrielle said. "Five, possibly even less than that."

"Fine, what is it?" Sasha said, staring at Gabrielle with a slight smirk.

"Have I done anything to you? Either of you?" Gabrielle said, alternating between Sasha and Alicia.

"Not me," Alicia said quickly.

"You don't bother me either," Sasha said.

"Then, why have y'all been acting the way you have toward me?"

"And how exactly are we acting? You mean because we're not running up behind you and bowing down at your feet? Because we're not telling you how marvelous you are?" Sasha asked. "What is it about people with the name Mercedes anyway? Whether it's the first or last name, what is it about people named Mercedes that makes them think people should bow down to them? My friend Mercedes in high school was just like that. Always thinking things were all about her. You know, the kind of people who become like sponges, soaking up everything they can around them, just because they can."

"Yeah," Alicia said, not having a clue what Sasha was talking about.

"I *know* this has nothing to do with jealousy," Gabrielle said. "I can't control other people saying nice things about me. What am I supposed to do? Tell them not to say anything nice or compliment me because I don't want other people to be mad?"

"Oh, that's not what we're talking about, and you know it," Alicia said.

"Shut up, Alicia!" Sasha said.

"What then? What did I do?" Gabrielle asked. "How can I make something right if I don't know what I've done wrong?"

"We've been hearing a few things about you," Alicia said. "Then, we started putting two and two together, and we were able to better understand how you were able to do it."

"Do *what?*" Gabrielle asked, almost exhausted with this game of *Guess Why We're Mad at You.* This was so juvenile. Grown folks acting like this.

"How you were able to just come in and take Doctor Morgan away from me!" Sasha blurted out.

Gabrielle held up her hands. "Hold up. Take Doctor Morgan away from you? What Doctor Morgan? I haven't taken anybody away from you, and least of all not Doctor Morgan. Unless you were planning on cleaning his house and you're upset because I got the job."

"What are you talking about?" Sasha said. "I barely clean my own house, let alone want to clean somebody else's. And I would assume Doctor Morgan would hire someone to come in and clean his house, so I wouldn't be cleaning his house either."

Gabrielle began to slowly shake her hands at Sasha. "Okay, apparently I'm missing something here." She put her hands down. "Could you *please* just tell me what you *believe* I've done that has you upset with me?"

Sasha put her hand on her hip. "I was the one who invited Doctor Morgan to come visit here during that Sunday we had our celebration. He comes, and what happens? I see him all up in your face. And I'm left wondering, what's *that* all about? Then I hear from Tiffany's husband that you have some special skills, which is probably why you were able to snatch him up like you did."

"Yeah," Alicia said, as though her word was a punctuation mark at the end of Sasha's sentence. "I heard this isn't your first foray into dancing on a big stage. I'm just still trying to figure out the difference between a stripper and an exotic dancer."

"Is that what Darius is spreading around the church about me?" Gabrielle asked.

"He didn't say exactly what kind of dancing you'd done before you came to put your dance skills to work here. Although someone did say you were an exotic dancer. But I have a problem with *anything* that might have been untoward," said Alicia.

"Not that I really want to dignify what you just said, Alicia, but the key word is *been*. Whatever you've heard or think you know about me, whatever that is, it's part of a past life. It's not who I am now. And according to the Word of God, I am a new creature in Christ," Gabrielle said. "My past is under the blood of Jesus now."

"Yeah, but if it's true, then you still did it. And honestly, I think you should still have to pay for what you did. I don't think you ought to be up here at church kicking your legs around and spinning, not when you know where you've done it before," Alicia said.

"In other words, you're saying that even though I came forward, confessed my sins, gave my life to Christ, am now forgiven, I am a new creature in Christ, that I'm not *truly* forgiven and that I should still have to pay for those sins regardless? Is that what you're saying?" Gabrielle looked at Alicia first, then over to Sasha.

"Listen, I don't want to get into all of that, because Lord *knows* I wouldn't want that standard applied to me and my life," Sasha said. "Even after being saved, sanctified, and filled with the Holy Ghost, I've messed up. I had a baby out of wedlock. Everybody knows I was doing something wrong. I asked God to forgive me, and I sure am not going to stand here and declare a set of rules that God didn't authorize and that I can't live under myself."

"I was just trying to make sure I understood," Gabrielle said. "We can ask God to forgive us and He does. But now, according to you two and some others, I have to worry about man thinking he knows more than God. That even though God has forgiven me . . . even though God has changed my life, I still have to prove something to all of you."

"Okay, I think I see where you're coming from," Alicia said. "Maybe I was wrong about that part."

"Maybe you're wrong about a lot of parts. Maybe when Darius brought that bone to you, you should have stopped him and had him carry it back instead of letting him bury it in your front yard. I can only hope and pray you haven't been carrying the bone and trying to bury it in somebody else's yard."

Sasha started laughing. "I don't think I've ever heard gossiping put quite that way before. That was a good point you just made. Dogs carrying bones and bringing them to your front yard to bury them there instead of in the back."

"Thank you," Gabrielle said, looking at Sasha. "Now, if you don't mind, I'd like to go back to something you said earlier. Doctor Morgan—how do you know him, and why did you say I took him away from you?"

"I met him when he came to close on his house a few weeks ago. We talked, I invited him to the celebration, and before I could get over to speak good, there he was chatting it up with you after services. He even joined the church that Sunday."

"Are you talking about Zachary Morgan?"

"Yes. Doctor Morgan. Some people call him Doctor Z. Some folks call him Doctor Z. W. I believe he said Z. W. stands for Zachary Wayne. Yes, Doctor Zachary Wayne Morgan."

"He's not a doctor," Gabrielle said, almost laughing at the obvious confusion.

"Okay, so now you want to be funny? Of course he's a doctor. He just finished his residency, and now he has started his own practice." Sasha looked at Gabrielle as her expression began to soften somewhat. "You really didn't know that Zachary was a doctor?"

"No. We never talked about what he did. I knew he worked," Gabrielle said.

"I don't get that," Sasha said. "The first thing you ask a man when you meet him is what he does for a living. You want to know where he works. And if you get close enough to him, you find out how *much* he makes, at least a ballpark figure. Personally, I want to know what kind of a car he drives, does he own or rent. If he rents, when does he think he'll be buying a house. If he owns a house, where is it and how many square feet. And you've been talking with this man, you came to church with him this past Sunday, and you had no idea he was even a doctor?" Sasha started laughing.

"Personally, even *I* find that hard to believe," Alicia said as she also laughed.

Gabrielle didn't want to admit that she hadn't pressed about where he worked or what he did because she didn't want him turning that question back on her. Besides, they weren't serious enough to dive into all of that just yet. Suddenly, Gabrielle felt herself getting sick. She quickly excused herself and rushed to the restroom. She arrived inside just in time to throw up.

*Zachary Wayne "Z. W." Morgan is Doctor Morgan. The Doctor Morgan I'm now employed by? Five-month-pregnant Queen's Doctor Morgan? That must be why he only gave me a cell phone number to call him on when we first met. He is married, and that's how married men keep their wives and potential mistresses in the dark. But how did this happen? How could she have fallen for such a lowlife that would cheat on his beautiful, pregnant wife? And, unlike the other married person I was involved with some years ago, I met Zachary in church. How could I have missed who he really is?*

Sure, he could quote scriptures, and he was good. She'd thought she'd found a genuine Christian man. Now it turned out, he wasn't any different from Darius Connors. No wonder he'd known so quickly what Darius was up to. They must have attended the same dog school.

*Darius.* The thought of him caused her to throw up again.

# Chapter 33

*As we have therefore opportunity, let us do good unto all men, especially unto them who are of the household of faith.*

*—Galatians 6:10*

Zachary had called and left a message on Gabrielle's answering machine. She had a real dilemma now. She'd fallen for Doctor Zachary Wayne Morgan, only to learn he was apparently married with a child on the way. Forget she'd just learned he was a doctor; that was a good thing. Now much of what he'd told her about his life made sense. Like being bogged down with college work where he didn't have time to date. Of course, if he was studying to be a doctor (college, med school, intern, and residency) that would be a lot on his plate. *Who* would *have time to date?*

Maybe she was wrong about Queen being his wife. Maybe Queen was just his girlfriend. Maybe they'd broken up. But if that was the case, why was she at his house that early in the morning? If they weren't together, why was she living with him? She wouldn't still be there, not in his house. And even if Queen was his girlfriend or an ex, she didn't want any part of that either. She then remembered Queen's wedding rings—the girlfriend theory was out. *Should I quit working there? Ask for another home to clean?*

That sounded like the best solution. She needed the job and the money, so she couldn't just quit. Surely the agency could swap her with someone else, and everything would work out. She would call tomorrow morning and ask to be transferred. *But what reason would I give if asked?*

Zachary called her again at ten PM. She sat and watched the phone ring. What would she say to Zachary if she answered now? *Accuse him of holding back the truth about what he did for a living?* She couldn't do that. She had never asked him what he did. She recalled that time the subject of doctors came up in their conversation. He'd asked her if she had anything against doctors. *Is that why he asked? Because he is a doctor?* Of course. But how could he be so public with her if he was in a committed relationship? It didn't make sense.

None of this made sense. She began to pray for guidance. She knew she needed to talk to Zachary at some point. She had to tell him what she knew, give him a chance to explain. That was the decent thing to do.

The phone stopped ringing. Not a minute later, it began to ring again. She picked it up, realizing maybe it was time to quit dodging the situation and face Zachary.

"Hello," she said as dryly as she could manage.

"Well, hello there, sweet thang," the man's voice said.

"Who is this?"

"Goodness, girl, don't be acting like you've forgotten me already," the male voice said.

His voice quickly registered. "Clarence!"

"How you doing, girl?"

"I don't know. I was excited today, and then everything seemed to have gone downhill quicker than clicking the send button on an e-mail you didn't mean to send."

"Okay," Clarence said. "I knew there was *something* I missed about you."

"Clarence, I don't understand. I just don't understand," Gabrielle said.

"Well, before you start to getting *too* depressed on me, why don't you come to your front door?"

"Where are you?" She got up, slipped on her slippers and her matching purple silk robe to her silk pajamas, and hurried to her front door. She opened it and stepped outside.

Standing in her driveway was Clarence, in front of her Toyota Camry Solara convertible. His 2009 red Corvette was parked directly behind her car. She clicked off her phone and slipped it in her robe pocket.

Ensuring that her robe was tied tight, she hurried over to him. "What is this?"

"Gee, it's been that long since you've seen it? Why, it's your car," he said.

"I know it's my car. What's it doing here?"

He held out the keys to her. She took the keys as she continued to wait for an explanation. He pulled out an envelope from inside of his jacket and handed it to her. "It's free and clear now," he said.

"Clarence, what did you do?"

"I got it back for you. And you don't owe anything on it anymore."

"Why did you do that? I told you I'm not coming back to work for you. I told you, I'm not coming back. Not ever," Gabrielle said, trying not to sound frantic.

"I know."

She calmed her voice. "I just don't want you thinking you can make a loan to me I can't possibly pay back, and hold that over my head to force me to come back to work for you."

"I would never do anything like that to you and you know that. It's not a loan. I'm giving it to you, free and clear. It's my gift to you."

She shook her head. "Unh-uh. Giving it to me is the same thing. I'll be indebted to you, and I don't want that. If I can't pay for it, then I don't need to have it."

"Wow, this is the first time I've seen anyone tell someone they can't give them a gift." He placed his hand on her shoulder. "Apparently, you don't understand the definition of gift. It means you don't owe for it. Look, I don't want anything from you. I don't. And I understand that you aren't coming back to work for me. I got that. But the car is yours. If you don't want to keep it, then that's on you. You can do with it as you please. Give it away. Give it to the church if you want. I don't care. But Gabrielle—"

She snatched away from him and took a step back. "What did you just call me?"

"Gabrielle," he said.

She wiped away a few tears with her hand that

were making their way down her face. "You've not called me that since I first came to work for you some eight years ago."

"Can we go inside?" he asked.

Gabrielle looked back at her open door. "Yeah, sure. Come on in." They walked to the front door and went inside.

"Do you have any coffee?" he asked.

She put some coffee on, making only four cups, since she definitely wasn't planning on drinking coffee this late at night. Clarence always drank his coffee black, so she didn't bother offering him sugar or cream.

He texted a message to someone, then took a sip of his coffee, having blown across the top of it to cool it. "Good coffee," he said after taking a few sips. He sat back against the chair, then leaned it back on its two hind legs before slowly setting it back down on all four.

"Gabrielle, you've changed. I began seeing it when you called that first time after you gave your life to Christ. I've always wanted to believe someone could be serious about their conversion to Christianity. You've proven it can be done. It's been something watching you struggle yet stick with it no matter whether an easier way was offered to you. And I must admit: you've touched me in a way I can't put into words. You've caused me to rethink what being a Christian is really about. It's not becoming perfect and then coming to the Lord. It's about the process of being perfected by the Lord. The process of trusting and believing God, no matter what man attempts to do to you to bring you down. Standing, no matter what."

Gabrielle leaned in closer. "I didn't realize you were paying attention to me."

"Well, I was. And yesterday, I was at a low place in my life. I was about to pour myself a drink and drown my misery in a bottle of spirits when I heard the Holy Spirit speak to me just as plain as you and I are talking right now," Clarence said.

"What did you hear?"

"'I created you for more than this. Come back to me. I'm waiting on you. I haven't given up on you. I won't give up.' That's what I heard. I promise you, I heard it plain as day. I was created for more than what I'm doing now."

"You actually heard the Holy Spirit say that?"

"Yes."

"I've heard people say they heard God speak, but I thought it was just a feeling they have on the inside, and they just *say* they heard His voice," Gabrielle said.

"Well, I heard Him. And I knew it was Him speaking. I want to make some things right. That's why I went and got your car today. I want you to have it, no strings attached. I promise you, I'm not looking for anything in return. May God strike me down if I'm not telling you the truth. I just need to make some things right with the Lord," Clarence said.

She reached over and touched his hand. "I'll take the car if you'll do two things."

Clarence laughed. "Oh, this is funny. I'm trying to give you your car back, and you're over there making conditions before you'll take it. Do you see anything wrong with this picture?"

She grinned. "I'm serious, Clarence. If you don't

agree to my terms, then you can call whomever you need to call, and y'all can take that car and do whatever you want with it. I still believe, somehow, God will provide for me."

"See, that's what I'm talking about. Look at you. Just look at you. I know how you were before: before you would have just said thank you. You're not the same woman I knew. When I was an avid churchgoer, we used to sing this song that said, 'I looked at my hands, and they looked new. I looked at my feet, and they did, too.' I never believed that was either true or possible. But looking at you, I do see a brand-new you. And you're not playing games either. I can see just how real God is, through you."

"So, does that mean you'll agree to my terms?" Gabrielle asked as she slightly raised her body up from her chair by leaning onto the table.

"Okay, let's hear them."

She sat back down completely and grinned. "First, I'd like us to pray, right here, right now. Just me and you."

He chuckled. "Okay. We can do that. What's the other thing?"

"Go to church with me. We have Bible study tomorrow night and church service on Sunday, two services, so you can pick either the early service that starts at seven-thirty or the ten-thirty service. Now, which would you like to go to?"

He shook his head. "I don't know about that. I *am* moving, but I'm not quite there yet. I'm taking baby steps. Bringing you the car, that was a baby step. Me and you praying like you're asking . . . baby step. I can do that. But going to church, I don't know about that just yet."

"Come on, Clarence. What are you afraid of?"

His look became serious. "That I'll end up becoming just like my father. That I'll be called to preach, and I'll end up letting others, as well as God, down. At least the way I am now, God knows I'm not a hypocrite. I'm not putting on a show. He knows I'm not leading anyone astray under the disguise of religion."

"So, is that a yes? You'll go to church with me on Sunday? Just once. One time. One." She held up an index finger. "Come on, say yes! And I promise, I won't ask you ever again. If you'll come just once."

"Thank you, Gabrielle." He smiled a sincere smile. "I realize your stage name may have been *Goodness and Mercy*, but I think that name just might have been prophetic of how you would someday demonstrate God's goodness and mercy through your caring about what happens to others. You care about sinners' souls. That's rare." He pulled out another envelope and laid it in her hand. "We all wanted you to have this."

"What is this?"

"Open it, and I'll tell you all about it."

Gabrielle brushed the tears away from her eyes as soon as she opened the envelope stuffed with cash. "I can't accept this, Clarence. This is too much." The tears continued to flow. She grabbed a napkin off the table and wiped her eyes.

"It's from all of us down at the place. I know you're having a hard time. You've said you're not coming back where you know you could make that much money in a week. Some of us wanted to do something to help out. Actually, we admire you for taking such a stand and sticking with it. Besides, I told you that I owed you." He laughed. "I cheated you out of some of your money early on. Consider this my retribution. Now, how about that prayer?" He bowed his head. She took his hand and prayed with him.

Gabrielle began to sniffle after the prayer. "Clarence, please come go to church with me Sunday. Please?"

He stood up. "I'll think about it and let you know. In the meantime, know that your labor in the Lord is not in vain. And please, don't become like those Christians who tend to blow with the wind. Stay rooted in the Lord the way you are now. Keep what you have and continue to grow it. Believe me: what you have is rare indeed."

He left. She stood at her front door and waved good-bye to him as he got into his Corvette and drove off. With a smile, she closed the door. Five minutes later, her doorbell rang. She hurried to open the door, figuring Clarence had forgotten something.

"Darius?" she said, shocked to see him. She tried to push the door closed.

He smiled, pushed the door open, and stepped past her. "Hello, Gabrielle. Mind if I come in?" He grabbed the door, closed it behind him, then locked it.

# Chapter 34

*Lest Satan should get an advantage of us: for we are not ignorant of his devices.*

—2 Corinthians 2:11

"What are you doing here?" Gabrielle asked as she stood near the door.

"I just came by to see how you were doing." He looked around the foyer. "Aren't you going to tell me to make myself at home? Isn't that how southern women are taught to be hospitable?"

She crossed her arms. "What do you want?"

"Hold up with the attitude. I just came by to apologize. Tiffany told me that apparently I'm the one being credited with spreading things about you through the congregation. I wanted you to know that even though I *did* threaten that I would do that, it wasn't me."

"Sure, Darius. You were the one who kept bringing it up. You were trying to use it to move in on me. And when I wouldn't play with you, you decided you would make me pay. I hope you're happy now."

"Secrets, secrets, so many secrets. You, of all people, should know that secrets generally tend to find a way of coming out. So, what did Johnnie Mae Landris say to you when she heard about what you used to do? I'm sure she's heard it now." He tried to appear concerned.

Gabrielle laughed. "Oh, so you're supposed to be bothered that Johnnie Mae might be upset about what you were spreading?"

"I told you, I didn't spread that on purpose. I asked a few people to keep you lifted up in their prayers that you don't slip back into what you'd been delivered out of. I praised you for your strength in doing what you'd done by putting your dancing gift to work in the Lord's house," Darius said, looking all sincere.

Gabrielle smirked. "Yeah. Just like you told me that Christians who want to spread something spread it when they don't want it to look like they're gossiping."

"You still haven't told me what Johnnie Mae said. Did she banish you from the dance ministry? Put you out? I hope not. That would be a travesty."

"Like you really care."

"I do care. How was I supposed to know that was going to travel the way it did? I thought maybe a few people would say something to you, let you know I was serious about the damage I could do if I wanted to. I sure didn't intend for it to get away like it appears to have done. And now my name is being attached to the mess. Big mouth folks. If they wanted to talk, they could have kept *my* name out of it."

"Well, not that it's any of your business, but I'd already told Johnnie Mae everything about me and my past. Everything."

"No, you didn't. You're lying. Why would you tell something if you don't have to?"

"I don't know," Gabrielle said. "But maybe you should try it. I suppose the biggest reason is that it can take a *huge* bite out of the impact of something getting out in other ways. Both Johnnie Mae and Pastor Landris were aware of my dancing career because I told Johnnie Mae. She spoke with Pastor Landris about it. They prayed about it. And in the end, not only was I allowed to dance in the ministry, but I was chosen as the choreographer."

"Yeah, okay. But that was *before* other people in the congregation started grumbling about it. There are lots of people, from what I hear, who don't think you should be allowed to continue dancing in church given your past life," Darius said.

"Well, you know what? I'm just glad these people aren't God. Because if they were, *none* of us would stand a chance. Now"—she walked to the door, unlocked it, and opened it—"it's time for you to go home to your wife. Tell her I said hello, won't you?"

He snickered. "Yeah. You think you're slick, don't you? I guess you want to tell her what I've been up to now, don't you? Get a little payback for what I've done to you?"

"Who *me*? Be the one to let your wife know what a jerk she's married to?"

"She won't believe you. She knows how much I love her. Tiffany understands jealous women. Women who are envious of what other women have are known to lie. When it comes to my wife, I'd keep my mouth closed if I were you. But you and I will talk some more. Who knows, maybe you'll confide in me some other little dark secret you haven't shared with anyone else. Or just maybe I'll stumble across some more information all on my own. So, we'll just say good-bye . . . for now." He leaned down to give her a kiss on her cheek.

She quickly pulled back before his lips could touch her. "Don't do that!" she said.

"Oh, so I guess it's okay for Clarence to come by, spend a little time here doing God only knows what and for how long, but not me."

"You were watching my house? You're spying on me, too?"

"No. I parked across the street. I was about to get out when three cars pulled up into your driveway. One guy parked your Solara, got out, then got into the car that pulled up behind the Corvette. The two of them left. Clarence got out of his Corvette and stood outside talking on his cell phone. With three cars pulling up in your driveway like that, I decided I should stick around and see what was going on in case you needed some help. I wasn't spying on you. Trust me: I have more to do with my life than follow you around. I was merely coming to apologize, and to try to make right what I may have inadvertently done. And I know you don't believe this, but I'd really like for us to be friends."

"If you want to make things right, then do me a favor: keep my name out of your mouth. Now, why don't you go home to your wife and quit trying to figure out how you can get me into bed."

"Because I know what I want, and for the most

part, I usually get what I want." He started to trace her jawline with his finger. She jerked back. He smiled. "You'll see." He leaned in closer to her face. "I'm a *very* patient and persistent man."

"Get out of my house. I'm not interested in you. And I don't know any other way I can say it to you. I'm not interested."

"I hear what you're saying. You think you want pretty boy," Darius said. "I've tried to tell you that he's not the right man for you."

She opened the door wider. "Leave now or I'm going to call the police. And I'll thank you not to darken my door again." She said it slowly, distinctively, and deliberately.

He grinned as he strolled past her and out of the door. Turning around once he had crossed the threshold, he blew her a two-finger kiss and grinned. She slammed the door in his face. She hugged herself, then quickly realized just how much her body was trembling.

# Chapter 35

*Moreover concerning the stranger, which is not of thy people Israel, but is come from a far country for thy great name's sake, and thy mighty hand, and thy stretched out arm: if they come and pray in this house.*

—2 Chronicles 6:32

Zachary wondered why Gabrielle hadn't called him back. He broke his own rule and called her again at ten-fifteen. Still, no answer. On another front, he was excited about the progress his house had taken. Queen had contacted an employment agency and hired someone to come clean and get the house in shape. The woman they'd sent had done an amazing job. Both he and Queen were more than impressed with her work and her decorating style. And if Queen was impressed, this woman *had* to be good.

Zachary knew Queen was good at turning on her charm, but she could be sneaky, too. She had a way of disarming a person's defenses so she could find out exactly what she wanted to know or what was really going on with them that they may not have intended to tell. But Queen had nothing but positive things to say about the new housekeeper. She couldn't wait for Zachary to meet her.

So, when Queen received a call from the employment agency Wednesday morning stating that after this week, Gabrielle would no longer be working in their home, understandably, Queen was taken aback.

"Did something happen?" Queen asked Ms. Daniels at the agency.

"No," Ms. Daniels said.

"Then why are you changing her out? I really like her."

"It wasn't us. She was the one who requested that she be reassigned."

"She asked? Did something happen here that I'm unaware of?" Queen asked.

"She didn't say anything happened. She just asked if she could swap assignments with someone else. But let me assure you, the person we'll be sending out next week will be equally as good, if not better. We want you and Doctor Morgan to be happy. In fact, I believe I have the perfect person to replace her. I think you're really going to like the new person as well. Unfortunately, she can't start until next week after she finishes a job that's due to end this week. But Gabrielle has agreed to finish out this week with you."

That bothered Queen. Maybe something *had* happened between her and Gabrielle. Maybe she'd asked Gabrielle one too many questions and one of those questions had offended her. She hadn't gotten that impression. In fact, they seemed to have gotten along splendidly. She'd been ecstatic that Gabrielle would be taking care of the house. She felt they could trust her. Now, she didn't know. Maybe she'd been mistaken about Gabrielle.

Queen decided she would talk to Gabrielle about it when she got there.

"The phone company is scheduled to come and put in the landline today," Queen reminded Zachary when he walked into the kitchen before leaving for his office.

"Yeah, I remember."

"It's sad how long it takes these days just to get a new phone. They couldn't even give me a specific time. Just said between nine and five, so I don't have a clue what time they'll be here. And I have an errand I *must* do today. But now I don't want to leave the new housekeeper here since she seems to be flaking out on us. I thought she was going to turn out to be someone we could trust when no one's here. Now, I don't know. So if I need you to come home for lunch today while I run my errand, do you think you could do that in case the phone company decides to show up while I'm gone?"

Zachary checked his watch to see how he was doing for time. "Yeah, sure."

"Great." Queen sipped her decaffeinated coffee. "I'll be *so* glad when I can get back to regular coffee. I don't care what anybody says, there *is* a difference."

"You need to keep doing what's right for that little one you're carrying," Zachary said. "Well, I need to get going." He grabbed a slice of bacon off her plate and ate it as he walked. "Call me and let me know if you need me to come home for lunch."

She nodded as she held her coffee cup in the air as a way of saluting him.

When Gabrielle arrived, she felt uneasy. She'd called Ms. Daniels and requested to be reassigned. Her hope was that they could do it today. Ms. Daniels had wanted to know why she wanted to change. She wanted to make sure there wasn't anything about that client they needed to know about. Gabrielle assured her it was nothing like that. In fact, she liked Queen. She'd been excited about working there, was looking forward to it even. Queen didn't hound her or act like some well-to-do people can act toward people they felt they were better than. And she could tell that Queen trusted her in her home. Queen was sincerely down-to-earth, in spite of her royal name.

It was *because* she liked Queen so much that she knew she'd have to make some changes. First, she needed to get out of their house as their housekeeper. Second, she had to kick Zachary completely to the curb. The last thing she needed now was to run into Zachary in his own house, although that would quickly take care of problems one and two.

Things just didn't fit. How could someone be so wonderful and be such a colossal cheat at the same time? She had totally misread Zachary, and she prided herself on being a truth-o-meter. She could usually tell when someone was lying. But she'd absolutely missed this one. He'd told her that he wasn't married or in a relationship with anyone;

clearly that wasn't true. And on top of everything else, his wife was expecting a baby.

Gabrielle knew she was being a coward by not answering her phone when Zachary called or by not calling him back. Anyone with just a little chutzpah would tell him what she knew and be done with it. But her plan was to first get out of their employment. Then she could let him know that the jig was up. She would bust him with the unadulterated truth. She could see God's hand here. How ironic that, of all the houses in which she could have gotten a job as a housekeeper, she would be assigned to Zachary's house and meet his wife. This *had* to be God looking out for her, protecting her.

When Gabrielle arrived at the Morgan's home, Queen didn't waste any time letting her know how upset she was that she was leaving them. She asked if there was anything she'd done to upset her or to cause her to leave. Gabrielle assured her it had nothing to do with her at all. She hated that Queen felt she was the cause of her leaving when she absolutely wasn't. But she couldn't tell Queen about Zachary—that would break her heart, not to say what it could do to their marriage. If Queen found out about Zachary, she would have to do it without her assistance. As far as Gabrielle was concerned, this was an *a* and *b* conversation, and she was going to *c* her way of out it.

That Wednesday, Gabrielle went about doing her work. She got a lot done. The house was really shaping up. She was amazed at just how many decisions Queen allowed her to make about where things should go. She would have thought Queen would have relegated her to more menial tasks while she put things in their proper places. But instead, Queen stressed to Gabrielle that how she arranged rooms or put things away was fine with her. The plan was to empty boxes and to make the house feel more like a home.

Queen had said she needed to run an errand. Gabrielle told her that since she was there, she could go if she needed to. Queen didn't respond to her offer to leave one way or the other. Gabrielle could tell there was a huge difference in the Queen of yesterday and the Queen of today. One, she was less talkative. Gabrielle was starting to see she'd likely offended Queen by asking to be reassigned. If only she could explain, then Queen would understand and even *appreciate* what she was doing. For sure, Gabrielle couldn't afford to lose her job. And if Queen was to find out about her and Zachary, she knew between the two of them, one would likely end up out on the street. And it most likely wouldn't be Zachary. It wasn't worth taking the risk. Being in Zachary's house like this, she and Zachary were bound to run into each other sooner or later.

Based on what Queen had asked her when she arrived, she deduced that Queen hadn't mentioned her name to Zachary yet. Otherwise, he wouldn't be calling her house and leaving those nice little messages on her answering machine. He would have figured out what was going on and most likely called her to say that they needed to talk, so he could further bury the truth from his wife. *Was it possible there might be two Doctor Morgans?*

Probable, but unlikely. She just needed to make it through two more days and she would be home free.

Queen came into the den to see how things were going. Gabrielle had to admit: she had a knack for cleaning and decorating. Queen acted as though she'd never seen some of these things before even though it was apparent they were items from a previous home.

"Look at this room," Queen said as she looked around and smiled. "Wow! You've done an *amazing* job. Amazing! But you know what this room needs?"

Gabrielle scanned the finished room. She was glad Queen was pleased and seemed to have warmed back up at least somewhat to her. "Pictures, maybe?"

"Precisely! But I believe all the photos are in one box. And I'm not sure where that box is." Her cell phone began to sing. "Excuse me a second," she said. "Hello."

Gabrielle busied herself so she wouldn't appear to be listening in on Queen's conversation. Still, she heard things like, "No, they haven't come yet. Whatever time you can come home, Z. W., will work for me. I told you, I don't have to be there at a certain time, just as long as I get there before five today. So, if you want to come now or an hour from now, either time will work for me. Whatever is good for you."

Gabrielle froze. *Zachary will be coming home before I'm out of here?*

Just then, the doorbell rang. "Hold on, someone's at the door. Maybe that's them now." Queen went to the window and peeked out. "It is. I know you're glad they made it so you won't have to come now. Yes, *Zachary*. I love you, too. Bye now," she said.

"Great, the phone company is here," Queen said to Gabrielle. She moved over closer to Gabrielle. "Hey? Are you all right? All of a sudden, you don't look well."

"I just need some water," Gabrielle said. The doorbell rang again.

"I have to get the door," Queen said. "Get some water, then take a break. Perhaps you've overdone it. I mean, by the looks of this room, you'd think you were trying to finish this whole house before you leave on Friday." Queen left and opened the door.

Gabrielle went to the kitchen and got some water. She pressed the cool glass against her forehead. Those words kept repeating in her mind. *Yes, Zachary. I love you, too.* She began to pray right there in the kitchen with the glass pressed against her forehead.

Friday afternoon couldn't come fast enough for her!

# Chapter 36

*It is of the Lord's mercies that we are not consumed, because his compassions fail not.*

—Lamentations 3:22

Gabrielle came home from work feeling good about what she'd accomplished. Two more workdays and she could walk away completely. After Zachary called and told Queen he loved her, for a minute, she'd felt like the wind had been knocked out of her. She didn't know why she cared. Sure, Zachary had been wonderful. But he'd also proven that he was a deceiver. She hadn't intended to, but apparently she'd fallen harder for him than she'd realized. The fact still remained, he belonged to someone else. So, that was that. She just needed to concentrate on God and His Word and let that be her main focus.

Her Realtor called and said someone had made an offer on her house. She had bittersweet feelings about it. She needed to sell the house. She'd prayed about selling it, even done a two-day fast. Actually, a week earlier, she'd tried fasting three days, but the hunger got to her on that second day. She later learned everyone had a hard time on the second day. And if you made it through your second day, the third day was such a breeze that some folks even went on to a fourth day. Still, her heart had been in the right place. She had fasted and prayed with her eyes on Jesus. Now, she was learning that someone had offered exactly what she was asking for it. That was a true blessing.

"And you're also not going to believe this," her Realtor said. "The buyer is paying cash, so you won't have to wait long for him to take possession. We just need the title search, an inspection, the two of you signing the papers, and that will do it. They've set the closing date for a week from today at five. I tell you: somebody up there must really like you. Things are moving *somewhat* these days in the housing market, but not moving for everybody. And for sure not like this. Most who are buying are still bargain hunting."

"Well, somebody does like me. In fact, somebody loves me," Gabrielle said. "And His name is Jesus."

"Okay," the Realtor said. "But lots of people are praying, and I'm sure Jesus loves them, too. However, they're not getting an answer like you just got with yours. You're getting the full asking price. That rarely happens in a good market."

"Is it possible we can close at six? I'm not sure where I'll be working next week, and I don't want to request to leave early my first week with my new employer just in case my shift there doesn't end until five."

"Six it is, then. I'll call and make sure that works for the buyer."

Gabrielle couldn't help but grin as she hung up.

Things were finally moving. She had been faithful through a few things, and now God was showing His faithfulness. She looked up, pressed her hands in a prayer like way, and said, "Thank You. Thank You."

Her phone rang again. She looked at the caller ID. It was Zachary. She watched as she allowed the phone to ring, then let the call go to her answering machine. From the tone of his voice, she could tell he was worried that he hadn't heard from her yet. He begged her to call him back as soon as she got the message. His worried sound didn't seem to have panic in it. He didn't sound like a cheating man who'd just found out he'd gotten caught. He sounded like a man concerned about the whereabouts of someone he really cared about.

Two more days . . . Thursday and Friday, and she could tell Zachary what was really up with the two of them. Two more days, and she could tell him what a wonderful wife he appeared to have, and how he should be ashamed of himself for what he was doing, not only to her and his soon-to-be child, but to the body of Christ. It was people like him who were giving Christians a bad name—him and Darius.

Well, as far as she was concerned, everybody could act up if they wanted to. But she was determined—to the best of her abilities—she was going to live her life for Christ. And if that meant she had to be all by herself, then so be it. She would just have to be all by herself.

# Chapter 37

*And shall not God avenge his own elect, which cry day and night unto him, though he bear long with them?*

—Luke 18:7

Gabrielle went to Bible study. She drove the Corsica to church so she could give it back to Johnnie Mae. When Clarence brought her car back to her, she'd called Johnnie Mae to tell her what had transpired. She hadn't been sure if it was right for her to accept what he'd done—paying to get it out of repo, then paying the entire loan off and giving the car (title free) to her.

Johnnie Mae had laughed when she heard it. "Well, the Bible does say that the wealth of the wicked is laid up for the just. Let me ask you this. Are you doing anything you shouldn't be doing in exchange for what he's doing?"

"Absolutely not. In fact, he's been trying to get me to come back to work for him, and even though, as you are well aware, things aren't going all that great in my life these days, I'm determined to do things God's way. If I lose my house, my car, and friends, in the end, I know that what I do for Christ is what counts. I know this and understand it. So, even though it may be tempting to go back into that world even just temporarily and with good reasons, I refuse to do it," Gabrielle said.

"I will tell you that for some people, that would have been more than tempting. To make the kind of money you said you were making, especially when you've been praying, and it feels like not only is God *not* listening, but that He's not even around. There are a lot of Christians who would have rationalized going back and even declared it to be a blessing from God."

"I can imagine. But I put one scripture down in my spirit, and I repeated that scripture when I knew I was in God's will," Gabrielle said. "First Corinthians fifteen fifty-eight: 'Therefore, my beloved brethren, be ye steadfast, unmovable, always abounding in the work of the Lord, forasmuch as ye know that your labor is not in vain in the Lord.' That part about being steadfast and unmovable keeps me grounded. People may laugh at me, they may talk about me, but I know who I am in the Lord. I don't want to do anything that would even give the *appearance* of wrongdoing."

"Well, I see nothing wrong with your taking the car, especially with your also telling me that he admitted cheating you out of some of your money early on." Johnnie Mae let out a chuckle. "Just remember this: the devil might bring it, but if it's good, then it's God who sent it. For every good and perfect gift comes from above. So that goes for that money you said he blessed you with as well. Just be sure you're not compromising God's Word. That's the rule to measure things: how does it line up with the Word of God?"

So, the plan was that Gabrielle would drive the Corsica to Bible study and Johnnie Mae and Pastor Landris would take it back home with them. She had asked Jackie, one of the dance team members she'd learned lived near her neighborhood, to drop her off at her house after Bible study to keep the Landrises from having to go out of the way. When she gave Johnnie Mae the key to the car, she told her the news about her house being sold. God was really working things out. Sure, some people at church were still whispering when she passed by. But she continued to hold her head up high.

Fatima was due home Friday. Gabrielle couldn't wait to see her. She would have a lot to tell her, that's for sure. That is, whenever she felt like talking, after having just lost and buried her mother.

Right after Gabrielle handed the Corsica key to Johnnie Mae, she spotted Zachary heading her way. "I'm sorry, I really have to run. I don't want to keep Jackie waiting," Gabrielle said, then quickly dashed away.

When Gabrielle got home, there was a message on her answering machine from Zachary. "I saw you at church tonight. I was coming over to speak. I thought you saw me, but I guess you didn't. At least I know you're okay. I was starting to worry about you since I hadn't heard back from you at all. I was wondering if I could come over to see you . . . to talk. Or maybe you'd like to go out to dinner sometime this week. Please call me back. Bye."

Gabrielle shook her head and looked upward as she took in deep breaths. *Two more days. Two more days. Thursday and Friday. Two more days.* "God, I can see this is going to be a lot harder than I thought!"

# Chapter 38

*And I myself also am persuaded of you, my brethren, that ye also are full of goodness, filled with all knowledge, able also to admonish one another.*

—Romans 15:14

Thursday and Friday came and went rather quickly. Gabrielle and Queen really bonded. Gabrielle learned Queen also loved to dance. On Friday afternoon, Queen asked Gabrielle to show her a few of her favorite moves, and she was more than happy to oblige. There was one special move Gabrielle hadn't done in a really long time. When she did that one, it affected Queen in a way she hadn't expected it would. Queen was fanning her face fast with her hand as though she was trying to keep her tears up.

"Oh, my goodness," Queen said. "Wow. That was wonderful. I've only seen one other person who knew how to perform that move like that, other than myself of course. I mean, you performed it perfectly, perfectly. Where did you learn how to do that?"

Gabrielle sat down beside Queen on the sofa as she tried to catch her breath. "I had a very special teacher growing up," Gabrielle said. She drank some of the cranberry juice that Queen had brought in for them.

"Did you grow up around here? I mean, in Birmingham?"

"Yes."

"You wouldn't happen to have known my aunt, would you? She's the only other person I've ever known who could do that move. That's who taught me. Her name is Esther Crowe."

"Esther Crowe?" Gabrielle said with excitement as she sat up straight. "Yes, I knew her! That's who taught me how to dance. Esther Crowe is your aunt?"

"Yes!" Queen began to smile. "Well, I'll be. You knew my aunt, and she taught you how to dance. Well, that makes sense now. What are the chances of this?"

"Oh, I'm getting goose bumps," Gabrielle said. "Queen Esther, so—"

Queen began to nod. "Yes, I was named after my aunt—Esther. My father adored his baby sister. When I was born, he wanted to name me after her. From what I was told, my aunt thought calling a child in my generation Esther was not the best thing you could do to her. It was *her* idea to add Queen before Esther since she couldn't talk him out of naming me that. I admit: I used to hate being called Queen or Queen Esther when I was growing up. Both my brothers used to tease me a lot. You know how brothers can be. But my brothers wouldn't let anybody else mess with me. And no one else had better make fun of my name either." Queen laughed. "Well, isn't this something?"

"I met Miss Crowe when I was eight. She rescued me really. Miss Crowe was truly an angel on earth, truly. She was in a car accident when I was seventeen. I never found out what happened after that. I never heard anything more." Gabrielle suddenly realized she couldn't bring herself to ask if Miss Crowe was still alive. As long as no one had said anything differently, she could always believe Miss Crowe was not dead.

Queen reached over and touched Gabrielle's hand. "She's still alive. She's in a nursing home now. Actually, she's been there since she got out of the hospital after the automobile accident. She doesn't say much, a few words. Some that don't really make sense to any of us. My brother and I used to go see her once a week before we left Chicago for warmer weather. We visit her whenever we go back home. My mother and father still live up there. My father is originally from here, but he moved up there right after my oldest brother was born. Of course, my brother doesn't remember living here, but my father has fond memories. We used to visit Aunt Esther about once a year until the family started having family reunions and my father used his vacation time to make the yearly rounds of reunions. With twelve children, the family reunion ended up in Alabama only once. And after Aunt Esther no longer lived here, there was no reason to come back. I tell you, Aunt Esther was the best!"

"I never knew what happened to her," Gabrielle said. "She and I were so close. She told me she had this surprise for me. She was so excited about it. I never got to find out what it was. She left around

Thanksgiving to go see about one of her brothers. There was some problem, I don't know. After that, I never saw her again. Somebody came and sold her house, but no one ever contacted me to let me know how she was doing or anything. I didn't know if she was alive or dead." Gabrielle began to pat her heart. "I'm so glad to hear she's alive. You just don't know. I would love to see her."

"Maybe you can go with me the next time I go. Possibly even learn what surprise she had for you. You never know what might happen. You could be just the medicine she needs. I know this is your last day working here, and to be honest with you, I really wish you would reconsider. You're just what this house needs. And I'd really like for you to meet my brother. I think the two of you would hit it off fabulously.

"He and Aunt Esther were real close," Queen continued. "He was the reason she was in such a hurry to come to Chicago during that time. He still blames himself for what happened. Everybody has told him to forgive himself and to let it go. He and my father had some major falling out. It got really bad. Bad enough that Aunt Esther jumped in her car despite the horrid weather report and drove up. She could have waited and flown in later in the week, but she was the baby of the family, and she thought it was her place to fix things when things got out of hand. My brother feels to this day that had he not done what he did, she never would have come when she did. And she would be okay today, most likely teaching a school of children how to dance those beautiful moves the way she taught you and me."

Gabrielle shook her head. "I remember she told me about her being from a large family. Her family seemed to mean everything to her. I can't imagine more than five."

"Oh, and they are truly close. My grandmother, God bless her soul, was quite the religious one. She named all twelve of her children with names from the Bible."

"Wow, that's something," Gabrielle said.

"Yes. Let's see: there's Deborah, Barak, Abraham"—Queen ticked off the names using her fingers to keep count—"Joseph, Zechariah, although he goes by Zachary, Naomi, Ruth, Rachel, Mary Elizabeth . . . she named Mary Elizabeth two Biblical names because she said Mary and Elizabeth gave birth to Jesus and John the Baptist and the names should be linked. There's Daniel, Priscilla, and Esther, the baby. Twelve."

"A quite impressive group," Gabrielle said. But what she was really thinking was how one of the children's names was Zachary, and how Queen must have a thing for the name Zachary, since she'd obviously married a man with that same name. Zachary was not all that common, especially among black folks.

"Well, I should get back to work," Gabrielle said. "I only have an hour left, and I don't want to cheat you out of any of your time."

"Please, don't leave," Queen said. "I mean, don't leave and go work for someone else. I really like you. I really wish you'd reconsider and stay. This house needs your special touch. I know I'm being selfish. And I can't help but think that I must have done *something* to drive you away."

"It's not you," Gabrielle said.

"But you're still getting your job going through the agency, right?" Gabrielle nodded to Queen's question. "And you were the one who asked to be changed, correct?"

"Yes," Gabrielle said. "But I promise you, my asking to leave has nothing to do with you." That was mostly true. Her leaving had more to do with her husband, Zachary.

"Is it the pay? Because I'm sure I can get that upped if I need to. Tell me, what will you be making with the other family you're set to go to on Monday? I'm sure we can match that amount."

"It's the same pay. Queen, it's not the money, okay? But I really appreciate your caring so much, and I especially appreciate your wanting me to stay enough to offer me more money. That means more than you'll ever know. You make leaving so hard."

"Won't you please tell me what it is, so I can fix it?" Queen said. "Please, or else I will be forced to believe it really *was* something that I did."

Gabrielle touched her hand. "Please, don't do that. It has nothing to do with you. I promise you that. If it was *only* about you, I tell you, you would have found it hard *ever* getting rid of me. Now, will you please just let it go? Please."

Queen stood up. "Sure." She flashed a quick, rather forced smile. "Why don't you go now? Take off an hour early. You've done more than a day's work already. Let this be my gift to you." She smiled again, this time with more sincerity. "But if you don't mind, I would like to keep in touch. And maybe you and I can work on your visiting my aunt when I go again. I have a feeling if she sees you, she'll absolutely perk up." She laughed a little. "There is this one phrase she says constantly. She's been saying it for years. It doesn't make sense to any of us, but from time to time she says 'book her.' I don't know, maybe she's thinking about her days when she was at The Juilliard School of Dance. Maybe she wants someone to book her to dance or possibly she wants to book them. I don't know."

"Book her?" Gabrielle said as she began to squint her eyes.

"Yes." Queen looked at Gabrielle quizzically. "Does that mean something to you? I mean, you did know her for quite a few years."

"This may be a stretch here, but before I changed my last name, I was Gabrielle Mercedes Booker. See? Book her . . . Booker. It's possible she may . . . *may* have been trying to say my last name: Booker."

"Book her, Booker." Queen repeated the two. She began to laugh. "I bet you that's it!" She laughed some more. "Aunt Esther has been trying to say your last name all of these years." She touched Gabrielle on her shoulder. "Now, I *know* you're going to have to go see her. I can't wait to tell my brother! And my father . . . oh, my father is going to flip! My father kept telling us that it meant something, that she wasn't just babbling words. She likely was trying to tell us to get in touch with you—Booker."

Queen insisted Gabrielle take the hour off early and leave. At the door, Gabrielle turned back and hugged Queen Esther. Whatever icy feelings she'd had about hugging folks, somehow somewhere, had slowly melted away when she hadn't even realized it.

"I pray the best for you and your family," Gabrielle said. And she meant it.

# Chapter 39

*Judge not, and ye shall not be judged: con-*
*demn not, and ye shall not be condemned:*
*forgive, and ye shall be forgiven.*

—Luke 6:37

Gabrielle had gone to Fatima's house on Saturday to visit her. She'd just gotten back after
burying her beloved mother. Wanting to get out of
her house and after learning Gabrielle had sold
hers—closing on Wednesday and possibly moving
out the next Saturday—Fatima decided to go to
Gabrielle's house to help her pack.

Zachary had called Gabrielle twice now, his second message indicating his belief that she might
possibly be listening to that message and was
merely refusing to pick up.

"I really need to talk to you," Zachary said. "It's
urgent that we talk. I'll be happy to come over. Just
please, please, call me when you get this message.
Okay? Please."

Fatima heard the message as Gabrielle played it.
She asked when Gabrielle stepped away without
picking up the phone, "Aren't you going to call
him back?"

"Nope."

"No? Why not? Because I'm here? Girl, you'd better call that man back. I can start putting your dishes in a box while you call him. I won't mind," Fatima said.

"I'm not going to call him back." Gabrielle primped her mouth. "At least, not yet."

"But he said it was urgent," Fatima said.

Gabrielle looked directly at Fatima. "I'm not going to call him back. So, let's just drop it, all right."

"No, I will not drop it." Fatima put her hand on her hip. "What happened?"

"Nothing. I just found out that he's not who I thought he was, that's all." Gabrielle picked up a folded cardboard box and began shaping it into an actual box.

Fatima picked up the tape and helped by taping the bottom of the box as Gabrielle held it together. "Okay, so he's not who you thought he was. Would you care to be a *little* more specific?"

Gabrielle picked up another cardboard flat and started the box creation process again as Fatima manned the tape. "For starters, did you know he's a doctor?"

Fatima stopped pulling the tape and gazed at Gabrielle as a smile emerged. "Get out of here! He's a doctor? What kind? Wow, a doctor. Who would have thought? Although, now that you mention it, I *can* see it. He has that doctor look about him."

"I don't know what kind of a doctor, because he's never told me what he does."

"Now, that's strange. Why do you think he kept that information from you?" Fatima finished taping the box.

Gabrielle got another cardboard flat and continued their routine. "I don't think he deliberately kept that information from me. I never asked him what he did, and I suppose he didn't want to sound like a braggadocio and volunteer it. I mean, what would he say? 'Hey, did I tell you that I'm a doctor?' No, that's not Zachary's style."

"So, how did you happen to find out?"

Gabrielle stopped and laughed. "My new job. Would you believe it was his house that I ended up being hired to clean?"

"Get out of here! He hired you to clean his house? Man, talk about tacky. He's interested in dating you, yet he hires you to clean his house? Well, I guess that was nice of him, since you *were* looking for work."

Gabrielle picked up two of the boxes they had created and took them to the kitchen. Fatima picked up the other one and followed her. "That's not exactly how it happened," Gabrielle said. "In fact, I'm not sure he knows I was cleaning his house."

Fatima dropped the empty boxes at her feet and stared at Gabrielle. "Okay, now this is starting to sound *really* crazy."

"Okay. I got a job through this employment agency. It was one Johnnie Mae told me about. She recommended me after she learned that I was looking for a job and that I didn't have a problem being a housekeeper. I reported to my place of employment on Tuesday, and I had a really wonderful time getting to know Queen Esther."

"Queen Esther? There was someone at his house named Queen Esther?"

"Yes, his wife. Only she generally goes by Queen. Although, I think one of her brothers calls her Q."

Fatima touched Gabrielle on her shoulders. "Whoa, whoa, whoa. His wife? Zachary has a wife?"

"Yeah, he has a wife. Oh, and did I mention she's pregnant? Yep. Five months."

"So, you're saying Zachary Morgan is Doctor Zachary Morgan, he has a wife, she's five months pregnant, and you and she chatted at his house, where you now work?"

Gabrielle nodded. "Yep, that about sums it up perfectly. At the time, I didn't know whose house I was going to. I knew I was assigned to clean a doctor's home. I arrived at the house, before time—"

"That's good. Before time is on time and on time is late," Fatima said, repeating what most of them had heard Pastor Landris say on more than a few occasions.

"Yeah. So, I'm there on time. She shows me what I need to do. Everything is going great. I'm excited about my new job. I get to dance ministry meeting Tuesday night. And Sasha Peeples and Alicia Cantor are there rolling their eyes at me."

"You're kidding? Sasha and her sidekick Alicia? As much as you helped the two of them back when we were trying to get that routine right, and they have the nerve to be giving you attitude?"

Gabrielle waved it off. "Any-hoo, I decided to confront the problem. You know, with love, the way Pastor Landris taught us we should do if it ever becomes necessary. I thought they were acting that way because of the stuff Darius started spreading throughout the congregation about me."

"Darius. Yeah, I've heard rumblings about that since I've been back. Tiffany called me, upset that folks are falsely accusing her husband of spreading that about you. She insists he was not the one who did it. It upsets her that Darius's name is being dragged through the mud by some who are saying he was wrong to have started it. Then, there are those questioning that if that *is* true about you, how Darius happened to come about that knowledge. It's a mess for sure. Darius is such a despicable little person to have started a lie like that. Especially since everybody knows it's not true. An exotic dancer. Please!"

"It is true, Fatima. It's true. In my past, I was in fact an exotic dancer. I'm not proud of that now, and I gave it all up once I came and gave my life to Christ. That's why I've been struggling so financially—trying to pay my bills when my income was cut so drastically all of a sudden. Still, I've been steadfast in the Lord and in His Word. I'm proud to say that the old person who used to do those things is dead and gone now."

Fatima sat down slowly. "*You* were an exotic dancer?"

"Yes."

"You'll need to give me a minute to process this. You danced in front of men—"

"Fatima, we don't need to go there, okay? That's who I *was,* not who I *am.* I made an error in judgment in my life, but now I've changed."

"I just can't wrap my head around that. I would have argued anybody down who claimed that was true," Fatima said. "In fact, I did argue a few people down. I don't believe it."

"Oh, so I guess you're telling me you've been holy all of your life? You've never done anything in your past that you regret?" Gabrielle held up her hand. "I'm sorry. That was uncalled for. I shouldn't have said that, especially not now. Forgive me." She went over, leaned down, and gave her friend a hug. "I know you're still grieving over your mother. I'm sorry. Okay? You came over here to get your mind off of things and to help me, and here I am saying something like this. I was wrong. Please forgive me."

Fatima stood up. "But you're right. I've *not* been holy all of my life. In fact, even as a Christian, I've done some things I'm ashamed of. So I really don't have any place to judge you or anybody else, for that matter. I'm sorry for having acted like I'm holier than thou," Fatima said, returning Gabrielle's hug.

Gabrielle pulled back and smiled at her. "It's okay. I guess it comes with the territory. I suppose I just thought Christians, of all people, would appreciate what it means to be a sinner saved by grace. I was a sinner, I admit that. I gave my life to the Lord. And now, my old life is gone, at least, not being held against me. That's how I thought it was supposed to work anyway," Gabrielle said.

"I suspect that proves we've all sinned and fallen short of the glory of God. It's why Jesus told us not to judge, so we wouldn't be judged by that same measuring stick." Fatima sighed. "Here I was somewhat throwing mud about what you used to do when my own hands aren't exactly mud free. I know I would hate for you to find out some of the things I've done in my past. I know that much."

"Don't worry about it," Gabrielle said. "But back to my Sasha and Alicia story. I thought they were looking at me funny because of what was being said about me. So I confronted them, trying to see if I'd personally done anything to them. That's when Sasha went off on me about taking a man she had her eye on—Doctor Morgan. Well, I'm arguing that I don't have a clue what she's talking about. I'm thinking she's referring to my new job where I'm working for Doctor Morgan. I'm completely confused, thinking that she wanted the housecleaning job I'd secured. I thought she had a job at the bank. Well, suffice it to say, she didn't know what I was talking about either. She didn't know I cleaned houses for a living. She only knew she'd seen me talking to Doctor Z. W. or, as she calls him, Doctor Z., after the celebratory service, and she felt I'd done her wrong. That's when we unraveled that Doctor Z. W. Morgan was my Zachary Wayne Morgan.

"I'm standing there in shock, discovering that the house where I'd just so excitedly left working earlier that day happens to belong to the guy I've started having a relationship with. Boy, did I feel stupid. And then, it hit me. Queen was the person I was dealing with at the house that belonged to Doctor Morgan. Queen is pregnant. Zachary was married, and that meant I was dating a married man." Gabrielle released a quiet sigh, then wiped her face with her hand. "You have no idea how it feels to know you're fooling around with a married man."

Fatima dropped her head slightly. In fairness, this would be a great place for her to come clean about the affair she'd had with Darius. After all, she and Gabrielle were friends now. But she just couldn't bring herself to show her scars to Gabrielle. Besides, it wasn't like it was a requirement for her to be forgiven. She'd confessed it years ago to God, and He'd forgiven her. There really was no reason to confess it to Gabrielle. But what she could do was tell Gabrielle how Johnnie Mae had helped her when she had had a problem and needed someone to talk to.

"Does Johnnie Mae know about what you did before? I'm sure she's heard, now that it's making its rounds through the church. Talk to her about it. You can even talk to her about Zachary if you feel you need to. You don't have to give her names. She's a great confidante."

"Yes, I told her everything after my audition. She knew before any of this got out. She had talked it over with Pastor Landris. They agreed that whatever I'd done in my past shouldn't be held against me in what I'm doing for the Lord now. Johnnie Mae said that God has forgiven me, so who were they to make me pay more than God was doing?"

"That's why I love Johnnie Mae and Pastor Landris. They are so real. They really get it. They get what Christianity is all about," Fatima said. "But this thing with Zachary, now that's messed up."

"So now do you understand why I don't want to talk to Zachary?" Gabrielle said.

"Yeah. But I know it can be hard to walk away. Most times, the best way to handle it is to cut it off completely," Fatima said. "Just like you're doing."

"You don't think I'm wrong or a coward because I won't talk to him and at least tell him what I know?"

"No, I don't think you're wrong. You don't owe him anything. The way it sounds, he's the one wrong. He's the one trying to pull one over on both you and his wife. I'm so tired of men trying to have their taco and eat it, too," Fatima said.

"Taco? I thought it was cake."

Fatima smiled. "I like tacos. Taco, cake, box of candy, it all means the same. They want to have what they have but be able to eat it, too."

"I won't bother calling him back then. I had said I would tell him what I knew after I left his house," Gabrielle said. "Now that you and I have talked, I'm not going to bother doing even that much. Let him figure it out. He needs to move on. Either work on his relationship with his wife or find someone else who's interested in fooling around with him. Sasha certainly sounded like she was interested. I'm not sure if she knows he's married or if she cares. You never know about folks. But I'm not going there with him or any other married man."

Gabrielle's phone rang. She checked the caller ID. It was Zachary again. "Humph," she said. "He's calling me from a different number now. Looks like a home phone number. I guess that must mean Queen isn't around."

"Ignore it," Fatima said. "Or you'll find yourself dealing with it as a stronghold."

Gabrielle sighed. "I just wonder how long it's going to take him to get the message?"

Fatima thought about Darius and how even years after breaking up, he still tried every now and then to talk to her. "Hopefully, soon," she said. "Hopefully, soon."

# Chapter 40

*Let your light so shine before men, that they
may see your good works, and glorify your
Father which is in heaven.*

—Matthew 5:16

Gabrielle started work at a different house on
Monday. The person there was not nearly as
nice as Queen. She really did talk down her nose
at Gabrielle and had specific ways she wanted
things to be done. On Tuesday, Gabrielle was told
it wasn't necessary for her to attend the closing of
her house Wednesday. Only the buyer was needed.
Wednesday evening, her Realtor called to let her
know that everything had gone smoothly, and that
she'd officially sold her house. When Gabrielle inquired about the date she would need to be out of
the house, her Realtor told her the buyer hadn't
specified that date yet. But he had her phone number. She could expect to hear from him soon. As
much as Gabrielle had needed this sale to happen,
still she cried. She loved her house. It was bittersweet indeed.

At Bible study, she could barely contain her delight in having finally officially sold her house. She
saw Fatima and told her the good news. She passed

Sasha in the hall, who was a bit warmer to her than she'd been even Tuesday during dance ministry meeting. Other people were a little more cordial, although a few acted as though if they were to accidentally touch her or get too close to her, they might contract some kind of a disease or something. When Mother Franklin and Mother Robinson saw her, they beckoned for her to come over.

"Baby," Mother Franklin said, "we just want to tell you not to let none of these prunes get to you. Folks are awfully good at pointing a finger at other folks. But they tend to forget that when they do that, they have three other fingers pointing right back at them."

"Trust me," Mother Robinson said, "the things I could tell on and about some of these folks right here in *this* church would make most of them run out of here with their holier-than-thou tails between their legs. You just keep blessing folks with your gift and keep on letting the Lord use you. That gift you have, it's from the Lord. He created you for *His* service. This is what He intended for you to do with it. Okay, so you got off track. Who hasn't? And now, you're back. Some folks don't ever get back. They take their God-given gifts and squander them in the world. You ever hear the parable of the Prodigal Son?"

"Yes, ma'am," Gabrielle said.

"Well, just like that child finally came to his senses and went back home to his father, people like you and others that went out into the world to see what it had to offer and come back make God happy when you come back to our Father in Heaven," Mother Robinson said, then beckoned for her to come even closer. She gave Gabrielle a big grandmotherly hug, complete with the usual "Mmmm-uh!" sound effect.

"She's right. You just hold your head up. Don't you dare let nobody get to you. God's gonna take care of those who judge you and do you wrong," said Mother Franklin.

When Gabrielle got home, Clarence's car was parked in her driveway. She knocked on his window. Apparently sitting there with his eyes closed, he jumped, then smiled when he saw it was only her. He opened his car door and got out.

"Hey, what are you doing here?" Gabrielle said as they started toward her house.

"I came to check on my investment," he said.

She stopped. "Clarence, now I told you: if you've done anything thinking you're going to get something out of it, that's not going to happen. I'm not coming back to work for you. I'm just not."

"Are you deaf? I said I came to check on my investment."

Gabrielle unlocked her front door and stepped inside. "I heard what you said. I just hope you heard what I said."

He started laughing as he followed behind her. "This is really nice," he said, looking around as though he'd never been inside of her house before. "Real nice."

"Yeah, well. I officially sold it today. So if you had wanted it, you should have bought it for yourself." Gabrielle set her purse down on a table.

"I agree. And you're absolutely right. And I did."

"You did what?"

"I bought this house," Clarence said. He walked over, opened the hall closet, then looked inside. "Very nice," he said as he closed it.

"What do you mean you bought this house?"

"I mean, I *bought* this house. Straight out purchased it. Completed the deal today. I have my paperwork with me, if you'd care to see it."

"No, I believe you." She looked at him, suddenly touched by his generous action. "Why? Why would you buy my house?"

He chuckled. "Why does anybody buy a house? You either need a place to live or think it's a good investment. I sort of need some new investment ventures. My daddy always told us that you can never go wrong investing your money in real estate."

"Clarence, you did this for me, didn't you. And you paid the full price." She shook her head as she looked affectionately at him and placed her hand on his arm.

"Now, don't go getting all sappy on me. You know I'm a businessman. I just figure it's time I expanded my stream of income. I was thinking I could buy this house and maybe rent it out or sell it on my own terms. You wouldn't happen to know anyone who needs a place to live, now, would you?" He grinned. "I'm a great landlord if they're looking to rent, or I can set up a nice payment plan if they want to purchase on friendlier terms. With the housing market like it still is, I'm willing to work with them."

"Clarence, what can I say?"

"Just thank God. Apparently, He's still working on me. Otherwise, even I can't explain why in the *world* I did something like this. It's crazy! Maybe I'm getting soft."

"Thank you," she said to Clarence. Then, looking up, she said, "Thank You."

"Now, do you think it would be okay if I see a little more of what I just bought myself?"

She laughed. "I'll be glad to give you a personal tour. This house has some great features." She stopped and looked at him. "You're coming to church with me Sunday, right? Please, say yes. Come one time, and I promise I'll not ask you anymore. Please."

"We'll see. If I do, will you promise you'll leave me the dickens alone about it?"

Her phone rang. She smiled at him. "I promise."

"You can get that. I can wait," he said, after she didn't move to go get it.

She went and looked at the caller ID. It was Zachary again. When it went to the answering machine, Zachary didn't bother to leave a message this time. She then took Clarence on a microtour of the house.

# Chapter 41

*God hath not cast away his people which
he foreknew. Wot ye not what the scripture
saith of Elijah? How he maketh intercession
to God against Israel.*

— Romans 11:2

Sunday, Clarence was true to his word. Dressed
in a dark blue, three button, notched lapel tai-
lored suit, he looked like he'd just stepped out of
*GQ* magazine. He came by and picked up Gabrielle. Gabrielle was also surprised to see Queen at
church. She was there alone. Zachary didn't appear to be with her. She and Queen hugged and
exchanged quick pleasantries before she and Clarence went inside and sat down. They were four
rows from the front. Clarence sat in the seat at the
end of the row.

Clarence fidgeted a little during prayer time.
Gabrielle could tell he wasn't as comfortable during that part of the service. But he really got into
the singing portion, standing as he clapped on
beat. During one song, he even did perfect double
claps. She knew that only experienced people
could double clap *and* keep time. He really did
have a wonderful voice with perfect pitch. Several

people turned around and looked at him, smiling, as they'd wanted to see exactly whom the smooth baritone sound was originating from.

Pastor Landris took the stand and began his sermon, using scriptures from Romans 8:1 and Galatians 6.

"I have been a bit disturbed about something over these past few weeks," Pastor Landris began. "Many of you have been hearing things that have made their way through our congregation. You may have been presented this information by someone who prefaced it under the guise of praying for someone who needed prayers. Well, if you ask me, I'd say that's just a phony cover for gossip. And what's *sad* is how many people are excited, thinking they've come across something juicy on someone else, and they can't wait to tell it to somebody else. Some of you have even said things to me, declaring that you don't think it's right that a sinner of such a caliber should be working in *our* church." Pastor Landris rocked his body back and forth a few times.

As he rocked, he was thinking about his conversations with a few members who had voiced their disgust and opposition when it came to Gabrielle having once danced as an exotic dancer before she became saved and was now being allowed to dance in church. He was thinking about Reverend Marshall Walker, who had called him to personally register his disagreement at his having allowed, let alone supported, such a disgrace to take place in the "Lord's house." Reverend Walker had even gone so far as to tell him that the young woman needed to be sat down and not allowed to serve, at least not in a capacity such as that.

"I'm not trying to tell you how to run your church over there," Reverend Walker had said, "but you need to put her on the usher board or have her join the choir. As the pastor, you need to set a standard when it comes to church and what people who have a past like hers should be allowed to do when it comes to the Lord's work and His house."

Pastor Landris couldn't believe how someone who had done what he knew Reverend Walker to have done in his own past could be such a hypocrite about others serving in the "Lord's house." But then again, Reverend Walker wasn't aware of the envelope in his possession that spoke to his own past secrets and misdeeds, secrets and misdeeds Reverend Walker believed long buried and now buried for good with the final interment three years ago of his friend (and the only person who knew) Poppa Knight.

Pastor Landris continued with his sermon. "Apparently, some folks didn't get the original memo, so allow me to text you a message real quick. Let me IM you. Allow me to send you an e-mail. 'You've got mail!'" he said. "Before you accepted Jesus, you were a sinner. In layman's terms, that means you sinned. Now, I know some of you want to dress up your own personal sins. You want to put lipstick on yours, put yours in a nice Armani suit with some classy Stacy Adams shoes. You want to stick a pair of Prada shoes on your sin . . . let it strut around like a male peacock. Now, I'm not saying that you're proud of your sins. It's just most of you think your sin was *not so bad* as someone else's. You know, I might have been a thief, but at least I didn't kill anybody—*that* kind of proud. Well, a sin is a sin. I've said this before, and I'll say it again: There are no big sins or little sins. Sin is sin. This means if you're saved right now, then you were once a sinner. And if any of you are working in the church, then that means we have former sinners working in church. No ifs, ands, or buts. Former sinners working in the church."

Pastor Landris paused for effect, then continued. "This is the place sinners are supposed to be able to come to get help, to get saved, to be forgiven. This is the place we come to get built up. But the way some of you have acted over these past few weeks, *you* have been walking in sin. And quite frankly, you need to come . . . No, you need to *run* up here when I open up the floor for people to come after I finish this sermon. Jesus came for the lost. Do you understand what that means? Jesus left Heaven and came to earth to save the lost. It means this is the place people *should* come for help. Not come to hear you running your mouth as you try to put them down. And when we have someone who has done exactly what Christ asked each of us to do, which is to repent, to turn from what you *were* doing wrong and to go in a different direction, what do you do? You run your mouth about them. Jesus said those who are well don't need a physician. It's those who are sick that need a doctor.

"We have people right here today in *this* church who have heard the Word, they came forth, confessed their sins, believed Jesus died on the cross for their sins, believed that God raised Jesus from the dead. And you who think you know more than God have the nerve, have decided to *still* condemn them for something that Jesus has brought them out of? That Jesus has forgiven them for? That's a disgrace! It is." Pastor Landris nodded.

"Some of you think you're something, when in truth, you're not any better than the person you're trying to put down," Pastor Landris continued. "God forbid, if some of *your* past secrets, and for some of you here, your *present* secrets ever see the light of day. Oh, yeah, I said it. God knows about them. Don't be fooled, don't be fooled. God knows.

"But, it's verse seven of Galatians six that you really need to be mindful of. People use this one for money all the time, but it's more than about money. It says, 'Be not deceived; God is not mocked: for whatsoever a man soweth, that shall he also reap.' What you sow, that's what you're going to reap." Pastor Landris shook his head slowly as he frowned.

"I'm not fussing at you if you were one who participated in this nonsense these past few weeks. If you were carrying this garbage or somebody brought it to you, and you allowed them to lay it down at your feet without making them pick it up and take that mess out of your sight, then you need to ask for forgiveness. We're running people out of the church, away from doing the Lord's work, because we're *wrong* in our thinking, because of a *spirit* of *tradition*. And I am telling you right here, right now, this needs to stop. The harvest is plentiful but the labors are few, and you're still acting like children all excited about a bunch of 'he said, she said' mess. Now, will we as Christians miss the mark sometimes? Yes. But when you know better, you need to do better.

"Church is not a clique. Church is not a social club where the goal is to keep out all the undesirables. Quite the opposite. We're recruiting sinners to give up their old ways and come over to the side of Jesus. I'm going to say this once more. Church houses . . . congregations are full of former sinners working, *working*. So, if you have a problem with that here, then you're in the wrong place. I'm not mad at you. If you don't like this fact, then you're more than welcome to leave here. Because we're not going to change it. Not *this* congregation of believers. Not this congregation." Pastor Landris paused as he began to wind down.

"There's somebody sitting here today, right here *today*, who's been hurt by Christians . . . Christians. They're sitting in *this* congregation. Sure, they may have been hurt by people in the world before, but these folks quit the congregation . . . left the church body because of Christians—people claiming to be followers of Christ. These folks have moved on because of something *Christians* have done to them. Such a loss, and for no reason. God's heart is hurting right now. When we do these things, we're hurting the cause.

"God, forgive us. Forgive us. Forgive us, Lord." Pastor Landris looked upward. "We didn't know what we were doing. We didn't realize we were doing the work of your adversary by running our fellow sisters and brothers away. Forgive us, Lord.

We didn't realize we were breaking Your heart when You were speaking to that man, that woman, that boy, or that girl, telling them to come to You. That lost child may have been on his way to You until we started acting just like, if not worse than, the world. It's supposed to be different with us. *We're* supposed to be different. We're called to be representatives of You and Your love. But instead, we've been selfish. Thinking only of ourselves— our needs, our wants. Forgive us for those we've hurt or run away. Please, give us another opportunity, Lord. We want to do better. We're striving to be a better people. Please, help us to be more like You." Pastor Landris stopped speaking. He couldn't continue. He was full now. He merely stepped forward and held out his arms.

After a minute, and finally able to pull himself together, he said, "If you're here today, and you're one of those who have been hurt, won't you come today? I may not have been the one who hurt you, but please accept my apology for the one who did. Forgive them, for they knew not what they were doing. And if you're here and you've hurt someone and you know you have: Maybe you didn't know what you were doing at the time. Maybe you did. Maybe you got swept up in the moment. But you realize it now, and you want to ask God's forgiveness. Won't you come as well? If you want to be saved, reconciled, forgiven of sin, to rededicate your life, or you're looking for a church home, won't you come now? Please come. He's waiting on you. God is waiting on you. He's waiting on *you*."

Clarence jumped up and almost ran to the front.

He was wiping his face when he got up there. Gabrielle started crying. She stood and started praising God. She had prayed for Clarence, but seeing it happen—she found herself overflowing with joy. It was the joy of the Lord. He'd actually gone up there. "Thank You, Jesus!"

Gabrielle then saw Queen get up and go forth and Fatima and Sasha, and she started shouting even more. The front was full, and people were still coming forward. Some asking to be forgiven, some asking for acceptance, some to become part of the ministry, too many to even begin to count— on their knees, praising God, standing solemn at the altar. There was something special taking place. Gabrielle could feel it. It was a joy that words couldn't formulate or speak. *Dance! Dance! Dance!* She heard that word bubbling up inside of her like a nice cool spring.

So, dance she did!

# Chapter 42

*For how great is his goodness, and how great is his beauty! corn shall make the young men cheerful, and new wine the maids.*

*—Zechariah 9:17*

Gabrielle waited outside the area of the conference room where they'd taken Clarence and the others who had gone forth to be saved.

"Hi," Zachary said, surprising Gabrielle when she saw it was him speaking to her.

"Hi," she said, unable to be mad with all the joy she now felt.

"I've missed you."

She ticked her head a little to the left without responding to that statement.

"I saw your friend go up today," Zachary said. "I know how you must feel."

"Words can't even begin to express how I feel," Gabrielle said, smiling.

"Is that why you didn't call me back? Because you found someone else, and you didn't want to tell me?" Zachary said.

She looked at him, disbelieving he was calling her on being with someone when he was married.

"I saw Queen go up there. I'm sure you're happy about that as well."

He smiled. "Yeah, I really am. I told her about the church that Sunday I came. She wasn't interested. She's one who's been burned by church folks. I can't tell you what that sermon meant to *so* many today. Goodness, that was a powerful message." Zachary touched her hand. "Listen, I'd like to talk to you. There are things I need to explain."

"You don't owe me any explanations, *Doctor* Morgan. A doctor." She shook her head.

"Oh, but I do," Zachary said. "I don't want to cause any problems with you and your friend. But you and I really need to talk."

"Come on, now. You're married, Zachary," Gabrielle said, allowing her frustration to shine through. "We're here in church, and you're *still* trying to talk to me?"

"Married? Who told you I was married?"

"Excuse me, but I've been to your house. I've met Queen. Queen Esther. I worked at your house for four days. She and I talked at great length. You know, Queen . . . your wife?"

He started laughing.

"Oh, so that's funny to you, huh?" Gabrielle began to walk away.

He quickly came up behind her and grabbed her by her arm and spun her around. "Gabrielle, please don't go." He was now chuckling. "Is that what's been bothering you? You met Queen Esther?"

On cue, Queen walked up and immediately fell into Zachary's arm for a hug. She turned to Gabrielle as she continued hugging Zachary. "Well, I see we meet again," Queen said, letting Zachary go to hug Gabrielle, then settling back comfortably in Zachary's arm, now around her shoulders. "I tell you, this *must* be divine intervention," Queen said. "So, I see you two have finally met. I've wanted you both to meet for so long. And then, that powerful message today from Pastor Landris, my goodness! I do believe I'm about ready to take wings and fly at this point. Wow, is all I can say!"

"Yes," Gabrielle said, not nearly as enthusiastically as Queen. "Well, I suppose I need to go find my friend. This is his first time here. I would hate for him to get lost wandering around this place. Queen, it was good seeing you again." She hugged Queen.

"Before you go," Queen said, grabbing her by the forearm. "I'm curious. What do you think of my brother?"

"Your brother?"

"Yeah. My brother." She smiled. "What do you think of him?" She looked over at Zachary. "I admit, he doesn't know how to talk to a woman. Say something, Zachary."

"*This* is your brother?" Gabrielle said, almost laughing as Zachary stood grinning. "This is *your* brother?" She pointed. "Him? Zachary is your *brother*? The brother you were saying you wanted me to meet? *That* brother?"

"Yes. When I told him on Saturday you'd been to the house, his house actually, and how you knew Aunt Esther, he was more than surprised, to say the least. Have you two not spoken yet?"

"No," Zachary said with a fake attitude. "But it hasn't been for a lack of trying. Apparently, there was some misunderstanding. Hopefully, Gabrielle will give me a chance to discuss things, now that we've cleared up that little misunderstanding." He looked at Gabrielle as he waited for her answer.

Gabrielle thought about what had happened. She started chuckling, then couldn't hold back a full laugh. "Yes, I believe we'll be hashing out a few things soon."

"Great. So I can call you later?" Zachary said to Gabrielle.

She smiled. "Sure. I'll be home. You can call me later."

Clarence came out of the conference room. Gabrielle waved so he would see her standing there. When he came over, she hugged him. "I am *so* happy for you," she said.

"God is good," Clarence said. "I wish I could express what and how I'm feeling right now." He shook his head and wiped his eyes. "Whew! I'm ready to get back to work in the service of the Lord."

"Clarence, I'd like you to meet Queen Esther . . ."

"Mabry," Queen said.

"Queen Esther Mabry," Gabrielle said, thinking that had she known her last name instead of assuming it was Morgan, she might not have jumped to the wrong conclusion.

"And this is her brother, Doctor Zachary Morgan."

"You can call me Z. W.," Zachary said.

Clarence shook Queen's hand, then Zachary's.

"And this is my friend, whom I'd like to say I am more proud of today than I've ever been since I've known him, Clarence Walker," Gabrielle said.

"It's nice to meet you. Any friend of Goo"—he stopped himself after almost slipping and calling her Goodness—"Gabrielle's is a friend of mine."

"Thank you for that," Zachary said.

"I'm just glad to be back on the battlefield for the Lord. I've not only decided to be baptized again, but I've also decided to join here. I'm excited about what God is doing in my life," Clarence said.

Clarence now knew he had to follow where God was leading him. And *this* is where he was being led. There was much in his life that would require changes. But he was grateful that Gabrielle had shown him not only that change was possible and could be done with integrity but just *how* it could be done. No matter how difficult, one had to be totally sold out for the Lord and trust Him completely. Clarence felt assured that God has a way of working things out.

# Chapter 43

*And I will strengthen the house of Judah, and I will save the house of Joseph, and I will bring them again to place them; for I have mercy upon them: and they shall be as though I had not cast them off: for I am the Lord their God, and will hear them.*

—Zechariah 10:6

People came up to Gabrielle and either hugged her or apologized. They didn't tell her what they'd done to need her forgiveness, but she knew Pastor Landris's sermon had hit home. She smiled, and to those who asked her to forgive them, her response was, "Of course, just as my Father in Heaven forgives me of my trespasses."

Darius walked over to Gabrielle. He appeared almost to drag Tiffany with him. At the time, Clarence wasn't standing next to Gabrielle. One of the ministers of music, having already been told of Clarence's beautiful singing voice, had pulled him off to the side to talk to him about possibly joining the choir after he officially became a member. As Clarence started back toward Gabrielle, he thought he detected hostility coming from Darius. When he walked up on them, what he thought was going on was indeed the case. Darius was telling Gabrielle, in a quiet but disrespectful tone, that he was *not* the source of the gossip being spread, in spite of what other people might be attributing to him. He felt that the entire situation was making him look bad when he'd had nothing to do with what was running rampant throughout the congregation.

Gabrielle wasn't interested in arguing with Darius. She told him she didn't know who had done it, but she was thankful Pastor Landris had handled it and hopefully put it to rest. But Darius kept repeating that he wasn't the one who had tried to start anything, and he wanted her to know he was innocent. And that if she happened to be the one telling people he'd been the one who began spreading that information about her, then she needed to put a stop to it and quit tainting his reputation and hurting his family.

"I don't have a clue *what* you did before you came to this church," Darius lied, "other than what I've heard myself. And this kind of gossip with my name attached to it is hurting my wife and children." He glanced over at Tiffany, who seemed uncomfortable and looked as though all she wanted to do was leave.

"Hey, man," Clarence said as he walked up and slapped Darius on his back. He grabbed his hand and started shaking it vigorously, even though Darius was trying hard to take his hand back. "Good to see you again."

"I'm sorry, but you must have me confused with

someone else," Darius said, finally able to yank his hand out of Clarence's big, strong hand. He took a step back.

"It's Darius, right?" Clarence said. "Darius Connors? Man, don't be trying to front me like you don't know me."

"Yes, Darius is my name. But I-I-I don't know you." Darius stammered as he spoke. He began to cut his eyes over to Tiffany, a well-designed signal for them not to say anything more. He was praying Clarence would pick up on the signal and not continue in front of his wife.

"Of course you know me," Clarence said. "Why, you practically *live* down at my establishment." He chuckled. "In fact, truth be told, you have pretty much kept my place in business. Okay, maybe that's an exaggeration on my part." Clarence leaned in as though they were the best of buddies. "But you're a regular, that's for sure. Of course, with me going up today to be saved and all and giving my life over to the Lord, I'll be closing up my little dance place. Yep. Yep, I just gave my life to the Lord for real this time around. I even plan on being water baptized again next Sunday night. Mostly because when I went up the first time to shake the preacher's hand, back when I was young and was made to go up by my father, it didn't come from my heart. And salvation is about the heart more than some empty action. Anyway, things are about to change big-time in my life, big-time. But I'm glad to see you here. So, did you go up front today to ask for forgiveness, too?"

Tiffany looked at Darius, then stormed off.

"Thanks a lot, *Clarence*," Darius said, then quickly hurried after his wife.

"No problem. My pleasure," Clarence said loudly, forcing the words to follow Darius. "Good seeing you again!" He looked at Gabrielle and started grinning.

"Now, you know you were being bad, don't you?"

"Yeah, well, *that* bad was for a good cause. I absolutely *despise* hypocrites. Always have. And then, for him to be over here trying to make you out to be the bad guy and him as some kind of a saint. Nope, I was *not* going to stand around and let him get away with that," Clarence said. "Not on my watch. So, are you ready to go?"

"Yeah," she said, smiling. "I have something important to take care of later today."

"And what's that, if you don't mind me asking?"

"I need to talk to Zachary. I need to see if there's anything there for me and him to pursue in the way of a possible relationship."

Clarence nodded as they walked to his car. "You really like that guy, don't you?"

"Who?"

"Don't be acting like you're an owl; you know who. Zachary."

"Why do you say that?"

"Oh, yeah"—he grinned—"you like him. You like him a lot!"

When they reached his car, he opened his door and slid inside.

Gabrielle opened her own door and got in. She couldn't help but smile as she thought about how Zachary always opened the door for her.

"Yeah, I do," she finally said, in answer to Clarence's question. "I really do."

But Gabrielle faced a dilemma. Would she tell Zachary everything he needed to know about her past? Everything? The fact that she had been an exotic dancer. Of course she would tell him that. But what about her other secret? The secret no one else even had a clue about. Was now the time for her to come clean with someone about it, for her to come clean with him? Or should she just wait and see how the relationship developed over time, and if things looked like they were getting serious, then she could tell him? God would truly have to direct her on this one.

# Chapter 44

*Beloved, believe not every spirit, but try the spirits whether they are of God: because many false prophets are gone out into the world.*

—1 John 4:1

Reverend Marshall Walker's cell phone rang. Surprised to see who it was when he looked, he hurriedly answered it.

"Hey, how are you?" Reverend Walker said, bypassing the customary greeting of just hello.

"I'm great. Doing *very* well, in fact," the deep male voice said.

"It's been a long time," Reverend Walker said. "I'm surprised you still have my cell phone number. It's good to hear your voice."

"Yeah, it has been a while. Look, I just wanted to call and let you know before you hear it from someone else, I went forward today and gave my life to Christ," the male voice said. "I'm scheduled to be baptized next Sunday night at six. I would love for you to come."

"You gave your life to Christ? You're being baptized? Why would you do that? You've already done that before. You joined the church, and you were water baptized when you were twelve years old. What's the matter with you?" Reverend Walker said.

"Nothing's the matter with me. For the first time, I feel like I'm actually doing the right thing. I would think you'd be happy for me. Proud even. Isn't this what you've been praying for . . . that I would come back to the Lord?"

"I'm glad you're coming back to the Lord. And yes, that is what I've been praying for. But if you were going to rededicate your life—"

"I'm not rededicating my life. I didn't dedicate it the first time around."

"Okay," Reverend Walker said. "If that's what you believe. But if you were going to do this, why didn't you come to my church and do it? Can you imagine the impact that would have had on my congregation? To see you returning home like the Prodigal Son? That would have been scripture coming alive for all of us. You know I'm not the only one who's been praying for you. We've all been praying for a long time."

"Well, I didn't intend to do this today."

"Where were you?" Reverend Walker asked.

"Followers of Jesus Faith Worship Center."

"Pastor George Landris's church? I should have known. What is that man *doing* over there?"

"Preaching the Word. Living the Word. Being a doer of the Word and not just a hearer only. Telling people what the Word says and not letting them live and do anything and think that it's okay."

"Don't take that tone with me," Reverend Walker said. "I'm still your father."

"Yeah, Dad. You're *still* my father."

"Clarence," Reverend Walker said, "I know things have been strained between us over these years. But I still love you. Listen, I'm happy something got through to you to make you see that you needed to repent. You know the Bible tells us if we train up our children in the way they should go, when they're old, they won't depart from it. I know your mama and I did our best, even if she and I did end up going our separate ways. I still love the children we had together. I'm looking for you and your other brothers to carry on the family name. I was hoping and praying one of you would carry on the family business—my church I've worked so hard to build. So, why don't you come on back home? Come back to Divine Conquerors Church, where you belong."

"Dad, I'm staying at Pastor Landris's church. There's something different there. I'm not trying to hurt your feelings, but I can't serve God sitting under you. I just can't," Clarence said.

"Fine. Embarrass me then. Stay over there and have folks talking about why my own son, who was a total disgrace by having that devil's dancing lair with all those women and pathetic men hanging out day in and day out, won't even come back to be under his father's ministry. Give people one more thing to drag my good name through the mud about. Of course, I shouldn't be surprised."

"Dad, I didn't call you for all of this. I called to let you know how much I love the Lord, and that today, He answered my cry." Clarence couldn't hold it any longer. He began to softly cry. "Dad, God is real. Do you hear me? God is real! He's real in my soul. He's not just an idea or a thought. He's real! And today was the first time I've actually seen that He's real for myself!"

"Oh, so what are you saying? That you didn't see God in my life? That you didn't know God was real after all I've preached and taught all of my life? I was eighteen when I was called into the ministry. Eighteen. I've been on the battlefield for a long time," Reverend Walker said. "I bet you Pastor Landris will have you working in that church before long. Probably up there singing like you ain't never done a thing wrong in your life."

"Dad, if God can use what He's given me for His service, then I want to be used. I don't want to argue with you. I just thought for some crazy reason that you might be happy for me. I suppose some things never change. But you know what, Dad?"

"What?" Reverend Walker said bluntly.

"I still love you. In spite of everything, I still love you. And I'm going to keep on loving you because I have the love of God in my heart. I don't wish any ill to come to you. Despite how awful you were to my mother. Despite the fact that you didn't do right by us after you and she divorced and you took a new wife and family. I still love you."

"Well, I love you, too. And I'm going to pray that God opens your eyes and lets you see that you need to come home to my church, where you not only need to be but where you belong." Reverend Walker tempered his voice. "Look, I need to get off the phone now. But I do hope we talk again soon. Good-bye for now, son."

After Clarence said good-bye, Reverend Walker

clicked off his cell phone. Looking at the now-silent phone, he nodded several times before slightly tossing it onto some papers on his desk.

"Yes, Lord, Pastor Landris has messed with the wrong one this time. My own flesh and blood . . . choosing this man and his church over me?" He shook his head before resting it against his over-stuffed burgundy leather chair. He then placed his fingers together in a steeplelike fashion and closed his eyes.

# Chapter 45

*And I will sow her unto me in the earth; and I will have mercy upon her that had not obtained mercy; and I will say to them which were not my people, Thou art my people; and they shall say, Thou art my God.*

—Hosea 2:23

Zachary couldn't wait to call Gabrielle. He was so relieved to find out this had all been a big misunderstanding. He and Queen laughed about it on their way home. How something so innocent could have gotten so blown out of proportion.

Queen had come to visit him from Pensacola, Florida, at his new house to help him get settled in. Actually, she and her husband were having marital problems, and she needed to get away for a little while . . . separate herself while they tried to work things out. She didn't know when she would be returning home since her husband didn't appear to be making any real efforts to do better. Zachary had told her she was welcome to stay at his home as long as she needed.

It had been all her idea to hire a housekeeper. Zachary didn't care one way or the other since he

worked so much and wouldn't be home that often
for it to matter. He knew he would get around to
unpacking things and putting them away eventually. And as for cleaning the house once things
were in their proper places, well, he knew how to
run the vacuum cleaner and how to dust. He had a
dishwasher, so cleaning the kitchen would be relatively easy. His dry cleaner washed and ironed his
white shirts. Besides, when Queen wasn't there, no
one was at the house to mess up but him. *How
much of a mess could one man make by himself?*

When Queen came, she knew she couldn't do
much unpacking, being five months pregnant and
told by her doctor she needed to take it easy since
she'd miscarried twice already. She couldn't put
away a lot, especially anything that required her
bending or lifting too much. So she'd asked a few
of the neighbors for a housekeeper recommendation, and she learned many of them used the same
agency to find great, dedicated housekeepers. She
decided to go with that agency.

Zachary agreed to go along with whatever she
decided, but he told her he had neither the time
nor interest in getting involved. It was all her pro-
ject. All he needed to know was how much to write
the check for. She could hire the person she
thought was right and direct the housekeeper on
what she wanted done. And maybe, just maybe,
after everything was set up, he might decide to
contract her to come in once or twice a week after
Queen went back home. But the way things were
going with Queen and her husband, it didn't look
like that would be anytime soon.

Since after Queen left, he would be there alone,

he actually thought once a week would be too often. But Queen informed him that he couldn't hire someone and only use them once every two weeks. At least, not someone from *that* prestigious agency.

"Besides, houses still get dusty, even if no one is there to make a mess," Queen said. "She'll still have plenty to do. Believe me, I know you. She'll have plenty to do."

But for now, there was enough work to employ a housekeeper for a month or two. So when Gabrielle showed up, it was Queen she'd met. And Queen was the one who told her what needed to be done and how. Gabrielle had learned Zachary was a doctor—something Zachary had failed to ever mention to her. He thought she had figured it out, so it wasn't like he'd tried purposely to keep that information from her. He just wasn't the type who bragged about his accomplishments—something Queen had told him more than a few times was a major character flaw. "If you've got it, flaunt it," she said.

When Gabrielle had put everything she knew together—Doctor Morgan, a woman, a pregnant woman at that, living at the house she was hired to clean—she couldn't help but arrive at any other conclusion except that Zachary Morgan was a liar and a cheat.

Zachary asked Gabrielle if he could come over so they could talk. She really didn't want to be alone with him in her house. She had strong feelings for him, and she just didn't trust them being alone for this particular talk. Besides, she'd packed a lot of her things when she'd first sold the house, thinking she would be moving out soon. Now, she was in the process of unpacking those things since she and Clarence had signed an agreement for her to buy the house from him at substantially reduced monthly payments from what she'd been paying to her mortgage company. *God was so good!*

What she'd been told was true. The devil may bring it, but if it's a blessing, it was sent by God. Every good and perfect gift *did,* in fact, come from above. And to think, in the process of her having not cut Clarence off completely after she became saved and he still wasn't, she'd helped win over a fellow brother to the Lord. Gabrielle had learned that as long as you stand strong on what you know is right and you don't compromise, you can become a light for Jesus to those walking in darkness. And the Bible says that if Jesus is lifted up, He will draw all men unto Him. That's just what had happened with Clarence.

Without her even realizing it, Clarence had watched her actions. He had heard her when she talked. He had seen the change in her life. She had prayed for him and with him. And on this day, when he heard the Word that had come forth, Clarence went running into the Lord's awaiting arms, asking what he needed to do to be saved. Gabrielle knew now, without a doubt, that this is what we're on this earth to do. Not just us getting saved, but that we become a light . . . a beacon, and hopefully help lead others to Christ. Dancing was the gift God had given her. But she now understood that the life we live before others was indeed the only Bible some people might ever read.

# Chapter 46

*He hath shewed thee, O man, what is good;
and what doth the Lord require of thee, but
to do justly, and to love mercy, and to walk
humbly with thy God?*

—Micah 6:8

Gabrielle was more determined now to live the way she believed God was calling her to. She decided, because of how she felt about Zachary, it was best they meet in a place where someone else would be present. Queen was still at his house, so she suggested they meet there.

They sat in the living room she'd so lovingly cleaned and decorated, and laughed at what had already transpired in their lives.

"May we begin again?" Zachary said.

"Sure."

"Hi, my name is Zachary Wayne Morgan. But a lot of people call me Z. W."

"Hi, Zachary. My name is Gabrielle Mercedes, although I was born Gabrielle Mercedes Booker. I dropped the Booker and legally changed my name to Gabrielle Mercedes because I liked the sound of it."

"I'm pleased to meet you, Gabrielle Mercedes," Zachary said with a quiet nod.

"And what exactly do you do for a living, Zachary?"

"I'm a doctor. I deal with burn victims mainly, although I'm quite proficient, and at home, in the emergency room whenever I'm called upon or needed."

"A doctor, huh? Wow, that's interesting. So, how long have you been a doctor?"

"I just finished my last year of residency earlier this year. I now have my own private practice. Many of my patients call me Doctor Z. or Doctor Z. W. There are a few who insist on calling me Doctor Morgan. I leave it up to them."

"So, what would you prefer I call you?"

He grinned. "Whatever you like," he said. "Zachary is fine. That's what my sister calls me when she's not calling me Z. or Z. W. You've met Queen, haven't you? She's my baby sister. I call her Q. when I want to mess with her. She acts like she hates it, but she loves being called a letter of the alphabet like she calls me. She's staying with me for a little while, helping me get my house in order." He turned more squarely toward Gabrielle. "So, Gabrielle, what do you do for a living?"

"Right now I'm a housekeeper. Earlier this year, I worked for a maid service. They downsized and ended up firing me, so I went through this employment agency that gets people assignments to clean specific homes exclusively. I loved the first house I was assigned to," she said, looking around the living room she'd recently cleaned and decorated. "I *truly* did. Nice place you have here, Doctor Morgan."

He nodded as he also scanned the room. "Yeah, my sister hired this off-the-chain housekeeper, and she really got things in order for me. Unfortunately, she asked to be reassigned, so I lost her, in more ways than I care to admit. I'm hoping I can somehow woo her back into my life. Any suggestions or advice?"

Gabrielle shrugged. "Well, you never know. I hear that God works in mysterious ways."

"It's true," said Zachary. "I'm a living witness." He raised his right hand.

"So, I take it you're not married, then?"

He shook his head and pouted his lips slightly. "No. Unfortunately not."

"Do you have anyone you're serious about in your life?"

He nodded. "You know, I have to be honest with you. I do."

Gabrielle looked at him as she tilted her head slightly. *"Really?"*

"Yeah," he said, smiling. "I met this woman back in January at this Inaugural Ball. She was the sweetest, most beautiful woman I'd ever laid eyes on. And on the inside, she was simply awesome. She and I talked. We danced a couple of times. Then at midnight, she suddenly had to leave. I didn't want to let her go. You see, I knew when I saw her that night that she would someday be my wife. But stupid me, I didn't get her phone number to contact her. I had nothing to go on except her church home and the way she danced.

"Then, one Sunday morning I was sitting in this

church, and right before me—dancing beautifully for the Lord—there she was. I was so ministered to by her dance that ushered us all into a place of praise and worship. After a powerful sermon, I went forward and joined this church. I'd been searching for a church home—I knew I had finally arrived. Afterward, I went in search of her, this woman who had danced into my heart, determined I would find her. There were others who tried to tell me that they were the one I sought. But the shoe just didn't fit any of them no matter how hard they tried to squeeze their foot into it, or slide their feet down to try to make it look as though it did." He took Gabrielle's hand.

Gabrielle looked lovingly into his eyes as he continued to speak. "But as only God can do things, we found each other again. It didn't matter the obstacles that came between us, I had found her. And she doesn't know this, but I knew I'd found *my* good thing. Because the Bible says that a man who finds a wife finds a good thing. I believe I've found my wife. We're nowhere near marriage yet, but I believe she's my wife. I know I'll have to court her so she'll know we're supposed to be together, and I don't plan to quit until she sees that she's my wife. No, I'm not a Prince Charming riding in on a white horse to take her away to live happily ever after. But I would like to give her the best of what I *do* have. I'd like to live as happily ever after as earthly and heavenly possible. I'd like the opportunity to love her the way Christ loves the church. So, what do you think?" Zachary said as he looked intensely at her.

Gabrielle removed her hand from his. "I think it

sounds like a classic Cinderella story, and I'm not sure that I believe in happily-ever-after endings either. But I do know that I care about you. And I would love for us to get to know each other better. It's just that I want to be sure we do it God's way. The sermon Pastor Landris preached today about people who talk about others and what they've done in the past, holding the sins of the past against one who is now serving the Lord. I have a confession to make. That message was partly prompted because of me."

"How so?"

"When I tell you this, I want you to know that I don't plan to hold you to anything you just said about me being your wife someday or you wanting to be with me." Gabrielle took a deep breath and released it slowly. "I used to be an exotic dancer . . . for close to eight years. My stage name was Goodness and Mercy. My last name, Booker, I dropped it also because it sounded too close to hooker. This year on January fourth, I gave my life to Christ, and I walked away from that life. And as only God can do it, I was able to put my gift of dance in service for God's Kingdom. Well, someone started the gossip throughout the congregation about my past life, my past job. And as you heard from Pastor Landris, that information was spreading like wildfire. Many people felt because of that, I shouldn't be allowed to dance in the dance ministry anymore. Before Pastor Landris's sermon today, there was the burning question: When people are forgiven of their past sins, are they truly forgiven, or should they still have to pay for those sins regardless? Pastor Landris addressed and answered that question beautifully today."

"So you were an exotic dancer?" Zachary said, obviously stunned as he sat up straighter.

"Yes."

"You mean a stripper? A real live stripper? With the pole and everything?"

"No. I didn't do the pole. Believe it or not, I actually approached my dancing, even there in that place, as though it was truly a craft. Funny mc. The woman who taught me—"

"Esther. My aunt. Queen told me about that. Of course, she didn't originally tell me your name. Just that the housekeeper who had just asked to be reassigned knew our aunt. I still can't believe it. Talk about six degrees of separation," he said, referring to the philosophy many held that most of us are only six people away from anyone we ever want to meet.

"Yes, your aunt Esther. She gave me so much. In fact, I dreamed of her earlier this year. And in my dream, she said there was more that God required of me. I went to church the Sunday after that dream, and I ended up giving my life to the Lord. And honestly, my life has not been the same since. I don't see things the way I used to. The old me died and was buried. This is who I am now. This is who arose with Christ."

Zachary nodded. "I see."

Gabrielle then took a deep breath and exhaled slowly. "There's one other thing I feel I need to tell you."

He looked her straight in her eyes. "There's more? All right. Go on."

She looked away as she gathered her courage. This was something she'd never spoken out loud before to anyone. She turned back toward him. "When I was eighteen, I had an affair with the father of a friend. He was thirty-three, self-assured, and quite the charmer. I had struggled most of my life to feel good about myself. My parents weren't around—my father, incarcerated for killing my mother. I had lived with my aunt and uncle, which is another story in itself. Upon turning eighteen, they told me I had to leave, get out on my own. Following that was this man telling me how wonderful . . . how beautiful I was, giving me all of this love and attention. Silly me. It was all just a game."

Zachary nodded. "Okay. So you had an affair with a married man who happened to be your friend's father. You were young. Look, I don't think you should beat yourself up about something like that. We've all done something in our past that we regret. I know I have. That's just the price of life."

She pressed her lips together tightly, nodded three times, then looked up before exhaling again as she looked back at him. "I got pregnant. No one knew about it except him. Needless to say, he didn't want me to have it since the baby would definitely mess up his sweet little life with his wife and family and all. He gave me money and told me to get an abortion." She continued to look at Zachary to gauge his reaction.

He merely nodded. "So, did you?"

"No. I went to a group home for unwed mothers

and had the baby." Gabrielle began to cry. "After I had her, a beautiful little girl, I kissed her, then signed papers to give her up for adoption. That was eight years ago. I was fine with my decision back then, but something has changed. I find myself wondering what she's doing now, what does she look like, is she being treated right, is she all right? And I have to be honest: it hurts."

Zachary reached over and touched her hand.

She got up and got a tissue, dabbing at her eyes as she sat back down.

"Are you all right?" Zachary asked.

"Yeah. Sure," she said as she shook it off and sat up strong. "So, if you've decided that the shoe really doesn't fit me either, then please don't feel bad. I won't feel like you're judging me. But there is a difference in judging sin and judging the person. Judging sin is fine; judging people is not something any of us should or are equipped to do. Only God can judge people's hearts. I realize that in being a doctor, you have an image you have to uphold. I just thought it only fair to lay everything out there before we proceed any further. I care too much about you to ever want to do anything to hurt you."

"Well!" Zachary said, slapping both his hands down loud and hard on his thighs simultaneously. "I suppose that's all settled now and out of the way."

"I suppose so." She held out her hand to shake his. "Still friends?"

"Gabrielle, I hope you don't take this the wrong way, but I really don't care to be friends with you." He stood up.

"Oh. Okay." She withdrew her hand and stood up as well. "Well, thanks for the talk." She reached down and picked up her slightly torn red Fendi purse, then started toward the front door alongside Zachary. Neither of them said a word as they walked.

When she reached the door, he opened it for her. "Well, I suppose this is good-bye," he said, matter-of-factly.

"Yes. I suppose so. Good-bye." She slightly dropped her head and turned to walk out of the opened door.

"Oh, Gabrielle, one more thing before you go," Zachary said.

She turned around slowly and in a weak voice said, "Yes?"

"What time would you like me to pick you up tonight?"

"What?" Gabrielle said, clearly puzzled.

"I have two tickets to the play tonight. You do know about the play tonight?"

"You mean the Broadway play that's been sold out for months now? The one *everybody* who can't get a ticket to is begging, borrowing, and trying to steal their way to? We rarely *ever* get a real Broadway play to come here to Birmingham. You can't possibly have tickets to that one!"

"Yes," he said, his chest stuck out, "I have tickets to *that* one."

"And you want *me* to go with you? Me?"

Zachary looked into her eyes. "With all of my heart," he said, his eyes seeming to dance with a slight twinkle. "I would be truly honored if you would go with me." He smiled.

"Even after all I just told you about myself?"

"Gabrielle, the Bible tells us that *all* have sinned and fallen short of the glory of God. Not *y'all* have sinned—all. That means all of us have something in our lives we wish we either hadn't done or could take back completely. *All* of us."

Zachary's mind quickly reflected back to his own past missteps. One in particular he hoped to someday soon tell her about. And in spite of her being so open and candid with him, now was not that time. Unlike her, he felt they needed to get to know each other better first. Then he would tell her all about what he'd done that had indirectly been the cause of his aunt being where she was now. He could only pray that Gabrielle wouldn't hold his misjudgments against him the way he wasn't holding hers against her now.

"And we need to plan a trip soon so you can visit Aunt Esther in Chicago. I think it will be wonderful for the both of you," Zachary said.

"Oh, I would love that! I have so much to tell her, so much to thank her for. I owe your aunt so much, so much. She absolutely physically saved me, even more than she'll ever know. I want her to know exactly what her being in my life has meant to me."

"So"—he snapped his fingers—"what time would you like me to pick you up tonight?" Zachary asked again. "And listen: I want us to court. Not date, court. The definition of court is to try to gain the love or affections of, especially to seek to marry. And like you, I want to do things the right way—God's way. Personally, I believe the man should find the woman. You might think that's Neanderthal or chauvinist thinking, but I believe it's biblical, as demonstrated in that verse I quoted to you earlier about a man who finds a wife finding a *good* thing. That's how I'd like to approach things with us."

"Me too. I don't want to do anything that would put us in a position to fail. So, how do you feel about no kissing between us except on the cheek, and keeping hugs brief?"

"Well, now, that's kind of radical. But I suppose if I could practically give up women for five years to pursue my medical credentials, I can go along with this with you for however long this courtship takes. But I'm telling you up front, it might be hard, because I'm *really* falling for you. Okay, so no kissing except politely on the cheek?" He shook his head. "I don't know, but for you, I'm willing to give it a try. Just please note the word *try*."

She smiled. "I'm falling for you, too, Zachary. Which is precisely why we don't need to tempt things. I can't promise you right now that I'm strong enough to fight the feelings we might develop even from something as innocent as a kiss. I can't promise I'm strong enough. That's how a lot of fires get started. An innocent kiss, then more kissing, passions begin to ignite, then before you know anything—poof! Fire!"

"But what if we get married and find out one of us is not a good kisser?" Zachary said, grinning at her.

Gabrielle laughed. "Oh, that's no biggie. If that should turn out to be the case, I'll just have to teach you how to kiss, that's all," she said, laughing.

He laughed as he shook his head slowly. He bit down on his bottom lip and slightly twisted his mouth. "Then, I suppose it's official." He held out his hand to her. "You and I are officially courting."

"Officially courting," she said. But when she took his hand and shook it to seal their agreement, she quickly snatched her hand out of his and began shaking it as though she'd been burned. "You know, we might need to add shaking hands to our list of things we can't do." She laughed.

He smiled. "Yeah," he said, also shaking off the shock of electricity he'd felt. "Maybe we should. The play begins at seven o'clock. We can go to dinner before we go to the play if you'd like."

"Dinner sounds good. I guess you can pick me up at five."

"We'd better make that four-thirty. I wouldn't want to chance us arriving late to the play. I don't want to have to fight somebody who might be in our seats. You know how folks are. And we have front-row seats—a perk, I'm quickly learning, of being a doctor."

"Four-thirty is fine with me." She stepped outside the doorway. "I suppose I'd better get going then so I can be ready, huh?"

"Yeah." He smiled. "I'll see you at four-thirty."

She took a few steps toward her car, then turned around and gave Zachary a quick hug. "Thank you," she said. "And I thank God for you."

He looked down at her, his eyes locked on hers. He didn't want to let go. "No, I thank God for you." And before either of them knew anything, they were kissing. He smiled as they both struggled to pull away from each other. "I'm not so sure how this no-kissing thing is going to work out."

She grinned as she bit down on her bottom lip, then scrunched her face. "Yeah. I know what you mean."

He shook his head as she walked away. "Lord, help us," he said. "Oh, man!"

Zachary went to pick Gabrielle up for dinner and the play. He laughed when she opened the door and performed a quick shuffle drawing attention to her shoes.

"Those look like real glass slippers," he said of her clear high-heel shoes.

She grinned. "Yeah. And you look like Prince Charming in that dapper suit."

He made a sucking sound with his teeth as he made a show of straightening his jacket. "I am rather charming, aren't I?" He closed her door, she locked it, and then he held out his arm for her to take. "Come, my princess," he said as they strolled toward an awaiting white stretch limousine. "Your carriage awaits you."

Gabrielle laughed. "Has anyone ever told you that you're a nut?"

"My sister Queen. More times than I care to count." He laughed. "And you know: sometimes I feel like a nut, sometimes it's Almond Joy." He leaned down to kiss her once again.

She shook her head and grinned as she only allowed him a peck. "Oh, I can see we're definitely in trouble. There's going to be a whole lot of praying going on down here."

He laughed and looked toward the sky. "Thank You, Lord. Oh, yes! I thank You!" He looked at Gabrielle and gave her another quick peck on her lips. "You're so right. There's going to be a whole lot of praying, without ceasing, I might add, going on down here. A *whole* lot!" He hugged her, then picked her up and began to spin around.

Don't miss
*Redeeming Waters*

In stores now

Here's an excerpt from *Redeeming Waters* . . .

# Prologue

*And he shall be as the light of the morning,
when the sun riseth, even a morning without clouds; as the tender grass springing
out of the earth by clear shining after rain.*

—2 Samuel 23:4

It was summertime, school was out, and with sky-high temperatures reaching near one hundred degrees, even the bees appeared to be chilling out from the smothering heat. Ten years old, Brianna and Alana were outside on the long, covered front porch playing a game of Monopoly—the board type, not something electronic like all the other children their age normally played. Brianna's father, Amos Wright, didn't believe children should stay cooped up in the house watching television and playing video games all day. Brianna didn't mind; she liked being outside. On the other hand, Brianna's mother, Diane, would have preferred her daughter do things inside, especially on scorching hot days like this.

Around midday, suddenly and unexpectedly, dark clouds rolled in.

"Girls, it looks like it's going to rain. You probably need to come inside now," Brianna's mother said as she stood holding the front door open.

"We're on the porch, Mother," Brianna said. "We won't get wet on the porch."

"Well, if it starts lightning, I want you to come in the house immediately. Do you two understand me?"

"Yes, ma'am," Brianna and Alana said in such perfect unison that it sounded like one voice.

"Older people sure are funny when it comes to rain," Brianna said after her mother closed the front door.

Alana loosely shook the two white dice around in her hand, then threw them on the board, rolling a double three, automatically garnering herself another turn. "I know," Alana said as she counted out loud and advanced her wheelbarrow six spaces. "Boardwalk," she said with obvious disappointment.

"Yes!" Brianna said, picking up her title deed card to that property. "Let's see now, with two houses, you owe me six hundred dollars!" Brianna held out her hand for payment.

Alana slowly counted out the money, leaving her with only a small amount of money to play with. "It's a good thing I'm close to passing go and collecting two hundred dollars," Alana said. "I just hope I don't land on any of your other properties on my next roll, or this game will pretty much be over—two hundred more dollars or not."

The rain started pouring down. And then the sun, just as quickly, came back out, brightly lighting up the sky even as the rain continued to fall.

"Look!" Brianna said. "The sun is shining while

it's raining!" Brianna got up and walked over to the top step. "Wow. With the sun shining like that, all of those falling raindrops look like diamonds bouncing all over the walkway. Do you see how they're sparkling as they hit?"

Alana stood up and walked over to Brianna. "You *do* know what this means, don't you?"

"Know what *what* means?"

Alana turned and grinned at her friend. "When it's raining and the sun is shining."

"No. What?" Brianna could see that Alana was pleased, knowing something that *she* apparently didn't.

"It means that the devil is beating his wife."

"It does not," Brianna said.

"Yes, it does. If you don't believe me, then go ask your mother. She'll tell you."

"Well, I don't believe you because the devil doesn't *have* a wife."

"Apparently, he does," Alana said with a snarky shake to her head as she moved her face in toward Brianna's. "That's why the sun is shining while it's raining: to let us know that he's beating her. I feel a little sorry for her even if she *is* the devil's wife. It's got to be bad enough to be married to the devil. Then to have him beat on you like that . . . Then again, she should have known better than to hook up with a creature like him. I mean, what did she expect when she married the *devil?*"

"Well, I'm not going to let any man ever beat on me," Brianna said. "Not ever."

"They say if you stick a pin in the ground, you can hear her screaming when he's beating her."

Brianna frowned, then winced. "Who would want to hear anything like that?"

"Hey, let's go get a pin and see if we can hear her. That way, you'll see whether what I told you is the truth or not."

Brianna and Alana hurried into the house. "Wait right here while I find two pins." Brianna started upstairs to her room, then stopped and looked back. "Does it matter what kind of pin it is? A straight pin, a hat pin, a safety pin, or is it actually a writing pen . . . ?"

Alana shook her head. "As long as it pierces the ground, it should work."

Brianna came back quickly and handed Alana a large safety pin. They started toward the door.

"And just where do you two think you're going *now*?" Brianna's mother asked as she walked out of the kitchen into the den, wiping her hands on a dish towel.

"To listen to the devil beat his wife and to see if we can hear her scream," Brianna said as easily as though she were saying that they were going to the kitchen to get a glass of water.

Brianna's mother shook her head as she smiled, but didn't protest—essentially telling Brianna that she had no objections to what they were about to do or the idea of it.

Brianna opened the large, lead-glass door and allowed Alana to go out first. Brianna grinned. She saw him before he saw her, and she ran full force, straight into his arms. "Granddad!" she said.

"Hey there," sixty-year-old Pearson Wright said as he picked her up and spun her around two full turns. He set Brianna back down. The two of them now stood close to the man who had come with him. "So where are you two going in such a hurry?" he asked.

"We're going to listen to the devil as he beats his wife and to see if we can hear her screaming." Brianna held up her safety pin to prove they were serious.

"Oh, that," her grandfather said as he looked back at what he'd just come in out of. "You're talking about the rain with the sun shining. That's a beautiful sight for sure: rain and the sun shining at the same time, a phenomenon that's always fascinated folks."

The good-looking man standing next to her grandfather began to chuckle as he smiled at Brianna.

"Gracious, where are my manners," Pearson said. "This is my granddaughter"—he placed his hand on top of Brianna's head—"the lovely and talented young poet and short story writer, Miss Brianna Wright."

"And *this*"—Brianna pointed to Alana as soon as her grandfather finished introducing her—"is my best friend in the whole wide world, Alana Norwood."

"Pleased to meet you, Miss Alana Norwood. And *this* is David R. Shepherd, aka King d.Avid," Pearson said, pronouncing it "King dee-Avid." "That's a small *d,* period, capital *A,* small *v-i-d.* You're looking at the next world-renowned recording artist."

"Are you a real king?" Brianna asked the tall man with black wavy hair and caramel-colored skin. She placed her hand in the man's waiting hand, which he'd presented to her to shake.

"No, not in the way you may be thinking," King d.Avid said. "But I do plan—with your grandfather advising and managing me—to rule the world of music someday."

"Sounds like a plan to me," Brianna said. "I plan on being the queen of something myself. Just not exactly sure what I intend to rule over. But I'm going to be somebody great, or at least produce something great one day, just like you. I promise you that. A lady at church spoke that Word over me last year. That's what she called it: 'A Word from God.' "

"I'm impressed," King d.Avid said, smiling at her as he continued to hold her young hand in his. "And I believe that." He gave Brianna a slight bow with his head, then let go of her hand. He reached over and held out his hand to Alana. "And you are the best friend of the queen to be?"

Alana walked over, shook his hand, and giggled. "Yes. Although, it's likely we'll both be queens. That's how a lot of friends roll, you know."

"Absolutely," King d.Avid said. "It's always good to be in the company of those who are going somewhere, instead of hanging around people who are going nowhere. That's precisely why I hang with Mister Wright, here, the way I do. The man is good at what he does." He glanced over at Pearson. "And I believe he's going to help get me where I'm destined to be." King d.Avid turned his attention back to Alana and gave her a slight nod.

"So, how old are you?" Alana asked.

King d.Avid laughed. "Why, I'm twenty-five."

"You're kind of old," Alana said, turning up her nose slightly. "Me and Brianna are only ten. Well, we don't mean to be rude, but we need to finish before the rain stops just as quickly as it started. Otherwise, Brianna won't believe that the devil really is beating his wife."

"Okay." King d.Avid sang the word. "But I don't *think* the devil really is beating his wife. Because I don't *think* that the devil is married."

"That's what I told her," Brianna said triumphantly with a grin.

Alana trotted down the steps into the rain and stood in the grassy, manicured yard. She looked back up at the porch, her eyes blinking with the raindrops before she eventually shielded her eyes with her hand. "Brianna, will you come on, already!"

Brianna hurried and caught up with her friend. They unlatched their safety pins, kneeled down, stuck their pins into the ground, and placed their ears over their respective pins with the rain drenching them and all.

Pearson shook his head, laughed, then escorted King d.Avid into the house.

# Chapter 1

*The waters wear the stones: thou washest away the things which grow out of the dust of the earth; and thou destroyest the hope of man.*

—Job 14:19

Brianna Bathsheba Wright Waters looked out of the window of their three-bedroom, one-and-a-half-bath house at the rain. A "starter home" is what her twenty-three-year-old (three years her senior) husband of eight months, Unzell Michael Waters, told her over two months ago when they bought it.

"Baby, I promise you, things are going to get better for us down the road," Unzell had said after they officially moved in. "I know this is not what either of us envisioned we'd be doing right about now. But I promise you, I'm *going* to get us into that mansion we talked about. I am."

She'd married Unzell at age nineteen, a year and a half after her high school graduation, as Unzell was finishing his final year at the University of Michigan. Unlike most women she knew, Brianna wanted to marry in December. The wintertime was her favorite time of the year. She loved everything about winter. It wasn't a dead period as far as she was concerned. To her, that was the time of rest, renewal, anticipation, and miracles taking place that the eyes weren't always privy to. Winter was the time when flower bulbs, trees, and other plants could establish themselves underground; developing better and stronger roots. Winter was the time when various pests and bugs were killed off; otherwise the world would be overrun with them. Brianna loved the rich colors she would be able to use in a winter wedding: deep reds and dark greens.

But she equally loved summertime. Summer was a reminder of life bursting forth in its fullness and full potential after all seemed dead not so long ago. Summer now reminded her of her days of playing carefree outside, *truly* without a care in the world.

So she and Unzell married the Saturday before Christmas. It was a beautiful ceremony; her parents had spared no expense. After all, this would be the only time they would be the parents of the bride. Her older brother, Mack, might settle down someday. But even if he did, they would merely be the parents of the groom, which was a totally different expense, experience, and responsibility.

Unzell Waters was already pretty famous, so everybody and his brother wanted to be invited to the wedding ceremony. Unzell was the star football player at the University of Michigan and a shoo-in for the NFL. As a running back, he'd broken all kinds of records, and the only question most had was whether he would be the number-one or number-two pick in the first round of the NFL draft the last Saturday in April. Unzell was on track to make millions—more millions than either he or Brianna could fathom *ever* being able to spend in *several* lifetimes.

Still best friends, Alana Norwood had been Brianna's maid of honor. Alana had grown wilder than Brianna, but Brianna understood Alana . . . and Alana understood her.

"Girlfriend, I'm glad you're settling down so early, if that's what you want," Alana had said when Brianna first told her she and Unzell were getting married in a year. "But I plan on seeing *all* that the world has to offer me before my life becomes dedicated to any one person like that."

Of course, when Alana learned *just* how famous Unzell was even *before* he was to go pro, then heard about the millions of dollars sports commentators were predicting he'd likely get when he signed— no matter which team he signed with—she said to Brianna, "God really *does* look after you! Of course, he's always looked after you. People on TV are talking eighty-six million dollars, over five years, just for one man to play . . . one man, to *play*. And you're going to be his wife? I know you used to say all the time that you were God's favorite. Well, I'm starting to believe maybe you really are."

"Alana, now you know I used to just say things like that. I don't *really* believe God has favorites," Brianna said. "The Bible tells us that God is no respecter of persons. We're all equal in his sight."

"Well, we may have the *opportunity* to be equal, but it's obvious that not all of us are walking in our opportunities. Not the way you do, anyway. So you're definitely ahead of a lot of us, not equal by any means. All I know is that you spoke that Word of Favor with a capital F over your life, and look what's happening with you so far."

The wedding was absolutely beautiful, every single detail and moment of it. But with the championship game being played the first week in January, Brianna and Unzell were only able to spend one day of a honeymoon before Unzell was off again to practice.

Michigan's team was the team to beat with number twenty-two, Unzell Waters, being one of the main obstacles standing between the other team having even a *semblance* of a chance. Brianna was at the game in Miami watching it along with her family. With two minutes remaining in the fourth quarter, Michigan was already a comfortable three touchdowns ahead. In Brianna's opinion, there really was no reason for Unzell to even be on the field. She, her grandfather Pearson Wright, and father Amos Wright were saying as much when that play happened—the play that would alter Unzell's career and life.

One of the other team's players grabbed Unzell by the leg as he ran full speed and yanked him down, pulling his leg totally out of joint. With him being down, everybody on the other team piled on him. Unzell was badly hurt. Instantly, his prospective stock for the NFL plummeted. Then came the doctor's prognosis. Even with the two necessary surgeries, Unzell would never be able to play football at that level again.

Brianna assured him things would be all right. "God still has you, Unzell."

"Yeah, but if God had me in the first place, then why would he allow something like this to happen to me . . . happen to us?" Unzell said as he lay in that hospital bed. "God knows both of us. He knows us, Brianna. He knows our hearts. God knows we would have done right when it came to me being in the NFL. So why? Why did this happen? And if God is a healer, then why can't he heal my leg completely? Why can't he make me whole again?"

"I believe that God *can* heal your leg, Unzell," Brianna said. "But right now we have to deal with reality. And from all that the doctors are saying, football is out for you, at least for now. So you and I need a new direction, that's all. We're going to be all right though." She lovingly took hold of his hand, then squeezed it. "We are." She smiled.

"So, you're not going to leave me?"

Brianna frowned as she first jerked her head back, then primped her lips before forcing a smile. "Leave *you?* Where did *that* come from?"

"Face it; I'm not going to be making millions now. In fact, I'll be doing well just to find a job, any job at all, in this economy."

"First of all, *Mister* Waters, I did not marry you for your money or your potential money. I've known you since we were in high school. You were in the twelfth grade; I was in the ninth. You didn't have any money then and I fell in love with you. So if you think I married you for your money, then maybe I *should* leave you." Brianna put her hand on her hip.

"I know, Bree-Bath-She," he said, calling her by the pet name he sometimes used. "But do you know how many women wanted me because they saw dollar signs?"

"Yeah, I know. I'm not stupid. I even think you thought about getting with a few of them. In fact, who knows, maybe you did. But still, I married you for you. And I married you for better or worse; for richer or poorer."

"Come on, Brianna. Nobody really means that part when they say it. Who truly wants to be with someone poor? Sure, we may feel that's where we are at the time, but all of us believe our lives are going to get to the better and the richer at some point—sooner rather than later—not worse or poorer."

"Well, if me staying with you now after you've lost millions of dollars—that if I'm not mistaken, you never really had anyway—means I meant what I was vowing when I said those words, then please know: I meant them when I said them. Okay, so those in the know were saying you'd likely get a contract worth eighty-six million dollars over five years with a guaranteed fifty million and now it looks like you won't. So be it. I'm just glad you're okay. You could have been paralyzed on that play. You and I will do what we need to be all right. Besides, you're graduating in May. You'll get your electrical computer engineering degree. Do like most folks and either get a job or start your own business. Regardless, Unzell, I'm here to stay. So deal with it." Brianna flicked her hand.

Unzell smiled, then looked down at his hand. "God has certainly blessed me richly." He looked up. "God gave me you."

"Oh," Brianna said, all mushy as she kissed him. "That was *so* sweet."

Brianna couldn't help but think about how far she and Unzell had come since that fateful day. Following Unzell's two surgeries and the rehabilitation period, she'd suspended attending college and gotten a job as a secretary, living with her parents while he finished his final months of college in Ann Arbor. After Unzell graduated, he moved back to Montgomery, Alabama. He was relentless about getting a job, even when it felt like no one was hiring. He was diligent, beating the pavement and searching the Internet. In four weeks, he landed a job as an assistant stage manager setting up stages for music concerts, but was told if he wanted to excel in this business, he needed to be in Atlanta.

So that's what he and Brianna did: moved to Georgia.

It didn't hurt when Alana told Brianna that she was also moving to Atlanta to pursue her dream of becoming a video girl. At least now, Brianna and Alana would each have a friend in their new city. Brianna especially needed someone after quickly learning that in his position, Unzell could be gone for weeks, sometimes even months at a time.

Brianna continued to stare out of the window. She suddenly began to smile.

"And what are *you* smiling about?" Unzell said, jarring her back to the present.

Spinning around, she kissed him when he came near. "I didn't hear you come in."

He embraced her. "You were gazing out of the window. It looked like you were in deep thought; I didn't want to disturb you. Then you broke into that incredibly enchanting smile of yours, and I couldn't hold myself back any longer. Did you just think of a joke or something that made you happy?"

"Look," she said, pointing outside.

He looked out of the window and shrugged. "And what exactly am I looking for? All I see is rain, the sun shining, and trees and other things getting drenched."

"Don't you know what that's supposed to mean? Rain while the sun is shining."

He laughed. "Here we go again. Another something you learned when you were growing up? Like not stepping on a crack so you won't break your mother's back. Not walking under a ladder or splitting a pole because it will bring bad luck. Not sweeping someone's feet or you'll sweep them or someone else out of your life."

"No. Not exactly like *those* things, which are merely superstitions. This is different. I'm not saying that I believe it, but they say that when it's raining and the sun is shining, the devil is beating his wife."

"Yeah, right." Unzell smirked. "Actually, the scientific term for it is sunshower."

"Scientific term, huh? Well, people also say that if you stick a pin in the ground and listen, you can hear her screams."

"Oh. So do you want to go outside and do that so we can put that old wives' tale to the test?" Unzell's eyes danced as he spoke. "I'm game to play in the rain if you are."

"Nope. Alana and I tested it out when we were younger."

He laughed. "And the verdict was?"

"I didn't hear a thing. Of course, Alana claimed that she did. She said the scream was faint. But honestly? I think she heard something because she wanted to believe it was true. Then she said we'd used the wrong kind of pin and that's why it didn't work right."

"Alana is something else, that's for sure. So how is she these days?"

"Still trying to get a contract as a video girl or whatever they're called."

"I wouldn't ever count Alana out. Before you know it, she'll be over here forcing us to watch her DVD, showing how she was 'doing her thing.' " He made a quick pumping dance move followed by the long-outdated Cabbage Patch.

Unzell wrapped his arms around Brianna. She fully submitted, lying back into him, then rubbing one of his hard, muscular arms that gently engulfed her.

"The devil beating his wife," he said with a sinister giggle as they both looked out of the window. "Well, now, I think I've heard just about everything."

Brianna broke away from his embrace and turned to face him, playfully hitting his arm. "Just don't *you* ever try that devil move on *me*."

He grabbed her and lovingly locked her again into his arms, gazing deeply into her brown eyes as they faced each other. "Never. I promise you I will *leave* before I *ever* raise a hand to you." He hugged her. "I would never abuse a blessing of God; I'm too afraid of what God would do to me if I did." He gently pushed her slightly away from him to look into her eyes again. "Besides, I love you too much.

We're one body now. So whatever I do to you, I'll be doing to myself. And I would *never* lay a negative hand or word, for that matter, on myself. Therefore, I won't ever do anything like that to you."

"See, that's why I love you so much." She cocked her head to one side. "You really get this whole concept of loving your wife the way Christ loves the church."

"I wouldn't want our life together to be any other way. Not any other way." He pulled her to him and squeezed her as he locked her in his arms, causing her to giggle out loud. He stopped, cupped her face, and kissed her with an overflow of passion.